# THE TEMPERED TURNS OF TIME

## THE KING'S SWORDSMAN BOOK 4

BECKY JAMES

A CIP catalogue record for this book is available from the British Library.

Ebook ISBN 978-1-9168774-9-8

Paperback ISBN 978-1-9168774-8-1

Book cover design: Timea Schwinger at Fantastical Ink.

Editor: Clem Flanagan at Red Pen Vigilante.

Section break illustrations: A. Bater.

Clarkenhome Press

Gloucestershire

GL2 5DR

For news from the author, visit www.beckyjamesauthor.co.uk

# ALSO BY BECKY JAMES

THE KING'S SWORDSMAN

Upper young adult / new adult sword and sorcery portal fantasy.

*The Tenets in the Tattoos*
*The Bind of Blood and Bonds*
*The Limit of the Lonely Man*
*The Tempered Turns of Time*
*The Mettle of the MasterMage*

DARK TIDES

Fantasy romance co-authored with Becky Tama.

*A Dram of Freshwater (prequel)*
*The Shadow of Death*
*The Thief of Souls*

For news from the author, check out www.beckyjamesauthor.co.uk

*For Laura and Jeff*
*Inspiring all the budding book dragons out there.*

The Unclaimed Lands
Dinahe
Mecah
Oberrot City
North Hold
Master's Palace
Skien
Skleratach
The Academy
Spiritshere
Dinerah
The Serene Sea
Jira
Summer Palace
Keltskarr
Peaks
Doblanshi
Nightcrest
Daron
Oberrot
Hanasta
Shiron
Lightreach
Mid-Ete
Rush
Al Shur
Rush
Temple Ruins

# CHAPTER I

Landing the flat of my father's blade with a thwack, I spun and launched three Artist blades with my other hand. Two sank into the practice dummy with a satisfying, solid thunk while the outlier bounced, clattering down the dummy's armour.

"Damn and blast." I scraped sweat from my face. Cool wind chilled my skin, the light fading fast. Soon, glowstones and torches would flicker to life in the city below, delineating the districts.

Glittering gems set in lords' and ladies' homes surrounded the castle walls, and, further down, the Dinahen district boasted concentrations of glowstones in the public spaces, highlighting the trees and long tables set out for the shared evening meal. The Rushia district had small fires, lighting their coloured fabric with shining blues, greens and pinks, and next to it the Daronian district was dark as usual, each family hearth kept behind their doors. Below it all, the warehousing district at the foot of the mountain was well-lit, as busy with deliveries through the night just as much as in the day.

I plucked the Artist blades out of the dummy. "Best three out of five, old friend?"

The straw-and-wood training man twisted slightly. I waited for it to settle, trying to calm and still myself, my mind turning on even so.

Liara was still nowhere to be found. She had escaped through a portal a mooncycle ago, tearing her way through someplace Evyn couldn't follow. Not that I would want her to; we wanted to ask the only portal travellers we knew about it, but they were absent as well.

I threw one knife to sink into the dummy's throat.

Soon, Gavain would arrive. Word had been sent that he was well enough to travel, and Gough had arranged official transport by barge. It was due to arrive in the city any day now. Gough would speak with him and determine for himself what responsibility he bore and what the punishment should be for his part in a hazing incident against me that nearly caused Evyn's death.

*Gavain tricked me.* I trusted him and he had made out he was trying to help me, and I fed her a sleeping draught mixed with bruswurt. It could have killed her. *He* could have killed her.

With a snarl, I sent another knife out. It sank dead centre into the dummy's forehead. I gave Gavain a second chance after Torgund, and he hurt Evyn. *He does not deserve or warrant a third chance.* I hefted the third knife, feeling out the balance.

The target for the third knife was the eye. Penetrating one would kill instantly; a blade to the brain guaranteed instant, painless death.

*People change. For good and for ill.* Even if I did not want them to, and wanting otherwise was childish and immature. Time marched on and so did the people around me, forging their own paths.

Like Aubin had.

I flung the knife. It spun, hilt smashing into the eye target. I growled obscenities, hunting at my feet for my waterskin.

"Here."

I spun around at my soul companion's voice. "Gods above. You've grown significantly in skill, you successfully sneaked up on me."

Evyn squinted up at me, my waterskin in one hand and a hot mug in the other. Small in stature, barely coming to my chest, my soul companion was the perfect height to enfold in my arms when she wasn't carrying boiling water.

"I said hi, hello and oi a few times." She blew on her mug, looking at me over the top of it. "I can tell you're feeling a bit rough."

Rough was a good way to phrase the turmoil inside, thoughts churning a constant pathway back and forth until it resembled an overturned trail. I tried to sort and sift through my emotions like I would assess and prioritise a small group of foes. *You, I can reach now, but you I have to deal with before you overwhelm me, and you over there can wait while I defeat and push these back.* Talking to Evyn would help, but I worked so I would not overwhelm her with my feelings, as she experienced them at the same time. As the two halves of the spirit we shared, we would feel and react to each other, in a way Evyn described as a feedback loop and I fancied resembled ripples in a pool merging and melding with one another.

I drank deeply of the water, gulping and gasping it down. Once I was sated, I admitted, "I think I am losing the skills Aglo's presence lent me. There should be *some* benefit to suffering him, so I am disappointed in that. I have to keep practising both the Art and Rushia so as not to lose them. Do you feel Ellen's memories fading?"

She nibbled the side of her lip. "That was different, she just gave me horrible nightmares—through no fault of her own, I think—and those are gone, thankfully. I guess we know what to look out for next time a stray spirit clings to me; Sabatha says it's not an active thing I can control, just a thing I can *do*, a passive ability." She turned up her other hand, acting rather blasé, in my opinion. Still, this was something we had discussed multiple times, and I knew she would not search out the spirits of the departed deliberately.

I turned over the next topic to bring up with her, a cloying weight sitting heavy on my chest. "In addition, Gavain will be here soon."

Taking another sip, Evyn winced at the heat against her lips. "Yeah. I have a feeling things will get worse before they get better." She touched my hand. "I'm ready to help. Don't feel you need to shield anything from me."

"So long as you know you can do the same." Putting my hand on her shoulder, a swell of warmth filled my chest and flooded my limbs.

She took another draught of her drink, the heat sliding down her throat. That I could pick up physical sensations meant our bond was strengthening. I curtailed my excitement, as this was a close range, but nevertheless I was pleased with our progress. We had found a way to each other at last.

Something else called to me from within her. A deep sadness pouring from the cracks in her heart, and the constant return of her thoughts to one subject.

*Aubin.*

I lifted my hand from her shoulder, unable to stop my anger flaring. How dare he break her heart by leaving! Fuelled by the edges of her and my hurt, I grabbed the knives and threw them again, one after the other. This time they all hit true, vibrating slightly from the force.

"Sorry," Evyn murmured.

"It's – no, don't be sorry, Evyn, it's not your fault." I ran my hands through my hair, sweat clinging to every strand. Evyn opened up when I did first. I could charge into a breach. "It will take time, but we'll move on from him."

Evyn's lips quirked. "You say that as if you had a relationship with him."

I frowned at her. "I did, he was my partner."

Evyn giggled.

I rolled my eyes. "Hells above, you know what I mean." Still, it was pleasing to hear her laughter and feel the weight lift off her, if only for a moment. We were close now, so although there would be challenges ahead, I knew we would face and defeat them in turn with her by my side. "I need to get really, disgustingly drunk. Want to join me?"

She nodded, draining her mug and walking in step with me as I put the training dummy away. Just as I exited the storeroom, brushing dust off myself, Captain Barlay rounded the corner. I saluted the late-middle-aged man with iron grey peppering his temples.

He studied our faces. "Ranger, Lady Evyn, well met. Can I see you two in my office?"

My stomach curdled. Last time Barlay had called me into his office, it was for a disciplinary matter, which he then took before the king. I was fairly certain I had committed no offences, but then again, I hadn't realised I had previously either.

Evyn stood in front of me, as if to shield me. "What for?"

Barlay's lips twitched in amusement. I relaxed in response; he wouldn't smile if his purpose was dire. He looked tired, his shirt collar askew. "Peace, Lady Evyn. I wish to ask something of you."

Evyn and I exchanged looks. "Yes, sir," I said.

Captain Barlay led us to his office, right at the very end of the barracks. The bunks of single soldiers lined up on either side, and it felt strange now that this public way of sleeping and resting had been my life for turns. I much preferred our apartment, and not only because now I drew looks from Special Forces wherever I went.

The chatter died down as Evyn and I paced along the rows. Evyn pressed her notebook to her chest. "Jeez," she muttered to me.

I put my hand on her shoulder, glaring either side at the men. They stared before looking away. It was like this at morning training as well, but after the warm-ups I could see to my own training, which I went to with a will.

Aleric polished his gear at his bunk, head down and mouth set in a grim line. He did a double take as we walked past. "Thorrn? I mean, Ranger Shardsson."

I didn't slow my pace. "The captain wants to see me."

"I... Right."

I left him behind, and Barlay swung his door open to admit us. The captain's office, once my father's, was a bare utilitarian office with maps on the walls. These featured the bluffs and craggy cliffs of

Skien, and above Barlay's drafting desk was a detailed map of the Oberrotian outposts on the Skienien border.

I turned my attention from them to Barlay. "Sir, you wanted to see us?"

"At ease, Ranger. I had a proposal which the king said might suit you both." His eyes met mine, exhaustion dragging at them. "I am in dire need of assistance. Philo is still on review and not able to assist in his capacity as sergeant. I have no other high-ranking staff that I can turn to. Ranger Shardsson, as you are not currently on a mission, I would appreciate more in-depth help with Special Forces. Remaining as a Ranger, of course, but it will give you some command experience."

My shoulders tightened somewhat. "The last time I had tried commanding these men and women, I mishandled it, sir. There is a deep wound in the corps that my presence will not serve to heal."

Barlay's mouth settled into a grim line. "I am aware, Ranger. However, they need to get used to you, and, to some extent, you to them." He tapped his fingers on the desk. "Sometimes you will need to command and respect men and women you do not actually like. This is also part of the role."

"Respect should be earnt," Evyn scowled. My heart warmed for her loyalty.

"I can show them all due respect, sir, but will they reciprocate?" I pointed out.

"If they have issues, I would rather they were ironed out here than on the battlefield." Barlay's gaze strayed to the maps of Skien on the walls.

I asked, "Is there something happening, sir?"

Barlay nodded. "You brought news from your foray into Skien of strong anti-magical sentiment gaining traction over there. Further reports indicate it is festering into another one of those horrific evictions. The MasterMage of Oberrot is also concerned, and she will arrive tomorrow to discuss what can be done."

I nodded. For Evyn's benefit I explained, "Skieniens hate magic and will run it out of the country. Every half a score of turns or so, they push all magic users, whatever their age or birthplace, out of the country. The refugees run across to Oberrot, where previously Waker MasterMage would take them in, or down to Daron." I pointed at the world map on the wall and the border where the sere mountains of Skien jutted up along Oberrot's low lush fields along our western border, all the way down to the southern border it shared with northern Daron. I turned to Barlay. "Daron will probably apply for help from Oberrot to secure their borders?" I guessed.

"That's the usual way they have to deal with it."

Evyn's jaw dropped. "Even... children and families?"

"Yes." I balled my fists. "It's slow to start, and the Battlemistresses keep corridors open for people to flee, but violence can erupt along those at any point. Last time this happened, Special Forces were asked to maintain order on this side, and we weren't allowed to help, even if something was happening a mere length from the border. Fortunately, the Battlemistress assigned to us wasn't that strict on distances, saying she didn't have time to measure things precisely."

"Hm, even so. Are we friendly with them?" The tone of Evyn's question bordered on unfriendliness itself.

I touched her shoulder to settle her. "Current relations between Oberrot and Skien are frosty. If Rush was a closed door, Skien is partly open, but only for trade."

Barlay added, "It's not hostile. We sit alongside one another, aware of each other, but not talking openly to one another."

Evyn nodded. "Alright. I'm sure there will be more to that, like there was in Rush."

"Perhaps, Evyn." My memories of maintaining that cordon to keep the refugees moving and assisting where we could were bleak, overlaid by the biting cold that permeated the country and seeped into my bones wherever I went and however I had dressed. That was nothing compared to the harsh looks on the faces of the Battlemistresses and the men they commanded.

Evyn said, "So you'd like some of Thorrn's time to help with the corps, but why do you need my input?"

"Lady Evyn, I would like to procure some of your time as a temporary record-keeper for the army. I'm finding that, being short on senior staff, I am besieged by paperwork. I need to free up some of my time to plan a deployment to Skien, if that's what ends up happening." He nodded toward me. "You assist Ranger Shardsson with his records, and this would be no different."

I patted her on the back. "Evyn, you would be part of Special Forces!"

Evyn snorted. "No, just the paper pusher in the back room. I do heavy lifting with words, Thorrn." She turned to Barlay. "I'm happy to help with drafting dispatches, note taking, that sort of thing."

Barlay nodded. "That's it exactly."

She smiled up at me. "I'd see more of you, so that's a plus."

"Yes, definitely." I had no doubts she would be exemplary at it. Barlay's choice was a good one, and she was already trusted with one of the king's most closely guarded secrets: her own origins. Evyn's homeworld of Earth was once just a fable to me, until she visited one day with her mother, the king's soul companion, Rose.

Barlay's exhalation held a cheerful tone. "Then it's settled. I look forward to receiving more of your support. I'll see you here at the usual time, Ranger. Lady Evyn, as is your habit, you are welcome to keep attending morning warm-ups, and then I can give you time to freshen up before you return to assist me."

"Great." Evyn eyed the stack of papers on Barlay's desk. "I can look now, see the size and shape of what I'm dealing with in the morning."

I gently touched her hand. "We have plans," I reminded her.

"But..." She pointed wordlessly at the filing to be done.

I grinned. I would never understand her deep love of information stored on paper, but I knew it brought her great joy. "Go to. Our plans can change." It would just be me racing her to the bottom of a bottle and winning, and I always won any race I entered. At least helping Barlay would be more productive.

Barlay's small, sad smile crossed his face again. "I need to remain here to get ahead of tomorrow's work, so I can be called upon to answer questions."

She flew toward the papers as I would rush toward a practice bout. "See you shortly!"

I chuckled. Judging by the size of the pile, she would be at this for a few turns of the glass at least. I could get started on that bottle somewhere in the city, come back to retrieve her, and have a nightcap with her in our empty apartment.

Saluting to Barlay, I marched back out. There were much fewer men on the bunks, those that wanted to turn in early or play quiet games in the room. Aleric was amongst those who had gone out, his bunk empty.

Gavain's bunk, close to the doors, was stripped bare, his effects stowed until such time that he returned. *If he returns at all.* My stomach surged with a mixture of anger and trepidation. It would be up to King Gough to determine his guilt or otherwise, and I did not envy him deciding that verdict. The burden of making sweeping decisions that affected the lives of the citizens of Oberrot included the intricacies of the castle forces and disciplinary measures where the captain felt necessary.

What could Gavain face? Gough had promised to review harsher punishments; no soldier would ever be lashed again after what had happened to me, but if Gavain was guilty of attempted murder, that was a capital offence. My stomach lurched. Despite my anger at him, I had no desire to see Gavain on a gallows.

I shoved that image out of my mind. Alcohol. That would help for a time, providing a little alleviation from my thoughts chasing each other round and round.

Outside, the air hung heavy with heat, a summery warmth that would dissipate shortly. A roar of laughter rang from inside the castle courtyard. The mess hall turned into a general bar for all levels of castle service at night, soldiers mixing with servants. My steps started toward it, but soon slowed. Special Forces were likely in there and, even though they might not stare, I had no desire to feel as though they might be watching.

I would go into the city. There were a few bars I frequented, many overlaid with memories of Gav and Al, but that couldn't be helped. If I let that stop me, I would never be able to set foot in the city again.

Passing under the gates from the castle grounds to the upper levels of the city, I pressed my fist to my heart in a salute to the small plaque to my father. At this time of day, the thoroughfare was busy with couples and soul pairs making their way to dinner and evening commerce setting up. This area would be cleared any time the king had to make discipline or an execution public. Here was where Torgund had erected a gallows for dissenters in Special Forces, and here Gough had built the dais for my lashing.

*In a few days, perhaps something else will happen here.* I shook myself. In a way, I just wanted the outcome announced already. Once that happened, I could deal with the situation in front of me. Having multiple ways this could go and preparing myself for every eventuality wore on me.

I paced on down a few streets to one of my favourite bars, but at the door I hesitated. Hot light filled the sitting area, the high ceiling in the main room exposing me to the last glaring rays of the day. The proprietor knew me, had probably seen me half-naked and twisting under the lash, and a wave of shame and anxiety washed over me.

A sensation akin to a light touch on my shoulder sent a wave of reassurance through me; Evyn Finding me. She felt like this every day and somehow battled through it. She really was stronger than me.

Hand on my father's sword to bolster me, I entered. The bar was quite empty apart from a pair of women at the bar and one lone figure in red in the corner. The back of his blond, short-shorn head was enough for me to identify him. Lips twisting, I prepared to turn on my heel and step back out before he saw me.

*I cannot avoid him forever.*

Girding myself, I approached his table.

Aleric had his chin in his hand, staring into the beer before him. He glanced up by reflex as I entered his reach, shoulders coming up in readiness. His blue eyes widened. "Thorrn! I mean, Ranger Shardsson." He stood up, sending his chair clattering to the floor.

"No brawling!" the barman snapped.

"We are not." My face heated. Damn it, but my back crawled, scars prickling as the women pointed at me, whispering to each other behind their hands.

"Did you come to find me? How did you know I was here?" Aleric's face brightened. "I'll get you a drink. Hoi, barkeep! Another round, and one for my friend!"

I grimaced. "I didn't know you'd be here, and we aren't friends anymore, Al."

He waved me to sit. "Yes, alright, well, why don't we have a few of these, you'll punch me, I'll slug you, we will both cry, and then..." He shrugged. "We will see."

That had been the weft and weave of our friendship. Hot disagreements over women or assignments, a screaming swearing fistfight, and then firm support and comradeship offered over that. My chest ached. "Would that it could be so simple. It's gone beyond that, Al."

"We can go back to that, if we want. What's to say we cannot?"

"How about your behaviour, the way you turned away from me the heartbeat I fell from favour?" My throat constricted.

His fingers flexed into fists. "How about when you intimated to Gavain I was a traitor, and the usurper king tortured me for no fault of my own?"

"That wasn't... I never meant..."

"You betrayed us first, you know, running away with your soul companion and leaving Gavain to face the heat for it." Draining his glass to half empty, Aleric set it back on the table with a firm slam.

"You are not occupying a moral high ground, so stop acting like you are."

Bitter anger seared my throat. "Where was this generous 'let's start afresh' magnanimity when I was disciplined and back to the bottom of the contingent? You choose to follow only those who are in favour."

"And? That's how it has always been. When are you going to say sorry?" Aleric glared at me. "You are so stubborn, clinging to your convictions like they prop you up."

"And you're a coward."

This time when the chair behind him slammed to the ground, it was because Aleric launched himself at me.

# CHAPTER 2

"Ow." I pressed the heel of my hand to my split eyebrow.

"Gods." Aleric worked his jaw. "I forgot how lethal your right hook is."

"I pulled that punch, otherwise you'd be in the infirmary." Leaning back against the cold stone wall of the street, I stretched my legs in front of me.

"Sure you did." Aleric slumped across from me, shifting his sword into his lap. He wasn't that hurt if he was able to grumble about it. "Drink, done, and spilled all over the floor. Punches, thrown, and earning us a ban from that establishment."

"I'll call round with some rubles for damages in the morning." I winced, feeling around my face. "When did you land a hit on my cheek?"

"I think that was when you dodged my swing. Perhaps you hit the table."

Truth be told, I had seen the blow coming. I hadn't touched a drop of drink and my reactions were honed to a sharp edge after the last mission. I had let him strike me. Either Aleric hadn't registered, or he was letting me save my pride.

He could have hurt me, too, if he wanted. Drawn his sword and run me through as the extreme, but I was sure he had pulled his blows as well.

I let the back of my head fall against stone. "How are your shoulders?"

"Better, but they feel like they aren't as they were before. I think they never will be. I'll have to work around it, Barlay has modified some moves to help keep me alive, but... if I ever get hit with an overhead strike, my arms will fail to block and I'll be killed."

My chest hurt. "I... I'm sorry, Al." My nose stung, and I scrubbed it.

"Time for the tears. My thanks, Thorrn. For what it's worth, I'm sorry as well." His voice hitched. "Thorrn, where are we?"

"Hm? Oberrot City of course." Was he somehow more drunk than I'd thought?

"What I mean is, I don't know how we've ended up here, like this, so I don't know how to get back." Wiping his eyes, he sighed. "Or how to go forward."

I didn't either. Part of me wanted my friend back. Another part recognised he had fallen short of what I thought he was, what I wanted him to be. Perhaps the same was true for Aleric, and he saw something in me now that he hadn't realised was there and did not want to see.

He curled his hand around the hilt of his sword. "What's going to happen to Gav?"

"I don't know," I answered truthfully, because I didn't know and, worse, I did not know what I wanted to happen.

"Rumour has it Gough is readying the gallows, but he would only do that for attempted murder, and it wasn't, Thorrn. You were there. Gavain said he only put bruswurt in it. Why did you panic over bruswurt?"

My heart pounded. Bruswurt was a benign herb, used in remedies for mild pain relief, but as it was native to our world, Evyn's body was not used to it. Any Earthian would have an extreme reaction against it, mounting an all-out assault that would have damaged her far worse than the herb itself.

It was not common knowledge, and it was a closely guarded secret that Evyn and her mother were Earthians. Gavain was privy to that restricted information and had looked up what would hurt her. It *was* attempted murder.

Or was it? I closed my eyes to recall the scene. When he had come into the kitchen in Dinahe to find Evyn flat out of the table, his face had given away his shock. He was intelligent and could lie with an aura of glib innocence, but that moment should have been the pinnacle of his achievement if he was aiming to cause her death. He would have expressed something other than complete horror.

*"Bruswurt... bruswurt cannot hurt anyone."*

My hands trembled. I forced them to stillness.

Aleric inched toward me. "There are some others saying he'll be hanged anyway, Thorrn, that Gough will do it because it was an attack against the daughter of his soul companion. I know he shouldn't have involved her at all, but Thorrn, he just meant for her to sleep, to get out of the way. I know he did. But Gough killed the apothecarist for stabbing Gav. He isn't going to extend Gavain any mercy, is he?" Aleric sniffed loudly.

As he broke into sobs, I got to my feet. He sniffled and snorted as I leant against the wall next to him, standing guard as he dropped his.

I did not relish seeing Gavain again, but I did not want him dead, either. I scanned the alleyway, marking the merrymakers laughing a few doors down and the footsteps of a couple passing by. The waiting was always the worst for me. I wanted to know now what would happen to Gavain, and then I could react accordingly. Until then, I was stuck, unable to put my feelings to any good use.

When the storm eased, the sobs turning to hiccups, I extended a pocket square to Aleric. He wiped his face copiously, mumbling behind the cloth. "How did we get here, Thorrn?"

I knew what he meant. I hunkered down next to him. "Through

the choices that we made, Al. But there are no more choices we can make and no way to affect the outcome. Now it's just the consequences." I held out my hand toward him.

He took it, grunting as he pulled himself to his feet. The sun had set fully by now, cheery glowstones winking on to light our path back to the castle. We walked in silence, both of us wiping our eyes and clearing our throats, and headed toward the barracks.

Aleric gave me a nod as he peeled off toward his bunk. I nodded back, rapping on Barlay's office door. "Come in," the captain called.

I shaded my eye using my right arm, hiding the no doubt burgeoning red bruise on my right cheek. "Bright in here, sir."

"Hm." Barlay snapped the ledger closed.

Evyn stamped up to me. "Who did that?" she hissed, tugging my arm down and gasping.

I put my finger to my lips. "People are sleeping next door, Evyn." I saluted Barlay. "Faced the issue head on, sir. I think there's been progress."

His lips thinned. "I suppose you are. At last."

Evyn's face went red. "I've had it with this sanctioned violence!"

I grinned at her. "Evyn, our whole lives are sanctioned violence." I put my arm around her shoulders. "Did you feel that? I'm sorry if you did."

She scowled. "Wait 'til we get home."

A small series of grunts escaped Barlay's lips. He was laughing. "I am very much reminded of Shard and Ista. Dismissed, both, and go well. I'll see you first thing."

I led a simmering Evyn back through the now darkened barracks. Aleric's red glowstone was dim, and I waved to him as we passed.

He smiled back, not the amiable smile of before, but something new, perhaps.

The apartment was dark when we arrived. It felt empty even though we lived here. I spent very little time in it, only to sleep, and I knew Evyn did the same.

Evyn clapped her hands, and the glowstones flared to life. That was something she had asked Tuniel to make the glowstones do, rather than respond to being tapped.

She planted her feet in the centre of our corridor. "Right. Is this happening again? Are you being beaten up as some kind of stupid ritual for acceptance?"

"No, I gave as good as I got. Aleric got his apology, and I've got mine."

Her eyes widened. "Aleric?"

"Yes, one on one. I insulted him to start us off, so the fault lies with me as well." I squeezed her shoulders. "The hazing nonsense will not happen again, Evyn. I don't believe it would help, and there are other ways to prove that I am an asset to a team than slavishly accepting their punishments."

"Hm." Her eyes narrowed. "Are you drunk?"

"I haven't touched a drop. Would you like some?"

She waved her hand. "Sure, I'll need some for that cut on your head, too." Her eyes strayed to the closed door next to us. Aubin's old room.

I gently brought her to my chest. "We'll be alright, Evyn."

"Mm," she murmured, small fingers clinging to my jacket. As much as she repeated in various ways over the last mooncycle she wanted to go forward, her heart and thoughts were dragged back to thinking of him and hurting. She pulsed with pain.

I was hit with a wave of love for her and an urge to run after Aubin and... "You know, when I see him again, I'm probably going to punch him."

She sighed. "What else is new, so no difference there."

"Oh, so it's fine by you if I punch *him*?" I rubbed my hands over her head.

Dragging sadness overtook me. She dropped her arms and made her way to the kitchen, standing alone. "We'll see. It's *if* we ever see him again, Thorrn. You can't hold out hope like that. Prepare for the worst, then be pleasantly surprised if it turns out to be better. That's what he'd say."

"Yes." Aubin never gave anyone second chances, least of all himself. If I couldn't reach the root of her problem, I would have to help her work her way through it. "Drink?" I asked her.

"Just a snifter." She settled on the sofa facing the floor-to-ceiling windows. The night sky was lit with two moons, red and blue, stars blanketing the rest, forming hazes of purples like streaks of water-colour paint. I could navigate without the glowstones. "I love seeing the stars here. You never see that many where I'm from."

I spared a brief look for the night sky I'd grown up under, turning my attention instead to my soul companion. She studied the sky as if she would be tested on it later, a keen interest piqued purely by her love of learning.

*Less than half a turn bonded and so much has changed, including ourselves.* Perhaps there would be a period soon where we could focus on each other and how the choices we had made had rearranged us. She was a decision I would make again and again, throughout all the worlds, and I knew that, sitting alongside us in all the different alternative timelines, the Thorrns and Evyns were all making the same choice.

*Whatever happens, we will be fine.*

"I opened it." Evyn's words floated out between us.

"Opened what?" *A portal?* There were no chill winds from Evyn's much colder climate. "Oh, another bottle? You are welcome to."

She put her glass down with a clink, picking up the parchment next to it. The paper held a hasty fold, badly askew and crumpled, spotted with something brown. She smoothed it flat on her thigh. "I drummed up the courage to open the letter Gavain sent to me from Dinahe."

Oh. That. I pressed my hands into the sofa, fighting back a surge of battle readiness. What could he possibly have to say to her, hiding behind words in a missive?

She rubbed her elbow, eyeing me, no doubt experiencing the wash of my anger. I expanded my chest, trying to call calm into my limbs.

When I could be sure of the foundations of my voice, I spoke. "Well? What does he say?"

She ran her finger along the side of the brief scribbles, her voice barely louder than the ripple of the parchment. "It's the exact dose of the bruswurt he gave me."

Righteous rage flooding my throat, I snatched it as if it were the poison. My leathers were too tight around my neck. I pulled them open, fighting for calm.

A stillness opened up inside me. I leant into it, into Evyn, taking each breath deep into my lungs as she smoothed the rage down with me.

The parchment trembled in my hand. I stilled it. "It's a confession. The king can... this is evidence. It's a full confession of what he did." The king would have to take this into consideration, and a full confession written in his own hand was damning.

*Gavain has signed his own death sentence.*

"Why?" My voice was a whisper.

"It's scribbled hastily. He wrote the dose out and got someone to send it." Her eyes filled with tears. "I think he meant it to help me."

That slammed into me, the edges of my vision dimming. "We have to give this to the king. He will know what to do."

"Right." Evyn plucked it from my fingers and refolded it along its proper edges with decisive strokes. "I'll show it to him tomorrow."

"Yes." Another mark against Gavain, or for him? Gough was charged with deciding, and yet again I was grateful it would not be me, for I did not know which way my heart would rule.

# CHAPTER 3

Aleric swung and his partner Kari blocked. Aleric's face twisted with pain as the shock reverberated up his arm to his shoulders, but he pressed forward, shoving Kari back.

"Good. Take a break for now," I said.

Kari slashed her practice blade to the side. "I'm not winded."

Aleric panted hard. "Nor I."

I kept my tone of voice light. "Does that matter? I said to take a break."

Aleric nodded and entered a ready stance, Kari following a few heartbeats after. This morning Barlay had explained to the corps that I would be working with them and they were to follow my directions and any orders. He strode the field now, Evyn keeping pace with him with steele and pad in hand.

I turned my attention back to the small group around me. "We're going into manoeuvres soon. We will need to develop something against hammers and Battlemistress blades."

Kari tutted.

"Yes, soldier?"

She flushed. "Battlemistresses are just dancing around. They are no match for Oberrotian steel."

I rubbed my forearms where Aubin had laid several slashes into me. "That kind of thinking will see you becoming a casualty on the battlefield, swordswoman Kari."

Aleric wiped his forehead. His jaw had to smart judging from the size of the red swelling. "So are we going to Skien, then?"

"The captain and I are having a meeting with the king later. Information will come from that. All in good time, swordsman Aleric." Barlay would want to prepare the troops as much as possible, after ascertaining with the king what our response to an eviction would be.

The metal embedded in my right shoulder warmed slightly, a thread tracing to my bicep. Sure enough, when I scanned the field I saw the delegation from the MasterMage's Palais: three serious-looking men and women in pale green, a tall thin woman with a rolling gait, a squat woman walking between them and then a silvrine-haired woman, younger than the rest, striding ahead of them toward the castle.

Tuniel did not look my way but the metal stroked my arm, as soft and cool as her touch. Knowing she could not single me out in public, I turned back to the contingent. The thought of her seeing me at work pleased me greatly.

Aleric wiped his brow. "You're faster than ever before, Ranger Shardsson. Can you teach us?"

That he had asked would help me to integrate with the contingent more, and for that I was grateful, but even still an irrational ire turned my stomach. Teaching Special Forces anything after the way they had treated me rubbed me the wrong way, as Evyn would say. Still, I considered what exercises I would use. How had I gotten faster? Practice and live fire experience, and working with Aubin everyday, whose speed put me to shame.

"I'll think about how to do that, swordsman. In the meantime, I think the captain will call for manoeuvres." Sure enough, Barlay raised his voice to call us all together.

I joined the scrum too until Barlay cleared his throat. Evyn motioned at me, and I pushed forward to stand between him and her.

"Special Forces," Barlay barked. "We need to look to the future. I know we have gone through some difficult times. Those are behind us now, but it is key that we learn and take from the experience, techniques and outlooks that will help us with future challenges. Growth is important, and we say that nothing grows if it is not challenged. But we were sent to the edge, and lost... lost so much. So many."

Barlay locked his hands behind his back. "We are stronger together. If whittled down to individuals, we will fail. Trust in the heart and strength of the person next to you and build on it. We have the strength collectively to defeat even magic!" he roared. A few people cheered, and I added my voice to them. "We will overcome the trials ahead of us."

"Which are, sir?" one man, Merritt, asked.

"We will ascertain the size and shape of that today, swordsman. For now, Ranger Shardsson..."

I snapped to attention.

"Set some exercises. I want the corps to be invigorated."

"Yessir!" Invigorated, eh? I ran through a few of my father's exercises that would get my blood to surge strength around my body. Keeping the contingent together, I bade them to gather round.

"Capture the flag. I know you're familiar with the war game. Divide yourselves and choose your team heads."

The contingent split evenly, one side choosing Grey and the other Kari. Aleric was on Grey's team. Grey did not spare me more than a glance, turning to whisper to Aleric. Al coloured but said nothing back.

"What am I taking notes on?" Evyn sidled up to me.

"I'll dictate. If you can capture the observations, I would be thankful." I cocked my head. "Do you have a title?"

"I'm sure I can make one up. Executive Mark-Making Technician. Chief Paper Wrangler. I'm getting a bad feeling about some of these guys," she added in Rushia. Very few of the others were likely to speak it; Ithnia, who was half-Rushia half-Oberrotian, was the only one I knew of.

"That might be me." I was likely bleeding through to Evyn. Grey and Merritt had been eager participants in my hazing in Dinahe. They wouldn't try anything overt with the captain nearby. "Stay by me, all will be well. There might be verbal unpleasantness, but you and I are old hands at that."

"Yes." She blew a stray lock of hair away from her forehead.

As I paced around each party, I listened in to their plans. Kari was hot-headed, but then so was Grey. It could be a near match unless one of them paid heed to one of the more strategic elements in their team. I asked Evyn to make a few notes on each.

When I neared Grey's side, he hissed, "Quiet," to his team.

I raised my voice. "I will not be sending intelligence to the other side, swordsman Grey. This exercise is to gauge and assess informally."

"Yessir. Didn't mean to imply otherwise, sir," he rapped off.

"I bet on malicious compliance," Evyn murmured in Rushia.

That was a good way of putting it. Grey essayed a salute but his fist was nowhere close to his heart. I saluted back, properly, my fist pressed above my heart. "I look forward to seeing what you come up with."

"Yessir." Grey turned back to his cohort.

As we made another slow circuit, Evyn tapped her steele on her paper. "Everyone seems a bit more tense than usual. Three guys nearly dropped their swords earlier, and another went the wrong way in drill, Barlay said."

"It will be the imminent return of Gavain." I fought to keep my voice level and quiet. "Aleric was saying that there are rumours in the corps. His fate is already sealed, apparently."

"Was he... sorry, *is* he a favourite then?"

"He and I were most often chosen as leaders in games like this. He's charismatic and very clever. He also has a relatable upbringing as the son of a baker and not the son of the captain." I tried to shrug that back as easily as I moved my shoulders now. Opportunity had seemed to rain on me and I seized every one that I could, all the while believing that others could step into the same deluge. Had they really been able to?

That aside, I focused on her question. "He was able to lead Special Forces during Torgund's reign of terror. That might lend him... I don't know, some kind of comradeship, as he underwent the same experience they did."

"And made the best of it," Evyn said, scowling at her steele. "A real lemons to lemonade kind of chap."

I did not need to understand the items she referred to in order to grasp her meaning. "Aubin had been of the same opinion, but I am not so sure," I admitted.

"Yeah, I can tell. You're an emotional seesaw right now." She touched my hand. "I don't mean that you should pull back, by the way, so don't."

I reined in my initial reaction to do so. "Very well."

"I'm sure it will all come out in the wash," she said with confidence, underlining whatever she wrote with a flourish.

"It seems to me that people reveal their true selves when they are under pressure. It was something my father impressed on me." I looked up toward the castle. "There will be plenty of pressure in the coming sennights, I feel."

"Yeah. Barlay's office is covered with all sorts of things about Skien. I suppose you'll be going soon."

"Mm. We can speculate, but for now, we have to focus on drilling Special Forces."

The exercise went well enough, with both sides taking an aggressive approach as expected. Three men were injured, but not badly, necessitating a trip to the infirmary and the healers there. Once that was squared away, my stomach was howling for the midsun meal, and Evyn's eyebrows looked rather pinched. She was liable to be snappish when hungry, and the jagged edge to her mood spiked and scraped along the sides of my awareness.

Pushing calm back over to her, I said, "The corps has been dismissed to duties. Let's away to baths and food."

"Yes please." Evyn tucked her papers away, and we walked in companionable silence toward our apartment as Evyn preferred not to sit in the loud company of people she hardly knew. Truth be told I was happy enough to indulge her preference for meals together, and tried to convince myself it was not because I felt similarly ill at ease amongst Special Forces.

As we gained the corridor to the guest quarters, two servants came running up. "Special Forces! Help!" the man shouted.

Now wasn't the time to correct my unit designation. "What's the trouble?"

The man rested his veiny hands on his knees, trembling. "The corridors are shaking! The MasterMage is attacking! Do something!"

*I don't believe that for a heartbeat.* "I'll investigate. Stay here." I meant Evyn as well, but she followed, a certainty settling into both of us.

I knew it would be useless to argue. "Alright, but stay close and do exactly as I say."

We made our way up to the guest level of the castle and I paced ahead of her down the corridors toward the suites for visiting dignitaries. The corridors were sumptuously decorated in the goods that Oberrot was famed for producing, and we hovered in the scant cover of decorative tapestries with our signature red and gold threads. They trembled, dust sifting from the ceilings. The stones *were* grumbling and shifting in their copings.

Something was dreadfully amiss.

Inlays of gemstones sparkled along the walls, but as we got

closer to the Hunter Suite they flared red. I halted in my tracks. Even the blues and greens were angry reds now, all glinting with malevolent ire. Tuniel probably knew we were here, she could use the very stones in the walls of the castle to detect people, but she had said once that the power in Evyn's blood could blind her senses.

I drew my father's sword and, when nothing happened, continued on. Evyn's steps beside me were quieter than usual but not nearly quiet enough; I motioned my hand for her to wait as I crept the last few steps to the suite.

I pulled up to listen at the door, keeping my back to it and watching up and down the corridor.

Inside was not the usual murmur of conversation of a visiting party settling in, but grunts of exertion. Unless they were moving the furniture, which I highly doubted, there was a battle going on inside Tuniel's rooms.

"You are limited within the castle walls, Tuniel," a woman said. "You care too much about collateral damage and the mundanes. Almost as if you think they are equal to magic users."

Her voice was clipped and cruel. Tuniel didn't bother responding, but the corridors flared red again.

Alerting Special Forces to a hostile mage within the castle was now a priority. I tried signalling to Evyn, *Go sound the alarm.* She knew a few hand signals and her eyes widened at 'alarm.' She started creeping back, when a choking sound froze my limbs.

"At last!" the enemy mage crowed. Whatever she was doing made Tuniel cough and splutter. She could be in agony!

Evyn was by my side in an instant, no doubt feeling the rush of my anger. "We have to help," she whispered, our hearts and intent aligned.

With a few quick but precise sweeps of her hands, she opened up two portals through the door, one to Earth and one again back to Oberrot. I leapt inside, sword drawn, and the portals snapped shut behind me.

The receiving room of the suite had been overturned, curtains shredded and chairs lying in splinters. Two women in pale green robes lay on the floor. Tuniel sat next to the bodies, skirts pooled around her and a quiescent collar glinting around her neck.

Hot anger surged up my throat. How dare someone collar her, cutting her off from her power?

A mage spun to face me, one of the ones I'd seen earlier in Tuniel's green livery, and my anger focused on her.

The mage paled when she saw me, but held her ground. "Special Forces, this is a matter within the magical community. I promise no mundanes will come to harm."

"It didn't sound like you were too bothered about mundane lives a heartbeat ago. Also, I am a Ranger."

She wasted no time and thrust her hand toward me. I braced, keeping my calm to assess her magic and her weaknesses. All flesh was weak against the sword, but the trick would be to get close enough to use it. I breathed deeply, but while my lungs expanded, I couldn't feel anything rushing to fill my chest. *She manipulates air.* Fighting the urge to claw at my throat, I launched forward. I had a minute at most before I would collapse from lack of air; I had to end her, and fast.

A strong wind shoved me back. I hunkered lower, pushing myself against the wall of force toward where Tuniel sat, locked in place by the collar. Her fingers twitched, reaching for me. *She is a stone and metal mage, perhaps she can fight the magic in the metal around her throat!* She might need time to do so; time I could buy her.

The mage dropped a table leg next to her own. It was picked up by the current and flung toward me, striking my right leg and dashing it out from underneath me. I slipped and the torrent shoved me to slam against the door with a boom, bashing out the remaining air in my lungs.

"Thorrn!" Tuniel's despairing cry barely reached me through the strong wind howling in my ears.

I scrabbled my hands along the lintel beside me, keeping hold of my father's sword, when the door vanished and I blew backwards over a heart-stopping five-length drop in the Earthian sky. It was grey and raining again in that realm, the chill rain washing over my limbs as I catapulted back into my own world, bashing against the back wall of the corridor.

Evyn's face was white. "Are you okay? How come her magic works on you?"

I leapt to my feet, able to breathe now the mage couldn't see me. "Wind caller. Her magic isn't directly against me, but on the air around me. Don't worry, they are wholly directional and can only attack one person at a time. She can pin me against the wall while stealing my breath, but she won't be able to deal with someone behind her at the same time. I need a handful of heartbeats for the mage to be distracted."

"So we both go in." Evyn's eyes were wide, but a determined streak as solid as an iron bar ran through her, through us both. We propped each other up, sending calm support and strong determination to one another. "I'll ping over the sky and give her a show."

"Run to the bedroom. It's the door to the left." My dry mouth could barely get the orders out. "Be careful."

Evyn stood next to me, inside my guard, and we both jumped forward at the same time. Two portals flashed before me, one after the other, and we were back in the ruined rooms.

Immediately Evyn ran for the bedroom, making more portals.

As expected, the enemy mage swung toward her. It still made my heart lurch. "Who are you?" She frowned, seeing no insignia on Evyn to identify her.

I darted for the enemy, sword raised, but the blonde did not even turn her head to look my way as she sent a strong gust at me. It knocked me off my feet, swirled me up with a twist and slammed me against the wall between the windows. The wind pressed relentlessly on my chest, pinning me, and I couldn't suck in a breath.

"Thorrn, eh." The enemy mage smirked at Tuniel. "MasterMage, now we reach an impasse."

Tuniel's face went pale, hands frozen in grasping toward me. "What do you mean, Renora?"

"Give up the mastery, or I kill him."

The wind pressed down, a relentless weight I couldn't throw off. *How am I going to get out of this?* I had battled wind mages and mancers before, but as part of the contingent. The last time I'd fought a rogue wind caller was with Gavain: I had been the distraction while Gavain went behind the mancer and ended him. At this moment, Tuniel was incapacitated by the collar blocking her from using her magic, and Evyn couldn't ping me through the castle wall; we were several lengths up on both sides of the worlds and I would fall to my death below.

Perhaps this wind caller would be enough on this one occasion, and I would never live down the shame of a Ranger being killed by a sail-filler. As well as being dead, of course.

"Thorrn!" Evyn stopped pinging.

*Keep going!* I fought to push myself from the wall, but the wind flattened me even further.

The mage turned her attention to Evyn. No! "What are you?"

Evyn flinched but squared her shoulders, as I'd taught her. "Let him go."

Flicking her hands, the mage sent another howl of a hurricane directly at me. My hair whipped my face, showering my cheeks and jaw with sparks of pain. Evyn gasped, starting toward me, and the mage's wind caught the edges of her shirt, flapping it.

It seemed as though the mage expected more, her jaw dropping. "You're an Earthian!"

# CHAPTER 4

Mages and mancers would kill to possess Evyn, using her for the power in her blood. I roared, but nothing came out of my mouth. *Evyn, run!*

Evyn scowled. "Magic doesn't work on me. Back off from my friends, or... or I'll..." She took another step toward her, but the mage was not intimidated.

Instead, she had a delighted smile on her face at an Earthian willingly approaching her.

Tuniel said, "Renora, stop your attack. Release the Ranger, do not harm the woman."

"You are not in a position to bargain, MasterMage," Renora said dismissively.

I mouthed wordlessly, my lungs starting to ache.

Tuniel stood up.

The mage gasped, mirroring my own shock. "But... you have a quiescent collar on! You shouldn't be able to move!"

"Yes, a quiescent collar, which is made of metal." The necklace shivered, shattering into links that cascaded down Tuniel's chest.

She brushed them away. "It took some time, but I convinced the metal to my point of view."

The wind mage took a step back, her right foot sinking into the stone made pliant and liquid. She toppled to her knees with a high-pitched scream, stone solidifying around her foot. The crack of bone turned my stomach.

The mage spat, "I'll kill him if you do not relent!"

That seemed a certainty if I couldn't free myself. I couldn't move from the wall and my chest heaved on nothing. My arms tingled. *I will not last long like this!*

Tuniel had a hand lifted, perhaps to ask more of the stone trapping the mage, but her fingers twitched. Her gaze flicked to me, a brief movement but enough that the wind caller caught it.

"Relinquish the mastery, or I will kill him," Renora said.

Tuniel's hand trembled.

"N...N—" I tried to cough out a refute. *We can still think of a way out! Don't do it, Tuniel!*

Tuniel opened her mouth just as the door to the corridor boomed wide. Behind it was the round short woman I had seen arrive with Tuniel earlier, red hair in one long braid. She jerked back in shock at our tableau, and instantly the doorway filled with black. A shining obsidian shape darted in, claws flashing from nightmarish angular arms and a wide jaw filled with rows of jagged teeth.

The wind mage screamed as the huge lizard seized the wind mage's head in her jaws and with a twist, the mage was dispatched.

The wind cut out immediately and I dropped from the back wall, drawing in gasp after gasp of air.

Evyn ran over to me and flung her arms around my chest. I drew her away from the bodies and the thing in the centre of the room as it hissed at the deceased enemy mage.

Tuniel smoothed her hair back. "Carreelee, really?" she said in Skienien.

The lizard twisted in on itself, curling into its coils. The black scales flashed pale and red, and then the squat mage stood blinking in the centre of the room. She flushed red, gesturing to me. "It looked like you were under attack," she muttered to Tuniel in guttural Skienien.

What kind of magic user was she? She could take on the form of a sinuous lizard; that kind of power was unheard of in Oberrot. Immediately I wondered how I would fare against something like that, and what a Skienien mage of all things was doing here, allied with Tuniel.

These questions would have to wait, but not my gratitude. My own command of the Skienien language was rusty and relied on simple phrases. "My thanks," I told her, moving onto one knee and catching my breath. The rush of air into my lungs had never been more welcome.

The mage nodded, peering curiously at Evyn. I tugged Evyn behind me, setting my jaw, and the mage looked away.

Tuniel sighed. "Mage Carreelee, you may leave me now."

She nodded, small beady eyes studying me briefly before she went into the dining room.

As soon as the door clicked closed, Tuniel ran over to me. "Are you hurt? I could monitor your heartbeat from the stones behind you, I knew you weren't close to dying, but that would have been unpleasant." She helped me to my feet. Her face turned from concern to a scowl. "Wasn't the colour change from the stones in the corridor warning enough?" She swiped at my arm. "And you brought Evyn as well!"

"I am capable of bringing myself," my soul companion said, putting her hands on her thighs and breathing hard. "Glad you're okay."

Grasping my upper arms, Tuniel pushed her face up to kiss mine, but then she reared back as if scorched. "This is too dangerous, Thorrn! We must make doubly sure that no one ever sees us together. She could have attacked you alone, all she needed to do was blow a hurricane at you until you became unconscious." She gripped her skirts, blinking away her tears and peering at me from under her lashes. "Are you truly hale and well, though?"

I bore the sweep and turn of her emotions. She was only angry because I had nearly been hurt, something she took personally. "The stones going red merely tipped me that something was amiss, but remember I charge into danger, particularly where my soon-to-be wife could be in peril."

She rolled her eyes but snuggled into my chest. "I was never at any risk. Renora was stupid enough to put a metal collar on me, but it took longer than usually to nullify it because I was trying to warn you away." Her hands curled around my biceps. "She killed the other two, and they were loyal to me. Serana was... was almost a friend." Her voice hitched, but she quickly brought it back under control.

I stroked her back, sadness swarming inside me. Tuniel had few friends, made fewer now. "She did not manage to defeat us."

The door to the corridor flung open yet again. I lifted my father's sword and stepped in front of Tuniel and Evyn, keeping a broad profile to fully shield them from the intruder.

An older Skienien woman marched in, grey braids swinging. She was whipcord lean, muscles packed onto her small frame. "Come to Oberrot City, she says. It will be a good season, she says. Cooler than the desert around the MasterMage's Palais, she says. There was no mention of rogue mages attacking, Lady Tuniel!" The woman fixed my chest with a glare, as if she could see through it. "Lady Tuniel, get out from behind that man mountain."

Tuniel scowled, sweeping around me. "Layloree, this is a Ranger of Oberrot Castle and Lady Evyn, a friend. Ranger Shardsson, Lady Evyn, this is Layloree, a long-term retainer for my family's homestead."

Layloree glared at her. "Retainer? I raised you, and you call me a *retainer?*"

This had to be Tuniel's nursemaid, a Skienien Battlemistress who taught Aubin their style of fighting. Smiling, I sheathed my father's sword and bowed to her. "It is a pleasure to meet you, Layloree of clan...?"

Layloree flapped her hand. "I claim no clan, not anymore. Not after what they did to my soul companion, Doresgere. Oh, do not fret," she cackled when I blanched, "he is retained too, as pretty little Lady Tuniel says. He's the best gardener in North Hold, with his magic to cheat."

Tuniel murmured to me, "Layloree fled Skien nearly two score turns ago when her soul companion developed magic, leaving behind her family and the men she had won to her side."

Layloree folded her arms tight. "Fled sounds too gentle, Lady Tuniel. Chased out, hounded, forced to fly. They burnt our homestead, my oh-so-loyal men, so they are no great loss, and I found another purpose." She tossed her head, braids flying. "Now, where is the *hellione*?"

*What does that mean?* I glanced at Tuniel to see if she understood that.

Tuniel's face fell, pushing her silvrine hair behind one ear. "Aubin is not here, Layloree."

I turned away from the conversation to arrange the bodies, putting the women's hands on their chests, even the one who had attacked us. Evyn helped, a similar disquiet simmering within us; we didn't need to hear this story.

"Not here? Where is he, then, the Academy? In his shop?" Layloree tugged at the expensive curtains on the floor-to-ceiling windows. With a rip, the fastenings tore, and she laid the cloth over the corpses with a flourish. She tapped her foot, and I looked up at her. Layloree raised an eyebrow at me. "Well? You know something, man mountain."

I sat back on my heels, waiting for Tuniel to explain, because to try and put my feelings on the matter into words was too painful.

Tuniel picked at her skirt. "Aubin went to Skien."

That was new intel for us. Evyn's surprise echoed with mine. "Skien? Why would he go there?"

Tuniel's lips twisted. "He wants to punish himself. If he wanted easy living, he would go to Dinahe for a comfortable life as an apothecarist."

Layloree tutted. "And if he wanted to put himself through hell, he'd go to Skien. Its rough edges have always rubbed him up the wrong way, being a small little *hellione* instead of a hale man like... well, like this strapping lad." She looked me up and down, giving me a gap-toothed grin. I straightened up, wanting to show well to this woman so key to Tuniel and Aubin's lives.

She went on, "As well, he fights using the Battlemistress blades. He is a laughing stock every time he brings them out. Real men don't fight using those blades; they use the hammer, or the axe."

"Hm." I tapped the hilt of my father's sword. The blades were traditionally used by Skienien women but they were effective in battle, and perhaps part of that was because it was unexpected to encounter a man using them. "He's probably chosen that option. He knows I wouldn't want to go back to Skien, not after that... incident." I winced.

Layloree frowned. "What incident?"

"The one that has inspired a new fashion?" Evyn gently teased.

My stomach fell. "What new fashion?"

Evyn smiled. "Apparently pairs of Skienien men are wearing each other's soul jewels on their right shoulder."

*Damn and blast.* I rubbed the back of my neck. "Yes. That incident," I muttered. Amare warmed, a low flare like a kiss, and I put my hand to Tuniel's soul jewel embedded up there.

Tuniel turned her face toward me, cool and calm, but I knew that she had stroked Amare just so to send me that reassurance. "So what is your plan to retrieve him?" she asked me.

I nearly took a step back. "Retrieve him? He... he quit the Rangers. He has left us, left the city. He clearly wants to be alone." *And much good may it do him.*

Still, my heart ached at Tuniel's words. *He wants to punish himself.*

Instead of making a new life, he was torturing himself with the past. "Does he... need us?"

She gave me a withering look. "Of course he needs you. He needs us all. I thought he wanted some time and space, but he still hasn't returned. I can feel he's hurting badly. He needs all of us, but he has run to the one place he thinks we cannot follow; myself because Skien will turn on mages, and you because of embarrassment." She raised her chin. Despite the wanton wholesale destruction around us, she looked regal and collected. "He clearly does not know us well enough if he thinks we will not follow him there."

A sour taste rose in my mouth. Chasing him down as if we could not live without him, begging him to come back, galled me.

It must have stung Evyn too. She gave a most unladylike snort. "Yeah, not sure I should hunt him down. I don't think he'd be pleased to see me."

"He will not be pushed, Tuniel," I reminded her.

She and Layloree both smirked. "We know," Layloree said, a twinkle in her eyes.

"So are you intending on kidnapping him to drag him back here?" Even though I said it partly in jest, I started to run through possibilities. "I mean, that would be the kind of challenge I would enjoy." The idea of slinging him bound and trussed to bounce on my shoulder all the way back to the city gave me a warm feeling.

Tuniel gestured to the bodies. "For the time being, these need to be removed and I will need to go to a different suite. I will have to apologise to Gough that a mage attempted to remove me on his property, and reassure him the situation is contained. He might want reparation for damages." Sighing, she laced her fingers together. "Then we will need to talk about the situation in Skien, and I shall introduce you and the king properly to Carreelee and Layloree and what they hope to achieve by being here."

I clicked my heels together. "Very well, MasterMage. I can return to escort you to the royal apartments in time for the meeting."

Her eyes glittered. "Thorrn, no. You cannot be seen to be close to me. Remember?"

I touched her elbow, but she pulled away from me.

I kept my hand raised. Given that her friend lay dead from an attack, her fear was likely all too real at present. "We can walk arm in arm, that's an acceptable escort," I pointed out. Friends and contemporaries of all genders and stations could walk arm in arm; it was hand in hand that was indicative of an exclusive relationship.

"Even so, I do not want to leave careless clues for anyone, Thorrn. I want nothing to tie us together in any way." Her gaze held mine, a sad smile on her beautiful lips. "Please. Even when I'm feeling weak, you have to be strong for us."

I lowered my head toward her. "Tuniel, it's just us and trusted allies here."

Her smile flickered and died on her face. "Can we ever really be sure of that?"

Layloree scoffed, squinting into the bright light from the high sun outside. "Can you be sure of anything? We could die of heart attacks at any moment, my girl. You must seize the air!"

Glancing at the outline of the bodies under the curtain, I nodded. "Yes. Seize the air."

Tuniel turned toward the bedroom. "I have to repack. Ranger, please go inform whoever you need to of the incident and that we will need a change of rooms." Behind her cold demeanour, I saw the tremor in her fingers. She was deeply shaken, needing time to compose her nerves.

She had proven capable of defending herself, and the other allied mage with her was a formidable opponent in her own right. She would be fine here, I reassured myself.

"Of course, MasterMage. I look forward to the meeting." I touched my fist to my heart and then tapped the stone atop Amare. Even under the leathers of the Ranger jacket I felt it warm. No doubt it was glowing as it was so close to Tuniel, resonating with the ebb and flow of her soul bond with Aubin, and the idea of that pleased me. I had missed that glow.

Holding my arm out for Evyn, I led her along the corridor to the servants, who were waiting with wide eyes. "The threat has been neutralised. Go tell the steward the MasterMage will need a new set of rooms. I'll inform the Regs and Special Forces."

The servants dashed off. Now that the fight was over and the surge of battle had receded, the swirl of our emotions intruded, mine and Evyn's both. I tried to lead our breathing and steady it, but a pool of unease rose within her, threatening to overtop our defences and flood through us.

I led her immediately downstairs to the ground floor, out into the courtyard and through the gatehouse. I changed direction from my automatic march to the barracks and stepped off the path, aiming us toward the castle gardens. Laid out in formal rows, the grounds were picked over with meticulous fervour by the castle's legion of garden-ers. Everything from the kitchen gardens further to the back and the decorative flowers bordering the castle walls was in formation, stems tall and tidy as a soldier on inspection.

I led us to bench. "Sit," I told her.

"You sit too." She lowered herself slowly, legs shaking.

I sat, shoulders blocking us from view by the thoroughfare. "Breathe. I won't go anywhere."

She tucked her head under my arm, hiding herself from the passers-by. I scanned them, staring down anyone who glanced our way, pushing down the urge to take her and fight my way out. As she breathed, the sharp edge to my sight receded. Her panic attack faded back down, and so too did my aggression.

She lifted her head. "Sorry. Thanks."

"No need to apologise. Cup of tea?"

"I've just seen a couple of bodies and watched someone get killed by a magic dragon, I need more than a cup of tea." Her voice hitched.

My brave soul companion. I sent a wave of reassurance to her, kneading my knuckles. "I need to walk only over there to the barracks, to explain what happened. I'll keep you within sight at all times."

Evyn gulped air. "What did happen? Who attacked Tuniel? Why?"

I settled back into the reporting cadence, trying to radiate calm. "It was an attempt on Tuniel as the MasterMage, a wind mage called Renora who chose today to strike at her. Likely because Tuniel is outside of her base of power here."

"Oh heck." She sat up. "Do what you need to do. I'll be okay."

"You're sure?" She did not yet feel as she usually did; there was a knot of tension in our stomachs.

"I mean, I will be. It's just a reminder that this place can get scary."

"Yes. You faced it bravely." I smiled at her. "Your training is coming along. We will need to get you a weapon soon enough."

Far from delighting her, she winced, but her face took on a determined set. "I suppose I'll need one. If I'm immune to magic, and you get pinned again, I want to be able to do something about it."

Her sentiment and determination pleased me. I stayed with her until she settled and began looking around the gardens with interest, relaxing into the familiar surroundings. She often spent time here marvelling, little prickles of wonder sparking up the bond as she stooped toward whatever ground cover flower had caught her eye, whether purple petals furled in a silvrine bed or taller stems with blousy blooms. Still, her wonder was coloured by sadness when she was here.

I knew why, and didn't need to ask.

# CHAPTER 5

I reported to the barracks and we had a quick bath and repast in our apartment before our appointment with the king.

Gough looked up from his desk as we reported in. "Lady Evyn, Ranger. Welcome."

"Hi, Gough." Evyn held Gavain's note to her out with a stiff arm. "I opened this at last."

Gough's brows lowered as he took it, gaze scanning the lines quickly. My stomach clenched, almost as tight as Evyn's grip on my fingers.

*What will the king think of this confession? What will he do?*

Gough turned it over to see if there was anything on the reverse, and rose slowly from behind his desk. "Thank you for bringing that to my attention. Before the MasterMage arrives and we decide a response to the situation in Skien, let's discuss Swordsman Gavain Gomoresson's return. He will be here by tonight."

I would struggle to keep my feelings from my face, and so I did not try. I squared my shoulders and set my stance to attention as anger followed by heartache chased themselves up my gullet. "Very good, sir."

He rubbed his temple, moving the creases on his forehead around, his deep brown eyes surveying mine and gauging my reaction. "I'm sorry to ask this of you, but you are familiar with him and with alternative versions both. I would ask that you interview him to ascertain his identity as the Gavain from this timeline."

Alts were rare but not unheard of, although the only ones I had met so far were versions of myself, Evyn, Tuniel and Aubin. They were the product of the twists and turns of their timeline, the unique events that shape us being different on their worlds. Despite that, I recognised a great deal of myself in my alternative version, and not just the physical similarities.

I saluted, two taps of my fist above my heart. "I will do so. I take it I am to stay away from subjects that will be brought up in any trial?"

"You have it correct. You have my complete faith, although I'm sorry to ask it of you. I know it will be difficult for you." Gough's brows dipped, scanning the note in his hands. "It would be useful if you both were to attend the hearing, along with Barlay and of course Gavain's soul companion, Zelora. I will particularly want your assessment, Thorrn."

My core went cold. My words would be added to Evyn's and Barlay's to decide Gavain's fate.

A wash of consolation surged up the bond, warming my heart as much as it was able against the chill of the difficult undertaking ahead. Evyn's fingers threaded through my left hand. I squeezed back for her.

The king saw, smiling briefly at us. "You seem to be adjusting well to one another. That's wonderful, and will be helpful in the coming days."

"Thank you, sir." We would need to draw on each other, our newfound openness tested.

Gough's smile fell, beckoning us to his door. "Come, let's await the MasterMage and her guests."

We moved to the king's receiving room where the MasterMage

and her guests were shown in by Captain Barlay. Tuniel bowed her head to the king and took a seat next to Evyn, arranging her skirts. Her face and dress were composed, showing no sign of the fight earlier. She brushed Evyn's fingers in what could be an accidental touch but I knew was anything but. It was gratifying to learn to decipher her moods, like a secret code or language that few people spoke.

Behind her came the new mage Carreelee and Layloree. Layloree bounded in, grinned at Gough and winked at Barlay, who coloured. Carreelee kept her eyes on the floor, toying with her long braid and shuffling to a seat next to Tuniel. Having seen how fast Carreelee could be, I stood just behind her.

"Well met. Refreshments?" Gough asked.

Tuniel inclined her head. "You know my preference for reds, Gough."

The woman I loved had an equal relationship with the king. The Accords between magical and mundane meant that Tuniel swore fealty to him, but she was the ruler of the magical community just as Gough ruled over the rest of the populace.

"I'll try some soft southerner wine," Layloree said, craning her neck to look at all the paintings on the walls.

"And for you?" Gough asked, ducking slightly to peer into Carreelee's face.

She twisted her face away, but spoke quietly. "Water."

"Me too," Evyn said, studying Carreelee.

"Very well." Gough's smile did not falter. "Barlay? Thorrn?"

"The red will be fine," Barlay grunted.

"Yes, sir." I had never taken a drink with the king before. The honour was only for high-ranking individuals.

*Which I suppose I am.* The thought both captivated and terrified me. Evyn looked over and I smiled for her, and together we smoothed out our emotions.

Gough ordered the drinks himself and came to stand in front of the gathering. "Thank you for coming here today to determine what our strategy should be, MasterMage. I look forward to meeting your retinue. Many of you will know me. I am the king of Oberrot."

"Well met." Tuniel inclined her head. "Layloree of North Hold is a Skienien by birth, but fled a score and a half years ago when her soul companion was targeted in an eviction. She will have some experience to add to this meeting, but, mainly, if we decide on an active response, she will be invaluable."

"Lady Tuniel speaks too highly of me." Layloree gave another gap-toothed smile. "I am a retired Battlemistress. Hardly invaluable."

"We will see, Layloree," Tuniel murmured. "Beside me is Mage Carreelee."

The squat mage flinched at the term, ramming her hands underneath her armpits.

Tuniel paused, face composed. "Carreelee, are you able to recount your journey and history to us?" she asked in Skienien. "All here can understand Skienien, I trust?"

Gough nodded but Barlay shook his head. Evyn stood, coming to stand next to me and Carreelee. The squat mage eyed her.

Evyn's welcoming smile pushed her cheeks into her eyes. "Thank you very much for saving Thorrn earlier. I was a bit in shock, so I'm sorry if we didn't introduce ourselves properly. I'm Evyn."

Carreelee uncurled slightly. "Well met, Evyn." Her Oberrotian was stilted. "Why are you here?"

Spoken with such a guttural accent it barked like an accusation. I bristled.

Evyn put her hand up toward me, calming me. "I'm a researcher, and right now I'm helping Special Forces. I'll take notes, if you don't mind."

The mage glanced from her to me and back again. Then she nodded. "Alright. I will try to speak slowly."

A rap on the door announced the drinks. I remained posted next to Evyn and Carreelee. The squat mage took a step closer, then another. She held her water glass with both hands, the water hardly trembling at all, until Gough said, "Carreelee, are you able to tell us?"

She nodded once, glancing at Evyn. "I grew up in a small town near Keltskarr. It is near to the centre of Skien, and it has many mines. My family are... were hunters." The catch and correction was not lost on me or on Evyn, who surged forward. Waves of compassion flowed from Evyn like a soothing song.

Although Carreelee would not be able to feel it, she did react to me relaxing, and eased a little herself. "I am a beastshifter." She lowered her head. A great deal of hurt hid behind that one word, being a magic user in Skien. "About a sennight ago, a band of rogue men moved in over the hills. The Keltskarr Battlemistresses offered a reward if they were encouraged to move on. I... I can frighten a great deal of people in a short space of time, as you can imagine."

Having seen a glimpse of what she could do, the capabilities rolled out before me. Shock tactics certainly, and she had moved fast against an adversary. How would she fare against a group? She would need support to push forward her initial advantage against a large amount of enemies.

Evyn chuckled. "Yes, I'm sure you can, and if you're not careful he —" she pointed at me "—will really want to have a friendly match sometime."

Carreelee squinted up at me. "Doable."

I grinned widely. "Capital."

She relaxed, letting her arms fall to her sides rather than wrapping around herself in a poor protection. "I confronted the rogue men but there were more than I had any hope of handling. They sent me home bloodied, but worse awaited me when I came looking for aid through the gates of Keltskarr."

She shivered, black scales shooting up along her arms. "A group had arrived, calling themselves the Hudau, those who oppose magic, extolling the dangers of those who wield magic, how they can manipulate you, steal the blood from your body, rip out your air, or make you do things by changing who you love or what your dreams are. They were led by a man called Brudamere and they had a lot of supporters, people I wouldn't even suspect harboured such sentiments: the baker's soul companion, who always had a kind word for me, the ratcatcher who sometimes used me to help wriggle into the smallest spaces, the town drunk who no one really listens to, but he had an intent look in his eye this time." Carreelee's arms shook.

Evyn put down her steele and gently touched her elbow.

The mage immediately stiffened at the touch, looking down at Evyn. She eased. "Everyone frightens everyone else with tales of the black beast, a dragon that comes out at night to eat men." She huffed. "Few people know it's me, but enough that if they told anyone, I would be routed for sure. I should have left, turned around immediately and run. There was nothing in my shack worth dying for, and my mother was long dead and gone, her men dispersed.

"Brudamere wanted to make an example, wanted to show that magic users can be killed just like anyone else. They had the crowd bring them people they suspected, saying they had a sure-fire test." Carreelee trembled again, a rumble resounding from her chest. "They had a row of people, all dazed and like they couldn't believe where they were, up on the town fountain staring down at the townsfolk they had seen every day. Some of them I knew had no magic at all, like the midwife, and some I'd suspected; someone whose tailored clothes came out a little too perfect each time, someone who responded to every single fire in the town and somehow it died down faster than we were expecting." Her hands flexed, claws sliding in and out of focus. "They wanted to hurt them all with hot iron, saying iron negates magic." She peered at Tuniel curiously.

"Of course not. Why would a particular metal interfere with magic? Only if it's imbued with another type of magic, as in a quiescent collar, and even then it's not the base metal. Nonsense." Tuniel flapped her hand.

Carreelee nodded. "But the hot part would hurt them, cause them to lash out, and they might use their magic to defend themselves or just because it hurt so much. And... it wasn't right. None of these people had done anything to hurt anyone. They hadn't committed any crimes, but here this Brudamere was, as if merely carrying magic was a crime."

My tongue felt too heavy. My thoughts had veered in that direction once, that no one who could command magic could be trusted to care for anything other than themselves. I glanced at Tuniel. I had since had my perspectives opened, but I could easily imagine another path that my heart could have taken.

"So I..." Carreelee scuffed her heel. "I transformed," she muttered.

"Into that big beast we saw earlier?" I asked.

"No. That beast is the one I can do quickly, but in theory, I could be anything." She straightened up further, and this time she kept going. Her height towered over my own, a muscled Skienien woman as lean as Layloree. She wobbled around the edges and her shoulders widened, hair flashing darker. A thickset version of me squared up to me.

I grinned again. "I'm used to seeing alts, so that isn't going to shock me."

Carreelee blinked in surprise, the expression looking lost in her face, and sank back down into the round mage. "I transformed into Desoree, to give me courage." Seeing the blank look on Evyn's and my face, she said, "Desoree is a legendary Battlemistress who even commands the current Chief of all Chiefs."

"Who is?" I asked.

"Grendamere the Great," she said. "I think. It was when I left."

"Yes, it has been two sennights," Gough grumbled.

"Commands...?" Evyn asked, gaze darting to me.

"Later," I signed. Evyn's questions about that particular element of Skienien society might tip off that she was not from this world. I would explain in private.

Evyn went back to taking notes.

Carreelee went on. "I charged up to the town square and

demanded the release of the prisoners. Some of the townspeople ran, some obeyed, but Brudamere called me out as a magic user. I... I tried to bluff, drawing Battlemistress blades, but I am no Battlemistress, and the blades were just extensions of me so they were soft to the touch. I could see this was not going to go well, so I changed into that big black beast you saw earlier. That caused a general panic, and a lot of people fled, but that just made the Hudau crow things like, 'See how destructive they are? How they revel in rampage?' But I wasn't the one branding people whose only crime was to exist."

Black peaks spiked up and down the backs of Carreelee's hands. "They surrounded me and threw ropes over me. They called for an axe and they had enough men there that they had a score of them. I can transform quick enough to wriggle out of and between ropes but I was tiring, and axes hurt. They began chopping, but I can pick up the pieces and put them back on. That just enraged... everyone, I think, even the prisoners on the platform looked stunned and horrified. I know it's not... normal, but I wasn't about to die just to satisfy their world view that chopped things stay chopped."

My stomach twisted, Evyn's and my sympathy twining together into a sensitive knot. Evyn held out her hand.

Carreelee took it with a grateful smile. "I might not have been able to escape. I panicked, too distracted that now everyone looked at me like I was a monster, but then one of the men tripped and went down, someone else slid away, and then there was a hand grabbing me and pulling. I followed after it in a kind of... ribbon that I can be, flat and flowing, because it was better than staying surrounded in a circle of axes.

"At first I thought it was a woman because of the height. They pointed me and the rest of the prisoners toward the gates and told us to go." She hunkered lower, as if the terror of that night were still weighing on her. "I helped the others escape, and once I didn't eat them three nights in a row they started to trust me, but before then it was rather tiring always being watched. I made them get to the border and we crossed it at night, and then we were in Oberrot." She shrugged a shoulder. "The best place for people who command magic to go would be to see the MasterMage, but she came to meet me just after we crossed the border."

Tuniel nodded slowly. "Yes. I met them in western Oberrot and helped to settle the refugees around the Palais in the east, but soon that will not be enough." Tuniel shifted to face Gough. "The situation is dire. Anti-magical sentiment is alive in this Hudau, well-organised by this Brudamere and most likely sponsored, supported or at least sufficiently ignored by the rulers of the country to spread. Tales like Carreelee's are probably playing out across Skien as we speak.

"As the MasterMage, I would welcome new talent. Being able to command magic is a rare skill, one in a hundred births. If both parents have magic that changes to one in fifty, but still a low chance. There is a wealth of skills and vocations that could use new magical talent, and this in turn can enrich Oberrot and the lives of all citizens." She raised her chin. "Of course, we will want to make sure all the magic users understand and pledge to the Magical Mundane Accords, but if we can offer them safety and a good life, we will win their loyalty."

Gough nodded once. "And, of course, it is the humanitarian thing to do."

Tuniel flushed, but instead of the light pink when she was complimented, it was a harsher burgundy. "Yes, of course," she murmured, gaze cutting away from the king.

She had prepared arguments for accepting the new magic users that were based on cold logic and benefit. She hadn't been sure enough of the king to know that he responded to the plight of people more than the promise of rubles.

Evyn's eyes shone with tears as she put the notes to one side. "I'm so sorry," she said to Carreelee.

"Why? Did you do it?" Carreelee frowned.

"That's just Evyn's way of speaking," I said. "She is sorry that happened to you. We are also pleased that you made it here and, frankly, I'm impressed by the abilities you've shown and the heart that your actions have revealed."

Carreelee's eyes narrowed at me.

Tuniel's composed face whipped toward her, assessing. "Before we go too much further, I will remind you that there are some cultural differences you must understand and adhere to, Mage Carreelee. The Ranger, for example, is part of Gough's retinue and is not available for you to claim."

I took a hasty step back, bashing into the back wall. "Oh, definitely not."

Another low growl rolled from Carreelee's chest, this one tinged with amusement. "I understand, MasterMage. Although I did save his life, so I could claim him if he had no other woman to look after him, if this was Skien."

Evyn raised an eyebrow at me. I shook my head once to forestall her questions in this company.

"But this isn't Skien." Tuniel's voice took on a hard edge, ringing through the room.

Carreelee looked between me and Tuniel, then at the king, who had a half smile on his face. "I accept he's yours," she told Gough. "I understand things work differently here."

"Thank you." Gough inclined his head, gaze darting to Tuniel.

She smoothed her skirts. "I can help you navigate the customs, Carreelee, as you can help us when we foray into Skien."

"Is that what we're doing, then?" Gough asked her, frowning slightly. "A foray, composed of who?"

"I would suggest a small party. Myself, Carreelee and Layloree at the least, to understand the operation there."

Tuniel would go herself? My chest tightened. "You'll be in great danger," I said. "If the Hudau were to realise the MasterMage was in their country, it is possible they would stop at nothing to get to you."

"I agree," Gough said. "The Skieniens have their magic sniffers, those sensitive to the use of magic, do they not?"

Tuniel tipped her head. "Yes, but as long as I do not use my powers, they will not find me."

"MasterMage, you are a strategic resource," I said. "Same as we would never let the king charge into battle, you are too precious to lose."

Tuniel's face went absolutely still, but I was certain that no one else would find anything amiss with my words. They were the truth; they just so happened to be true in more ways than one.

"Very well," she said, stiff hands smoothing her skirts. "But the same risk applies to Carreelee."

Relieved, I nodded to her, then turned smartly to Gough. "Your Majesty, I recommend that Oberrot sends support with Mage Carreelee. If she cannot use her powers, she will be vulnerable."

"Not that vulnerable," Carreelee said with a smirk.

Gough swirled his wine. "I agree with you, Ranger. A small, discreet party I can quietly authorise, along with Special Forces to keep the borders between Oberrot and Daron flowing as before."

"Nothing announced widely, of course." Tuniel's eyes swept over me. "But we must help the people under persecution, those who cannot escape from the Hudau."

"And bring them back to Oberrot. Mm." Gough set his glass down with a pleased smile.

Barlay clicked his heels. "We will need to venture into Skien along the southern edge, and that's where the parties can split, sir."

"Good thinking." Gough looked up at me. "Are you in agreement, Ranger?"

"Yes, sir." My heart pounded with certainty. Finally a job for the Rangers. *Well, one Ranger.* My stomach twinged, and Evyn met my eyes. I smiled for her. "Although getting to each and every settlement in Skien quickly enough will be a challenge." It was possible that we could dip in and out of Oberrot and travel via Earth, with their much faster, propelled methods of transportation, but we could not with Carreelee and Layloree along with us.

"You won't need to visit every settlement. Activity is being coordinated from the Skienien side," Carreelee said.

"Oh?"

Evyn glanced at her notes. "Oh yes, the woman who helped you."

"Woman? Ah, no. I only thought they were a woman to start with, as he was so small and he used Battlemistress blades."

A surge of surprise rocked through Evyn and I, rippling through us in little shocks.

Carreelee said, "I had help from an Oberrotian. He said his name was Tabreksson. He led us to the border and assured me the Master-Mage would be waiting on the other side."

The sting of hearing Aubin's fathername was tempered by the fact that he was fighting to protect innocent lives. *Aubin cannot help himself. He saw an injustice and needed to remedy it.*

I gaped at Tuniel. She nodded once. *That's how she knows Aubin is in Skien.*

Evyn's delight and trepidation matched my own. Our complex knotted feelings of betrayal, disappointment and sadness had been joined by buoyant hope.

"Wonderful," Gough said, his chest puffing out. "Then I assume you will want our Ranger to meet with, ah, *your contact*, and help escort as many as we can out to the border. Captain Barlay, I leave the planning to you and your staff, but assume that we will be contacted by Daron to help them with their northern border with Skien, and proceed on that basis. I have no doubt the Duke will reach out soon if he's seeing what we are seeing."

"Yes sir." Barlay saluted.

Gough turned to Tuniel. "Thank you for bringing this to my attention, MasterMage. I can give you resources to assist and my support in rehoming the displaced and their families. I will require your agreement that our direct intervention is kept from the officials of Skien. This will be the action of Oberrotian citizens on their own initiative."

She inclined her head.

Gough levelled a look at me. "Shardsson, you'll be taking leave shortly. I suggest you prepare for a vacation from the city."

I saluted with a wide grin. "Yessir."

Barlay nodded to himself in agreement, but his shoulders slumped with tiredness. He had hoped to use me to plan the deployment. "I can help you, sir, until my vacation," I reassured him.

"Yes, but you should also be focused on said... vacation." Barlay rolled the word around his mouth, like it tasted foul.

Gough smiled. "We can call it the mission here, amongst us, Captain."

"Very good, sir." Barlay fell into silence, no doubt already thinking of the Spiritshere-sized mountain of work ahead of him. "How long until we go?"

Gough looked to Tuniel for the answer.

She stared deep into the reds of her wine glass. "Within the sennight would be best."

Gough raised his eyebrows. "Barlay? Thorrn?"

"It will have to do, sir," Barlay grunted.

"I can be ready faster, sir, once... once those other duties you mentioned are completed." I stretched my fingers out behind my back to steady them. *First is Gavain's trial.*

The door rapped. Gough nodded to me, and I paced over to open it a crack, blocking the view of whoever was outside. "Yes?"

It was the king's steward. "Message from the docks. There's a request to bring the king's barge up to King's Lake, and His Majesty asked to be made aware."

My stomach twisted so hard that Evyn gasped behind me. *Gavain.* He was here, he had been returned to the city, and now Gough would want to get to this as fast as possible.

The steward frowned at me.

I cleared my throat. "My thanks. Is that all?"

"Yes, Ranger." He continued to stare at me. "You've gone rather pale."

"Ah, well." I willed myself upright, grasping for anger to fuel me rather than shock to gut me. "That will be all."

"Of course."

I closed the door, and immediately Evyn was there at my side. I smiled for her as best as I could.

Turning, I saluted the king. "Sir, I have a message for you."

He seemed to know, perhaps from the timing or my demeanour. "Thank you, Ranger. MasterMage, Mage Carreelee, Layloree of no clan, may we wrap up this meeting on that note of coordination and cooperation to assist the beleaguered citizens of Skien?"

Tuniel swirled her wine around her glass. "Yes. I will be in the suite your stewards are setting aside for me." She drained her glass. "On an entirely different note, I can offer the assistance of one of my highest ranking medimage or mancers, Gough. Do keep that in mind." Her hard ice blue eyes met his. "You might need it."

# CHAPTER 6

The walk along the passageway to the cells was quiet aside from a harsh, regular noise that started and stopped in time with my rapidly beating heart. Grasping the hilt of my father's sword, my march slipped into the same rhythm, echoes from my boots clipping down the corridor.

The panting became clearer and louder the closer I got. I nodded to the gaoler, who gave me a hesitant salute back. None of the other castle forces really knew how to react around a Ranger. My Ranger leathers were a darker red than Special Forces' bright crimson hues, the stiff collar digging into my neck as I turned my head to search out that sound.

My stomach rolled. I quelled it before the sensation could seep across to Evyn, but I felt a reassuring touch on my shoulder, my soul companion Finding me. Not for the first time, I was both grateful and embarrassed that she experienced the same as I. We were both feeling rather a lot of trepidation, Evyn's nerves mingling with mine until they became a mass too compacted to pick through and separate. I had to carry that as well, feeling as though my stomach jutted up under my ribcage to elbow my heart.

The cells were clean, dry and warm, well-lit by glowstones. As I neared a closed cell door, the pants resolved into breathless effort in a low male voice. Perhaps he was exercising, doing push-ups or similar in his cell.

I rapped my clenched fist against the door as I passed it, entering the next open cell along. Between the cells were bars so prisoners could be visited or interrogated, or soul companions brought in and stowed separately but still within sight of one another. Zelora sat on the bunk in this open cell, her arms around her knees. She wiped the heel of her hand against her red eyes, but saluted me. She was thinner from recent strain but strong.

The man in the next cell was standing, lifting his arms up and down. "Three-score nine. Three-score ten." His voice shuddered. Blond hair pulled back into a queue stuck to pale shoulders showered with sweat. He had taken his shirt off. "Three-score eleven. Three-score twelve." He glanced over his shoulder, and when his blue eyes met mine, Gavain locked into place.

*He looks terrible.* His skin had flushed as if with health, but his legs were swollen and his belly bloated. He had lost condition in his upper body, the usual firm outline of his muscles now obscured by swelling. It was understandable; he had sustained a usually fatal injury.

I tried to sort through my emotions, the flurry of feelings at seeing this man again: outrage, yes, hot and choking, for what he had done to Evyn; a bitter taste to my tongue that he had betrayed me yet again; and while he seemed to pay for it, there was disappointment in him and in myself that, somehow, we had let events come to this.

Heartened that he was alive, that the face I'd seen every day for turns and travelled along the same path as me for so long was still one I would see again.

Dread, for the actions and events of the next few days would determine his fate, and whatever the outcome, it was going to be emotional turmoil. *I hope you're ready, Evyn, because I don't know if I can shield against this.*

Gavain hobbled to sit on his bunk. It was no act, his jaw locked in a grimace and sweat trickling down his temple. Once he sat, his gasps continued to ring harshly around the cell, and he fixed me with an unfathomable glare.

What were his thoughts on seeing me here, bearing witness to his indignity? No one had sent word of my coming to him, so it was a surprise to him. Zelora was wide-eyed, staring at me, but I couldn't discern if she was reacting to Gavain or whether this was her own disquiet.

Taking a reporting stance, I fixed my gaze on Zel rather than Gavain. "I'm here to ask a few questions, as authorised by the king. You are welcome to stay, or you can get some rest."

She shook her head and smiled sadly. There would be little rest for her over the coming days as well, and my heart went out to her.

Clicking my heels together, I paced to the centre of the open cell. Keeping my feet shoulder-width apart, hands balled in front of me in a ready stance, I stared down at Gavain.

He tipped his head back to look at me, blue eyes searching mine. His blotchy face was pale, deep circles under his eyes and lank hair falling into his face. Left-centre of his heaving sweat-streaked chest sat a horizontal scar, an unobtrusive and unnaturally uniform small rectangle, as long as half the size of my smallest finger. *This is where Aubin's knife pierced, spearing Gavain's heart.* Thinking about Aubin, however, made my chest hurt. *Probably not as much as getting stabbed there would.*

Gavain placed his hands on his thighs, his voice reedy. "Thorrn. Well met." He wiped his brow with a shaking hand. "Lady Evyn, how does she—"

Anger flared hot at hearing him speak her name. *Evyn could have died.* Saving her had been a struggle, and at any point I could have lost her thanks to this man. "The king sent me to ascertain your identity," I said loudly. "There have been a few alternative versions in evidence, and as I am familiar with them and with... you..." I paused to regroup as memories assailed me; sparring with the man in front of me day after day, knowing how he moved and how to best him, and how he changed to best me, the pair of us in constant challenge to better ourselves. I had thought it healthy competition, but maybe he had not.

*Only one way to discover for sure.*

I continued. "Anything you say will be used to help me form my conclusions for the king. He will interview you himself, but know that I will make a full report of anything you disclose to him."

"I understand," Gavain said, gaze dropping to his hands loose in his lap. "I could decline to answer." A statement. He knew as well as I that Gough did not condone torture to wrench answers out of people.

"You can decline. I'll note that to the king, and it will render my report rather inconclusive." Although it was a Gavain tactic to take. If I suspected he was an alt, a person from a different timeline to ours, it was likely that Gough would have different questions for him, and then he wouldn't be on trial for a near manslaughter.

Gavain sat back on the bunk. "I will not decline. I'll answer as truthfully as I can, Thorrn."

His hard but earnest gaze was hard to parse or, indeed, bear. He looked drawn, yes, as if troubled or bearing a heavy burden, but also determined. Was I genuinely seeing that, or was I interpreting him as I wished to see him?

On with the questions. Gough had left it to me to decide what to ask. "Where were you born?"

"In Oberrot City, where I was raised by my father." He took another gasping breath. Even talking was wearing for him. "The woman who bore me left to find something more for herself, searching for something better to be than a mother and a baker's wife."

This was true. "Why did you join the Regulars?"

He frowned slightly. "When, or why?"

"Why," I affirmed.

A flush darkened his temple. His jaw worked. "Perhaps I am more like my mother than I would wish. I wanted something more for myself."

"What do you mean by more?"

He looked away. "A place. A story. A tale of adventure to my life rather than the drone of the everyday. Who knew that even adventure could become everyday." A smile twisted his lips, brief and fleeting.

That chimed with what I had seen, the baker's boy striving to keep up with me, following me until he could surpass me in some areas. The army welcomed his talents, a strategic mindset and logic not often seen in soldiers. My father, Shard, had been pleased that he joined the extra training he subjected me to, bringing us both along.

"Why did you apply to Special Forces?" I asked.

Snorting, he looked at his closed fists. "Honestly, I said, and honest I shall be. I joined because of you."

I stared at his lowered profile. *Gavain joined Special Forces because of me?* "Explain."

He glanced up. "I want... wanted..." Swallowing hard, he dropped his head. "When I met you, I wanted to be with you wherever you went."

That was new intel to me as well. "Why?"

"Why?" He shook his head. "Ridiculously skilled, handsome and born into a family who loves you? It was not an option for me, of course, so then I wanted to beat you as the next best thing." That smile returned, a temporary flash that made his face sadder and more serious.

I turned that over in my mind, a flare of anger searing my lungs. He had taken the first real opportunity that presented itself to do just that, to side with the usurper king who helped the former Master-Mage Waker to depose Gough rather than follow me.

I pushed my feelings aside. It was a gaping hole in his story to explore. If he joined for me, why did he torture me? "Outline what happened when Torgund became king."

His face darkened. "The king suddenly changed to someone hanging people all around. Minor infractions were punishable by death." He paused to regroup, red trickling up his chest. "Shard and Lori refused to bend the knee and were executed swiftly. Newly made captain, Barlay told us to hold to our tenets. I do not need to remind you that the first one is abject obedience. When you returned, I helped Barlay administer your test because the usurper king insisted on it. I counselled you to obey his every word because he was set on hanging you, Thorrn. He asked Barlay and I to report any slight deviation, anything at all, from marching out of step to looking at him the wrong way."

My skin tingled, crawling with unease. Torgund had wanted me dead. Gavain had seemed frightened, that morning outside my cell, telling me to obey as fully as I could.

Gavain leant back, gasping now. "He insisted that it be a genuine charge, I think to shore up Special Forces' belief that he would be a just king, but he would make anything a genuine charge for you." He had to recover, hands flat on the bunk and a dark expression on his face. Hatred? Shame?

I took a deep breath. "And then?"

His gaze hardened. "And then... you rebelled. I tried to stop you."

"Why?" *Why didn't you come with me if you joined Special Forces for me?*

Gavain shifted his legs in front of him. They were swollen and bloated as well, and looked painful to move. "You know me. I do not press a fight I am sure I will lose unless ordered. That is a sure way to get you killed and, if you are a commander, throw away the lives underneath you." He met and held my eyes. "You had no chance to escape, not with the abilities I knew you to have. I suppose I did not have the full information; I did not appreciate what Evyn could do or your... new friend."

Cowardice, or calculation? I turned that over in my mind, rolling my fingers over my thumb. It rang true for Gavain, and I was known to press against incredible odds. Not everyone would or could be expected to, but he was my closest friend. I would have expected his support, even into death.

*Is that really something I can expect of others?* Aubin had given me that kind of support, but even he was gone now.

Gavain looked away. "My staying helped to calm Special Forces. You rebelled and we had to distance ourselves from you. I did so quickly, lest the usurper decided I had a hand in helping you escape. I rallied and supported the remaining troops." His hands curled around his knee caps. "For good or for ill, that pleased Torgund."

My emotions must have passed across my face, because he glanced at me and scowled. "Yes, Thorrn, because pleasing him was the only way."

"Hence your promotion. Alright." I ran my tongue behind my teeth. Gavain was either a cold opportunist, or a man trying to stay ahead of the waves around him.

Aubin's observation about Gavain had been drawn from a singular incident. Despite the pain now, I trusted Aubin's instincts over my own, and it was another tack to try Gavain with. "During your test to enter Special Forces, you let Zelora be pushed into water you believed boiling. Did you hesitate?"

He frowned, probably wondering how I knew about his test. "No."

"Why not?" Cold sweat trickled between my shoulder blades. During my own test, Torgund had revealed that the water was not boiling, but asked me to push Evyn in wearing chains so she would sink and drown. He meant for me to retrieve her against orders to the contrary and kill me then, but instead I begged him to save her, revealing she was from Earth so he would relent.

I still did not think I would have let Evyn be pushed into what I feared was scalding water, but according to Aubin, Gavain had chosen the king over his own soul companion without a care for her wellbeing.

Gavain and Zelora's eyes met, their shared spirit united. "I knew she would be fine. Gough was present and he would not devise a test where she would be in the least hurt. It's not only a test to follow orders but a test of trust in Gough."

I had not considered it in that light before. With my experience being related to Torgund only, I saw it only as a torturous choice underlining how ruthless the corps could be. It unsettled the motivations that I had been reading into my one-time friend. What if he was not truly as cold-hearted as we thought? *What does that change for me?*

Gavain watched me. Questions bubbled in my mind, full of too much bitterness to voice while charged with an official duty. *Why did you continue to hurt me after Gough's restoration? Why did you hurt Evyn? Why did you involve her in our squabble? What is our disagreement even about?*

I tamped down my anger. Tomorrow, Gough would question him and I would learn those answers. "That will be all for now. I have all the information I need." This was the Gavain that belonged to this timeline, of that I was sure.

He lurched to his feet, staggering to the side and crashing into the bars. "Thorrn, wait. I want to talk."

"I have all the information I need," I pressed.

"I don't." He licked his lips, shuddering from the effort of merely standing up. My heart twisted painfully. "That uniform you're wearing, I heard you had a new status, a new part of the army? A Ranger?" His hard face was almost accusing.

That much I could divulge, as I would to any enemy forces who managed to capture me. "I am a Ranger, yes. A new part of the castle forces defending the king and Oberrot."

"And it's just... you?"

Pain flashed across my chest briefly. There had been two Rangers. I kept my face stoic and clear of emotion.

Gavain's eyes dropped. "Then it's as I feared." His hands wrapped around the bars between us.

I needed to get out of here, breathe some of the air outside. I saluted to Zelora who nodded back, hand pressed to her mouth, and I turned to leave.

"Thorrn. Thorrn, wait!" Disgust scrunched his face, as if he were lowered to begging from me, or perhaps ashamed at being so out of condition before me.

I halted.

"Lady Evyn. Is she alright? I want to see her."

Anger roared through me, demanding that he shouldn't be allowed anywhere near her. "No," I spat.

Shoulders slumping, his grip on the bars slipped loose.

Barely holding on, I made my way out of the cells at double-time pace, not stopping to acknowledge the gaoler. My steps quickened along the corridor to the atrium, ears ringing with my heartbeat.

Outside Barlay waited, and he turned and matched his pace to mine to cross the wide space. "Slow down, lad," he said, voice low.

My heart pounded so hard it was a wonder I wasn't seeing red and black smears across my vision. Anger and fear clawed at me, demanding that I run back in there and howl at my friend, fight him, rip him apart, even though his condition meant it would be an utter rout. Evyn would be feeling this for certain, and sure enough I felt her Finding me, a light touch on my shoulder.

I pulled myself back from the brink using that anchor point.

"Good." Barlay's steps slowed, and so did mine. "How did the meeting with Gomoresson go?"

I flexed my hands. "It's him, sir. He's very ill, but it's him."

"Mm." Barlay grunted. "It must have been difficult to do, but important. My thanks." He drew up, and long instinct drilled into me had my feet stopping as well, taking an attention stance.

Barlay looked up at me, his gaze taking me in. I probably had a flushed face, maybe an agitated set to my jaw. I hated that Gavain could provoke such a response in me.

Barlay met my eyes in turn. "Breathe, Shardsson."

I did, sinking into each rise of my ribs, trying to pull in cooler air even though everything around me was too close and too hot.

When I properly came back to myself, I noted we were on the upper level of the atrium. The mosaic depicting Oberrot and its immediate surrounds was at my back, and Barlay was studying the eastern edge, where our country bordered Skien.

Barlay glanced at me. "There, that's better. Your pupils were wide enough to swallow me whole, lad. Your control over your berserker issue is admirable."

Usually my chest would swell with pride, but it felt too battered and bruised at this moment, as if I'd spent a turn of the glass in a Skienien fighting ring. "Thank you, sir." Even the platitude felt too hollow.

Barlay continued to survey the map. "Thorrn, it is hard to watch you go through this. It was harder when that usurper was in charge." His mouth worked, as though he fought not to spit at the mere mention of Torgund.

I rocked back a little on my heels. As captain, Barlay had to balance the needs of all the men and women under his command. I had not much thought of the pain wearing on him to watch individual journeys.

"I'm sure it will all... turn out for the best," I said. One of Evyn's phrases, and one that was supposed to fill me with serenity. Instead, it felt like someone was screwing their fist around my guts. Either Gavain would be executed or he would not, or he would be banished, or he would be restored to Special Forces, and I did not know which outcome I wanted. "I just want to know, now, so I can react. I hate not knowing," I admitted.

Barlay's gaze focused on the entry and exit roads in our borders with Skien. "Part of my role is seeing multiple ways how an engagement can unfold, preparing for the most likely or the most disastrous turns of events. During that time of Torgund, I had to try to navigate to save as many of the men and women under my sudden command as possible. That included you *and* Gomoresson, as well as all the others. I... I lost so many because they were not wary, because they kept pushing their beliefs and principles when the time was not right." He rubbed his red eyes.

I fixed my sight on the mosaic of Oberrot Castle, the centre of the map and indeed my world. All of this had happened so quickly, lives turned askew between one heartbeat and the next. Barlay had had to do so much, be so much, in a short space of time.

He cleared his throat. "I counselled him to obey, because the king was watching him. I would have given you the same orders. When you escaped, I tried to think of where you could have gone, how to help you, but you were using methods I did not understand. Cut off from you, the only one I could help was Gomoresson.

"When Torgund ordered a contingent to the Palais I sent a rough patchwork one, made up of different members from the gutted cohorts. Gomoresson was somehow able to form them into a unit, a remarkable feat. I was delighted in that, except it was brought to bear against you, but again you had allies I was not aware of and couldn't account for. All my planning and worrying were for naught when it came to you."

Barlay faced me square on. "I learnt that you can and you will surprise me, but you will stick to your chosen path with both hands and every fibre of fire inside of you. Gomoresson... he will do what he needs to do to survive. He will adapt and he will thrive, even in circumstances most consider too dire. Where others lay down, give up and die, he will fight. He's rather like Tabreksson in that respect."

A bubble of dark mirth rose up in me. "I could well imagine what Aubin would say if he was compared to Gavain like that."

One side of his lips tipped up. "So can I. The man did have a way with words." He turned from the map, clicking his heels. "I will continue to try to help all of you to find your paths. Some will be in your way, Thorrn, but it will be the right path for them. It's not personal. You always were too quick to think that it was your fault, your mistakes that led to an outcome."

*Other people's choices are not my fault. It's how I react to those choices that matter.* Another phrase from Evyn, and this one did settle me.

"Thank you, sir." I tapped my fist above my heart. "I genuinely mean it, and I value your support for everybody."

"As you were. The MasterMage has asked that she be allowed to examine Gomoresson, and the king has granted that request. She'll be along shortly... ah." He saluted, looking behind me.

I turned as well, my head still swirling, and faced my beautiful promised. Her eyes searched mine briefly, narrowing at what they saw there.

Tuniel inclined her head. "Captain. Ranger." Amare gently squeezed against my tense shoulder. I tried to relax into it, shooting her a small smile that sank away. We could not greet each other with anything more than cordiality in public, and while I would welcome her touch right now as a comfort, I was a strong swordsman and I would bear up without it. Nevertheless, I wished there was some way I could signal back to her that I was pleased to see her.

Behind her strode a person almost as tall as me, eyes bright and studying mine as though searching for a trace of recognition.

Tuniel gestured to her colleague. "Captain Barlay, Ranger Shardsson, this is Journey Mage Hepzibah."

Hepzibah inclined her head. "For this day. Well met, Captain, and it is good to see you up and around, Ranger Shardsson."

I frowned. I couldn't recall meeting her before, and what did she mean by "this day"? "Do you go by a different title on other days, Journey Mage?" I asked.

She puffed, pleased. "You're one of the very few to ask! Sometimes I feel more he than her, so I might introduce myself as Journey Mancer." She shot a look sideways at Tuniel. "I'm working on the MasterMage to make an all-encompassing title rather than have it be based on gender all the time."

That flummoxed me, but then again, I had met a shape-changer today. "Well met in any case, but I am afraid that our previous meeting escapes me." I tried to recall. Had they been one of Waker's minions, perhaps?

Tuniel laced her fingers in front of her. "Journey Mage Hepzibah holds the title because she is one of the foremost healers in her field. She assisted your recovery, Ranger Shardsson."

"My..." *After my lashing.* "I had not realised I had received magical healing." I had been so consumed with my recovery, both physically and mentally, that I had not even thought to ask. "My sincere thanks."

Journey Mage Hepzibah nodded, smiling broadly. "It is not often that I get to heal such extensive damage. It's quite pleasing to see you walking around and back in service again. Believe me, it was not certain that you would be."

Remembering that time made the skin on my back feel tight, the scars tugging as I fought not to hunch my shoulders. "Then my thanks again, for your incomparable skill and your generous time."

The Journey Mage flexed her hands, turning to Tuniel. "It was an interesting problem, so when Tuniel asked me here again, I could not resist."

Tuniel's eyes glimmered with rare warmth as she smiled at her friend. "I asked her here to give her assessment on the chances of recovery for the swordsman Gomoresson."

"And maybe assist with a new phenomenon."

I frowned. "Me?"

Hepzibah threw back her head to let out a deep laugh. "Oh, you I have already solved, and while you needed acute treatment it was relatively simple to aid you. No, this is something else, something entirely new." She nearly vibrated with excitement. "I reviewed the medical notes from Dinahe. It's clear they were astonished at his recovery, but it's only temporary. The patient presented with all the symptoms of a fatal stabbing, with severe blood loss and damage to the surrounding tissues. He went into shock, heartbeat slowing, and the notes are quite clear that they expected his half-spirit to leave his mortal body."

My stomach twisted. She was talking about Gavain, and the immediate aftermath of Aubin stabbing him.

Hepzibah went on, "But then they started recording signs of some stability, and some little but remarkable improvement. It took him sennights to recover to the point of consciousness, and by that time his pulse readings were commensurate with struggle." The mage rubbed her hands, as if that were delightful news. "That is why Tuniel called me, and, as well as responding to an order from one's MasterMage as a loyal mage should, I find it quite intriguing. He might be the one we are looking for."

Looking for? *Who are Tuniel and this mage looking for?*

Tuniel turned her face away from me. She remained completely composed, giving me no signs to her inner thoughts. "Shall we?"

Captain Barlay said, "Let's examine the prisoner. Ranger Shardsson, do you have somewhere else to be?" His gaze averted from mine, allowing me to retreat if I wished, to not have to see Gavain again.

*I do not retreat.* "I would be interested to learn the answers to these questions as well." Facing Gavain would reduce my reaction to seeing him and help me acclimate to being able to confront him again.

We walked all together, but naturally Barlay led and Hepzibah walked alongside him. Tuniel's steps slowed, and after we passed the gaoler and turned into the corridor with the cells lining either side, she straightened her skirts. Her knuckles brushed against the back of my hand, another accidental touch that was filled with purpose.

I lowered my head, staring straight down at the floor. "Thank you," I whispered. She was reminding me she was here, walking beside me, with me.

She made a soft noise in the back of her throat. "Mm." *Of course.*

With her by my side, facing Gavain would be much easier.

Barlay went into the cell where Zelora maintained her vigil and quietly explained that we were here to examine Gavain. "Swordsman, lay on your bunk," he ordered Gavain.

"Yes, sir." Gavain, still shirtless, sat on the edge of his bunk. He turned and lay down, body shaking and coursing with sweat as if he had just completed a hard workout.

Barlay opened his cell door and went in with Hepzibah. Tuniel paused a moment before following, and Barlay locked the door behind them. I went to stand in the adjoining cell, maintaining a ready stance.

Hepzibah wasted no time in holding her long-fingered hands above Gavain's chest. Gavain lay perfectly still, but his breaths came a little shorter, his eyes shut as if he rested, keeping himself relaxed.

Hepzibah cooed, cried out and swore. Finally she exclaimed, "This is perfect, MasterMage!"

"What are you seeing?" Tuniel asked, leaning over Gavain.

"The heart is faltering, failing, enlarged and bloated. The muscle tissue is damaged. It's a slow death sentence."

Gavain shuddered, and Zelora let out a little sob.

I stilled. No matter what Gough decided, Gavain would die.

*Good, he deserves it.* I expected relief that the decision would be taken out of mine and Evyn's hands, or more specifically our words. This was a natural consequence of the choices of his life and Aubin's blade that likely led to this, nothing to do with us.

Instead, I was consumed with sorrow. *He's going to die.*

Barlay's face fell, grey and drawn. "MasterMage, Journey Mage, what is it you intend with this swordsman?"

Hepzibah spoke. "A whole new possibility, unlike anything we have seen before."

She snatched Tuniel's hand and, far from tugging it back as I expected, Tuniel allowed her to twine their hands together. I bit back my surge of protest. *She isn't my inamorata here, in public. She is the MasterMage.*

Hepzibah's hand glowed, and then so did Tuniel's. Above Gavain's chest there formed a concentration of light, as if motes of dust had been made to glow. It formed something the size of my fist, four regions pulsing and twitching.

A human heart. Two of the chambers were striated, lined as I knew muscle to be, like strata in sandstone. The other two were smooth, each one a bright solid mound, as if it were...

"Amare," I said. The armour deployed smoothly and wrapped around me, sliding into place from my shoulder to embrace and support my torso, warm and comforting.

Tuniel looked over her shoulder at me. "Yes," she murmured.

Hepzibah's grin was so wide I could see every tooth. "What we are planning here is a new breakthrough. Some of the MasterMage's living metal fused with the fibres of this man's heart, a magical undertaking the likes of which the world has never seen."

"But how?" Barlay peered over the mages' shoulders at the image floating in the air. "How will your metal get there, MasterMage?"

Tuniel put her hands in her myriad pockets, pulling out a small silvrine ball of liquid metal that puddled into her palm. She handed it over to Barlay, who took it with both hands. "First, you hand him over for experimentation. Then we will work out these details. I expect the best way to insert the living metal into his body would be to introduce it via a wound, given the way that the shoulder armour bonded to the Ranger."

A wound? Did she mean to torture him? "No, stop. You can't," I said.

Tuniel's eyebrow raised. "That will be determined by the king and the captain, *Ranger.*"

"Why him?" I asked before I could stop myself.

Her gaze flicked to Hepzibah and back to me. "He will die other-wise, or perhaps be sentenced to death. A previously hale subject with an inner strength to keep surviving."

I tried to sift for any deeper meaning behind her words, but I was overwrought and could not clearly see any. I could read the meaning behind her gaze however – *later.* "Very well," I said, in a tone that implied that this conversation was not yet through, but my stomach settled. I knew my wife-to-be. She did not revel in the pain of others and she would not cause him overmuch distress.

Tuniel tapped her lip, looking at the shape hovering above Gavain's chest. "It will truly be incredible, a world-first: metal and living tissue working in concert. Think of the many lives this can save."

The glow to her face, a flush of triumph and excitement in discovery, warmed my heart. She was excited to begin, that much was clear. She wanted to help.

She shrugged. "If we can get it to work."

"Indeed!" Hepzibah smiled broadly. "And even if it doesn't, we will learn much from the attempt."

The attempt, meaning that Gavain might die. He didn't seem to react, lying still and silent as though already dead.

"That's enough." My voice was firm. Discussing his fate when sentence had yet to be passed was abhorrent.

Amare gently pulsed. Even though Tuniel did not look my way, I knew she had meant it as an apology.

Hepzibah seemed not to notice. "I wish I had paper and steele."

Barlay looked up at me from his study of the metal ball shining and wobbling in his cupped hands. "Shardsson, please request such from the gaoler, and then I expect you'll have duties you need to get to elsewhere."

I nodded, saluting, and paced out, trying to frame it as a strategic retreat. We had the pre-trial with the king soon, and I would have to get composed for that.

I welcomed the breathlessness of walking up the stairs to the living areas of the castle, my mind vibrating like a plucked string, thoughts reverberating and bouncing around inside me. My usual way of burning off emotion was to exercise, but what I wanted now was to see Evyn. She would be at the pre-trial as well and would need help with her own emotions.

I entered the apartment and pulled off my boots, stacking them with controlled hands. *I will not shove this turmoil down, but I need to be able to function and speak coherently.*

"Hi." Evyn's quiet voice from the sofa. "I can tell it was a challenge."

"Very. I feel like I've been punched in the gut multiple times."

She padded up to me, hot mug in hand. "Kettle is on. What's your fancy?"

"Something stronger than tea," I said, eyeing her mug.

She nodded. "Irish coffee, coming right up."

"What's that?"

"Caffeine and alcohol."

"Skip the caffeine bit, and give me the alcohol."

"Right. One Irish, then." Leading the way into our small kitchen area, she poured me a little sniff of spirits. I thanked her and took the bottle. "Oi!" she protested as I took a swig.

"Here." I put the bottle down on the counter.

She peered up at me. "Was it really that bad?" She could feel this as well as I, and I straightened and laid out the different strands of my feelings.

I closed my eyes briefly. "He was terribly ill, with a small scar but a wasted body to tell a tale of a long recovery in Dinahe." I wanted to sound triumphant, to feel exonerated and exhilarated by his discomfort. Instead all I felt was empty.

Evyn touched my hand. "How did he... survive? Is healing magic powerful enough to heal any kind of wound, then?"

I shook my head. "Tuniel and another magic user, Hepzibah, examined him. His heart is failing. Well, I knew that. He's going to die no matter what. That's what the medimage said, and Tuniel wants to use him, to push the living metal Amare into his heart."

Evyn's eyes widened.

"Oh, I deployed it already." I tapped my chest.

"I'm not amazed Amare didn't deploy or whatever, I'm just... wow. So she wants to put living metal in his heart? It would help him?"

"Tuniel and Hepzibah seemed delighted to try, if not entirely certain it would work." I tipped the glass back, searching for any more droplets in the glass. "He was different, but, I mean, anyone is out of sorts in the cells."

"Did you recognise him?"

An interesting question. I turned that over slowly. "He's not an alt, he is from our timeline. And... I suppose I did. I recognised enough of him that I see him as my old friend, even sick as he is."

And I wanted my friend back.

# CHAPTER 7

Morning training the next day was rote, unnaturally so. None of the men or women broke formation, but neither did anyone have any breakthroughs or excel. They came, they trained, but everyone had fallen back into old patterns.

I did exactly the same, so I could not fault them. All my thoughts were consumed with the interview in Gough's office immediately after training. My gaze drifted toward the cells. Right about now, Gavain would be washing and pulling on a fresh uniform, preparing himself.

Barlay was dressed crisply, his collar tight, and he seemed preoccupied with watching the sun cross the sky rather than the training. Evyn trailed after him, fanning her face with her notes and shooting me small smiles, but even she stared into the middle distance more often than usual.

At last Barlay called for the training to end and Special Forces to get to duties. The men and women drifted together in silence, but Barlay, Evyn and I turned and made our way inside. Evyn clung to my hand, but despite the proximity her touch seemed distant.

The coolness of the castle interior drenched my overly warm

skin, the sudden shock grounding me. I was too much in my head and not enough in my body, and Evyn was the same.

When Barlay broke off to supervise Gavain being led from the cells, I leant toward her. "Talk to me."

She startled, a spike of shock thrumming down the bond, and then she too grimaced as she realised what had happened. "Alright, but it's a real mess. I'm scared because I don't know what's going to happen, and I don't know what to do for the best."

I nodded. That chimed with me, so much so I rang with an echo of it. "All we can do is breathe through it. We will cope. Believe in our ability to do that."

Her cold fingers in mine trembled. "If you're sure, which I can feel you are. Or you'll just say it louder and louder until it becomes so." Giving me a shaky wink, she wrapped her free arm around her notes, pressing them close to her chest like a shield. "Let's do it."

We stopped three times to catch our breath before continuing to climb the castle staircase to the royal apartments, and each time I kept imagining I heard the clink of chain as Gavain was led up after us. Barlay would bring him, and they might be catching up, but I did not want to hurry Evyn along. We had to do this at the pace we could manage.

I flashed my tattoos at the Special Forces guard on duty and he waved us in. Gough waited at his open office door, brows bunched together and wearing his reds. As the ultimate commander of the Oberrotian army, he had a uniform as well, emblazoned with badges and sashes rather than tattoos.

"Sir." I saluted.

"Ranger, well met and welcome. Lady Evyn, good morning." He hurried to the sideboard. "Can I supply you with some waters?" When we shook our heads in unison, he frowned. "Today will be rather trying, I'm afraid. You should make sure you are prepared." He unstoppered a bottle with a pop, holding the neck over a glass. It wavered in his hands.

I had not seen him in a tremulous state before. "Very well, thank you, sir. Yes, it will be a trying day, but then it will be over."

He grunted, lips twitching. "Typical Ranger response: only way to do it is to go through it."

I tried to smile back, but my face would not hold it.

Setting the bottle down, the king gave an exasperated huff. "Ranger, would you mind pouring the waters?"

"Of course not, sir."

Gough watched as I essayed the task. "I have always rather envied the steady hands of my swordsmen and women. Look at that, not a drop spilled, yet I can tell you're nervous."

"It's the training, sir." I passed the king and Evyn their glasses. "I wish there was similar training for composing my face at times."

Gough's own expression was neutral. "Ah, yes. It's a skill learnt, not taught." He knocked back the water as if it were a dram of something stronger.

I set the bottle down with a clink. "Sir, what's to become of him? There are rumours it's a foregone conclusion."

"Rumours, eh. Gossip spreads further and faster than flames, sometimes." Gough folded and unfolded the note along its crisp edge. "The evidence is irrefutable, and this acts as a confession, but the outcome will be determined here, same as I did for you, because of the nature of the secrets he knows."

My stomach swooped. The dressing down I'd had in this room followed by sentencing had been unimaginably unpleasant.

He put a hand on my shoulder, brown eyes meeting mine. "Thorrn, lad. Your trial was not fair, and I saw what I feared rather than what was truly there. Barlay counselled me against it most strongly. As much as I want to go back through the turns of time and change it, the best I can do is promise you its like will never happen again. I want to learn from that experience."

My shoulders loosened under his hand. We had both learnt a great deal from that time.

Gough went on, "I want to learn from this as well. I want to listen to Gavain's reasoning to understand why he made the choices he did, so we can prevent men and women from following a similar path again. Then, depending on what he says and what Ellesmere Reads in him, I'll have to weigh the crime of attempted murder against misadventure." His voice dropped. "It might not come to it, but if he is guilty, we will pass sentence accordingly."

I bowed my head, throat tightening. "Sir," I croaked.

Evyn slumped lower in her seat, guilt bubbling up, sharp and stinging.

"It's not your fault, Evyn," I reassured her.

Gough smiled at us, genuine pleasure in his face before his face grew stern once again. "It is a hard responsibility, but I want you to hear his words directly and give me your unvarnished thoughts on them." He placed the note square and centre of his desk, the sun's light from the window picking out the glint of grey in his black hair and beard. It had to be a heavy burden on his shoulders, but he bore it well, hardly ever letting any strain show on the set on his shoulders and sure steps.

The door rapped again. "Enter," Gough called, pulling himself upright. Gone were the nervous motions, and he was still and serene.

In came Captain Barlay and Zelora, and two Regulars dragging Gavain between them. Gavain staggered and panted, his reds soaked with sweat and his cuffs rolled up to accommodate the heavy manacles on his wrists. My gut twisted with shame; I would be mortified to be presented to the king like this.

Zelora's fingers curled around Gavain's elbow. He gasped for breath, lips white and quivering, but he quickly scanned the room, noting the threat points as we had been taught. When he met my eyes, a surge of anger and pity kindled in me, seeing him like this and that we were here, in this place, having to go through this.

A matching scowl passed his face. His gaze dropped to Evyn beside me, his face slackening. "Lady Evyn—"

"Silence, swordsman," Barlay snapped. "Your Majesty, I bring here Gavain Gomoresson to discuss the charges against him."

Gough motioned them forward. "Swordsman, sit." The Regulars gave him no choice, escorting him to the seat. Gavain folded, sitting with his elbows on his thighs, wheezing as the Regulars left.

I planted my stance wide but avoided eye contact with Gavain. I had to listen and try to contain my anger, a burgeoning sadness brimming up inside me.

Evyn's hands wrung together before she stretched out her fingers and wrapped them around the steele. She was likely feeling the same, focusing herself on a task.

*I wish I had a task rather than stand here and feel.*

Over Gavain's blowing and panting, Gough turned to Zelora. "Zelora, you're here to ensure fair treatment. I will ask that you are silent throughout the proceedings."

She stroked Gavain's hair from his face.

Gavain said, "Leave, Zel. We are going to need to mention state secrets, and I do not want you involved." His eyes flickered with pain as he faced the king, sweat trickling down his jaw. "She knows nothing, Your Majesty."

Zelora bit her lip. Clearly this was an argument they had already had.

Gough brows raised. "That is a sensible suggestion, if you're sure, swordsman. Zelora, you are free to stay so long as you swear under pain of death to maintain these secrets."

"I'll go," she whispered. It seemed they were aligned on this issue, and it broke my heart to see her backward glances at him as she departed.

Gough paced behind his desk, gaze fixed on Gavain's face and his battle for composure. Everyone waited on the king's word, including me. The future would be set in these moments, and the weight of it made my chest ache.

Gough came to a stop opposite Gavain and levelled a glare at him that, if used against me, would strike me down with shame. "Swordsman, Captain Barlay will assist during the interview, and Ranger Shardsson and Lady Evyn are here to observe. The charges that we are discussing here today could be as serious as attempted murder. Now then, we will start with—"

"No." Gavain's sharp voice made me jolt. "You can stop this charade, Your Majesty." He sat up, chains clinking.

Barlay started forward, but Gough raised his hand to forestall him. He stared down at Gavain, face utterly expressionless.

Gavain's harsh pants rang through the room. "I'll save you the time. Pass sentence of execution, give me to the MasterMage to torture to death, and have done with it. I only ask... one mercy." His hard blue eyes bored into Gough's gaze. "Give Zel time to find another match. Let her separate from me before the MasterMage... before she starts on me," he finished, but much more quietly.

*Good, he admits it!* But far from victorious triumph, despair locked me in place, unable to speak even if Gough would allow me.

Gough folded his hands in front of him. "So if I were to raise a charge of attempted murder, how would you plead?"

Gavain's voice wavered. "Guilty."

Shock shot through me, sharp and cold. Evyn beside me gasped.

With his shoulders slumped, his head lowered over his bound hands, Gavain looked defeated.

Gough stayed quiet for a handful of heartbeats, his gaze penetrating. "Guilty, swordsman?"

"Yes, sir."

Gough and Barlay shared a look over his head. Now Gough let his shock rest on his face, and Barlay's was transparent, as bereft as I'd ever seen him. *He felt for us all.*

The king gathered himself, calm once more. "I will continue to ask questions, swordsman. The captain and I want to understand."

"If you want, sir."

"And I want you to look me in the eye, swordsman."

Gavain lifted his head, face blotchy with anger and shame. His words when he spoke were soft. "Yes, sir."

The suddenly quiet rote responses tore into me. *Where is your fight, Gavain? Why are you lying down to die?*

Gough motioned to me. "Ranger Shardsson, please move my chair, if you would be so kind."

"Yes, sir." I picked up the heavy seat, moving it around and placing it where he pointed; next to Gavain's.

Gough sat down slowly, mirroring Gavain's posture, lacing his fingers between his knees. "What happened to you under Torgund?"

Gavain's lower lip trembled. He bit down on it hard. "We've discussed that, sir. I obeyed orders. You demoted me but determined my actions were compatible with the first tenet."

"Yes. But what happened to you?" Gough shifted forward in his seat. "I said I would follow your career with interest, but what transpired in Dinahe is… something I would never have expected. I want to understand. Now, a great deal of trauma from Torgund's rule is rippling through Special Forces, and it's finding outlets. Outlets that I don't like, cannot condone and must punish under the law. But I cannot keep hurting my swordsmen and women; I need to address the malaise and salve it."

That echoed within me. *Someone needs help.*

The pinched look on Gavain's face remained. "Your Majesty, I can see how this ends, I know what the logical conclusion is. I know too many secrets, and I hurt someone close to you." He let his gaze rest on Evyn, steele purling across the pages, and then back to Gough. "I heard you nearly banished Shardsson, and you executed the apothecarist for my attempted murder."

I looked up at the ceiling, keeping my face clear. Gavain might be able to read the truth from my expression if I let it sit there. Gough had bestowed mercy on Aubin, but Gavain would not see that from the story we told.

"Thorrn isn't nearly banished," Gough said. "The Rangers is a corps that I trust implicitly, and who trust me in return. It's true, you do know some of my secrets, and you used that knowledge against her." Gough passed a hand over his face; when next he spoke, his voice was clear and calm again. "I'm doing this out of order somewhat. Captain Barlay, the evidence please."

Barlay clicked his heels together. "Using secret knowledge against a charge of Special Forces. Placing a harmful substance into a vial and deceiving and coercing its administration to the victim. That much we have evidence and a confession for."

Gough pulled out Gavain's letter, dropping it to flutter into Gavain's lap. "Barlay and I are disappointed that your potential was used in this way. Swordsman, you are highly intelligent. What were you trying to do?"

Gavain crumpled the letter in his fist. "I did not mean to kill her, or even to come close. Dinahen is hard to translate and the texts on offworlders were in the mythology section in that library. I looked up something that would work on her, and saw it was perdure but then... then I saw bruswurt listed and that it would hurt her. She would be asleep, so she wouldn't feel it, but Thorrn would. The apothecarist had accompanied her and Thorrn, so he would be able to easily reverse it, I thought. My plan adapted."

Gough's brows bristled. "What were you trying to achieve in the first place?"

"I wanted Thorrn to go to... that other place." His eyes slid to Evyn, her head down over her pages. "I wanted him out of Special Forces and away. I wanted him gone. I had to make him snap and rebel again so he would have no choice, and this was an easy way of achieving that."

*Why does he hate me so?* Resentment brewed up to match his.

"Why?" the king asked.

"Why? It's hard to explain. I... I hate him." He glared at me, and my first reaction was to glare back, to meet his hatred with my own. If he loathed me, then so be it!

Gavain met my eyes. "I hated that... that you were right. I hated that you rebelled and it *worked*. It meant that I had chosen wrong. I... I couldn't face that until recently. I obeyed the tenets, yes, but they were wrong." He turned his face away, twisting the manacles on his wrists. "They were wrong."

My heartbeat rang in my ears. *Gavain regrets his choice!* This was tantamount to an admission of treason to anyone else, but it chimed with what I had done, and Gough had seemed to understand that. What would the king say to this?

Gough took up one of the spare water glasses. "How did you expect me to respond when you hurt Lady Evyn?"

Gavain's face coloured, an ugly shade of puce that clashed with the sick white pallor of his cheeks.

The king's expression softened as he offered out the water. "Well? You would have thought it through to the end. What did you intend when I inevitably spoke to you about putting bruswurt in the perdure that Lady Evyn drank?"

Taking in a long breath, Gavain met his eyes over the glass between them, hands limp and not reaching out to take it. "Two scenarios. Either Thorrn would escape, taking Lady Evyn with him, and no one would ever even mention the bruswurt, or if he stayed and told all, as he did, then I fully intended to talk my way out of it."

The back of my neck went cold. *He admits he would lie to the king.* He amassed more evidence for treason, and from his own mouth.

Gavain continued, "I could say I did not know, that I didn't realise bruswurt would cause her pain. When I saw her laid out, the apothecarist working quickly, the medimancer in a panic, I knew... I knew then it had gone too far. I shouldn't be plotting to remove people." He glanced up at Evyn, red eyes welling. He choked on a sob, coughs wracking through his body and shaking his once formidable frame.

*Of course he wishes this had never happened.* His body was ruined, his heart faltering from the damage it had sustained. *From the choices he had made.* Not running from Torgund had broken him.

Gavain clutched his chest, coughing, the chains rattling with every hard-won breath. Gough gave him time to compose himself, the water glass trembling in Gough's outstretched arm.

Wiping the spittle from his mouth with the side of his hand, Gavain sat back. "I recognise you gave me time to recover enough to return to my home. I made peace with my death. If you want it to serve some greater good with the MasterMage's experiments, then by all means." His watery bloodshot eyes met mine. "Do what you want."

I frowned. Defiance mingled with defeat within him, and all the while his damaged heart beat closer to his death.

Gough sat back, drawing the untouched water back to his chest. "Is execution truly all you expect from me?"

"Yes," Gavain said quietly. "It's all you can do. The law is clear."

"Yes, it is. For attempted murder, in any case." Drumming his fingers on the arm of the chair, he sat up. "The queen will Read you now. Ellesmere, if you would? Thorrn, please let her in."

I opened the door to find Ellesmere walking down the corridor toward us. As a Reader mage, she could listen in to our surface thoughts, and evidently had been doing so to respond now when Gough asked her to enter. She smiled warmly, clasping my forearm, and her brief soothing touch brushed my mind.

She held out her hands for Gavain. "There, it will all be well."

"I don't think so, Your Majesty." Gavain lifted his arms for Ellesmere to slip her small hands into his. He kept his head tipped back, looking deep into her blue eyes. I knew from previous experience that the touch of her mind was discreet and he was likely only seeing flickers of memories as she gently probed.

A tear rolled down her cheek. "Gough, this one is hurting, and he has lost his faith. He just wants the pain to stop."

Gavain dropped his head, his shoulders bunching.

Anger had entirely left me, although Evyn still wrote notes with furious focus. I ached to turn back and undo what had happened. Something had gone deeply wrong with my friend Gav, and the path he was on was not what he was capable of, not who I wanted him to be.

Gough stood. "Thank you, my dear. Captain, Ranger, Lady Evyn, a word outside, please."

# CHAPTER 8

I held my hand out for Evyn, who slipped hers into mine and followed as Gough led us toward the corridor. Two Special Forces guards stood outside, and with a few terse instructions they kept the office door open to supervise Gavain sitting alone. Gavain's hunched back slid lower, his hands curling around the armrests of the chair.

The king led us into his sitting room, waving for us to sit down as he escorted Ellesmere to a seat. Neither Barlay nor I sat, but Evyn perched against the dining room table, leafing through her notes. Her emotions were unformed, circling around her stomach, but slowly they distilled as she looked at the words underlined harshly and studded with exclamation points, as if giving them a name solidified them.

Gough folded his arms. "Well. Your thoughts and impressions, please."

Barlay said, "He admitted that he intended to lie to you."

"He said he intended but he did not in actuality. I think he's been quite open with the truth with us today."

Ellesmere nodded. "He is. Make no mistake, I can be deceived by surface thoughts if I brush an intelligent person's mind who is aware of my ability and has prepared themselves. But touching now..." Her eyes unfocused slightly, hands raising to her chest. Gough's brows lowered, watching his wife exercise her powers. Ellesmere took a shuddering breath. "He's conflicted. He doesn't know if he can trust you, any of you. Gough, he thinks you executed Aubin and expects the same treatment."

"There's little point in telling him otherwise for now, until we work out what the charges are and our response to this incident." The king strode to the table, by Evyn's shoulder. "Evyn? As the injured party, what are your thoughts?"

"I was more mad at Thorrn than at him to start with. I think he definitely meant to hurt Thorrn by poisoning me."

"What do you feel now?" Gough asked her.

She smoothed out her pages, scanning her notes as though they held the answers rather than within herself. "I'm not sure if I believe him completely. From what I've seen and heard about him, he *is* smart enough to lie to us." She chewed her lip, spikes of soreness from it striking me. She folded her notes. "I do think he wants Thorrn gone. He's super jealous of him, and that's turning to bitterness. As soon as he got some power and authority, he abused it to bully Thorrn."

"Hazing is to be expected," I tried.

She rolled her eyes at me. "Well, what do you think of his excuse?"

I collected my thoughts, speaking slowly. "Gavain is intelligent, but in there he pled guilty and made statements that can easily be interpreted as treasonous. Why would he do that?"

Gough said, "To make us think he had changed, if I were to interpret it in shadow, or because he genuinely feels guilty. If he had acted brash or stupid, I would not hesitate to level a charge against him and remove him from the corps, but his demeanour speaks of..." Gough turned to Ellesmere. "My dear? You might be able to give insight and name this better than I."

Wrapping her hands around herself, Ellesmere said, "He wants the pain to end. He knows he has made choices that cannot be changed. He can't go back, and he cannot see any way forward."

A way forward. What way forward could I see from here? It depended too much on the king's choice, what he decided to make of Gavain's statements.

*Can I really trust his words are sincere?* Whether he meant to harm or not, he had, damaging my trust in him in the process, but Al said I hurt them first, running off without a backward glance. They didn't know I had been trying to find the true king. Gav and Al had to make the best they could, along with the rest of the corps, under Barlay's new but thankfully steady leadership.

*They hadn't trusted in me enough to know I would come back for them.* That hurt, stinging like a deep cut salved with salt. I *had* returned, and that should have solved everything, except choices had already been made and paths taken. *Gavain cannot get back to where we were before.* He took my father's life and tortured me, refusing to commit treason for me.

That was the heart of it. "He's the model swordsman," I pointed out slowly.

Evyn turned a slack-jawed look at me.

"I mean, he followed the tenets. He is the perfect Special Forces swordsman who held to his duty above all else."

"No matter what it cost him," Gough mused. "Like the others."

"He was not following the tenets when he moved to harm Lady Evyn," Barlay said, bristling.

Gough shook his head sadly. "By then the damage was done. He lost trust and faith."

"His heart is broken, and I don't mean medically. I mean the… thing that drives me forward." I tapped above my heart, putting a hand on Evyn's shoulder. Our bond renewed with a cool relief. "He broke himself to do it, to follow the tenets under Torgund. He was hurting, and I did not help him. He tried to speak to me while I was a Sergeant, and I turned him away each time."

"It's not your fault," Evyn said. "At some point people have to take responsibility for their own actions."

"Then I am taking responsibility for mine. I should have listened." I bowed my head.

"Thorrn." Gough squared his shoulders to face me. "Do you believe he is sincere? Do you think he has changed or will change?"

"I… want to believe." That sounded too weak, too desperate, and also too close to a truth I held to my chest. I locked my gaze with the king. "I think my behaviour as a sergeant damaged the corps."

Gough's eyes softened. "Thorrn, not every problem has its root in you. You are too quick to shoulder other's burdens and their mistakes. People make their own choices too, just as Evyn said."

I shook my head. "I said I gave him a chance before, but it wasn't a true chance. I didn't listen to him. I didn't listen to… to Aubin." I swallowed hard. "I have to learn to do that. It seems to be important."

Evyn touched my wrist, soft sadness seeping from her.

"I don't know, sir." I let out a shuddering breath. Admitting a failing was still hard for me. "I don't know, and I cannot give you an answer that is not bluster. He could betray us again, that's my fear. He could be…" *Plotting something*, I nearly said. The Gavain I knew was a talented strategist, but the steps he had taken led him to the edge of the gallows, the noose around his neck. Gough had only to turn away from him and his fate would be sealed.

If my words were to have reaching ramifications, I had to be certain they were the right ones, directly from my heart. "He could do great wrong with another chance. He could also do great good. I cannot tell which way it will go. I wish I could look ahead to the future and see." I stood straighter. "Maybe the alts can. They did say it was possible."

Evyn leafed through her notes. "They said it would be the same for us anyway, that we had to commit to a course of action and they would report back to other versions of us from the past." She rubbed her forehead.

I still didn't understand, but I trusted Evyn's judgement. The king was also nodding along as though he grasped it.

Gough said, "Here we have a man who followed the tenets no matter what it cost him, but who made a mistake and is guilty of a misadventure and of deceiving Thorrn. Although he caused a great deal of distress, no one died, and indeed it was another way through which we were able to come back together, Shardsson."

Evyn lifted her hand into the air.

Gough bowed his head to her. "You are correct in that you experienced distress, Lady Evyn, for which he has paid a price, and we – and he – are much thankful for your recovery."

She shook her head. "The bruswurt didn't have a lasting effect on me, it was the Rushia spirit tangle causing those issues. I mean that, well, someone *did* have to die."

Gough tipped his head. "You are right, of course. The façade of Aubin's death served a purpose, to reassure the corps that attacks against them would never be accepted. It was my only recourse, and I will not apologise for it, but you are correct that I have to weigh how it plays into this."

Gough turned in place. "People are capable of great good or great evil, depending on what drives them. They are also capable of change. He will either learn from this or not. If he does not change, then I have only one recourse, but it seems he has taken and will take these lessons to heart." He winced. "Ah. In a way.

"He was a member of Special Forces. He followed the core tenets, which ultimately ended up killing and harming men and women loyal to me, even going so far as to torture his friends. You can see he did not enjoy it, but he had to find some way of enduring it. It has made him harsher in some ways, which points to the burden he carries."

I turned that over in my mind, watching the king pace back and forth. This was one side of the story he could paint. "My own judgement is obscured by childhood memories. In general, Aubin is a better judge of people. He told me there was something off about him, that he had a sadistic streak, because of how Gavain had responded during his test to enter Special Forces. But I asked Gavain about that same incident, and he said it was a test of loyalty to the king, to trust that you wouldn't hurt an innocent, sir. He did trust the king once, but when Torgund stepped into that role, that trust was broken."

"Yes, just the same as the rest of Special Forces." Nodding eagerly, he turned to Barlay, a spark returning to his eyes. "Do you think this is it? Can we fix this?"

"Time and consistent action will heal the wound. That horrible lashing was a step back, but this will be a step forward. It would be very good for Special Forces to see a path to redemption. He inspires loyalty from his men and women, and he is also very good at his work, putting together ingenious manoeuvres." Barlay rubbed his chin, no doubt thinking of ways he could use those talents.

My heart beat harder. Did I want this? I felt lighter than I had before, with hope unfurling in front of us instead of an execution looming.

"So... you're just going to let him back in?" Evyn set her pen down with a *clack*.

"No, not precisely." Gough studied the pattern on the carpet for a handful of heartbeats. "Ranger, do you think you can trust him again? What do your instincts say?"

I blew out my cheeks, stomach falling. "I... I'm not sure, sir. So that would be a no, at this moment."

"What do you need to see to trust him?"

"Well, like Barlay said, consistent action. If he's taking the right steps, and if I can see those, well... People stumble at first, don't they?" I smiled at Evyn, my stomach twisting. "I've made mistakes. The people that matter have been generous enough to give me the grace to make up for those mistakes."

Gough beamed as though I had said something noteworthy. "I believe he is telling the truth now, and in a situation where it does not benefit him to do so. People can be brought along and shown a better way. This is a good opportunity to see it first-hand. He needs healing, Captain, Ranger. The *corps* needs healing."

Gough poured more waters on the counter, and this time his hands were still.

I leant down to Evyn. "What are you feeling?" I whispered to her.

"Same as you." She shot me a hard look. "We are not sure, but I think this is a turning point. Maybe it's your hope coming through, but we're still going to have to stay sceptical for a while."

My stomach trembled with anticipation. "I think... I hope this is the way forward."

One person was missing. *Aubin doesn't believe people are worthy of second chances.* What would he say about this? He wouldn't give Gavain a second chance and he would not give me or himself one either. He wouldn't let me prove myself able to lead him, and he wouldn't forgive himself for his mistake.

"Look, I... I know what he did was really stupid and dangerous. And it was wrong of him to trick you and convince you to drug me." She squeezed my hand to reassure me that we had dealt with that latter part. "Teresa did some bad things too. Not on the same level, but your world kicks things up a gear when it comes to brutality, your world tolerance is a lot higher or whatever. But she still... hurt me.

"Somehow, we walked through that and out the other side. She's needy and clingy, but... that's okay. She still says the first thing that comes into her mouth and thinks a perfectly tuned insult is the height of friendship, but... I don't know. I don't know what it is about her, but seeing her makes me smile more and more each time." She smiled now, a fondness in her eyes that heartened me.

"It's because you are a very patient and loving person, and forgiveness is something you extend to the lost." I clutched onto the edge of the table. The wood creaked in my hands. "I gave Gavain a second chance. What damage could he do with a third?"

"Or, maybe…" She pushed her notes to one side, their usefulness spent. "Maybe what good can he do with a third?"

I raised my eyes to Gough, who held out a fresh water to the queen. "His fate isn't up to us, Evyn."

"Mm. I can tell you don't know which way you want it to go, though," she whispered.

"Yes. I hoped something would be said or an action taken that would help me draw a strict conclusion, but right now all I feel is…" I searched for a name for my feelings.

I wanted my friends back. *I want Gavain and Aleric, and I want Aubin.* A searing pull tugged at my core, loneliness and hurt in a cold spike. I had lost them all, the old friendships unable to survive the fire of Torgund and the new unable to develop and stabilise on a foundation of trust.

Evyn looked up, eyelashes heavy with tears. We were feeling this together, and she was far too familiar with this loneliness for my own comfort. Folding her in my arms, I held her close. *We will be well. We can stand together.*

The king straightened up. "I think I have it. Let's return."

Ellesmere took his offered arm, and Gough escorted her as far as the office before she peeled off to return to her pursuits. Evyn and I disengaged to walk side by side, and Barlay followed behind.

We filed into Gough's office, Gavain watching us, slumped in the chair and brows drawn tight, as if bracing for pain. "Sir." He saluted Gough.

Gough sat next to him and thrust a water glass into his hands. "I've come to some conclusions. You were right in that, if in the course of this interview we determined that attempted murder was the correct charge, I would not hesitate to apply the law. However, I do not think that attempted murder is the correct charge to lay against you. Misadventure which could have led to manslaughter, perhaps."

Gavain frowned, looking from the king to Barlay and then me. His fingers wrapped around the glass.

"That charge is still quite serious, but here is what I am proposing." Gough put his hand on Gavain's armrest. "You will return to Special Forces."

Gavain gaped at Gough, and again looked up at me. What was he looking at me for? Permission? Reassurance?

Verification?

I nodded once. Gough spoke the truth, and surely Gavain could hear that.

Gough continued, "You will need to work to win trust back, and that will be represented by two things. One is your pay. That will be stopped for at least a turn, maybe more. Secondly, your sword will be handed over to Barlay while you are in the castle."

I gripped the pommel of my father's sword hard. A swordsman without his sword was not quite defenceless, but certainly at a disadvantage. He would also be noticeable around the castle, almost as if he were not fully dressed.

Gough seemed satisfied by both my reaction and Gavain hanging his head. "Good," the king said. "We will also need to work to win trust from you, but I think this will lead to a new beginning in Special Forces."

"I... but I..." Gavain screwed his fists closed. "This is but a stay of execution. I'm dying anyway."

"The MasterMage seems to think she can help," Barlay told Gough.

"But she... my actions led to her soul companion being executed." He studied Gough's face. "Is that my fate? Sanctioned torture?"

"Of course not!" Gough stood, affronted. "The MasterMage is a trusted ally. She will not deliberately harm one of my assets."

The water sloshed from Gavain's glass. He righted it, eyes wide.

Gough moved his hand to Gavain's shoulder. "There will be consequences, but what do we have to do to prove ourselves to one another, to win your trust back as you must win mine?"

The shock on Gavain's face drained it white. "I... I don't..."

Gough smiled. "You didn't think about this being a possible

outcome, did you? That's because your trust, the belief in me that I wouldn't hurt you or yours without just cause, needs to be restored. Make no mistake, Barlay and I see potential in you, but you will be brought back into the behaviours we expect." Gough's face hardened. "I hope I don't have to point out that this is a chance we are offering you. Work with us, not against us, and all will be well."

Barlay fiddled with his manacles to unlock them. "I've got your sword already, and that will be locked up for the foreseeable. You'll do work that you are capable of for now. There will be a foray into Skien to prepare, and I'll work you from sunup to sundown figuring that out."

"Skien? Is that because there is another eviction?" The chains clinked between his hands as he cast them off. "Of course I'll help, sir. I... yes." His voice was breathless, and this time I did not think it was from his damaged heart. Being close to Barlay like that would be like being his Second.

My stomach twisted, hands clutching my father's sword on one side and Evyn's on the other. *If Gavain is helping Barlay, and Evyn and I are helping Barlay...*

We would be working together again much sooner than I thought.

"Good. I'll have you escorted to the barracks," Barlay said. "Get settled back in and get your thoughts organised. You will need them for tomorrow."

The big blond tapped above his heart. "Thank you. I... I can't..."

I needed time for my own thoughts to organise. Fortunately, Gough said, "You're free to go whenever you like, Lady Evyn, Ranger. Thank you for your assistance."

I saluted. "Thank you, sir." Taking Evyn's papers, I put them under my arm and walked straight for the door, keeping my gaze averted from Gavain's shock at his reprieve.

Special Forces locked onto me as I passed them, and I had to force myself to walk and not drop into a reactive stance. They wanted to know Gavain's fate and would be among the first to see it for themselves. I tried not to let any emotion sit on my features, lest they report that as well, because I needed to feel this for a moment before I tried to explain it.

We walked along the corridor toward the staircase in silence but not quiet. Our emotions surged and flowed along the bond, mixing and reforming, levelling out to be consistent across us both. We did not need to speak; I could tell what she was feeling, and it was the same as me. Relief, as cool as a drink of water; a nameless anxiety, a foreboding of ill; an ache like a broken rib, sharp and hurting; and then hope, bright and brassy. Would we be naive to feed the hope? Would we be betrayed? Or would a new friendship open up, like Teresa's?

We entered our apartment to voices inside. I put my hand on my father's sword but instantly relaxed when I heard Tuniel. My heart surged at seeing my promised sat on our sofa. "Well met, MasterMage."

Sitting across from her, his back to me, was a tawny-haired figure. I'd know that profile anywhere.

"Aubin." My voice came out as breathless as Gavain's.

Evyn's hand tightened in mine as Aubin turned. Sharp amber eyes raked over us, taking us in. "Well met, both. You're looking hale—"

Evyn dropped my hand and the papers. She bolted forward, knee bashing against the side of the sofa as she swung around it and pulled up within striking distance. "Right. You're fine. Good." She backed away, a crashing tumult of grief and anger rising inside me and a sharp snap as she snatched up her feelings.

"Evyn?" The sudden halt of the backcloth of her feelings made me stagger. She locked her emotions down deep inside herself, away from me. "Don't shield, please!"

With a low breath, she relaxed slightly and a trickle of hurt filtered out to me. I wanted to snatch her up and take her away, and definitely punch the man standing there, the cause of all this.

It was all because of *him*. Aubin stared at her, unmoving and unmoved, and that heart of his had to be broken to not react to the pain pouring out of Evyn.

Evyn stepped back next to me, twining our hands together but never taking her eyes off Aubin. "I'm sorry," she whispered to me. She raised her voice. "Excuse me, but I can't do this right now."

She shivered, but not with fright or excitement. It was anger, a sharp nettled stinging sensation that prickled throughout her and across to me. I smoothed the emotions down, stretching them out across the bond, dispersing and calming her anger.

He held up his hands slowly. "There's been a case of mistaken identity. I'm not who you think I am. I'm not your Aubin, I'm who you call the Assassin."

I glared at him. They looked exactly the same, but slowly differences filtered in: he had stubble on his jaw that our Aubin would never tolerate, and his severe face spread into a wider smile than our Aubin would ever give. I wanted to knock it off his face, for how dare he smile in the face of Evyn's pain?

He sobered. "I'm very sorry to have caused you any distress."

That phrase in that voice from that face tore pain and longing into me. *It's the wrong one. It's not him saying this to you. Do not forgive him!* An apology was what we wanted to hear from Aubin, desperately, and to have it now but not have it was maddening.

The Assassin said, "We need to talk. We're in trouble."

Out of the kitchen shambled another me, his height lowered by the bent way he held himself. His face reddened and he took a step toward Evyn, then halted, fists bunching. His shoulders shook, pain and grief etched across his stance and tear-streaked face.

My shoulders slumped. "Oh. The Assassin and alt-Thorrn, well met."

Evyn gasped. "What's the matter?" She dropped my hand and raced up to alt-Thorrn, putting her arms around his neck. He clung on to her, pressing her close to his chest.

Jealousy and sadness for him stole across my heart. "What trouble? What has happened?"

"She's gone." Alt-Thorrn's sob tore through me. "My Evyn is missing."

# CHAPTER 9

Clanks and clatters rang around our small kitchen, Evyn rampaging about in it while I watched from the entrance, out of her way. Her mood, stoked by Gavain's pre-trial, had caught aflame on confronting who she thought was Aubin. Now she felt both hard and brittle, like fresh glass blown and brought out of the mouth of the furnace. Would it crack and shatter into angry shards, or cool and temper into her usual capacity for compassion?

She pushed plates into the sink with a cascading crash. "Don't stand there like a lemon, go ask what people want to drink while I try to find some biscuits. I have no idea what we've got to offer, but we have to give them something."

I retreated a step back over the threshold of the kitchen. "Evyn? They've come to see us, not be fed and watered."

She hissed, "We have to give them *something*."

*This has to be a cultural thing.* I winced for our crockery, pouring out proper measures of alcohol. "It seems we will need it." Fingers splayed, I picked up all five of our only matching set of tumblers, something Evyn insisted we use, and beat a tactical redeployment out of range.

Setting the glasses down on the central table caused alt-Thorrn to flinch at the noise. I raised my hands in apology, and he dropped his head back to the sofa, shivering with repressed tears. The Assassin sprawled in our chair next to the bookshelf. He was much more self-confident than our Aubin, foot bouncing in the air as he peered through Evyn's books, nodding or shaking his head at the tomes.

I passed a glass to Tuniel. "It's wonderful to see you here."

Her fingers brushed mine as she took the drink. "You were distressed yesterday. I wanted to see how the events of the day had impacted on you, but when I arrived I found... interlopers." Her gaze slid toward alt-Thorrn, curled in misery, and the Assassin, who held a glass up to the light to study the garnet liquid inside.

My heart warmed for her concern and that she had risked the ruse to come here for me. "My thanks. We are well, Evyn and I supported each other through it. It is a new experience, having an open soul bond with room for one's emotions to spread out."

Tuniel shifted in her seat. "Yes. An open soul bond is rather... helpful."

I wondered how her soul bond with Aubin was faring. They were always apart from one another, but it must be strained, with Aubin in Skien.

Another bang from the table sent alt-Thorrn darting upright and me into a defensive stance in response. Evyn had dropped one side of a plate, and biscuits lay scattered on the floor.

"I'm sorry," she said, ducking to pick them up. "I didn't mean to scare you."

"I... you didn't, I'm sorry, I..." The big man slumped to his knees, fumbling to put the offerings back on the plate.

"Here." The Assassin held a handful out to Evyn.

She ignored his outstretched hands. "Those are yours now."

The Assassin turned the biscuits over in his hands. "I for one am glad to see you're looking hale and well, Lady Evyn."

Ire flickered up along the bond. I tamped it down, straightening it out for her.

"Yes." My double's hand hovered over her shoulder, as if he desperately wanted to take it and was holding himself back. "I heard you weren't well. What happened?"

Her expression softened toward him. He really was in a sorry state, wrought into a wreck. She spoke to him, ignoring the Assassin. "We went to Rush and found out that, far from it being some kind of magic, it was an angry Earthian spirit. I talked to her and helped her fight back, then brought her home again. I guess the Spirit Shaper thing means I was a taxi service, and it was very noisy in here for a while." She tapped her forehead.

Alt-Thorrn's cheeks went pale underneath his ruddy tan.

"Meanwhile, I got claimed as a slave," I said. "The Rushia Princess owned me, though she's given me back now. I disguised myself as one and spent a day breaking metal. Our description is circulating down there as an escaped slave, so, if you're planning on going to Rush, don't," I told him.

"You were a slave?" His white face turned horrified.

"And what of your Lonely Man?" the Assassin asked, jerking his chin toward Aubin's room. "Still playing soldiers?"

An arc of irritation soared through me from Evyn. She busied herself replacing the biscuits, but she was truly struggling to stay calm around him.

I gathered the feeling between us, shaking my head at the Assassin. "No. He's handed in his resignation."

"He's gone off to be really lonely somewhere, and we don't know where," Evyn said, each word clipped.

Tuniel leant forward to take a biscuit from the plate, watching Evyn's reaction underneath her lashes.

The Assassin's brows twitched. "When was that?" he asked me.

"A mooncycle ago. Four or five sennights."

Evyn huffed at my imprecision. "Four sennights and three days."

The Assassin's frown deepened. "That's a long time."

I tried to smile. "Well, we needed him to do what he does best, but he doesn't want to, so he left." Saying it so flippantly was supposed to smooth the edges off the pain by now. It had not.

The Assassin nodded slowly, the pile of biscuits marooned in his lap. "He left you both?"

"He rejected my marriage proposal. Said he could do better." Evyn slammed the biscuits on the table. "There. Who wants one?"

My blood surged, looking for the threat in response to her anger. Long and low, deep breaths helped to mitigate the spikes of her irritation and stop it from escalating into a rage, but my limbs tingled, ready to fight.

A trickle of red traced up Alt-Thorrn's throat in response as well, and he levelled a glare at the Assassin as though he were at fault.

The Assassin placed his pile of biscuits next to the plate, brushing crumbs off his palms with slow movements. "Unfortunately... we need him. We need all of you. Evie has gone missing."

I locked my fingers around Evyn's. "How long?"

The Assassin rubbed his forehead. "It's been a sennight and we're out of ideas. We figured a fresh perspective is what we need."

"Is she hale and well?" I asked alt-Thorrn.

"She's alive and unhurt but I can't Find her." His shoulders rounded, defeated, and the bond twinged with something akin to physical pain at seeing him shrink so small. A wave of pity knocked into me, souring my stomach. I would be bereft and lost if Evyn were to go missing.

Evyn opened her arms to him. "May I?"

Nodding, he gathered her close to his chest, choking back sobs in her hair.

The Assassin watched with a grim set to his face. "Tuniel... Our Tuniel, that is, she thinks that indicates she's on another world or in a magical cage somewhere."

I balled my fists. "Then we will endeavour to rescue her."

"I was hoping you'd say that," the Assassin said. "But we do need you three – by which I mean Thorrn, Evyn and Aubin."

"Why the three of them?" Tuniel asked, biscuit half raised to her lips and forgotten.

The Assassin spread his hands. "You're welcome to come too, MasterMage, it's just that our Tuniel is always too busy to come jaunting around time and space with us. She has all that Master-Maging stuff to do."

Tuniel's lips thinned, and I knew that meant she was suspicious of something. Our Aubin had also been wary of the alts and taking them at their word. "Where was she last seen? What was she doing?"

"She was hunting down your loose Liara," the Assassin said, an accusing edge to his voice.

*Liara.* All of us tensed. "Damn and blast. Her again."

"Indeed. It seems like she escaped your timeline and is on a jolly jaunt." The Assassin spoke lightly but his face held no mirth whatso-ever. "It's a real mess. Your Luc is after that Liara as well. It's always fifty-fifty whether those are vanilla murderous or evil murderous, and our Evyn really doesn't like to buddy up with them."

I could understand that, but while our Luc had a gruff exterior, he could and would use all his power to protect Earth. "It's good our Luc is on her trail." I grasped hold of my father's sword, in the absence of Evyn's hand.

Tuniel came to stand next to me, Amare warming through my right shoulder muscle.

The tension there relaxed as I let go of holding myself so stiff. I asked, "What is Liara's objective? Do you know?"

The Assassin's lips took a bitter twist. "I don't know. My Evyn was the one after her."

"And you let her go alone?"

He shot me a deadly look. "No, I did not, as it happens. When I catch up to her, there will be a great deal of 'I told you so's'. But first, we have to find her, and for that, we need your Aubin."

"Why?" Tuniel asked.

"Because I was told that we need him to find her."

"By who?" Tuniel pressed.

"Never you mind." The Assassin sighed at Tuniel's frosty look. "When we catch up to Evie she'll break my legs for telling you, just in case it affects the trajectory of your timeline. If it will affect Evie's safety, I will tell you, but suffice to say that I trust the source of information." He let his hands fall limp in his lap. "We just know she's not in this timeline right now, because my Thorrn cannot Find her, but we suspect she might have been, to start tracking down your Liara. As well, the Lonely Man and the Spirit Shaper are drawn to each other. She is most likely to appear near him if she calls in."

"If she drops into this world near our Aubin, and he's in Skien, then she might get caught up in this Skien business." Tuniel's face gave little away, but her eyes widened slightly.

My stomach tossed its few contents toward my throat. Evie and Evyn were not magic wielders, but they could open portals, and, from a distance, a Skienien mob would not stop to differentiate.

It seemed Tuniel came to the same conclusion at the same time, standing and moving toward Evyn, as if to pull her back into safety. *It isn't my Evyn but another in danger.*

"What Skien business?" Alt-Thorrn's arms shifted to wrap around Evyn, his voice high.

"Skien is starting another eviction of magic-users. The Oberrotian response is to provide a safe corridor for people who use magic to get to safety, and then assist their settlement. Aubin is out there too, and so we can double up this mission. I swear, we will do all we can to get her back safely." Tapping over my heart, I felt Evyn's echo of determination, and beside me Tuniel nodded firmly.

"Good. My thanks," the Assassin said, relief in his voice. "Now, technically, if she's in another time and place, we can bend time somewhat so we can spend however long we need to here. Having said that, I'd like her back as soon as possible, as would he." He pointed his thumb at alt-Thorrn, a distinctly Earthian gesture. Perhaps he had spent more time there to pick up more of Evie's mannerisms and way of speech. It was a stark reminder that he wasn't the Aubin I knew; even how he held himself was different.

One similarity remained in how his gaze strayed to Evyn. Even scanning the room, he would centre himself on her before looking around. He addressed his remarks to her even when she wasn't the one who had spoken, and his body oriented to face her whenever he moved. I wondered if, were alt-Thorrn to allow Evyn to move, he would turn to face her without thinking, like a plant following the sun.

Tuniel would do the opposite to me. Still, I was starting to be able to read her more public face and the meanings behind her words, relishing the moments together when I, and only I, was granted to see her heart and her true feelings flowing free. And at this moment, she seemed to be struggling with something.

The Assassin yawned, fist over his wide mouth, and then shook himself. "What do you need in order to chase off after your Lonely Man and drag him back? I can help track him, and between the two of you, you Thorrns should be able to contain him."

Evyn muttered, "I would hope we could just talk to him and ask if he could help us, but if he doesn't, then at least we know that about him."

Tuniel said, "While talking to him would be a lovely idea, he might need a little more persuasion. As soon as he sees us coming, he will vanish."

"Even you?" I asked her.

She stood very still behind alt-Thorrn and Evyn. "Aubin is in a difficult place. He thinks he needs to be alone to sort through it, or he has already condemned himself to be alone. I... He's difficult to read in any case." She pushed her hair over her shoulder, stroking the soft strands.

I glanced between Evyn and Tuniel. Evyn was preoccupied with helping alt-Thorrn, her anger ebbing and flowing in waves that she was managing admirably. Tuniel, however, was closed to me; not only would I never feel what she felt the same way as I would with Evyn, she was guarded with her emotions in any case. Nevertheless, I felt she had something hurting her, and I resolved to assist her first. She had no one else.

I waved a hand toward Aubin's old room. "For right now, you can stay here, we have a spare room."

The Assassin barely spared it a glance. "Ooh, lovely. And it has its own bath. Fancy."

Evyn turned a dark look onto me, the bond twanging with resentment.

*Ah.* I lifted my hands in apology. They were allies in need of assistance, but I should have realised Evyn would struggle to have the Assassin being so close to her.

Her choler spluttered out when she turned back to my double. Grief twisted his face into expressions painful to look at, let alone endure, and Evyn's open heart ached for him.

While she looked after him, I would see to my promised. "Perhaps you can help me prepare the spare room for these guests, MasterMage?"

She raised an eyebrow at me. "I would think you have servants for that, but I will consent to speak with you in private."

I rubbed the back of my neck. "I'm not good at the whole hidden message subterfuge thing!"

The Assassin smirked. "Indeed. Don't worry, I won't get offended and assume you're talking about us."

"You two go ahead," Evyn said, stroking alt-Thorrn's hair away from his sweaty forehead. "He needs me."

Her presence was helping him, his shoulders relaxing. Was there the smallest echo of the soul bond within the different versions of ourselves? My drive to help Evyn and keep her safe expanded to Evie, and indeed all Evyns, for they were all precious, every single iteration and facet of her.

I led Tuniel into Aubin's old room and closed the door. She glanced toward the soul stone which had fired to life, a soft green glow that hardly pushed back the shadows. Aubin's soul jewel, resonating with their bond. I stared at it for a heartbeat, at the fissure that ran through it, splintering the light to scatter on the wall. The room had been stripped back of all his personal effects, which had not been much; some old tomes on plants and herbs, well-thumbed and well used, which Evyn had donated to the library rather than keep in our apartment. He had left his Ranger uniform, which had been sized for him and was useless to me, and that remained hanging in its set pieces in the wardrobe.

She sat on the edge of the bed, hands folded in her lap. "Well?"

I shifted my stance. How could I encourage her to share her innermost thoughts with me, given that I could not discern how she felt on the matter?

I settled for the direct approach. "How are you feeling, seeing the Assassin?"

She tilted her head. "You are correct in assuming it has stirred up some emotion. You two reacted quite… interestingly."

She has parried that, turning the conversation back toward me and Evyn in a neat riposte. I took two strides to sit next to her, my leg close to hers. The bed dipped her toward me, and she put a hand on my thigh to halt her topple. I took it into my own. "It's just us. You can talk freely."

Her eyes met mine, softening. The soul jewel flickered, dimming; she glared at it, and it snapped back to its meagre brightness.

Perhaps we should talk in generalities first, to warm up. "Given how concerned you are of people finding out about us, how is it you have come directly to my apartment, MasterMage? Not that I'm complaining, far from it."

A small smile pushed her cheeks up to dimple. "I came up here using a method you might like to know about. There are servant corridors containing small compartments where goods can be lifted up and down in shafts using mechanical hoists. These riddle the walls and I was able to follow one up onto this level. Few lead into rooms, apart from the one in the suite that I had been assigned."

"Very handy to know, I suppose, but are you sure it was really necessary to squeeze in there? I am having trouble imagining you navigating these spaces. You actually rode up one of those mechanical hoists?"

She scowled. "I *am* a stone mage. Small dark spaces do not trouble me, and I had the walls around me to assist."

Not for the first time, I wondered what it would be like to have the very stones of the walls bend themselves to respond to me. If she were to get very angry as I did, I had no doubt she could cause significant structural damage to wherever she was.

She was very strong and careful of her abilities, keeping constant control of her emotions, but at a high cost. "You do not have to shoulder this alone."

"Shoulder what alone? I've been balancing with Aubin since before you were born."

Despite winning a stride in the right direction, that gave me pause. "Er..." She didn't look that much older than me.

She chuckled. "A score and six to our names, and we found each other at four turns, if you recall."

"Ah." Seven turns my senior. "Well, then you'll know infinitely more than me about soul bonds and sharing across them. I haven't even a turn with Evyn. Perhaps you can teach me."

She shook her head. "Every pair is different, Thorrn, and our needs change throughout our lives. They... they change." She dropped her gaze down to her hands, one screwing her dress fabric in her lap, the other tight around my hand.

I did not look directly at her, stroking the strands of her hair and waiting. If I spoke now, it might turn her thoughts away from what she needed to put into words, and as I could not know her mind, I might never understand what she truly wanted to say if I interrupted it. It would be like blocking a blow before the opponent's sword even moved.

"My needs have changed," she whispered. "I... Maybe I am too confident, but it has felt safer to bring him closer to me, to work directly with him, to be near him. When he brought me into this to help you, I thought being so close to him would be temporary until it ended up changing my fate entirely. When I assumed the mantle of MasterMage, I knew it would be important to push him even further away. But then Gough came up with a way to hide him entirely, to make everyone think he was dead, and... and I felt he was safer. More than that, working with you and alongside Evyn, I thought he had found a place to be. I thought he could be... happy."

My nose stung, the precursor to tears. Tuniel kept her face away from mine, the light dimming so I wouldn't be able to see her. She was so unused to unburdening that this could only be revealed to me, one of her closest confidants, under cover.

I listened, handing her a pocket square, wanting to soak in every word she entrusted to me.

She wiped her face as she continued. "I saw he was happy, for a time, inasmuch as helping you two avoid death can be its own reward. He meant something to you, and I thought that would bring him fulfilment. As well, I... I saw what it could be like to be near to him and not endanger him." She pressed her fists to her forehead, using the back of my hand to hide herself. "I want that," she whispered.

I leaned in close. "It's alright to say you want Aubin back too."

She buried her face in my hand. "It's not what he wants, but it's what he needs. He's hurting, badly, and shutting me out anytime his control slips. I keep Finding him and he moves, as if he's evading me."

My stomach twisted. "He's even pushing you away?"

"Yes." She raised her tear-stained face to me. "We need to find him. Knowing him, he blames himself and will take all responsibility for what happened in Rush."

Anger seared through me at his selfishness. He was hurting Tuniel and Evyn with this idiocy! "What happened in Rush was, he forced the spirit out of me. He was the only one who not only thought of what would work but could follow through. Without him, I would be dead, or driven mad."

"He knows that. He sees that he had it in him to hurt you, and you would be better off without him."

Anger stumbled, overtaken by fear. If he was consumed with the thought that he was the only one at fault and that he could take all the bad things in our lives away by removing himself from it...

There was only one conclusion to that line of thinking. I hunkered closer to her in the dark empty room, and put my arm around her shoulders, for her and myself. "I had no idea he had shut even you out. He must be much worse than we thought."

"Why would you? I'm only now telling you, and only because you're holding space for me to be open. I... We have to help him, Thorrn. Somehow, if only I knew how to reach him."

If Tuniel did not know, then what could Evyn and I do? Except that we had to try, and hope that something revealed itself.

Tuniel turned over my hand. "It seemed seeing the Assassin stirred some emotion for you and Evyn as well. You were stunned into silence, but she seemed... angry."

I would return her openness with my own, but naming emotion was new to me. "It was a sudden shock to see who we thought was Aubin. Evyn was angry, yes, and she had shut me out. Probably so it would not affect me, but it was hard to lose that contact even so."

The jewel brightened. "Ah, yes, the push and pull of wanting to protect them against balancing your needs. I can understand her anger, of course. Being refused is one thing, but having that person cut you out of their life must be difficult."

"It certainly hasn't happened to me before." Or had it? "Unless we count Gavain and Aleric."

"Ah, yes. How did that resolve?"

That. I fought not to fall back into reporting cadence and instead remain open. "He is back in Special Forces. Gough thinks he can be a valuable asset and that, while he made the wrong choices, he can change." I stared at the crack in the soul jewel, a black path through the green depths. "I'm not sure I will be able to trust Gavain again, but... he said something about the tenets being wrong, and he was wrong to follow them."

She frowned. "Pretty words that he can roll out, given that he saw what you did and where you are now."

"I... he said that he hated I was right when I broke the tenets to rebel and find the true king. He's having trouble reconciling it, I think."

"Understandable, when you are lashed for stepping out of line." Tuniel's hand slid into mine. "It is a time of change, of Gough changing how he interacts with and perhaps even what he feels about the corps, but don't fear. I think you'll always be his favoured."

While that sentiment made my heart lift, it also sent a barb through my burgeoning pride that made me wince. "That's the whole problem from before. Do I truly deserve his favour?"

Tuniel frowned. "The man who rebelled against the false king to save him? The man who pieced his broken heart together to protect him?"

"Fine, yes, but... what about my father's?"

She twined our fingers together, her soft skin brushing against my hard calluses. "I don't know what shape that took, Thorrn, so I cannot determine that for you. My own father loved us each exactly the amount that we could bring fortune to the family, and used my powers to further the family wealth. He certainly showed me favour above my siblings, my older brother and my younger sister. Perhaps they minded; Nedant is dead now, and Sora is too preoccupied with the family holding to do much navel gazing. The women of North Hold have always been the most practical.

"We can't change the past. Whether he showed you favour or not, you are where you are. No amount of training or favour could have prepared you for the tests you faced, both with Torgund and with Gough. You showed your true strengths then, I feel. For that, you are worthy of... some praise." Leaning forward, she swept her smile against mine.

"Just a little, mayhap," I murmured into her mouth. She tasted of the spirits I'd poured, marzipan foremost.

She drew her teeth across my bottom lip, then sat back. "And so, you have mixed feelings about his return?"

I dragged my thoughts back to the issue at hand. "Who? The Assassin or Gavain?"

She cocked her head. "Both, I suppose."

"I... Yes." A tumult of feelings, each needing to be straightened out with Evyn so we didn't crowd each other.

Tuniel's free hand stole into her pockets. "It is interesting that Gavain chose to disclose something like that to the king, and interesting that the alts have decided to visit now."

"They need help." I stretched my long legs out into the empty room. "So does Gavain, it seems. And..." I swallowed hard. "Aubin."

"Hm. There are sure to be ways I can help. Starting with the swordsman." She pulled out a small blob of quivering silvrine.

"What did you think of Gavain's condition?" I asked, staring at the metal. As pleased as I was to have Amare on my shoulder, the idea of it sliding further into my body had prickles pinching my skin.

The metal slid over her fingers. "Hepzibah and I have been looking for a strong subject. We have observed that the living metal can fuse with the human body." Amare warmed. "They quite passionately believe that the metal could be a replacement for flesh and muscle, but while it is pliant and tensile, the metal still needs to respond to commands. Hepzibah assures me there are signals and commands in the heart, so I would need to investigate how these can work with the metal to get it to, in essence, pump."

Her intent gaze fixed on the silvrine shimmering in her hands, already no doubt turning over the problem and searching for solutions. "That's... interesting." I shivered.

She frowned at me. "There is, of course, a great deal of uncertainty. We will not enter into this lightly, but it seems he will die without intervention."

"Is it likely to work?"

"We will try." The silvrine blob crawled along her wrist. "We will need to experiment, and I was hoping to work on something a bit less complicated than the human heart to start."

"Yes. It is complicated." I smiled at her. The edges of her lips tipped up, and it was strange to see her in this room that reminded me of Aubin, pale and silvrine to his tawny gold. My own heart gave a judder. "Why... why do you want to help Gavain?"

Her lips pursed. "It seems to have come together rather perfectly. I spoke with him, you know, when he formed part of the contingent under the other Sergeant."

I stilled. This would have been when my contingent left me while I recovered to go on to Dinahe and start the investigation into murders against Oberrotian officials.

Tuniel went on, "He asked after you and seemed bitterly satisfied that you would pull through and potentially return to the contingent. I found it... interesting."

"You find a lot of things interesting of late, it seems." I winced at the brusqueness of my voice. "I did not mean it to come out so harsh, MasterMage."

One perfect eyebrow arched. "This was interesting in the way that his feelings about you were hidden behind bluster, laid bare if one knows how to look. I know myself how to hide deeply what one truly thinks and feels, and I could see the signs within him. When I stayed silent about you he practically begged me for word of you, then when I said you would survive he seemed both relieved and disgusted, talking about how stubborn you are with affection and bitterness both."

Relief and disgust, two emotions that rode within me now when I thought about his return to the contingent. Had I found fellowship with Gavain in this way after everything that had happened?

Tuniel noticed, putting the metal away and touching my hand. She traced her nail along the tendons of my hand, brushing over the calluses. "Potentially that war within him still remains. At the time, I was fighting a similar war within myself, to allow myself to admit deeper feelings for you than mere physical attraction. I thought there was strength in standing alone, but there is no greater strength than being surrounded and bolstered by my loved ones." A pink colour hastened to her cheeks. "There, I said it."

I chuckled. Her hand was smaller and softer, but it too had worked edges where she melded metal to form her creations.

Her eyes met mine from under her long lashes. "Then Aubin set out to murder him. That in itself is interesting. He had much quieter ways of solving the problem, but it seemed that he was driven to it through despair. I know it is far too pithy to say that soul companions balance completely, but I feel a certain kind of satisfaction in Gavain nearly being killed by one half and restored by the other half. I feel that... if Gavain lives, a good deal of Aubin's assumption that he is a murderer would be unfounded, that belief shaken, open to being replaced by something else."

I let that settle within me. Would Aubin be pleased Gavain was still alive? He did not believe people deserved a chance to redeem themselves. If he saw that Gavain had changed, what would that open up within Aubin?

"The last reason is entirely and utterly selfish." Her eyes went hard and flinty. "If he ever hurts you, or Evyn, or Aubin, if he uses the chance that we give him for new life to instead further his old feuds, then I can end him."

She clicked her fingers, the sound ringing in the room. Amare went instantly cold on my shoulder, and I flinched away from it.

She ran her hands over my shoulders. "My apologies." The metal under her hand warmed gently, a burst of heat that soothed the sudden surprise of cold.

"Well. I suppose you do have something that protects us in everything you do."

She smiled. "Yes. So do not fear. I'll give you the word to say should he threaten you, and I can make it so he feels no pain."

*I could cut him down with a single word.* That was a dizzying thought. The power of life and death of my opponent had always been my choice but within the limit of my skills. Magic changed that, shifting the field to my advantage. Again. Always, it seemed the deck was stacked in my favour.

I swallowed hard. "Will you let the king know?"

"I probably should." She stretched her arms over her head, her pale green gossamer sleeves cascading down her forearms. "Ever the obedient soldier."

"Always." I was not above nakedly admiring her position, shifting closer and taking hold of one of her arms. Lightly pressing kisses up from her elbow to wrist, I revelled in her warmth and the small, contented murmurs she made. "Can I see you later? Which suite are you in?"

"The Armington set of rooms. I have blocked off the servant's compartments, but I'll feel Amare getting closer."

"Very well." Pressing a kiss into her palm to take with her for the day, I stood and offered her a hand up. "Shall we return to Evyn and the alts?"

A considering look settled on her face, as if she puzzled out my hand. "What do you think of their story?"

"What do you mean? Evie is missing and may be in peril."

"So why search you out?" Glancing at the door, she lowered her voice. "I came and found them here. Your double was inconsolable, and the Assassin looks rather perturbed and unsettled, but if they were truly worried, why are they not on her tail themselves. You know Aubin through and through, and the only times he is not composed, he is out of his mind with grief. That other Aubin especially cannot be trusted."

A cold feeling settled in my stomach. "That was what Aubin said as well. Why do you two mistrust them on sight?"

"Because someone has to. What reason have they for moving across the worlds? Are they mere travellers, exploring the multiverse? Are they prospectors looking for something? They won't tell us, ostensibly to protect our timeline, but is that the truth?"

"Well..." I scrubbed my hair, unease at her questions bubbling in my chest. "We have no reason to doubt they are telling the truth either. They helped Evyn by studying the effects of bruswurt on her, and they definitely saved us during the campaign against Waker. We could not have defeated her without their intervention."

Tuniel's eyes unfocused slightly, and Aubin's green soul jewel flickered. "Mm. That they did." Standing, she sent a small warm flare to Amare; a kiss right at my shoulder, deep in the heart of something that protected me. "In any case, all we can do is wait and see what comes to fruition."

This time I tugged her toward me, and when she pressed her hips against me I had to lock my knees to stop them from bending.

"Tonight?" she whispered.

"Yes, absolutely."

She smirked, glancing over my shoulder at the jewel. It simmered down, dimming the room. "I will be breathless with anticipation."

I was fairly out of breath myself.

Returning to the others, I found Evyn still within alt-Thorrn's reach but at least out of his arms. His head was lowered, and the shadows under his red-rimmed eyes and lines etched into his jawline spoke of his disquiet. Evyn sat close to him on the sofa, gaze fixed on the untouched offering of biscuits between them. A pile of linen slumped next to her; she must have retrieved it while Tuniel and I were talking.

The Assassin turned from his slow walk around the room, hands underneath his armpits as Aubin did sometimes. "All matters settled? We still have your support, I trust?"

Alt-Thorrn's head jerked up sharply.

"Of course," I reassured my double. "If Evie, or indeed any Evyn is in trouble, we will help."

Tuniel eased in front of me. "I hope this gesture will encourage you to extend trust back to us in turn, and enable you to tell us what you're doing here."

The Assassin's eyes narrowed. "Of course. Let me just break the laws of space and time so we can have an open-door policy with each other, and while the multiverses crash into each other in a heap of superheated flame and agony, at least we can say that we were open with one another." He threw up his hands. "And here I thought you at least understood."

Evyn flushed, an angry tick to her jaw.

Tuniel's hands went stiff in her skirts. "So you say, and therefore I shall not press the matter. For now." Her tone made it clear that it was only for now. "I have to return to my rooms. Ranger, I shall arrange to have Layloree meet you first thing tomorrow morning as her creed is to rise very early, so expect her before your training. I will also ask Carreelee to attend, but that is less certain, as her habit is to rise late. Lady Evyn, good day."

She left without a backward glance, but Amare flared again and I pressed my hand to my jacket over the metal. She would return the way she had come, the idea of her regal bearing shuffling and twisting into tight spaces making me smile. There was more to the MasterMage than she ever showed to anyone else.

The Assassin broke through my thoughts. "Any more interrogations before we take our rest?"

I shrugged a shoulder. "Just to ask if you wanted to join morning training."

The Assassin snorted.

"That's a no. How about you, Shoulders?"

The version of me from another time and place frowned, looking around behind the sofa. "You mean... me?"

I smiled at his confusion. "Everyone else is getting a moniker. I think it suits you, unless there's someone else around here with an enviable shoulder span. Join us for morning training. Evyn will be there."

"Yep." She became animated, patting his hand. "I've heard it's probably good for you or something. No one ever told me that exercise would help with mental things too. I have been feeling better recently. Well, sort of." She shot the Assassin a glance under her lashes, then quickly looked away. My solar plexus twinged with pain, as if I'd pulled a muscle there. That was usually where I felt a hesitant bubble of Evyn's feelings for Aubin, but there was no warmth there.

Slapping her knees, she stood up. "Can I get anyone anything before we turn in?"

"I... no." Shoulders wrapped his arms around his chest, head bowed.

His demeanour dredged up the dark time after my lashing, when my thoughts were grey and confused. I touched his back. "We'll find her. Please don't worry, although, knowing me, you will."

He flinched from me but then nodded, misery in every line of him. Heaving himself off the sofa, he stumbled into the spare room.

Evyn's sympathy surged after Shoulders, her heart cracking deep inside to see his pain. *She would have looked like this when I was hurt, felt like this.*

Evyn turned away from me, grabbing the armful of linen. "Here." She shoved it at the Assassin, anger spiking through the bond.

He caught it, rocking back on his heels. For once, he was wrong-footed, mouth working and mute in the face of her simmering resentment, and I almost laughed. At close range, Evyn could be fearsome in her own way, her disappointment a bitter burden to bear.

He attempted to regroup. "My thanks. I... can tell my presence here in particular has caused you some distress. For that, I apologise." He looked utterly sincere, all his insouciance dropped away.

All that did was stir more anger in Evyn to thrum across our bond. Stepping behind her, I put a hand on her shoulder. *I'm here.*

Evyn raised a hand to placate me, her tension tempering. She raised her chin to face him directly. "I just can't right now. It's not your fault, and I know it's not your fault, but... Maybe I'll feel better in the morning after a good night's sleep, just... Not right now."

"Of course." The Assassin struggled for a grip on the linens. "My double has a lot to answer for. Usually, people who upset my Evie end up regretting it. I'm tempted to make the other me pay for it in this case as well."

I frowned at him. Sentiment like that stirred up something in Evyn, hard for me to categorise except it was confused. "All right, Assassin. That's enough from you."

He left without smart comment, just a murmured, "My thanks." That in itself was remarkable, but he had seemed tired.

"Come on, let's get to bed," Evyn said. "It's been a long day. And no, I'm not in the mood to talk about it. I need some alone time."

She meant to abandon the used mugs and plates where they were, unusual in the extreme for her. "I'll tidy up here, then be up," I promised.

She gave me a small smile. "Thanks, but I know you're going to see Tuniel. Don't stay up too late."

I saluted her, and she smiled for me, but it was pasted on for my benefit.

# CHAPTER 10



THE NEXT MORNING DAWNED FAR TOO EARLY. IT FELT LIKE I HAD ONLY JUST managed to get back to my room after completing an admittedly satisfying visit with Tuniel. Rubbing my eyes, I heaved myself upright, sore throughout my body from navigating the tight service shafts. "Morning, Evyn."

She yawned and turned away from me, burrowing deeper into her covers. "Kettle on, please."

"At once." I should have known better than to try to talk to her before I had her drink in my hands.

Padding downstairs, I hissed from the cold of the stone floors. The noise made someone start up from the sofa; I dropped into a defensive stance before I recognised my double. "Oh, it's you, Shoulders. Good morning."

He got to his feet in intense silence.

My gut twisted. "It may not feel like a good morning for you. We will make all haste to Skien to intercept our Aubin and help Special Forces rescue those people who are in need. Once we make that contact, we'll persuade Aubin to help us." I rubbed the back of my neck; every one of those tasks would take a huge amount of effort.

"No small feats, any of those, but we will manage it all, and faster than you would think. I swear."

He shook his head, his massive shoulders slumping. "She's not here. I can't think of anything else except getting her back. I know I should be focused on the things that will help her, but..." Shuddering, he let his hands go limp. "I just need to know she's safe."

A sudden need to stand near Evyn seized me, but I reined myself back. He was suffering, and it wasn't as if misplaced soul companions was catching. Still, if our places were traded, I did not think I would ever stop until I knew Evyn was safe again. I wouldn't be able to. "She is very capable. More than I know I give her credit for." I touched his shoulder. Thinking of any Evyn, small in stature as they were, facing down some kind of threat without me, made my heart stutter, no matter their ability to ping out across worlds. Perhaps Evie couldn't use hers if she was not back yet and trapped in some way.

He must have seen my fear cross my face. "She's capable and careful, but whatever has her must have outwitted her. All it takes is one slip-up, one mistake, and my Aubin won't..." He closed his mouth slowly with a flush to his cheeks. "I'm pretty sure I'm not allowed to tell you," he said bitterly.

"What? What won't he do, or say?" My grip on his shoulder turned hard, Evyn and Tuniel's and even the echo of Aubin's misgivings screaming up at me. "Is there some way he can help and he isn't?"

Shoulders looked back at the closed door, shut tight against the early morning. "Aubin, he can... he has this..." He frowned, and I had to force myself to wait for him to herd his thoughts into words.

"He can change things, accidentally or on purpose, when we visit places. He says he can't right now, so he can't just go back and stop her from going." He flexed his hands. "I'm not explaining it properly, I... I don't know the right words."

I secured my patience. "That's alright. I can try to understand,

and my Evyn can do an even better job. Let's get her a cup of tea, shall we?"

He nodded fitfully, still looking over his shoulder at the closed door. Was that a flicker of fear in his face? It was quickly replaced with resolve. *Good.* I knew he would do anything to keep her safe, and perhaps we could learn something at the same time.

We boiled some water and brought Evyn her morning drink. She sat up, knuckling her eyes as we both tramped up the stairs. "Hi. Oh, hi, Shoulders." She tried his nickname with a small flush. "Did you sleep well?"

He shook his head, rendered mute by seeing another version of his soul companion hale and well, but not his Evie. That must be some kind of refined torture.

Evyn tapped her bed beside her and Shoulders stumbled to get to her.

I passed her the hot drink. "At some point, Shoulders here wants to explain something to us." I returned to the stairway, listening for noises downstairs. "Something the other version of Tabreksson knows or can do that he's not doing."

"Sounds suitably ominous." Evyn patted his back. "Whenever you're ready? I can skip morning training if you need me to."

"I... I need to think about this. The knowledge might hurt your timeline and I... I would not want to hurt you."

I pulled on my Ranger jacket and handed him a clean shirt. "Come to training, then. I've always settled my thoughts through hard work."

Taking it, he moved with shuffling steps into the bathroom to change.

Evyn watched him. "What was that all about?" she asked me as soon as the bathroom door closed.

I kept watch on the stairs. "He intimated that his Aubin could do something to help Evie, but he isn't. Perhaps your suspicions about them are founded, or at least they are bleeding through to me." It felt wrong not to trust allies, but lately we had been in a place where it turned out allies were not worthy of our trust.

She blew on her drink, the surface rippling and threatening to overtop the sides. "Hm. Could just be grief talking, and as we know Aubin isn't all that great at the whole sharing feelings thing, so Shoulders might not feel supported."

"No, not for feelings, but his support went beyond that." Aubin would work tirelessly to find the solution and do it, no matter what it cost him. Meanwhile, Gavain's support went only as far as the law and no further. It should have been that that line would never need to be crossed, and therefore his support would be steadfast; but it underlined that Gavain's trust went only so far. Aubin's went beyond that, until broken irrevocably.

I straightened my cuffs. "Possibly it's nothing, but I know you are investigating the multiverses when you have time. Speaking of time, I need to get down early to meet Layloree."

"We'll see you down there for morning training. You better let Barlay know we're bringing an alt."

"Good idea." I went downstairs, pulling on my boots. The door to Aubin's old room was still closed, and no sounds issued from within. The Assassin could be sleeping, but part of me doubted that.

Blowing out my cheeks, I trotted down the corridor toward the stairs, a nagging, gnawing unease lapping up against my stomach. It was probably Evyn's and mine together, and we would feed off each other's suspicion until we put the matter to rest. I tried to calm it, promising myself that the rougher edges of the emotion would be smoothed off by sweat to allow for clearer thinking later on.

Besides, I had to prepare myself for Gavain's first day back in the contingent. So much had happened last night that I had had little opportunity to think and prepare, but charging into the breach was what I did. Relaxing my jaw with a click, I resolved that, whatever happened, I would be calm and polite. He would have to take my orders for now; a little warm flame fanned against my heart. *Perhaps he will try some malicious compliance, and I can write him up.* The thought made me chuckle."

The castle courtyard was quiet as always at this time of the morning, but people hurried about their business in industrious fashion. The cooks were already hard at it, warm smells spiralling and bright light spilling across the cobbles from the kitchens attached to the mess hall. I marched through it double quick time while yawning messengers darted out of my path and gossiping bakers hoisted up their wares to move aside. I passed out of the gates with a nod at the Regular on guard, who sat up straighter at her post.

No one was on the training field this early, not even Layloree. I might as well train to pass the time, but if I tried pulling out a practice dummy I risked waking someone in the barracks, and they needed all the rest they could get.

I started a bodyweight workout, moving through some of Aubin's more challenging poses. Having my entire weight resting on my arms was one thing, but moving the rest of me while I balanced precariously, constantly shifting my hands to stay upright, was another. *How does Aubin stay still and calm doing this?*

Perhaps he only appeared to be calm. Maybe all this time his body was shaking and trembling just as mine was. I was tense in some parts, relaxed in others, and, as I moved, those areas shifted up and down my core with a deep ache. I tried to relax into it, rather than fight to maintain my balance or avoid the pain of holding myself upright.

"Oh. So you like that, eh."

I moved my head toward the speaker and overbalanced. My legs hit the ground, and I sat back on my heels in front of Layloree.

She had her arms crossed, tapping her fingers on her skinny elbows. Her braids swept to the same level, each one with blades woven into the plaits. If she spun, those blades would dissuade anyone from getting into her guard.

I saluted. "Good morning, ma'am. I hope I didn't disturb you, asking you to meet me here."

She put her hands on her hips. "Yes, you did disturb me, with your partial painful knowledge of the poses." She tutted. "Who taught you?"

I opened my mouth, hesitant to mention Aubin's name to her. The knowledge of the Battlemistresses was a closely guarded secret, their training completed on remote mountaintops in central Skien. No Battlemistress I met would impart their knowledge to an Oberrotian, and perhaps she had trained Aubin on some strict agreement that he would never pass on his training.

She cocked her head. "The *hellione*? His work is all over this, stripping movements down into sections and areas, organising and ordering. It's heartless." She stuck out her tongue in disgust.

I settled my hands on my lap. "While we journey into Skien, could you teach me?"

She frowned. "Teach you to fight properly? You're too old. Too inflexible."

"I would definitely challenge you on that. I am a keen student and I will do whatever you tell me to do," I said quickly. I couldn't lose this chance!

"Oho, *anything* I say? Tempting. You're a pretty boy." She clucked her tongue, circling me. "You are too set in your training ways to change now. You have been cast into a mould, forced into a single shape, and set in one frame."

I stood up slowly. "I'm learning all the time. The Ranger style of fighting was being developed by me and Aubin. So far we've included the Oberrotian sword, yes, but also the Dinahen staff, the Rushia Art, and of course Aubin's Battlemistress movements feature prominently." I hoped they would, in any case. Perhaps by training myself in the way Aubin had been trained, I could understand him a little better. I ventured a smile. "I would be honoured to work with an expert such as yourself."

"What a lovely mouth you have. Be careful, man mountain, saying things like that to a Battlemistress." She folded her arms, tapping her chin. I had seen Tuniel in exactly the same pose. This woman had imparted a great deal to both of them in their formative turns. "Well, we will be up and down all those mountains for a while, so it might be interesting, especially if you really *will* do anything I say." She gave me a wicked grin.

I grinned back. "Try me. I'm not all that inflexible." I leapt into a handstand, twisting and landing my feet on the other side. I wobbled but stayed upright.

"Mm. Very pretty." Layloree said. "Consider it done. Now, Mistress Tuniel said you wished to speak to me. Was it just to show off your exuberance, or was there another purpose?"

I composed myself. "Yes, my thanks. Do you have everything you need to enter Skien? Are there any provisions you recommend or would want, and where do you think we should enter the country?"

"Well, I want a palanquin to traverse that blasted hellscape of a snowstorm-cursed country, but we don't get what we want, do we?" Layloree's mouth twisted, her expression sour. "Warm clothes, nothing for fires. I suggest we walk along the *heta koller*, the hot waters that crack the country."

I nodded. "I wondered the same."

Layloree flapped her hand. "Then I am not sure why you need an old Battlemistress with you if you already wondered the right thing. Dragging her down to this sticky hot city, what cruelty, and then not using her expertise, what woe!"

I ducked my head. She did not seem overly upset. "We need your expertise, Layloree."

She snorted. "You need my trail cooking. I can feed man mountains, I remember the despair trying to feed all mine. Constant demands, never ending." She rolled her eyes. "The *hellione* had one thing going for him; he was a small streak of nothing that existed on barely any food, no matter how many times I tried to feed him up."

I could well imagine that, but she had lived it. "He was a small child, then?"

Layloree huffed. "Small he was and small he remains, sliding out from the corner of your eyes when you aren't paying attention. I remember clearly the day the master brought home two children when he went down to the city with one. He was delighted that Tuniel had burst forth with magic, and then distraught that she'd claimed a limp little rag as her soul companion. I couldn't find the second child at first until Tuniel moved aside and there he was, hiding behind her, big eyes staring from his head. At least he wasn't full of lice, but he ate too much at table come dinnertime and was sick all over the floor. I had to chuck him in a bath, and he fought me as if I was trying to drown him." She chuckled at the memory.

"Sounds..." Hard. Heartrending.

She glared at me. "Now you pity him, and he won't want that at all. I won't lie and say it was easy for him after that, mind; the mistress, the mother of the household, she was a mage of little power but great ambition for her daughter. She imagined Tuniel to be safer without her soul companion and wanted him gone. Oh, the times I had to thwart that woman from slipping poison in his food. So no wonder he wouldn't eat much."

"That's terrible." My heart lurched in my chest.

Layloree shrugged. "He lives, does he not? He survived everything Mistress Antry tried, and perhaps it did them good, as Lady Tuniel and the *hellione*'s bond is one of the strongest I have ever seen." She scowled. "He's hurting her now, though, with this self-indulgent mannish behaviour."

I looked down. Did he know that? If he did, why did he continue?

"So you will knock him on the side of the head to stop him," she said. "That'll bring him to his senses."

Despite my heartache, I chuckled. "Will do, ma'am. Now then, we aim to be ready as soon as possible, within the next few days. Will that suit?"

She shook her head, braids flying. "I am ready now, always, I carry my ready with me. So no, it does not suit to be laying about, Oberrotian. When will we go?"

My eyes widened slightly. "I need to make sure you and Carreelee are ready, and Evyn. She's coming with us."

"Oh, is *she* going to hunt down the *hellione* and bring him to heel? Ah, yes. I can see that." Layloree's eyes sparkled. "So small but so determined. It is the quiet ones that bear watching."

I rubbed the back of my neck. "I'm not sure Evyn would even be pleased to see him right now, but we have to get him out of the situation he finds himself in, whether he wants our help or not." I let my hand drop. "One thing at a time. We need to get in there and meet up with him and the magic users under threat, so we need to prepare as best we can."

"Do not worry about us, man mountain. The monstrous mage and I will carry out Lady Tuniel's needs once we get to Keltskarr. You're there to lift the heavy things." She patted me firmly on the cheek.

"I hoped we would pack light," I hazarded.

"Oh, I meant the *hellione*." She mimed wrapping something in mid-air, then tossing it over her shoulder.

As much as that idea made me smile, disappointment dropped into my stomach. "I'd rather he choose to come back with us of his own free will. Forcing him to do something he doesn't want to do does not sit well with me."

Layloree nodded. "He can choose to come nicely and be tied comfortably, or not nicely and be upside down. That's a good choice." She clucked her tongue impatiently, in a well-practised gesture. "Men don't know what is best for them sometimes. Best to look to your matriarch to decide." She frowned at something behind me.

"I don't have a matriarch," I reminded her, turning to face whoever was walking up to us.

The round mage Carreelee waddled slowly up the field, blinking sleep out of her eyes. "Tuniel MasterMage told me I was needed," she mumbled. "Are we doing something at last?"

I saluted. "Well met, Mage Carreelee. Thank you for coming to meet me."

She halted a few paces away, chewing her lip. "Well?"

It seemed all Skienien women were short-tempered, especially when woken early. "I'd like to know whether you feel ready to re-enter Skien, what provisions you know are needed and whether you agree with our approach. I would also like to train with you if possible, to understand your capabilities."

Carreelee's eyes narrowed.

Beside me Layloree started speaking Skienien, the syllables guttural and ricocheting off the castle walls. I could catch some words such as *"heta koller"* and "Keltskarr."

The mage nodded. "I understand that," she responded, slow enough for me to follow. "He's asking me to pack for him and fight with him."

"I'll handle the packing. Well, I'll requisition," I reassured her.

Layloree shook her head with a clatter of blades. "Carreelee, they do things differently here."

The mage's smile pushed her cheeks into her eyes. "I know. It's funny, though." She winked at Layloree.

The retired Battlemistress snorted. "Yes, he is very funny." She slapped me on the back. "Be aware, man mountain; asking a Skienien woman to do things for you is fraught, especially if you offer to fight her straight afterwards."

*This again.* "Then my apologies, it's a simple question here. I wouldn't want to begin the mission without using your expertise."

Layloree hooted. "You flirt! Such pretty words from a pretty face."

This was starting to get tiresome. "Can we focus on what we need to get done, please?"

"And what do *we* need to get done? *We've* been ready for days," Carreelee said, putting her hands on her hips.

"Good, wonderful. I do need to understand your capabilities so I know how to work with you."

"You cannot fight me alone," the mage said.

"It would be a practice bout, so low to no contact, if you feel that's appropriate."

"No contact is best," Layloree muttered to me, voice and face stern. "That thing is a true monster and you'll be cut to ribbons. You belong to Mistress Tuniel, and she'll never let me hear the end of it if you end up as ribbons."

"I don't belong to—" Breaking off, I took a deep breath. "Look, here in Oberrot, a man is his own."

"He is in Skien too." Carreelee eyed me. "He just is better with others." She craned her neck around. Dawn was approaching but still about half a turn of the glass off. "Are you sure you want to do this? Alone, no one to help?"

"It's just a training assessment, we aren't going to hurt each other."

Claws sprang from her fingers. She took a step forward, her toes digging into the ground and elongating, darkening from brown shoes to black. "I cannot always control her. My monster." Her arms lengthened, stretching out and turning inky, as if underneath her skin was darkness.

I took a step back. "Does your monster have a name?"

She prowled forward, spine elongating and stretching out behind her. Her hair and clothes melted down, disappearing into her skin and smoothing to scales. Her eyes flashed red, jaw lengthening into a cruel, hooked smile, incisors glinting. "Whatever name you have for a demonic goddess in your heathen religion."

I drew my sword.

She laughed. "I'm hungry. You can call me that."

She sprang forward. I put my sword up to guard and she slammed into it. Twisting, I shoved her back. She wasn't abnormally strong but she had a lot of weight behind her.

She sat back and snarled, her spine lengthening until she was half again as tall as me, claws flexing above my head level.

I moved under her talons and hit her stomach with the flat of my blade. "You're done."

She stopped where she was and looked down at me. "You... what?"

"If this was a real fight, I could have skewered you. You left your stomach unguarded."

She thumped back onto all fours, pushing her head into mine. Her eyes had moved to the side of her head and her jaw had lengthened considerably. "Usually they are running away screaming by now. You knew I wouldn't hurt you. This doesn't count."

"You rely on shock tactics. Do you have any fighting ability at all?"

Hissing, she snatched at me.

I batted away her curved claws, careful to keep the sharp side of my father's sword away from her flesh. "That's a no. Is there anything else you can do?"

She looked down at herself. "Isn't this enough?"

I smiled, wiping my face. I wasn't even sweating. "Yes, I suspect it is against civilians, but against a trained fighting force, you're going to run into problems." Sheathing my father's sword, I turned a slow inspection around her. "This is incredible, though."

"Is it?" She cocked her head.

*What I wouldn't give to have such capabilities onside.* I probably should not voice that sentiment like that, however, not the way these two seemed to be around compliments from men, no matter that they were true statements. "Shock tactics is one thing, but with a bit of knowledge on the basics of fighting, you could be a wonderful asset to any team."

"Team, mm?" She picked up one clawed arm. A long tongue crept out of her mouth and she licked her paw.

"What is your skin like? Is it tough, chitinous?"

She rippled all over, spikes standing out in the wake of the surge. "I can make it look like this, or this." Her skin smoothed to be as shiny as glass. "But either is just as soft as normal skin."

"So it isn't its own armour. Can you thicken the skin at all?"

The huge thin beast closed her eyes and shrank down. The slim lines took on bulk, becoming chunky and rounded. "Yes, but now I'm smaller." She stood at the size of a horse now.

"The extra protection would be worth it." I rubbed my chin, thinking.

The beast elongated again, twisting and turning, and more ideas thrust forward for my consideration. "Can you fly?" I asked.

"No. I cannot make wings that work." Two sails grew out of her midsection, peeling up. The skin underneath immediately sealed over, and she stretched wide two wings either side of her. Tail lashing, she bared her teeth at me. "They look impressive, though."

"Hm. I wonder if Tuniel could come up with a design you could follow."

Layloree peered at the castle. Shading her eyes, she waved. "Man mountain, I think this exercise has attracted friends."

I glanced over. Barlay stood, arms folded, next to a hysterical night watchman. The Regular blanched when the beast glanced their way, and nearly toppled backward when she shook her neck, stretching all her limbs again so she was long and sinuous.

But I was distracted by the man beside Barlay. Gavain stood next to him in a brand-new red uniform. From a distance, his swollen chest looked like he had packed on more muscle rather than bloating. He was clean, his chin and jaw freshly shaved and hair tied back in a neat queue. *He looks more like himself again.*

I shook myself. "Oh, damn and blast." Perhaps parading a monster in the training grounds wasn't the best way to start the morning. I saluted, sending Barlay a hand signal for "stand down" and "all is well".

The captain patted the man on the shoulder, pacing up to us. Gavain followed at a distance and much slower, as if reluctant.

Rubbing his eyes as he pulled up, Barlay stayed at the edge of the practice field. "Well met, Ranger. Ma'am. And, uh..." He stared up at the beast.

"Hungrig, sir." I flashed a smile at the beast. "That's hungry in Skienien, is it not?"

Sitting on her haunches, Carreelee slowly shrank down, coils of black curling and thickening, and pale pink and dark red emerging until the squat mage stood before us. "It is true, as I missed breakfast."

Barlay continued his slow blinking, as if he couldn't shake off the shades of sleep from his eyes. "Remarkable."

I bounded up to report to him. "It really is, sir."

"I wouldn't know where to start with a skill like that," he said in a low voice.

"Well, sir, it's like any recruit, I think. Try to find the edges of what they can do and how willing they are to expand beyond that, and then work out how to help them do that."

Barlay raised an eyebrow at me.

A twinge of anxiety twisted my belly. "Was that close to any truth, sir? Or have I got the wrong of it?"

"No, that's it hit squarely in the centre. I just usually hear more aggressive words applied to it; test, push, pull. I've always believed that some people like the pushing and testing and grow under it, and others will wilt and fade with it." He patted the wooden fence post between us, a pleased smile on his face.

My chest swelled at his tacit approval. I refocused. "Captain, last night our alternative versions visited. Just two of them, my version and the alternative version of Tabreksson. My version is about to come down now to join training. I've been calling him 'Shoulders' to help differentiate him."

His smile faded. "Thanks for the information. I'll let the guards know to expect them, and I'll have to insist on increasing checks on your codes. Nothing personal, just protocol."

It pained me that Barlay did not trust my alt, and that pulled my pale doubts out of my mind. Shoulders had saved our lives and fought to keep my Evyn safe. What did he have to do to prove himself to me?

"They are here because they need our help. Their Evie is missing —the alternative version of Evyn—and they need me, Evyn and Aubin to help."

Barlay's brows lowered. "Help, you say. And just you three."

"Help we are minded to give them, after all the assistance they have been to us." I met his gaze steadily. Our nascent doubts about them looked ungrateful in that light.

Barlay said, "I know you think of them as allies, Ranger, but their motives in their continual visits are unclear."

"Motives? We are friends. They came to visit to spend time with us."

Barlay's lips twitched down. "I can see you're preparing to hunker down and defend this one to your grave, Shardsson, so I will not press it now. Just... be careful. Your training as a swordsman, Lady Evyn's ability and then Tabreksson's specific skillset is a powerful combination."

"Yes. The perfect deployment to help their Evie."

"A lever that would work on you every single time," he pointed out, voice calm and almost gentle.

"She was chasing after the Liara from our timeline, sir. Liara disappeared between the worlds, and we do not have the ability to follow after her. They do."

Barlay's eyebrows raised. "Ah, well, in that case... I suppose that is a legitimate ask back to you."

I felt almost magnanimous as I said, "It's alright, sir, you didn't have the full picture, and you have Skien to worry about."

"Yes, but don't think you cannot come to me with these things, Shardsson. I cannot even begin to fathom these people from another world, so I will always err on the side of caution as the safest route to proceed. I trust your judgement, of course I do, but..." He scratched the stubble at his cheek. "First things first. You'll need to get to Skien before we deal with any of that. Focus on that, and I'll keep the bigger picture in mind."

"Yessir." I rapped off a salute.

Gavain gained the fence line as Barlay turned. "Gomoresson! Report to the training field."

Gavain nodded, jaw tight, not meeting my eyes as he turned

away. Already the underarms of his uniform were stained darker with exertion.

I drew my mind from Gavain and back to Carreelee. I needed to focus on her and her capabilities, so we could be prepared for Skien.

I walked back up to Carreelee, her thick red braids standing stiff over her shoulders. "Well?" she asked.

"Can you make other shapes?"

"I can be anything – and anyone – you want me to be." She grew taller, clothes melting into her and springing out as burgundy over-lapping scales. The face shifted into a hard jawline, red beard sprouting along the curves. Her green eyes glared down at me. "See?" Even her voice had changed, going rougher to match the weathered man standing before me.

"Very impressive. Could you disguise yourself like this in Skien?"

"As a man?" Her nose wrinkled.

I nodded. "The Hudau might be looking for you as a woman. They are likely to overlook a Skienien man."

"I can just be another woman." The beard receded, fleeing along the sides of her face, and her hair lengthened. Hips and breasts shifted, flowing easily.

Layloree's bony elbow nudged my arm. "Stop staring, man mountain."

"Hm? I'm just watching the... oh. Right, yes." I stood straighter. "Apologies, Mage Carreelee."

She smirked, now an eight-foot tall Battlemistress with corded muscle. "If we were in Skien..." She left the rest unsaid.

"He isn't yours to claim." Layloree threw her hands in the air, then turned to me. "You're going to need a matriarch in Skien to keep you in line and represent you to anyone else we meet."

"And who else is in our party?" Carreelee asked, leaning on one leg and thrusting her hip out.

I counted on my fingers. "Me, another version of me we call Shoulders, another version of Tabreksson we call the Assassin—"

Layloree sliced her hand down to cut me off. "Another what, man mountain?"

"*Fordubbla*?" I tried, thinking of what the word could be in Skienien for an alternative version from another timeline.

"You have your *fordubbla*?" She whistled. "And they stay, they don't vanish away?"

"So far they've come and gone but right now they've been here a few days."

"And Mistress Tuniel, she has hers as well?"

"Yes, but she visits much less."

Layloree's mouth dropped open in shock. "She did not say anything! That girl keeps her secrets close to her and her alone."

"It's not exactly a secret, they'll be walking around shortly."

Layloree rubbed her hands. "Battlemistresses watch for *fordubbla*. They come at key points in your life to mark turning points, choices to make. Meeting one means you are close to the edge of importance, a twisting fork of your time. To meet your own *fordubbla* means *you* are the key to whatever will happen, and your choice, made or unmade, will bring about the turn." She looked back at the castle, where dawn light had started to trace down the Last Tower, standing as the highest peak for miles around. "I cannot wait to meet them and discern the differences between my *hellione* and this *hellione*, piecing together the clues of what choices fashioned him." She looked genuinely animated by the prospect.

"You are the first person who has expressed delight at an alt. Usually they get treated with suspicion."

"I can see why. They are an omen, man mountain."

"They are also just people," I said firmly.

"Ah, yes. The worst of all." Layloree nodded sagely.

Carreelee's eyes cut away from me. She had been on the receiving end of the darkness in men and women's hearts only recently.

Layloree stretched her limbs. "We return to the fork we travelled down, and get on right path; who else is attending with us to the lovely crunchy mountains of Skien?"

Crunchy was a good way of putting it. "Aside from those two, there is my soul companion, Evyn. She is much more learned than I."

"And she is needed to tame the *hellione*." Layloree pursed her lips pensively. "Quick, now, dawn is coming and it's getting too hot for these old bones, so let's get this agreed in principle. I say keep me in the back, as an old Battlemistress who's nothing special, a mother with no teeth who needs feeding by her daughter. So Carreelee and Evyn are matriarchs."

Carreelee scowled. "Two matriarchs never works. Men look to both, and if they are not aligned, there is chaos. I am interested to try being a man, but I will be the top man." She glowered at me.

Layloree gave an acquiescent grunt. "Put it in a rough order, we can sort on the way."

"The rough order is: me on top." Carreelee squared up to me, beard blooming along her face again. "We are agreed?"

"Yes, indeed, if you wish. If it comes to a fight, however, I expect you to listen to me."

Carreelee bristled. "You will listen to *me*."

Layloree tutted. "This is already like men. Look, set the hierarchy. Worst fighter at the bottom, best at the top."

"That's me," I said.

"Or could be me, we haven't tried properly yet," Carreelee said, breath hot on my face.

She lunged to grab my shoulders but I was already moving, ducking down and under. I yanked her leg out from under her, and she collapsed in a heap to the floor.

I rolled to my feet. "You need more combat training, and in all the different bodies you can do."

Picking herself up, Carreelee scowled. "Fine. I submit to that."

I frowned, looking to Layloree to see if she understood.

Layloree burst out laughing. "You beat her and then gave her a suggestion, but as the higher ranking male, your 'suggestion' is law."

*Oh, wonderful.* "Can we please focus on the mission?"

"Yes," Carreelee intoned.

Layloree snorted.

"It's not fun, being a man," Carreelee groused.

I didn't know quite what to say to that. "I need to get to training and finalise the plans, now that I have your input. Perhaps we can see you later on today?"

"Bring our new matriarch!" Layloree said, delighted. "And those *fordubbla*."

# CHAPTER II

Turning to follow the gravel to the barracks and the field, I scanned the lines of men and women in red and their soul companions. I walked faster, close to being one of the last there this morning. The ranks murmured to one another, but all stood straight when they spotted me and parted sharply to let me through. For once their attention was fixed ahead rather than on me.

I approached Captain Barlay. "Apologies for the later fall-in this morning, sir..."

Gavain stood next to Barlay, his blue eyes meeting mine unflinchingly. I lifted my chin in return. To see him here again, back where I had always seen him, back where he belonged, sent a strange mixture of relief and regret to tingle on my tongue. A greeting sat there, unformed and rendered mute by uncertainty. *What do I say now?*

Barlay put his hands on his hips, nodding toward the men and women in rows facing us. "I'm just about to welcome Gomoresson back into the troops."

Ah, yes. I would have to speak to Gavain if we were to work together effectively for Barlay. To refuse would be churlish; if he was to prove himself to me, he needed to be able to talk to me without me shutting down.

I cleared my throat. "Well met, Gomoresson," I croaked, turning about-turn to regard the corps before Gavain could react.

They were restless, some shifting their stances from ready to attention and back, some openly talking to their peers. A few faces I picked out, Aleric and Grey especially. Aleric's eyes were wide and his face pale, while across the field Grey looked between Gavain, Barlay and me with wariness. I met his gaze and his eyes narrowed.

"Excuse me, coming through." Evyn's voice barely reached me. The corps parted, then flinched backward, a murmur rolling through them in a wave. Everyone's attention snapped toward the shambling figure making his way through them.

My alt stared at the ground, his hand firmly encasing Evyn's and his face reddening. He trudged forward, following her as she coaxed him onward, but his steps slowed as he neared the front.

Evyn looked at me, her face also Special Forces red, and I motioned to the space between me and Barlay. Tugging Shoulders forward with gentle motions and soothing platitudes, she stood close to me, almost hiding behind my arm. The fact that the two of them had managed to make it this far was nothing short of incredible. I held out my hand behind my back, and Evyn slipped hers into mine with a grateful squeeze.

Barlay took a step forward. "Special Forces, well met. You'll notice we have familiar faces back with us. First off, the easiest one: this man here." He pointed directly at my alternative version.

The poor man instantly paled. Evyn scowled, stepping in front of him.

"He is easily identifiable by demanding to see tattoos. Please do make sure you know who you are speaking to before you disclose information or accept orders."

*Damn and blast.* Of course Special Forces would revel in demanding to see my identification each and every time I opened my mouth or tried to go anywhere. I met Evyn's eyes, and she bit her lip. *Malicious compliance indeed.*

Meanwhile, Shoulders stared at the ground, red trickling up his shaking jaw. Gavain glanced at him and away. Across the rest of the corps, Aleric looked confused, but Grey was staring at my alt with a gaze that unsettled me in its intensity. *What is he thinking?*

Barlay raised his arm to point at Gavain. "You'll also notice that Gomoresson is back. He has been granted a rare opportunity to return to service after recent events, including critical injury. He will be assisting me in planning and strategy, and will not be able to join training for the foreseeable. His sword has been removed. He will, however, be observing manoeuvres. You are to treat him as the lowest-ranking member of the contingent – but let me make myself clear: I do not want to see any initiation or ordeals imposed by yourselves. Such behaviour will put the swordsmen or women involved directly on review, and we do not have time for it."

Barlay paced in front of us, talking directly to the men and women and projecting his voice over them. "On to the briefing I can give you. The king has assessed the latest intelligence from Skien. It indicates that shortly we will need to provide a humanitarian response to keep the borders flowing and allow refugees to enter and resettle in Oberrot. We will also likely be asked to support Daron's border in the same capacity."

The troops stayed absolutely still, warm clouds of air puffing from each open mouth. This was a large undertaking, and many of the corps had seen the last eviction only four turns ago. However, we were only a fraction of the force that we had been then, due to Torgund's own purge removing experience and compassion from the ranks.

This was going to significantly stretch Special Forces as it was now.

Barlay nodded, his face grim. "For now, forward with training. Ranger Shardsson, if you would be so kind as to assist."

"Yessir." Taking in a deep breath that stretched my sore chest, I let it out in one long bellow. *"Run!"*

The corps turned as one and broke into a run, the formation breaking up as the front runners charged ahead. Evyn and Shoulders shambled along behind; I trotted with them briefly before putting on a burst of speed, rushing through the pack of runners, dodging through them to get toward the front.

On the return journey I spotted Gavain. He was walking toward the turnaround point, head high with sharp puffs of steam coiling around him. Red-faced already, he kept his arms swinging in a quick march.

*Is this wise?* He knew his own limits, presumably, but judging by how much stairs taxed him, this could put him in the infirmary on his first day back.

He stumbled. *Or the cemetery.*

I pulled out from the pack and peeled off to run up to him. "Soldier, what do you think you're doing?"

His fists bunched as he drew to a halt. "Morning warm-ups to the best of my current ability. *Sir.*" The glare in his eyes definitely bordered on hatred as he slammed a fist against his heart in an angry salute.

*So much for wanting to start anew.* I grimaced. "I'll suggest to the captain that we check with the medimage treating you on what's appropriate for you. For now, turn and walk back, but *slowly.*"

A frown darkened his face. "Slowly, eh? And be late for the patterns?" He marched on, heading toward the top of the field.

I rounded on him. "Stop right there, soldier."

He growled under his breath. "You couldn't even wait for the warm-ups to start in on me. Well, fine. Have at it. Give me a hundred punishment laps, take away my rations, put me on latrine duty." His breathing was harsh and strained, sweat trickling down his face.

I moved into his path, arm outstretched. He bumped into it, rocking to a halt. Already he was swaying, sucking air in and gasping it out between his pale lips. "Take a moment," I said, voice low. "I'm not starting anything on you, I just don't want you put straight back in the infirmary. Barlay needs you for desk duty."

"And lifting a steele is strenuous." He made as if to move around me, but his knees sagged.

I darted forward, and underneath my hand on his chest, I could feel the sharp shallow breaths that shook him. "Gav. Stop. Turn around and go back. I'll come with you and give my report to the captain."

He shoved my hand away. "A report that I couldn't make it half a field, that I begged to stop." His glare was hot. "I'm not stupid, *Ranger*."

"No, you're just stubborn." Shaking my head, I jogged back to Barlay. "Very well then, die on the field, see if I care," I muttered to myself.

The captain was with the rest of the corps, who were doing warm-up exercises in batches. I fired off a salute. "Gomoresson is making his way the best he can, sir, but I suggest we ask the infirmary what he can and cannot do."

Barlay inclined his head. "Make a mental note to ask Lady Evyn to take a physical note of that." He nodded toward where Evyn was with Shoulders. He was moving smoothly enough through the warm-ups, and even had a broad smile on his face as Evyn wobbled all the way up on a full press-up. She sat back, face flushed with triumph, and he grasped her shoulders with pride.

That warmed me, but also hurt just a little. It should be me supporting and encouraging her, and then celebrating with her. I paced up to them. "Well done, Evyn!"

"Thanks." She gave me a delighted grin, and my heart lifted. "Did you see it? My first real press-up!"

"It was magnificent!"

"Well, maybe not that good." With a roll of her eyes, she held out her hand for me.

Taking it, I felt our bond renew, a balm that warmed and soothed me as I pulled her to her feet. She felt it too, leaning into me, and I put my arm around her shoulders.

"Pair up!" Barlay called. "You too, Ranger, we're doing old patterns," he said as he passed us.

I glanced down at her. "Do you fancy doing some pair work?"

Her smile went wider, if that were possible. "Yes please! It's been ages since we last paired up."

I beamed, pleased.

On his knees still, Shoulders wiped a hand across his face. "I'll... wait for a partner," he mumbled.

Damn and blast. I should have offered that he partner with Evyn. Glancing at her, I saw her draw her bottom lip into her teeth as she fretted. I was just selfish enough to want to partner with her today. "Maybe we can rotate. I also need to keep an eye on the corps, of course." They would be fine during pair work on older patterns that they could flow through innately, it was only with manoeuvres and new patterns that Barlay needed help assessing the corps. Evyn knew that as well, nodding slowly.

My double looked away. "I don't want to come between you two. I know... I want..." He curled his hands into his trousers, head bowed.

Evyn and I moved as one, putting our hands either side of his shoulder. His head jerked up in surprise.

I hunkered down. "It's alright." My throat hurt. "If it were me where you are, what would you do?"

His eyes went wide, the whites contrasting sharply with the deep browns. They were somehow darker, much sadder than the eyes I met in my mirror. He couldn't seem to speak, his jaw working but no words forming. He stood slowly, with us either side of him, and the smallest smile twitched his lips.

A drastic wheezing like a set of bellows with a hole in it and the slap of feet behind me made me look up. Gavain had finally arrived back at the contingent and immediately bent double, hands on his knees, gasping like a fish landed on the side of the Mid-Ete lake.

We three shared a glance. I disentangled myself, shaking out my hands. "I'll return momentarily."

Slick with sweat, Gavain slid to his knees.

"Oh, hells." I pulled up next to him. "Can you speak?"

"What..." he panted "... do you think?"

I rolled my tongue in my mouth. "I think you're trying to goad me."

His rheumy glare snapped toward me. "Write me up. Do it."

I folded my arms, tamping down the rush of irate responses that I could snap at him as his superior. I settled for, "I'll have to at this rate." Why was he angry with me, when yesterday he had seemed neutral? *What have I done now?*

Unless...

Did he expect me to exact some kind of revenge on him while he was in this vulnerable position?

He had done so to me. When I limped back into the contingent in Dinahe, the hazing had begun immediately, led by then-Sergeant Philo. Gavain expected the same treatment now.

I put my hands on my hips. "Swordsman, I have some work for you."

He nodded, jaw set and eyes hard, waiting for me to order him to do something ridiculous.

I waved my alternative version forward. "Shoulders, Gomoresson will help you review and perfect those stances we learnt a few mooncycles ago. Gomoresson, I'll be checking later to see how he has improved." There. Now my alt would have a partner, and if Gavain decided to teach him incorrectly, it would only be a turn of the glass's worth of lessons that I'd be able to address. If he did do something so disgustingly petty, then I would be glad to cut him out of my life entirely.

Perfect.

My alt approached cautiously, and Gavain frowned as they sized each other up. Gavain looked back and forth between us, then nodded. "Alright. Shoulders, is it?" He settled to the floor, folding his legs. "I can see why you earnt a nickname like that."

Fanning the red shirt at his chest, Shoulders gave a small nod.

"I'm Gavain. Well met, I suppose, now that we're on the same side and I'm not arresting you for existing." Smoothing his hair back, Gavain pressed a fist to his chest in a salute. This one was sincere at least. "So then. Show me the basic stances."

Satisfied, I brought Evyn to partner with me close by, and she smiled, equally pleased by my solution. I focused on her and developing her unarmed proficiency, given that she was not happy carrying around a weapon.

"But you may need to carry something sharp in Skien," I mused. "You'll be expected to."

She frowned, blocking my slow punch and knocking my arm aside as I'd taught her. "I'm happy you're automatically assuming I'm on the list to go, but also, isn't it a bit dangerous?"

I nodded. "Which is why you should be prepared and able to defend yourself."

"I don't know if I want to go." Her lips twisted. "I could just be on the other side ready to ping you across," she murmured in Rushia. She meant to follow along on the Earthian side.

Straightening up, I adjusted her left leg with a nudge from my own to improve her balance. "You could do that, if the geographies align," I whispered in Rushia. "We would need to be even more careful if you were to use what would appear to be magic in that country, should you appear in front of natives. If you fear harm coming to you, you will be surrounded by me, Carreelee, Layloree and probably the alts, and if I can arm you as well, then you will be as safe or safer with me than you would elsewhere." I wanted her with me, where I could see her and provide assistance if needed. Perhaps seeing Shoulders so bereft was gnawing at me, but I did not want her to leave my sight for long.

I settled back into an attack stance and lunged for her.

She knocked my forearm aside again. "I suppose." That darkly hopeful but also uncomfortable bubble in my solar plexus bubbled up.

"You're worried you'll see him again." I did not need to specify who I meant with her.

She nodded once, then let her arms drop. "Yeah. I am. You got me. I'll get over it and pull up my big girl socks." A tremulous smile was my reward for finding her out, but the hurt and heartache that washed over me made me wrap my arms around her.

"We will be alright," I reassured her. "Together, we can face anything!"

"Yes, sure, of course." Sniffling, she gave me a final squeeze and let go. "I'm all sweaty, and you don't want that on your jacket."

"I don't mind." I did mind sweat staining clothes in general, but I would wash it off for her.

The pair work was winding down. Gulping down water and passing Evyn her waterskin, I quickly scanned across the rows. "Nearly time for you and I to get to work, after a quick bath, of course."

"Okay. I submitted the packing list today, comparing records from a few campaigns ago." She rubbed her hands.

"Sounds..." *Like torture.* "Um. Well, if you will enjoy it, then by all means charge ahead." In any case, it couldn't be as bad as the shoulder torture that Gavain employed against me.

I scanned the field to put eyes on Gavain and Shoulders a short distance away. Gavain sat, arm raised and running a finger down his own forearm onto his hand; he looked to be demonstrating a neutral hold to the wrist versus a tense one. My alternative version flexed his own wrist, eyebrows lifting as understanding percolated through to him. He shot his instructor a delighted smile; Gavain's cheeks suffused with red.

"Spot inspection," I said, marching up. "Go on then, Shoulders. Show me what you've learnt."

He did not hesitate, flowing into the basic guard stances and into the more intermediate ones.

I nodded, satisfied. "Now all that's missing is a weapon, so you can get used to stabilising and positioning yourself with the weight and heft of it." As for Gavain, apart from the pink flush to his cheeks and his shirt soaked with sweat, he looked to have recovered his breath.

*My thanks.* It was a simple phrase said so often as to be rendered meaningless. Thanking him for doing his job, the work I had asked him to do, when there were still words to be said and weighed between us?

It was the right thing to do. "Thank you, swordsman."

Gavain blinked slowly at me, blue eyes searching mine. Once more he was at my feet looking up. "Yes, sir." He slowly put one foot flat on the floor, preparing to stand.

He might need help to rise and would be too proud to ask for it. My hands flexed uselessly at my sides as I stood mute, unable to offer and unwilling to walk away.

He stood on his own, slow but stable enough, brushing his uniform as he straightened up. "I suppose it's time for manoeuvres, sir, but you and I will be planning the deployment."

"That's right." I stared over his left ear toward the barracks. What would it be like trapped in an office with this man? I wasn't prepared for it in the least.

I could turn on my heel and walk off without an explanation – it was within my rank to do so – but that felt uncomfortable. Not that these stilted words masking our muddled emotions were in any way comfortable to endure.

"I'll make sure Shoulders is suitably employed, away from the planning session, of course." That twinged, deep in my chest. He was not and could not be trusted even still. "And I'll make sure Lady Evyn is ready." Not that she could ever be ready to face the man nearly convicted of plotting to kill her and converse politely with him a day later.

Gavain nodded sharply. "She needs bracers," he said, the words accompanied by a smatter of spit. He wiped his mouth, disgust turning his lips.

I put my hands behind my back. "Bracers, swordsman?"

"Lady Evyn would benefit from some bracers if she is going to use her arms like that, and if they can be made out of the metal in your armour, they would repel attacks." He looked at the churned ground beneath our feet. "What would the MasterMage charge for such a thing?"

"That's an official discussion between her and Lady Evyn." The idea of bracers took hold; those would suit Evyn very well and be unobtrusive as a weapon, protecting her as much as they could be used offensively.

"Very good, sir," he said, wiping his face.

I returned to Evyn and Shoulders. "Time for baths. Evyn, would you lead Shoulders back to our apartment?" I knew he preferred to bathe alone, and this would also remove him from critical areas of the army.

Evyn gave a little salute. "Will do."

Running his hands through his hair, Shoulders nodded, keeping his eyes lowered from the gaze of the men and women around him.

Perhaps I was becoming more sensitive to the stares, as I was quite often the recipient of them nowadays, because it seemed as though we were garnering extra attention from Special Forces. Grey especially kept looking over, but whether it was me, Shoulders, or Gavain as the focus of his interest, I could not be sure.

# CHAPTER 12

I washed in record time, showering off outside the baths and dipping in for a quick immersion in the warm waters, keeping my back and the scars away from Special Forces. Aleric nodded to me, which relaxed my stomach somewhat, but I was too busy to linger.

Pulling on a fresh uniform, I towelled off my hair and set it with a quick glance in the mirror. Chatter rang from all sides of the tiled bathing room, and naturally it centred around Skien. "Difficult" and "cold" were mentioned of course, but I also caught bitter breathings of the words, "rogue magic users." Turning that over in my mind as I walked to the barracks, I wondered what they had heard. The king had not mentioned anything of the sort.

Entering the cool of the barracks, I tried to relax my tightening stomach. Evyn wouldn't be here yet, and I would watch the main door for when she came in so I could escort her up through the bunks. Not that there was anyone here right now, not even Barlay and Gavain. I could have stopped for some food, but the twists and turns of my stomach made it difficult to tell whether I was even hungry.

Every bunk lined up along the pathway to the office looked the same. It was only through experience that I knew who slept where. Gavain's bunk now had possessions stowed in the cupboard, so it was closed, and that was the indication that he was back in my life.

"Hi." A small voice and smaller footsteps.

"Well met." I turned to face my soul companion, padding down between the bunks toward me. The morning sun at the open barracks door streamed in behind her, lighting up her hair and lending her skin a glow. My heart swelled, as if it too glowed and warmed like some kind of soul jewel when she was near.

She met me halfway. "Nice bath?"

"Yes, on the whole. I picked up some interesting rumours about rogue magic users, and I'm not sure where the corps got that from."

Evyn slipped her hand into mine and led me confidently up toward the office. "I heard some stuff during morning training too, everyone was talking about the refugees. A lot of the louder ones were muttering about why Oberrot has to take them, it was awful."

I halted. "They're questioning the refugee settlement?"

"From what I could gather, yes."

"But why?"

She shook her head but a voice behind me said, "They're magic users."

I spun to face Gavain, pulling Evyn behind me. There was a small bathroom in the barracks, with enough water to complete a standing bath rather than a full immersion; I should have realised he would have to use that.

He pulled his shirt closed over the paunch of his belly, hiding the pink and red mottled skin of his chest. Shaking fingers fumbled over buttons, but his voice was calm. "I overheard them pointing out that the refugees are magic users being displaced from their country. They're going to be angry and grief-stricken, and we all know magic users with high-running emotions are not in full control of themselves. Special Forces are asking themselves, *Why are we being used to get rogue mancers and mages into our country?* Think about it. All the worst engagements we had were in Skien."

Disbelief warred with the calm logic in his words. "That's not... They aren't rogue magic users, they... they're people." I tried to push my fingers open, to run tension through them so they wouldn't ball and form a fist, but anger filled my chest with the taste of sickening bile.

Evyn peered around my arm, looking Gavain up and down.

He straightened slowly under her inspection, his sunken eyes glittering in the shadows over by the bathroom.

She touched my hand. "I think he's just reporting it, Thorrn."

Gavain nodded. "The corps' view is distorted by the engagements we are sent on, and the bloodiest are always in Skien, so it seems. The constant suppression of magic and anti-magical sentiment makes the magic users born there feel hunted and desperate, more likely to slide toward violence. Perhaps it's always been to protect themselves, but when everyone is casting you out and calling you a monster, then maybe one day you decide you'll show them a monster."

I stilled. The rogue mages and mancers we had been sent to contain or kill were all victims in some way, I knew that. I just hadn't thought it through. "Skien's policy is really stupid," was all I could come up with. "They're creating the problem they are trying to solve."

Gavain inclined his head. "Indeed, but changing international policy isn't our job, it's Gough's, and we need to give him the space to do that." He gestured toward the office. "We should get started, but first... Lady Evyn, may I speak to you?"

I resisted the urge to pull her back behind me. "What for?" I barked.

"Thorrn," Evyn admonished softly. She clung to my hand, taking it with her as she came forward to face him. "You can speak, and I'll listen, but I can't promise you anything will come of it," she said.

He pulled his jacket on, movements jerky and face grimacing from pain. "That's all I want, Lady Evyn, and more than I could ask for." He sat on the edge of his bed, chest heaving.

"Alright then." She folded her arms, weaving mine in with hers. "I think Thorrn will need to stay, or he'll wear a groove in the floor pacing or listen in anyway. He can *be quiet*, though." She raised an eyebrow at me.

I nodded once, holding my jaw shut tight. What could he say to balance the fact that he brought her into our disagreement? What could he say to address that?

His jaw worked as he fought something deep within him. "Very well. In that case, I..." He dropped his gaze. "I need more time."

Suspicion prickled across my nerves. *What was he going to say to her, if I cannot be there as well?* Putting my hand on her shoulder, I steered her away from him.

Evyn glanced back at Gavain. "Er, okay. Office, work, come on. Anyone want a hot drink to get started?"

I could use a drink, but one with slightly more inebriation potential than what she was offering. "If you are making one for yourself, which I know you are."

Gavain said nothing, stumbling after us.

Evyn tentatively touched the small, cold heatstone next to Barlay's desk. The flat stone flared a deeper red, and she put the tin pitcher filled with water on top of it. "Right. I'm on the job." She stayed staring at the stone for a handful of heartbeats, her feelings churning inside her, a nervous swirl of dread. She glanced at me and it intensified. *Oh, she's worried about how I will react.*

Taking a deep breath that expanded my chest and filled my lungs, I tried to send calm waves down the bond between us. *He won't hurt us again. I'm watching him, and I will never give him the chance.*

Although she wouldn't ever be able to hear my thoughts, she perhaps sensed the sentiment, for she gathered herself and bustled to the bookshelves.

Keeping my gaze on Gavain, I pointed at the desk. "Well then. I suppose we better get started."

"Yes, Ranger." Gavain limped toward one of the two chairs,

mopping his forehead and cheeks with frustrated swipes. "So you're a separate unit. Do I need to put provisions in place for you in the plan?"

I shook my head. "No, I'm planning a separate operation to Special Forces maintaining the border. I'll let Barlay brief you."

"What is the Ranger corps? What do they do?"

"It's King Gough's unit for when he needs something a bit... different to Special Forces. A corps that can make decisions in the field, adhering to the spirit behind his orders, and breaking off where necessary to aid the helpless and the innocent."

Gavain gained the chair, hands flexing on the back of it. "Are you the first out in battle?" he blurted.

"No. That would be stupid, to go alone in the field." My hand closed around the well-worn hilt of my father's sword. That was the reason why I hadn't been sent on any missions on my own.

*To go alone against an enemy is suicide, but that's what Aubin has done.*

He frowned. "The way I've heard it told, it sounds like a berserker corps."

My throat tightened. "Oh, no, nothing like that at all. Where are you getting your information?"

Settling himself on the chair, he stretched out his legs, wincing. "Damn that hurts... Well." He glanced up at me. "A few people wrote to me while I was recovering. Aleric for the most part, and Grey." He pressed his lips together.

"Oh, of course. Well, we didn't want it to seem like some kind of promotion." I recalled Barlay introducing the corps to the concept of Ranger, saying I was unit apart, and would be kept working until I perished. The latter, of course, was true for all members of Special Forces; they would only be released from service by Gough if they were medically discharged, or if they were convicted of a crime and either banished or executed. Barlay had that clever way of making the words work for him, something that Gavain had in his gift as well.

"So it's not a punishment? It's a promotion?" He eyed my leathers. "You got a new uniform, you act as Barlay's Second—"

I held up my hands. "More like something of a sergeant. I'm helping Barlay more nowadays because Philo is on review, and he has this big campaign to plan. Which you should, you know, probably make a start on." I gestured to the well-worn drafting desk, the glowstone throwing steady orange light onto the blank parchment.

Gavain grunted. "One more question. Are there other Rangers?"

I kept my eyes averted from his. "There was another one." What would Aubin think of this strange ceasefire, this uncomfortable understanding? Immediately I imagined him glaring darkly at Gavain and plotting his demise, but Aubin wasn't like that. Would he ignore him, perhaps?

No; he would calmly take in everything he had done to Gavain, carefully listening to each halting breath and memorising every wince he made. He would make himself confront what he had done, and if it was too much, he would leave. Leave for a life of exile, of living away from his errors but never being able to remedy his mistakes.

Evyn poured and passed out the drinks, and then Barlay arrived, face dark. "Ranger, Lady Evyn, swordsman. We will have to draw up our route quickly; the Duke of Daron has reached out with his usual convoluted asking-without-asking request that Oberrot send aid, but they are reporting incidents of violence within Skien and very strange occurrences. They're using a word that Gough had to ask Lady Saleski for help translating." Barlay glanced at me.

"Mother?" She was the only Daronian noble in the castle, and one of the very few Daronians at all living in the city. They had an enclave area near the bottom of the hill, beneath the cemetery, keeping very much to their families and their neighbours. It made sense she would be consulted on the meaning of a word. "What did she say, sir?"

"She said they were talking about dhampir." Barlay's brows

lowered"We know the Duke especially would not speak in jest or exaggerate."

"But dhampir are stories for children," I pointed out. "Like dragons and... and..." I swallowed hard.

Earthians had been a legend and a myth lost to time for me only a few mooncycles ago.

Barlay and Gavain's eyes also passed over Evyn.

She noticed, looking between them and then up at me. "What? What did I do?"

"Nothing, just that a legendary creature is starting to look more... plausible." I cleared my throat. "Can the legends be true?"

Barlay said, "If so, we need more information, and reliable information. Lady Evyn, I need you to scour the library, please, and put a report together on the veracity of information there pertaining to dhampir. I don't need to tell you how to do your work, but I need to know what traits these things might have based on correlating accounts."

Evyn brushed her sweaty hair back from her forehead. "Cool, yes, great. I can start work immediately."

Barlay inclined his head. "Gomoresson, you're with me. We need to plan two deployments: on our western border somewhere to assist the evacuation into Oberrot and a resettlement team there, and support to Daron's northern border, which will take refugees safely across the mountains into southern Oberrot. The king is putting together the resettlement elements with the MasterMage, so we don't need to worry about that, we will only need to coordinate with it." Barlay glared at the distances on the map as though they had laid a challenge against him. "Lady Evyn has done a wonderful job of pulling together the notes from the last several such missions, so we can build on learnings there, but I fear this will be a massive undertaking. We still need to maintain protection on the royal family, of course, so we cannot send all our experienced troops to Skien. We need to maintain supply lines for an indefinite period of time, and—"

"Can we enlist the help of mages and mancers, sir?" Gavain interjected.

Barlay shifted back on his heels, sucking his teeth. "I suppose this is a joint mission. You're talking about mingled operations, which we've never done. But I suppose dire times call for unusual measures. I cannot see the MasterMage protesting that, if I'm honest." Barlay slid a look toward me.

I shook my head once. Tuniel would see the sense of it, understanding that it would strengthen how mundane forces and magic users worked together in Oberrot on an effort such as this.

"Good," Barlay said, smiling briefly. "Get with drafting, Gomoresson. Meanwhile, Shardsson, get to planning your foray with the MasterMage's team."

I scanned over the map. "We won't be able to use magic to travel."

"Why not?" Evyn asked, curious.

"Skien's magic sniffers would be able to tell if someone was using magic, and then pinpoint us for targeting and removal. It would be like clashing cymbals that we were here. As well, Mage Carreelee will not be able to use her powers in Skien for the same reason."

We might be able to use Evyn's ability to ping, but that would mean taking Carreelee and Layloree onto Earth. That would be an emergency only, I decided.

Barlay shuffled his feet. "Now then, the issue with matriarchs. Special Forces has some women in the ranks to put forward. Shardsson, I'd say your team was... rather heavy with matriarch potential."

Ah, yes. "Good. Travelling in pairs was always a bit... fraught."

Barlay stared somewhere above my right ear. "Right. Yes."

Evyn put her hand in the air. We all stared at it. "Yes, hi. Matriarchs?"

How to explain? "Skien's family units are... a bit different, Evyn. You'll know that men cannot travel alone together, because they'll be seen as rogue men. A man always has to have a woman with him somewhere. She's his matriarch, and she will have as many men around her as she can inspire loyalty from."

"Oh." Her eyes went wide. "Interesting."

"Indeed." With Evyn, Carreelee and Layloree in tow, I would have a different problem than the one Aubin and I faced. Perhaps they would think me a fearsome man, needing three women to keep him in line?

I could hope.

"Ah, so that's what Carreelee was on about in that meeting." Evyn's eyes sparkled. "She could have claimed you as hers, she said."

I tried to push back the warmth from my cheeks. "I suppose so, but we live in Oberrot, where a man isn't something you can just pick up off the street and decide is yours to keep for as long as he amuses you."

Evyn chuckled.

Barlay clicked his heels together. "Lady Evyn, I can escort you to the library if you'd like."

I looked up sharply. Being left alone in a room with Gavain? *No thank you.* Judging from the look on Gavain's face, he felt the same way.

There was a rap at the door. "Or I can." Lounging at the side of the open door, black headscarf in hand, was the Assassin.

Barlay moved in front of the drafting desk, despite there not being any plans there yet, and Gavain's eyes widened. "He... The apothecarist, he's not dead?"

# CHAPTER 13



The Assassin grinned, incisors flashing.

"This is an alternative history version," I explained hastily. "*The* alternative history version, in fact. The one you fought before." Perhaps not the best association to make between them.

The Assassin wagged his fingers at Gavain. "Hello again. I'd say you're looking hale and well, but…" His cruel smile widened. "You're not." He nodded to Barlay. "Forgive my intrusion, but I am looking for these two, and my friend assured me they were to be found here."

Barlay squared up to him. "You are barred from entering the barracks, as of now. Ranger Shardsson, escort him off the premises."

"And probably wear the headscarf, yes, I know." The Assassin donned the Rushia attire, covering his hair and face completely with just a slit for his eyes. "I just couldn't resist the look on the oaf's face. It's as if he saw a spirit come to life before his very eyes." The Assassin rubbed his hands.

"Come on, out," I said, just loudly enough to be considered an order but not shouting. I held out my arm for Evyn, who took it.

As we paced down the bunks I said, "We should get you a lodestone so you can talk to us rather than entering sensitive areas of the army."

"If you wish. I must say, the security around here is appalling. One thing I'll say for Torgund on my world is he cultivated a nice rich culture of distrust. Someone entirely dishonest with nefarious intentions could do a great deal of damage here."

I baulked at the door to the barracks. "Is that a... threat?"

He leant closer to me. "Consider it a freebie. If alternative versions start bleeding through onto your world, you're going to have a great deal of trouble containing them." Glancing back over his shoulder, the Assassin held out his arm for Evyn. "My lady, shall we be off to the library?"

"Uh..." She pushed her damp curling hair back behind her ear, eyes flinty. "I'm okay walking and working on my own, thanks."

Folding his arms, the Assassin nodded. "Very well. I'll see you safely there and then wander off to create mischief elsewhere. It's not as though I'm up to no good." He studied his nails. "Yet."

Evyn sighed. "Come on then, if you really want to. But I have work to do."

"Oh, work, how terrible. I try not to catch that myself." He nodded to me. "As you were."

"Right." I tapped my fingers on the lintel. He was doing that thing again where he reacted to her, but this time in a protective stance around her. He surveyed the grounds with quick eyes from the shadow of his disguise, his hands on his blades. Evyn would be safe enough with him.

She walked off, chin high, refusing to take his arm, and he hesitated only a heartbeat before falling into step behind her, silent and shadowing her every move.

Returning to the office, I found Barlay and Gavain deep in discussion. Gavain hadn't moved from his chair, bending forward with his elbows on his knees. Barlay wrote at the drafting desk, rapid notes that sprawled from his steele.

I turned in place like a sentinel. The office was packed with knowledge won from campaigns in the past, but the most vital information I needed to know was whether Aubin had moved. "I need to ask the MasterMage a few questions," I informed Captain Barlay.

"Very good," he murmured, gaze intent on his map.

Gavain's glance slid off to the side of me. Was that a smirk, or a grimace? It was hard to tell.

Doing an about-turn, I marched out, just as much of the contingent returned to their bunks to either get something before their shift or for rest before their work began. Their smiles dropped as I passed through them, and while they stepped aside I felt their attention on me, hard and searching.

I couldn't imagine living in here now. That would be hellish. My separation from Special Forces has been well-received by the remaining corps, and from me as well. Living alongside men and women who hated me would have been torture.

"Oh Ranger?" Barlay called.

I halted, spun around and marched back. "Yes, sir?"

The captain lowered his voice. "The MasterMage will be in the infirmary. Remember to ask the medimage what she thinks." *About how much exercise Gavain can handle*, I recalled.

"Yessir."

Behind the captain's shoulder, Gavain struggled to his feet in the office. "Ranger, if I can be of assistance during your planning phase, please let me know." He kept his face to the drafting desk; all I could see was the determined set of his jaw.

"My thanks." Simple and sincere. It was getting easier to talk to him while I was targeted on the tasks he completed for me now. Whether or not I would ask him to help, I hadn't decided yet, but refusing it if I thought it would be valuable would put my mission at risk, and that was stupidity at its finest. I tried to reconcile Gavain's actions with the person who stood before me. *He hates me.* He was being truthful, at least I could trust in that, and now I knew that I could proceed. I could acknowledge that, and still appreciate his talents as a strategist. I did not have to like him to work with him.

Saluting the captain, I walked back through the dispersed men. Aleric gave me a small wave, quickly hidden. I didn't want to embarrass him or cause him difficulty with a public greeting, and just gave him a nod, but at the door I looked back to see if he had understood that. He wasn't looking at me, however; he was looking at Grey with twisted lips. Grey faced the open office door, so I couldn't see his expression, but he slowly folded his arms.

The swordsman had never liked me, of that I was sure, vocally opposing my inclusion in the ranks despite not being able to complete Special Forces' test. My father had had to discipline him, and now that stuck in my throat. Had that completely been warranted? It was my father and perhaps Gough's decision, not mine, but I had benefited directly from it. When other people's decisions opened doors for you, were you not supposed to go in? Special Forces trained to make the most of every advantage, no matter how small.

Having my father as captain had been as much a big advantage as a curse, a chore. I had to uphold his name while I built my own, and the fact that I shared the same foundations as everyone else was overlooked. I thought Gavain and Aleric had seen that and understood it, but apparently not, and now I couldn't see anyone ever taking the time to understand it. *Poor you, having the captain as your supporter.* What they didn't see was that every one of my actions reflected on him just as much, if not more. *Had he really pushed that?* He gave me extra training until I could perform every action perfectly, he drilled the stances into me, he didn't let up even when I vomited, shaking and sobbing. *The enemy will be relentless, so the corps must be as well. You have to keep up with your contingent or risk losing them.*

Now I was a Ranger, set aside and standing apart again. I hoped that his spirit was pleased with this turn to his legacy. I was contented with it most of the time, but sometimes, the lonely edge to the station chafed.

✳ ✳ ✳

MARCHING TOWARD THE INFIRMARY, I marked the slower pace of the messengers flowing around in their white livery up and down the overwarm corridors of the castle courtyard. The heat of midsun hung low over the castle. With the biggest meal of the day over with, the mess hall was quieter, as if resting after a large meal. Servants took breathers in the shade, drinking cold pitchers of water and trying to encourage a breeze by flapping their hands at each other.

The infirmary corridor stretched from an inner courtyard; a waft of strong lyneal from it sent a spasm of memory to shriek across my nerves. Usually, a visit to the infirmary was preceded by pain, whether a training accident or an encounter that cut too close, and it was hard not to feel a twinge of dread just by being in these echoing halls. The infirmary itself was welcoming; a big round space with a glass dome overhead which sat inside one of the rear courtyards. As such, the dome received a muted light and never got too hot. Soft murmurs echoed from the rooms set around the atrium and made a soothing susurration, almost like a trickling river.

I hailed a nurse who pointed to one of the side rooms when I asked about the MasterMage. He may or may not have had magic; all medimancers and mages did, manipulating tissues, knitting torn muscle and setting bones faster than would be achieved by natural healing alone. The nurses seemed to have a different type of touch which may not be magical in nature at all: that of soothing and reassuring. Certainly after speaking to him and gathering myself I felt more settled. *I'm not here for me, after all.*

Rapping my knuckles on the door to the room he indicated, I listened hard. "Enter," Tuniel called.

Inside the well-lit room, Tuniel stood over an empty bed, utterly engrossed by a sparkling shape in her hands.

I slid inside and closed the door. There did not seem to be anyone else in the windowless room, but I addressed her formally even so, just in case. "MasterMage, well met. Are we alone here?"

Her eyes flicked to me briefly. "Yes, Thorrn."

"Mm. Then people will talk."

A smile tugged at her lips. "We should maintain the ruse anyway, just in case someone else should come to find me here. Now then, please be quiet, Ranger." The silvrine shape turned slowly in mid-air, the bright light from the al athmadi clear glowstone overhead flashing off glossy surfaces, each as smooth as a rounded orb.

Thinking of rounded surfaces, I paced closer to her, trailing a finger up her arm. "What are you up to, MasterMage?"

"Prototype designs of the heart for your colleague." The metal slid closer to us, and my own heart seemed to lurch in my chest. Smaller than my fist, it comprised four interconnected chambers. "And what part of quiet don't you understand, Ranger?" she murmured, her voice low and thick with promise.

Hooking soft strands of her hair back from her ear, I pressed my lips over her jumping pulse. "I could ask you the same question, MasterMage. Our surreptitious meetings aren't all that quiet at all. Not that I'm complaining."

She arched back, our breath mingling together. My blood rose, my heart surging, and the one in Tuniel's hands started to beat faster as well.

"Interesting." She placed the heart down and spun around in my grasp, tipping her face for a kiss. "It's responding to my magic, but..." She broke off as I kissed her.

When I let her come up for air, I grinned at her. "My apologies, MasterMage. I hope I didn't interrupt the run of your thoughts."

"Only in a good way." She put a finger to her full lips. I took it to kiss it. Her eyes softened. "I was wondering how to replicate the pumping using the natural spark signals that Hepzibah says the body gives off. The metal will need to be responsive to those signals. For now, I have to do that via a reservoir of magic, rather like the lodestone that is installed in your armour, and I will need to refill it often, as I cannot do it remotely like I could for you."

I glanced at my shoulder, a familiar pang echoing through me. Without Aubin close by, Tuniel couldn't use the resonance of the soul jewel to help retract Amare remotely. "Then you'll have to visit the city more frequently than you do, and for a legitimate reason. What a shame."

She smiled at me, then sobered. "It does also mean his life is tied to mine. Without a stone mage as powerful as me, a medimage or mancer acting as the focus to renew my power in the metal and the stone in the centre of his chest, he will die. At least until we think of something else."

"Mm." I pulled her back close to my chest, bending to rest my chin on her shoulder.

"And what of you?" She gave another twist of her wrist, and the metal started to turn over, spinning on a sideways axis. "How does your day fare?"

I stared, enthralled, at the delicate metal pulsing in mid-air. "I need to plan for this so-called leave I'm taking into Skien. I want to understand Layloree and Carreelee's capabilities."

"I see." She pushed her hips back against mine.

I bit down on a groan, stepping back. "I need a clear head," I confessed.

One eyebrow raised. "Don't start an engagement you cannot win, Ranger."

Admitting defeat, I bowed to her.

She chuckled. "And how was it, then, seeing your comrade in arms back in the family, or whatever you call yourselves?"

"Contingent, and yes. Difficult. Strange." I leant against the bed, folding my arms. "It is as we discussed before. I stand apart from the contingent, and I still don't know how pleased I am by that."

Tuniel nodded slowly. "Standing alone is always difficult. When everyone else seems to be moving in one direction, lifting your head and planting your feet where you need to is a lonely thing. Moving against them, even more so." She shrugged. "You can do what I do, and show that you do not care. Ignore them and do not grant them the power that their words and deeds can hurt you. They will have their truth, but you will have yours. You can take what you have been given to the best of your ability and live it as your truth while letting them have theirs."

I let that flow into me, like sand percolating and settling around the rocks of my conviction, giving it strength. "I like that. I like it so much I might take it as a tenet."

Her cheeks warmed, crimson. "Well, good." She held up her hand, and the heart halted in the air. "Now I need to do repeat volume tests to confirm the amount of liquid this can pump in a turn of the glass, and—" She lurched forward with a cry, the heart dropping to the bed.

"Tuniel!" I pulled her behind me, looking for a threat in this empty room.

Her back arched, face locked in pain, and I turned her over, looking for something, perhaps a thrown knife or a bolt, never mind that we were in a windowless room. *She is hurt somehow and if there is a wound I need to deal with it now!*

She gasped. "Aubin!"

My heart seized. *No.*

Sagging, her fingers dug into my arms. "He's pulling back now, shielding, but something hurt him, something big. What if the Hudau found him?"

"Is he still hurt? What can you feel from him?" Horrific imaginings of him fighting a mob dashed into me, red slicing across my vision. He would tire quickly and be overwhelmed, especially against the Skienien hammer or, worse, an axe, and my chest hurt, bursting with anger at his foes. I pushed back the rage; it couldn't help him, not if he was hundreds of miles away. We would never get there in time.

She shivered against me. "He's shielding. He's safe enough at the moment that he can do that successfully." Her hand reached out and knocked into a water glass.

I held it up to her lips for her, willing my own hands to stillness.

Wiping her brow, she squeezed my hand a final time but then stepped clear of me. "Is the heart damaged?"

"How would I know?" I still had those terrible images chasing themselves around in my brain. I squeezed my eyes shut but they would not depart.

*He's alone out there. He has no one for support.*

I opened my eyes. "We have to get to him, and quickly."

Tuniel nodded once. "By the end of tomorrow, you need to be ready to go."

"Aye, MasterMage." I saluted, pressing my fist to my heart. We would go ahead of Special Forces and rescue Aubin.

Whether he wanted to be rescued or not.

# CHAPTER 14

The rest of the day passed uneventfully but fraught all the same, as the frenzy of packing and preparing became all consuming. I returned to the apartment with dinner to find Evyn ensconced with books she had pulled from the library.

"Evyn, well met. I need to check with you on everything the previous mission took and what we might need for our smaller outfit. Warmer clothes, as Skien is much colder, and we'll need trail rations for journeying between the towns..."

Evyn took the roll that I passed her, eating it without really looking at it. "That's the basics, but what else?"

"Useful things like rope. No tinder and flint, because we won't want to light a fire, that'll put up smoke leading directly to our position."

"Isn't Skien cold?"

I drummed my fingers on our dining room table. "It's too cold to sleep outside without a fire, but Skien is riddled with hot springs. We'll be walking from spring to spring."

"Great." Evyn spread out her research. "I need to finish my report for Barlay tonight on these dhampir, then I can help you with your list?"

"Yes." I looked around the empty lounge, strewn with books as usual. "Where are the Assassin and Shoulders?"

She nodded toward Aubin's old room. "They were here earlier, but then Gough asked to see them, so they went up to the royal apartment."

"Good. I'll requisition supplies for them as well." Perhaps the Assassin would fit in Aubin's Ranger uniform. That idea made my stomach clench; seeing him but not seeing him, a mere copy and not the real thing.

She looked up at me, heartbreak in her eyes. "He's not doing so well. Shoulders, I mean. He's really struggling."

My heart squeezed. "We're moving as fast as we can. We need to get to Aubin, and quickly." I rested my hands on the table. "Tuniel felt pain from him earlier."

Her face paled. "Is he alright?"

"For now. He can't keep doing what he's doing, though. Sneaking around trying to free magic users from the mundane mob and organise them toward Oberrot is not something you can do with just one man."

"Maybe he'll realise that too. You never know." She turned over a page, staring past it. "All we can do here is what we're doing, so let's get to it, Ranger."

A rap at the door. I answered it to two messenger boys, both grinning at each other and panting as they caught their breath. Clearly they had challenged one another to a race, but I was unsure who had won; they both looked exhilarated by the run.

"Message for Ranger Shardsson!" they sang out in unison.

"That's me." My voice came out rougher than I anticipated. Maybe one day these boys would see each other as obstacles standing in each other's path rather than friendly rivals pushing each other to greatness.

Shaking off my morosity, I took the pieces of paper and brought them to Evyn. I peered at them both; one in writing and the other in code. The code one I could read. "Do not react to that other message," I said aloud. Handing the other sheet to Evyn, I frowned.

She opened it. "It's from Aleric. 'Meet me for a drink in the mess hall?'" Folding it, she looked on the other side. "It's signed from Aleric too."

I turned over the coded message. "This is blank. Could be sent via the automatic authority of Special Forces."

Evyn set her research aside with a grim look. "The station mistress will know who sent this, hopefully."

I ran back to the door, flinging it open. "Messengers, get back here and answer my questions!"

The boys turned, one holding his hands up. "Look, I just go where I'm told to go and say what I'm told to say."

"Who told you to come here?"

"The station mistress!"

"We will see about that. Come with me. Evyn, you come too." I wasn't going to leave her here alone if this was a ploy to get me out of our apartment and away from her.

The boys scowled and muttered as we tramped down to the message station. "We are in so much trouble," one moaned. "Do you know how many messages we have to deliver? It's not just you, you know, we have a round to do."

I pounded down the stairs. "They can wait. Tell them it's Ranger business."

The other boy trotted at my feet. "They won't believe that, they'll think I'm lazy, I won't get any rubles for fast delivery."

"I'll give you some rubles if you stop talking."

The boy clamped his mouth shut and did a little mockery of a salute. *How easily they can be bought.* The message system in the castle was not secure, yet operations relied heavily on it.

Thudding down each riser, I approached the message station on the ground floor, next to the stewards. A swarthy woman with a red face and collar undone came to the message desk when I rang the bell. "What do you want?" she barked, one eye on the line of boys and girls in white lined up against the wall behind her, all fidgeting and elbowing one another as they giggled.

"Ranger business." I pulled my right sleeve up to bare my forearm, covered over with my tattoos. I tapped the swirls of the Ranger one. "A message was sent to me, just now. Who sent it?"

Muttering, she flung open the book beside her with a bang. "Destination Rangers, Rangers..." She tapped the entry. "There. Three quarters of a turn of the glass ago, mind you." She glowered as she turned the book around and shoved it toward me.

I tried to focus on the lines, the hastily scribbled script illegible. Evyn pushed next to me and gasped, eyebrows drawing down into a firm line. "Special Forces." She frowned up at the bristling woman. "But that isn't a name."

"Special Forces has an automatic warrant, Evyn."

The station mistress nodded in agreement, barking, "I can't write a name if he doesn't give me one, but this one was noticeable. Big, blond, and sweating and panting like he'd climbed the castle before coming here. I had to mop up the desk after." She slammed the book shut, barely missing Evyn's fingers. "Happy?" she snarled at me.

"Not really." *Gavain.* He sent those messages? Was he even now trying something to manipulate me, to make me think that he had changed when in reality he was using this fresh chance for more vengeance?

Evyn steered me away from the desk. "And the message was very specific. Don't react to the other one. What could he be trying to tell you?"

"Don't meet Al for a drink? Refusing to respond to a message like that would put Al's back up." Such a petty action made my bile rise.

"Right. So, I think we need to see what's in the mess hall."

Beckoning Evyn, I led the way to the hall. "Get ready to ping," I whispered to her.

"Yes, alright." She jogged to keep up, but I could not afford to slow. "What do you suspect?"

"Trouble."

"Well, yes, but, what kind? The framing-you kind? The sneak-attack kind? The... I don't know, you do this more than me."

"Just trouble. Get ready to ping in and out of the mess hall. The back wall adjoins to the courtyard, so someone might see us. Let's approach it from the kitchens entrance."

I walked cautiously down the corridor, Evyn at my back. At this hour, just after dinner, the mess would be turning into a taproom for the troops. The clink of glass and the murmur of conversation was at a usual level. Pacing up the corridor with one hand on my father's sword and the other holding Evyn close, I tried to assess whether there was a threat here. This was my home, its rhythms as familiar to me as my own daily patterns. Anything out of the ordinary wasn't necessarily a hint of something dire, but in this mood suspicion ran high.

The kitchens should be quiet at this time, when service turned from hot meals to serving cold drinks from the bar hatch on the other side. The bakers had indeed set their loaves to rise and gone to bed, ready to wake in the pre-dawn and bake, and the cleaners would have been and gone. The heatstones threw off light, red and low, and while shadows bathed the corners, they were innocuous.

"Alright, let's listen to the mess hall at the serving hatch." Feeling increasingly foolish, I hunkered down in the kitchen underneath the closed hatch.

Evyn settled next to me. Perhaps her nerves were mixing with mine, for my heart rate increased even though all we heard was the normal ebb and flow of conversation in the mess hall on the other side of the wall.

The more time flowed by, the lower my tension ratcheted. I had an itching sense that something was going to happen, but that seemed more and more unlikely. "This seems to be a waste of our evening, and we have too much to do as it is. If a baker comes to turn some pastry over, or whatever cooks do, they might scream the castle down when they find us lurking under the serving hatch."

"Yeah." She stood up with a pop of her knees. "Why don't we—"

A clatter rang out from the corridor toward the kitchen, a tramp of boots I knew only too well. Grabbing Evyn, I bundled her under the serving table, rolling over with her and then getting myself into a crouched, ready stance. We froze, hidden. *Is this what we were waiting for?*

Men in civilian clothes piled in, five that I knew as part of my contingent. Grey led, his face shadowed in the dim light, and Aleric's blond hair flashed out as he got closer to a heatstone. He looked over his shoulder at the hatch to the mess hall, shifting his weight. His gaze passed over us; we were utterly concealed in the dark under the serving table.

My breath came short, but not as short as Gavain's. He panted in the midst of them. Out of uniform he looked bloated, his face a dark puce under the light of the heatstone.

"Gavain," Grey said. "Time to welcome you back."

The big blond sucked breath between his teeth, long hair straggling across his face blowing back and forth.

Grey's face hardened. "You're hideously out of condition. Fat and sick. You're a disgrace to our unit."

Gavain nodded, glaring at Grey.

*He's sick. He needs a new heart.* My disquiet and Evyn's compassion formed a hard knot in my stomach. *This is wrong.*

Once he could breathe evenly, Gavain said, "Get this over with. What do you want, Grey?"

"I saw you with the Ranger. I can help you, sir, anything you like, sir." Grey mimicked Gavain's growling tones. "Now that he's back in favour he's insufferable. He's back to his old ways, lording it over us."

My hand tightened on my father's sword. *No I am not!*

Evyn's cool touch on my hand startled me, and I relaxed my tendons. *Grey has his truth, a story that he will adhere to, and I have mine.* I couldn't change his story about me if he wasn't open to hearing a different side.

Gavain continued to hold Grey's gaze. "What of it? It's my task to help Barlay plan for the deployment. That's all it is."

"You're softening in your stance. No weakness in Special Forces, Gavain." Grey sneered at him, looking him up and down.

Finally Gavain's gaze dropped, fists bunching uselessly. "He's changed, Grey, it's different now. I need time to work through the implications. There's more to the situation."

My chest grew lighter. *Gavain recognises I've changed.*

Grey leant in until his nose nearly touched Gavain's. "You're trying to worm your way back in with him, aren't you?"

Instantly Gavain went utterly stiff as if stabbed through the stomach with a pike. "No, Grey. But I can see it differently, that's all."

Chuckling, Grey flicked Gavain's nose with his index finger. Gav surged forward but men either side dropped their hands on his shoulders. Forced to settle, Gavain's head drooped.

Aleric opened his mouth as if to speak, but one glare from Grey made him close it again. Aleric's head swivelled back to watch the hatch, above where Evyn and I crouched.

"What do you want, Grey?" Gavain asked heavily.

Grey stopped his pacing. "Your pay for the next turn, to start."

*What was this?*

Gavain gulped, but his gaze never left Grey's movements. "What for? Hazing? I can't, the king has taken it. I... my father, he needs that."

Gomore's bakery in the mid part of the city did well enough, but Gavain probably did send his father part of his wages to make him more comfortable.

Grey nodded slowly. "The king took your wages and your sword. A slave in all but name, now."

That realisation struck me hard in the chest, as it did for Gavain, whose mouth dropped slightly.

Grey's smile widened. "Now then, to the real reason we're here. We need to know if you have what it takes, Gavain."

"Do I have a choice? I'm here, back in the unit. The king decided to let me return, Grey, it's not your decision to make." Gavain chuckled, the sound a harsh bubble. "Now I know how Thorrn felt."

Grey hissed. "What he feels is entitled. You won't get special treatment from the king, Gavain, because of who you are." Grey pointed to the ranks of unrisen bread. "There's your beginnings, dough boy, and that's all the king will ever see. Common, poor, ten a penny, and expendable."

"That's not true. The king does care, believe it or not."

Grey laughed, the sound ringing in the pans hanging from the ceiling.

Gavain lifted his chin. "It's the truth. He asked me what he could do to win back my trust."

"Nonsense, he's spinning you a lie. Men like you and me, we don't get a look in."

He didn't trust the king? That did not bode well at all.

Grey said, "Now then. We need to test just how committed you are to returning to be one of us."

Aleric finally opened his mouth. "Grey, Captain said he didn't want any hazing."

"He said he didn't want to *see* any hazing. I caught the distinction there." Grey swaggered to the table where the unbaked bread sat. "I think the dough boy should remember where he came from, grubbing around to get by. Perhaps a taste of it would remind him." Picking up a ball with his bare hands, Grey's face twisted in disgust as it sagged and melded around his hand. "Soft and flabby, just like you."

While choking down raw dough was unlikely to hurt Gavain, it would be unpleasant, and Grey's manner made bile burn up my throat. Browbeating Gavain to somehow test him was an excuse; Grey wanted to domineer him.

I shot an incredulous look at Evyn, who bared her teeth back at me. "So what else is new," she mouthed.

I had to agree with her sentiment.

Gavain turned his head away, flexing his hands as Grey

approached with the ball of sticky dough held aloft. Grey gave a curt nod to the other men, waiting while they took his arms either side of him.

Gavain struggled briefly then sagged. He could have thrown them off before, but with his heart the way it was, he wouldn't be able to resist them now. He was trapped.

Evyn grabbed my arm. I turned to her, motioning for her to stay put. Her lips thinned and she waved her hand, pointing behind us. She seemed sure of something, so I followed.

Aleric backed up toward the hatch, his attention on the men huddling around Gavain and sending furtive glances toward the pots and pans above them.

Grey lifted the dough. "Open wide, dough boy," Grey whispered. Another man curled his fist in Gavain's hair, immobilising his head.

Gavain's nostrils flared, blue eyes wide as the dough pressed against his sealed lips.

Grey shoved. "You'll open up or it goes in through your nose."

Evyn's hands flickered and a portal snapped open behind me, just the perfect size for my crouching form. I rolled through it into the cold forest, back and sides crackling along the leaves and bracken on the ground. She rolled with me as behind us a crash sounded, pots and pans cascading to the floor.

"Gods, Aleric!" Grey hissed over the cacophony, and Evyn made us a larger entrance back. I stepped back onto Oberrot and the portal sealed shut behind me. She would go back to her hiding spot, and she allowed me to enter the fray standing and ready to fight, pulse pounding and anger thrumming in my veins.

"Stop this right now!" I bellowed.

All the men snapped into a defence stance, faces as white as the dough Grey pressed to Gavain's mouth.

Grey dropped it to the floor with a splat. "How did you... what?"

Al took a step back, next to me, Grey's glare following his shift of stance.

Gavain could breathe at least, heaving with coughs and a splutter. "Go away, Ranger," he spat, but rather than a snide sneer at me, his eyes were lowered. "I'm not helpless, and I'm certainly not an innocent."

I could argue strongly on the former but not the latter. "You aren't innocent, but neither am I. This is wrong." I squared up to Grey. "You will stop this immediately. I'm reporting you to Captain Barlay. All of you." My gaze swept them all, outrage burning the sides of my lungs.

Grey put his hand on his sword. "That's if you leave this kitchen, Ranger."

# CHAPTER 15



I sank into an attack stance.

"Don't be stupid, Grey," Aleric stammered.

Grey swept his hand to the side. "You obviously told him where we would be. You'll be cut down as well." He drew his blade. "The rest of you, we have to fight. He'll tell the captain we were planning treason and the king will see us hanged."

I faced the others, all white-faced and arrayed behind Grey in a loose protection formation. "I can swear on my soul companion that I'm going to report the hazing, but I will not lie. I'm apparently not very good at it."

The other men glanced at each other, each seeing what the other would do. It could go either way, and none were willing to stand alone.

I straightened up out of my stance. *I hope this de-escalates proceedings.* "Lay down your arms and let's talk. It's obvious there are things to be aired out here, so let's—"

"It's a ploy," Grey said, scorn dripping from every word. "He knows he cannot defeat the four of us, not even with that turncoat Aleric on his side."

Four trained swordsmen, all with their swords. It would be a stretch, a level I'd never taken before. "Are you sure about that? Two at a time I can do, handily." Despite my boast, I kept my hands away from my father's sword. Far from eager to fight, nausea at the implications rolled up my throat. "I don't particularly want to, though. If we fight, you'll be arrested and tried."

"Is a brawl now a hanging offence?" Grey sneered.

"No," Gavain croaked. "But a deliberate attack on a serving member of Special Forces is."

As far as the troops knew, that was what Aubin had been convicted of. The men with Grey shifted their stances, each taking a slightly different pose to make an uneven defence. They were starting to realise just how badly this could go if they allowed it to continue.

Grey growled, sword in hand, but Gavain grabbed his arm. "That's enough," he said roughly. "Stop this now."

"Yes. This ends here." One of the men threw his sword to clatter at my feet. The others dropped their swords soon after, locking their hands behind their necks in surrender. Relief poured through me.

Grey spun in Gavain's grasp, wrenching free. "Recreants, all of you! Whatever happened to strength standing together? We cannot let weakness enter the corps."

The others wouldn't meet Grey's wild eyes, their gazes lowered and jaws locked.

I kept my hands open, my voice low. "Grey, put up your weapon."

The tip of his sword raised toward me. Odd sparks in the corner of my vision made me frown, strange green shapes sliding in and out of focus. I kept my attention on Grey, putting the edge of an order into my tone. "Lower it."

Grey's stance was unwavering, the grip on his sword firm. "You aren't worthy. You disobeyed the first tenet. You should have been banished, just as..." Pain swam in his eyes. He collected himself, mastering and shoving it down as I had done myself, many a time.

"Just as?" My gaze slid past the tip of the sword to meet Grey's eyes. Evyn's fear snarled inside my stomach; he was frightening her, and that couldn't be borne. "Speak plain, man. What do you mean?"

His face reddened. "Not what, who." He shifted his fingers, the blade dipping slightly. "You don't even remember, do you? You don't care beyond your own immediate surroundings."

"You don't know me." I shouldn't goad him, but damn if it wouldn't be satisfying to challenge him here and now. Grey might hate me, he might even want to kill me, but I didn't know why. We had hardly had any interaction of note, yet his anger against me blistered up over and over again.

Those distracting shapes were getting more and more frequent, as if green pressed in from outside…

*Evyn is trying to make a portal to Earth!* But she was under the table, and we stood in a deadlock ten paces away; she made portals directly in front of herself, not at range. She might give herself away, and if she was scared enough to come out, she might be hurt.

I breathed calm into my stomach. *All will be well.* Not for the first time, I willed that I could push my thoughts to her as I would my feelings. Her fear stoked my anger, panic welling in my throat; I took it and smoothed it out between us, reaching past it for her calm compassion.

"Tell me, Grey," I said. "Talk. I'll listen."

"A stalling tactic." His foot squelched in the dough. He seemed not to notice or care. His sword hovered an inch from my throat.

"What's to stall? No one is going anywhere." I gestured to Gav and Al and the men with slow movements, so as not to antagonize Grey. I didn't want Evyn more frightened than she already was. "Talk to me. Who, Grey?"

His chest rocked with short sharp breaths. "Frosh." At my uncomprehending look, his face darkened. "I knew you wouldn't remember. My older brother, a model swordsman, five turns my senior and infinitely wiser, stronger, faster. He was the best of the best. I joined to follow him. 'There is no cause more noble than

Special Forces, protecting our king.'" Grey's voice shook but his hands were steady.

I waited, open and listening. Gavain's pants echoed, ringing against the pans above us, and Aleric kept still beside me.

"He was... He was convicted of misconduct. Him." Grey's eyes shone. "He went to tell the king something, and the next thing we hear is that he has been arrested. The trial was brief, and by the next morning, sentence was passed.

"He was banished, his tattoos flensed off by the Lorekeeper, and turned out with nothing but a change of clothes and a water skin. No one could help him, no one was *allowed* to help him, and he was hounded out of the city, bleeding. He was a strong man, Shardsson, but he fled weeping."

Grey's voice broke, just as I imagined his brother had. *Why was he banished?* Banishment was reserved for misconduct, failing to face an enemy head on or not upholding the behaviour expected of swordsmen and women. Breaking the tenets themselves resulted in execution; whatever Frosh had done was bad, but not bad enough to warrant his immediate disposal.

Banishment, however, could be a fate worse than death, a slow demise if one tried to stay in Oberrot. Citizens would be penalised if they interacted in any way with anyone with the scars of banishment. Grey's brother would have been ostracized, cast out and shunned by all.

Grey dashed the tears from his face. "Captain Shard told me he wasn't cut out for Special Forces, so he was cut from it. My brother was strong, he was perfect, but it wasn't enough. We have never tolerated weakness, and then there was *you*." Swallowing back his sadness, anger pulsed in the tight set of his jaw. The tip of his sword trembled; he stilled it. "You were promoted to the corps despite not passing the test to enter. It was against the rules, the same laws and restrictions that condemned my brother. Your father said you would show you had what it took to be part of Special Forces. The first thing you do when he's killed? You disobey the first tenet.

"You should be banished. You broke the rules. You shouldn't be here, you are not one of us. You are not strong enough to sit by and do nothing when ordered to."

*None of that is my fault!* I never asked my father for any favour, I worked harder than everyone else and it showed, and disobeying the tenets to rescue the true king turned out better for everyone. My skin heated, ire rising ready to match his truth against mine, to rail against him until he accepted my version of events.

If only he would see that, but Grey was not open to me.

I let out my anger in a rush of breath. "That must have been hard," I said.

Grey evidently expected something along my original reaction, mouth opening ready to shout back at me. As my words reached him, confusion robbed him of momentum, as if I had tripped him up. "What?"

Embarrassment prickled my cheeks, an unpleasant sensation curdling my stomach. Empathy hurt sometimes. "It must be hard trying to reconcile what happened to your brother with... with what you saw happening to me." Whether or not it was my doing. The key would be his trust in Gough. Was it still intact? "The king we follow is just. He has his reasons." I believed in that, wholeheartedly. Gough must have made a difficult but correct decision.

Grey's face hardened. "A reason to leave my niece without her father? I had to step in and raise her. She thinks her father is dead."

My heart tugged at the idea of a young girl without her father, when I knew the hard sharpness of that pain myself. How did a child hold up under it?

"Yes," I said. My trust in Gough had been hard won. "Gough is just, for everyone and against anyone. You saw what happened to me when I stepped out of line as a sergeant. Gough has a reason, I am sure of it, but I know well that living with his justice can be hard to bear."

Breath catching, Grey met my eyes. His sword wavered, but I

focused on him. Pain, yes, spurring anger, but without a target, the anger drained away.

He put up his sword, sheathing it at his hip. "What now?"

A bright wash of Evyn's relief soothed over me. "I'll have to report this," I said. "Go to the barracks, but as the captain said earlier, consider yourselves on review. Al, go with them."

"Yes." Grey saluted, two brief but correct taps. "Sir." He and the other men turned and marched out without a backward glance; Aleric followed, steps fumbling as if he were drunk with relief.

I skirted the swords and the dough on the floor to duck under the table underneath the serving hatch, holding out my hands. "Well done."

Small shaking ones took mine. "Thanks."

I wrapped her fingers in my strength and warmth to help her out, pressing her briefly to my side. "Were you trying to help?"

"I'll practise," she whispered.

Gavain leant against a table, lank hair in his face and blowing back and forth in front of his wide mouth as he panted. His jaw snapped shut as Evyn stood, dusting herself off. "You... You helped?" he asked her.

"Yep. Are you alright?"

Trembling, he nodded, and then he slid from the side of the table and onto his knees. The thunk when he landed made me wince; he would be feeling that all up his thighs to his hips.

Evyn and I both darted for him, but he held up his hands. "I'm fine. I meant to do that, so I can do this." He met and held Evyn's eyes.

She took an uncertain step back into me, and I wrapped my arm around her shoulders. *What is he doing?*

When he bent at the waist and pressed his forehead to the floor, I gasped. "This is how Daronians apologise, prostrating themselves," I explained to Evyn, my voice shaking. I was half-Daronian and old enough to recognise that my mannerisms and expectations were

180

wholly Oberrotian, but even so something stirred inside me at the complete and abject nature of this apology.

He had to be sincere. There was no way his pride would allow him to do this otherwise.

His voice was muffled. "I'm deeply sorry. Deeply and truly." He lifted his mottled pale and red face to meet hers directly, raw regret and sorrow shining from his eyes. "I'm sorry I used you against him. I'm sorry I thought to put that stuff in there to hurt you. I'm sorry I followed through with it. I'm sorry…" He lowered his head, curling his hands into fists. "I'm sorry I did not try to help you when Torgund demanded you for his own. I'm sorry I followed orders and locked you away. I didn't know you, your life didn't balance against the ones that were important to me, and… and I'm sorry I thought that about anyone.

"I'm sorry I tried to recapture you. I'm sorry that I continued to pursue you. I'm sorry… I'm sorry I had to help the previous Master-Mage under Torgund's orders. I'm sorry I couldn't recognise her as a rogue mage rather than the ally we thought her to be."

Taking a shuddering breath, Gavain pushed off from the floor, climbing his hands up the side of the table to maintain his balance.

Evyn darted forward to help him. She was open to him, and she did not enjoy another's pain, like me.

The big blond man shook at her feet, staring at her small open palms. "I'm sorry I belittled you," he went on quietly. "I'm sorry I used you to rile and anger Thorrn. I should never have joined in scorning you. I know what it's like to start from the bottom, with no one around you believing you can achieve anything of substance. I'm sorry I did not welcome you or help Thorrn come to terms with you. I'm… I'm sorry."

Warmth flooded my chest, hers and mine. "I started it. You were following my lead. I suppose… I wasn't a very inspiring figure back then. No wonder you wouldn't break tenets to follow me." I rubbed the back of my neck. No one would risk death for assisting some entitled, arrogant bore. Even though I hadn't really recognised that about myself, I had to accept it was what others had seen and thought of me, and apparently still did.

Gavain tilted his head at me. "You've changed a great deal." He ventured a smile at Evyn, a flash of red in the light of the heatstone. "I wager that's your doing, Lady Evyn."

Evyn snorted. "Thorrn is too stubborn, he doesn't go anywhere he doesn't want to go. He wanted to change, I guess."

"Yes, he is stubborn, and he never would be the first to apologise."

"I won't apologise for saving Evyn," I said. "I won't ever be sorry for breaching the tower and helping her down against Torgund's wishes. I will never regret that. I won't repent for saving our true king, and I cannot be contrite for opposing you to do it."

Gavain's gaze dropped, his hands flexing as he stared at the flagstones.

"But…" I rolled my tongue around my mouth. "I am sorry you didn't feel you could trust me enough to accompany me. I'm sorry for everything that happened to you under Torgund, and I'm sorry I was a bad sergeant after it all ended. I'm sorry I never spoke to you when you asked to see me."

"I… I'm sorry too." He looked up, eyes shining. "I'm sorry I killed your father. I'm sorry that I chose the wrong side, and I'm sorry I chose to pursue retribution rather than understanding."

His chest juddered. Mine felt like my ribs were about to crack under some kind of pressure both inside and out.

Evyn looked between us. "We just needed a bit of compassion here, guys."

I nodded stiffly. He looked from her to me, clearing his throat.

Evyn smiled at us. "Alright, let's talk it out, but probably not just now, because I think I'm going to be sick."

Gavain took her hands to steady her. "You're doing very well under the pressure of combat, Lady Evyn."

Evyn chuckled. "Thanks. Come on, Thorrn, I can't help him up on my own."

"Right." I shuffled over, grabbing under one of his arms and pulling the big man to his feet. "There."

"Right." Gavain did not meet my eyes.

"Yes."

"So."

Evyn rolled her eyes. "We probably need to tell someone about this mess, right? Give some statements or what have you?"

"Yes, indeed." I helped Gavain to the doorway. Post-battle, or rather post-confrontation, I calmed and quieted my breathing and my heartrate. Gavain couldn't seem to control his, gasping between clenched teeth and then panting when he couldn't take anymore, a twisted type of torture.

"Did you send the letter? Just nod or shake your head."

Gavain nodded. "Saw Aleric looking uncomfortable with Grey's promise to talk to me tonight. He rushed off and I followed. Damn near killed me to keep at his heels. He sent you a letter. Whatever it said, I didn't want you involved." He sucked in a deep breath.

I waited patiently, slowing our pace. He had more to say and I would not interrupt his thoughts with mine.

Gavain continued, "If you got involved, more men would be put on review, which Barlay doesn't need, and the enmity between you and Grey would deepen. I didn't expect him to turn against *me*."

"No. That bit is always a surprise." Unease twinged my stomach. "You think they have your back, but we know very little about them apart from how they do in exercises. I'm starting to wonder if my father's maxim about a man or woman showing their true heart in training is even close to the truth."

"Training is only one aspect of a person, Thorrn," Evyn reminded me, coming up on Gavain's other side.

I said, "Correct, and the test to enter Special Forces is only one as well. So is the time under Torgund, I suppose. Basing our conclusions of a person based on singular incidents is myopic at best and disastrous at worst." Gavain leant heavily on my shoulder, his breath coming sharp and fast now. I readjusted my grip on him. "Everyone needs to be given a chance to tell their side of the story. It's such a waste and inconvenient that more men are under investigation for conduct issues, but important to pull all these to the fore now, rather than in battle." I shuddered. "I'm glad it was sorted now, as these tensions would only increase under the pressure of the icy shale mountains."

"Yes." Gavain halted.

"And we need to—" Gavain fell into me so hard I slammed into the wall. "Gav? Report!"

He gaped, mouth ajar, the pink and red of his inflamed flesh draining from his face, replaced by a sick off-white.

Roaring, "Get him to the infirmary!" as if I commanded a unit and not just Evyn, I grabbed him around his shoulders and pulled him off his feet, dragging him backwards.

Evyn ran after us. "The corridor turns right! There's a straight! And... oh!"

Other hands swarmed in, grabbing hold of Gavain's limbs, and I looked up into my own face. I blinked away the surge of red across my vision. "Shoulders, help me get him to the infirmary."

"I'll endeavour to contact your Tuniel." Behind my shoulder, the headscarfed Assassin turned and ran back toward the main staircase.

Shoulders and I lifted Gavain, heaving and twisting in our arms as though he were in agony. His crooked fingers clenched above his breast, tearing the air above his faltering heart.

"Hold on, Gav," I called. "Keep pushing strength to your heart and stay calm, we'll be there soon." Calm was far from my own heart, beating fast as we hustled to the infirmary.

A nurse took one look and shouted, "Aid!" Three medimancers poured from the surrounding rooms, including the tall Hepzibah. Hair pulled back and makeup gone, their angular features were more pronounced.

Raising a hand over Gavain's torso, Hepzibah frowned. "This is not good. We were hoping for a good few sennights at least."

"Help him," I rasped.

"I'll certainly try. Where's the MasterMage?" Hepzibah herded us to the empty room Tuniel had occupied earlier, and Shoulders and I dragged Gavain there.

"On her way." I hoped the Assassin could get there fast. Lifting Gavain onto the bed, I tipped him onto his back.

"Then I'll keep him alive until she can get here. As for you, you've done all you can." Hepzibah tugged Gavain's shirt open and pressed their hand onto his chest.

Gavain's eyelids flickered, fighting, and then he slumped, asleep.

A tug at my wrist made me turn. "Come on," Shoulders whispered. "Where's his soul companion? We need to let her know what happened."

I nodded, mouth dry. "Zel. Let's go find her." Having something to do galvanised me. Taking Evyn's shoulders, I steered us out.

The disarray of my thoughts was matched by the flurry in the infirmary. It seemed that every single medimage and mancer had been impelled into action, dashing about with quick sure steps. Although it was meaningless to me, their steps were as practised as my stances, and I had to leave them to their craft.

Tuniel rushed past us as we exited the corridor. Her initial look was filled with trepidation, but quickly tearing her gaze away from us, she brushed past me without a word.

I forced myself to march on. The ruse was in force, and I would maintain it in line with her wishes. Evyn tucked her hand into mine, and I eased my fist open. I could and would share what Evyn was feeling, remaining open to her as she was to me.

The Assassin lounged at the end of the corridor opening out to the castle courtyard. He peeled off to walk alongside Evyn.

"My thanks," I told him. "Tuniel arrived very quickly."

"My pleasure. I love running up stairs at a breakneck pace."

Evyn switched to my other side, walking close at my right hand.

"Evyn?" Underneath our singing nerves of the past turn of the glass, I could feel mounting disgust, a strong emotion that threatened to overtop her.

"Carry on, I'm fine," she said, her serene words at odds with the storm inside her. She squeezed my hand and shot me a quelling look.

I inclined my head. *Very well.* If Evyn did not want to speak of her emotions in front of others, then I would allow that, just so long as she talked it through with me later. "Come on, Evyn. We probably have to report everything that has happened to Barlay after we find Zelora."

"And we'll stay out of the way." The Assassin reached out to take Shoulders's arm, the big man grinding to a halt. "We shall see you later."

"Yes, thank you." Evyn's high sing-song voice made me wince. Yes. Definitely put out by something.

❉ ❉ ❉

ZELORA NEARLY CAREENED into us on the way to the infirmary. We reported all that had happened and she tore off. After her hurried a friend, so she would not be alone at least, and we reported everything that had transpired to the captain.

Evyn needed to talk to me, at least to help sort and categorise the emotions inside her just as she would define and line up her notes and books. I followed her up to our apartment, where Aubin's old door was still tightly shut, sending a pang of recognition and loss to echo through us.

She didn't need that from me. She bustled into the kitchen. "What a day."

"Indeed." I settled into a ready stance as she pulled out some vegetables. Taking the paring knife, I peeled with fast motions, the knife slipping fluidly around the roots. "It has been a long and trying day." I reined myself back from jumping in and naming the swirl I could feel in my midsection. Breathing deeply, I sat with it.

She mirrored my position, chopping with brisk strokes, head bowed so her long hair became a curtain between her and the world.

Except I didn't want to be shut away, outside from her. I could stand being shut in with her, though. It seemed that while we were in the castle, we stood separate from all around us. Evyn had felt like this since the beginning, of course, and even further before I met her. It was a new sensation for me, but perhaps it shouldn't have been. Apparently my friends hadn't accepted me at all. *No, that isn't fair.* They had accepted the version of me that I had pretended to be, a model soldier who believed appearance equated to one's worth and losing anything was an unacceptable failure.

I ran my hands over my tattoos, each one once a point of pride that now rang hollow against the achievements that mattered. Where was the tattoo for finally bonding with Evyn? With reconciling a terrible wrong in Rush? With surviving an assault that still haunted my nightmares?

I stepped closer to her, close enough that she could touch me if she wanted. Slowly the feeling in my belly settled its incessant swirl, and Evyn took in a breath with me. I smiled; I didn't think she noticed. I was the calm one today, it seemed.

"We should be preparing to enter Skien," Evyn muttered.

"Yes. I just hope Aubin can hold out until we do," I replied, but my stomach twisted hard, the air punched out of me by Evyn's sudden surge of feeling.

"What do you know?" she demanded.

I lifted my hands in apology. "Only conjecture and extrapolation. If he is playing an active role, he will be in danger."

Relief flooded over me from her, loosening my limbs. "Oh, thank god," she managed, voice weak. "But we do need to get there. How soon can we be ready?"

"I've chosen an approach, and Carreelee and Layloree have approved the route. I need to check they are well-equipped. We won't have significant magical assistance right with us in an emergency, so we have to plan carefully."

"Um..." Evyn pointed at herself. "I can just ping us out."

"Only to be used in a dire life-or-death emergency."

"Is there ever any other sort here? Yes, I understand. I won't ping everyone over for fish and chips." She scowled, resuming a rough handling of the unsuspecting roots.

My soul companion was usually level-headed, but she was snappish when pushed to her limits. I backtracked. "I apologise for pointing out something that is obvious to you. You are one of the best guardians of this secret, and I know you do very well to keep it."

Evyn nodded, relaxing slightly, but her eyes reddened around the edges.

I put the roots and my knife to one side. "Evyn, I'm sorry if I upset you—"

"It's not fair," she blurted.

"What isn't?"

"That he can have so much of an effect on me and not even be here to do it." She swept her roots to one side, yanking a fresh bundle onto the counter for their fate.

I didn't have to ask who she meant. I waited.

She leant her hip against me, and as she spoke, the closeness helped to shift and align my feelings with hers. "He was so suddenly in love with me, but that was sort of okay. Emotions were running high, I know that. I kept thinking about that stupid legend you've got about Earthians being so beautiful you fall instantly in love with them, and... I guess I wanted that. I've never had a boyfriend, Thorrn, and then suddenly this guy is giving me flowers and saving my life and supporting me and... and all the things you're supposed to do when you love someone.

"He was also doing the other things. Not the world-shattering things, but the more humdrum things, the stuff that doesn't get glorified in fairy tales. No one ever writes home about the guy who realises your love language is chores and makes sure the place is sparkling for you. He replaced our herbs every day, did you realise that?"

She smiled, and it lifted my heart.

She went on, lifting her hands as she spoke, as if she wove the words around us. "He would always listen whenever I came home babbling about what I had learnt that day, and he'd ask me questions about it, which would help me think more deeply. He loved hearing my insights on your culture, because I could see it from a fresh perspective and see where it had been based on some hundred-year-old tradition or whatever, and he did the same for whatever I told him about Earth."

Her hands fell. Cold stole into my—our, at this range—stomach. "I'm trying to take that good stuff with me, I really am. But seeing the Assassin made me realise... it hurts. It hurts and I don't think I will ever forget how much it hurts. Learning to love or whatever isn't worth this, Thorrn, I could have done with learning that with someone else, someone who will stick around. Because my other love language is sticking to the course, and... and he didn't."

My heart ached for her, a crushing pain heated by anger. I tamped it down, pulling it out from the bond.

Her shoulders softened in response to what I was doing. "I tried to be all open and patient and stuff, but I don't think I can be. I just want to clock the Assassin whenever I see him. Uh, sorry, punch his lights out. Argh." She dropped her face into her hands. "Bloody idioms."

"I get it. You wanted to hit him, to make him feel a fraction of the pain you feel, or to punish him."

She winced. "I wasn't thinking about it that carefully, I just wanted to smack him and feel my hand hurt and know I did that."

I eyed her. "Goodness, we really are starting to share perspectives, aren't we?"

She chuckled and my heart eased, but quickly her face lost its lustre. "Every time I see him, it just makes all these feelings boil over, and I want to get away, or make *him* go away. It's not like I can even talk with him to sort it out, because it wasn't him who did anything." She shook her head, decapitating the greens. "I know it isn't fair on the Assassin. He's innocent."

"I am absolutely certain he is not innocent in the least."

She laughed this time, and my heart soared. "Well, okay, but he hasn't broken my heart. That sounds too dramatic. I mean, he hasn't seemed to want a relationship and then ran away screaming when I asked if he did."

Both perspectives crashed into me, Evyn and Aubin's pain. Did I try to justify him to Evyn? Was that what she needed from me? "He's hurting," I tried. "Tuniel can feel it. We need to help him."

Her fist curled tighter around her greens. "Sure, I'll help him. That's fine. But I hate that he has some kind of power over me to feel like this when we haven't even been in any kind of relationship. It's pathetic, is what it is. I'm such a stupid, pathetic girl."

"You are not stupid or pathetic." I had to consciously unclench my shoulders. "I'll challenge anyone who calls you that, so watch yourself."

She smiled at my efforts, tipping the stalks in the colander and scraping off the board with a rasp. "I'm being realistic and honest. What kind of person mourns what never was? Someone with too much time on their hands, that's who."

I gathered her hands. They were cold and slightly damp. "Love can be like that. It is giving power over to someone else to say, here, you have the potential to hurt or lift me."

"I want it gone," she whispered. Her fingers curled around mine. "Oh, don't worry, not me and you. I just don't want him to be able to do this to me. Maybe I've got to reclaim my power or whatever, but I want it gone. Help me do that, to walk around cool as a cucumber like you."

"Cold as a... vegetable?" I glanced at the greens in the sink.

She giggled. "Oh, boy. This isn't so much a language barrier as an idiom barrier." She squeezed my hand at last, a wave of happiness breaking over me and her. "I feel better. But we only just got to a good place, and now I'm unsettling us again."

"Something will always happen in our lives, Evyn. It's not ever going to slow down, and I learn best on the front line of action anyway." I grinned down at her.

190

"Thank you for listening."

"Anytime. I... Forgive me for being forward, but I wish to reassure you that you are not at fault in this instance."

She pulled her hands free to wipe them on a towel. "Thanks," she said, her voice as low as her mood, both striated with layers of determination and thrust. What hurt me was that I felt she didn't quite believe me.

Aubin's door opened, and Evyn and I glanced at each other. Shoulders stumbled by the kitchen to sit slumped on the sofa, barely lifting his head in greeting as we filed into the lounge to see him.

"Still nothing?" I asked him.

"Still nothing." He dropped his head into his hands.

Putting her towel down, Evyn moved over to sit next to him, stroking his back. He shook, silent sobs wracking him.

I could only stare. I would be the same if Evyn ever vanished with no way for me to find her.

"What's the latest?" the Assassin's voice floated from Aubin's dark doorway behind me.

My heart accelerated so fast I gasped. "Damn and blast, I didn't know you were there."

A smile pulled at his lips, revealing a flash of teeth. "Not very many people realise I'm there either."

I considered him. As tense as I was, I would never get to sleep and, given the feelings Evyn had just disclosed for me, I determined to help ease her burden as well as meet my own needs, so she did not have to. "I need a drink. Let's go to the city," I said.

He shrugged. "Suits me."

Evyn waved me away, her attention firmly on the other version of me breaking his heart in her hands. I felt irrationally jealous of her spending time comforting another me, but also strangely heartened.

# CHAPTER 16

Rather than the bar in the mess hall — I'd had my fill of that — we walked in silence out of the castle courtyard, pacing down the path that ran alongside the training fields. In the castle and its grounds behind me, dozens of stories rose and played out.

Grey and the others on review, awaiting the morrow. Barlay going over plans in his mind, acutely aware that a misstep would be bought in the lives of swordsmen and women. The men and women in the barracks, wondering what the immediate future would bring. Gavain, laid out in the infirmary fighting while unconscious, and Tuniel and Hepzibah working furiously in concert on something entirely new, the challenge both exciting and intimidating. So many lives on the tip of a ruble, and those were just the ones I knew about, and all so focused on the answers the future would bring to them.

I was no different. *Where is Evie? Is she safe? Where is Liara? Can she be stopped?*

*Where is Aubin, and will he come back?*

I had slipped into companionable silence, Aubin's preferred mode of travelling. The Assassin moved like him, quiet but loud enough so I knew he was there, with me.

"Any preference on drink?" I asked.

"I can be convinced to try any number of things. Just take me somewhere which will allow me to take this awkward headscarf off."

I did a quick head turn. The streets were empty, glowstones fitful in the warm evening light. "I did know a place, but I'm possibly banned right now."

"Let's test that assumption."

I led him there and, although the barman's nostrils flared, he didn't immediately cast me out. Rather he banged the drinks on the table and said, "Any noise from you two, and I'm calling the Upholders, rubles or no."

"Yessir, not a peep from us, sir." I saluted to placate him.

He grumbled, wiping his hands in the dirty cloth slung over his shoulder.

The Assassin watched him go and then pulled off his headscarf. It ruffled his hair, dark in the light of the stones. "That's better. I can see why your Aubin left, forced to wear that thing all the time."

I tapped the cold side of my glass, the beer foam already dissipating. "It was hard for him. He managed it."

The Assassin leant back, making the chair creak. "Then he's more adaptable than me. I suppose the Rushia do it, but damn, I'm not one of them."

The feeling of a familiar conversation and moment tipped into me. *"But I'm not Rushia, am I? I'm not a soldier, I'm not even an apothecary anymore."* A similar man had spoken eerily related words to me, and I hadn't truly taken them in.

I stared into the glass, my reflection thrown back upside down at me. "What am I supposed to say to him?"

"Hm?" The Assassin leant in, avoiding putting his elbows on the table at the last heartbeat with a sneer at the sticky surface. "Gods, you know how to show a tourist a good time. Now, what are you supposed to say to whom?"

In the glass I could see the Assassin's intent concentration on me. Aubin tended to sink backwards, not letting his target know that they had his full attention. He would watch Evyn from underneath his eyelashes and react to her without even realising it, like the Assassin. The man in front of me felt like some kind of facet of him, yes, but not the full man. His familiarity clashed with the differences, making me dizzy.

The Assassin snapped his fingers underneath my nose. "Is this some kind of guessing game?"

I scrubbed my cheeks. "I'm thinking about my Aubin and wondering what I can say to him, that's all."

"That's all, eh. I'd say that's a pretty big moment. If he's anything like me, you'll have one chance and one chance only to speak. After that, he won't want to listen." The Assassin put one leg over the other. "Why do you think he left?"

I frowned. He knew this story. "He quit the Rangers because he didn't want to kill anymore and he thought we would make him."

"And will you? If he comes back and wants to play again and all of that, would you want him to kill for you?"

The thought of Aubin back again made my heart surge. "I kill if the situation demands it. I carry the responsibility of ending lives too, their stories stopping with me, so he cannot pretend he is the only one in the world who carries those burdens. At the same time, Gerlay the Dinahen prince doesn't kill, and I respect that."

"Do you really?" The Assassin's gaze turned intense, becoming hard to meet. "Would you really respect that as a choice, or would you expect there to be some clauses where you would want him to break that tenet?"

I swirled the beer around the glass to lap against the sides. "Yes, because it's him. He *is* more flexible." If he had been near to Liara instead of me when we were in Rush, he would have been able to end her and the threat she posed, and then Evie wouldn't have been waylaid. I swallowed another gulp, enduring the bitter taste of failure.

"And now he doesn't want to make those kinds of choices, but you still expect him to do what you need him to do. What you don't want to do yourself." He looked over his rim of the glass at me. "You expect him to do the dirtiest work for you, so you can keep your hands clean and your tenets of only killing when you need to nice and tidy."

The beer lurched in my queasy stomach. His observation had thrust like a knife into one pillar of my reasoning, revealing a rotten foundation. "I suppose I will need to do some thinking before I see him."

"You'd better, but I think there is another matter at the heart of this. What you're describing isn't an insurmountable problem if all parties are willing to come together and discuss it openly."

I waited for a handful of heartbeats. "Well? What's the other matter?"

He set his glass down untouched. "Just that. He thought you wouldn't listen. He didn't think you were willing to see his truth of the matter."

"I am! He just needed to talk to me."

"And when you talked before, what were you doing?"

I scowled. "Look, we talked all the time. He told me things he's never told anyone else."

"Like his love for your Evyn? Did he confide things like that to you?"

Heat flooded my cheeks. "Well, I observed that and confronted him with it." The wooden chair creaked as I shifted in it. "And actually Gerlay had to beat it out of him, practically."

He smirked. "I suggest you think through how you intend to confront him, or rather *approach* him."

"Without him running off immediately." I sent another slug of beer sliding down my throat. "Do you know how I could do it?" I asked.

"I can only tell you how *I* would react. We are different, you know."

"No, I mean… Evie said she could do a thing where she jumps forward in time to see and comes back to tell us."

The Assassin's eyes flickered. "She did. We also mentioned that she is the only Evyn who can do that."

*Is that the truth of the matter?* Beer fizzed along my senses, blurring the edges of my perception. I couldn't always tell if someone was telling the truth, and certainly not for someone like Aubin, who could control his features down to the smallest muscle.

The Assassin finally took a sip, swallowing it with a shudder.

"Can you... do that?" I asked.

He rolled his tongue around his mouth, leaning back. "Evie tends to get all excitable about telling any alts things."

"So you've talked to lots of alts."

He gave me a look. "That's one of them." Tapping the table with an unsteady rhythm, he seemed to be weighing something in his mind.

I leant in as much as I could without touching the sticky table. "You are probably aware that very few people on this world trust your intentions are benign. Your attitude doesn't help you any."

He moved forward to meet me, forearms nearly brushing against mine. "That's not new for me. Very few people on my own world trust my intentions. I will tell you one thing, though." Beckoning me closer, he craned his neck.

I shifted in my seat to lean right over the table, turning my ear toward him.

He lowered his voice. "Your uniform is soaked. This table is disgusting."

Scowling, I slammed back in my chair, lifting my forearms to inspect the damage. My shirt sleeves were dripping. "Fine, don't say anything, and perpetuate this stupid air of mystery. It'll get you locked in the cells before too long."

He chuckled. "Your king doesn't imprison innocents, unlike some of the rulers we have come across in our travels. We've been doing this for a long time. Everyone always wants to know how it ends. *'Do we end up married? Do we survive the next day? Do I get my promotion?'* Countless questions, and all about the future. No one ever has the same curiosity about the past, or how the patterns of the past lead into the future. And what happens if we spoil the end? Well, it might not happen. Your swaggering confidence that you'll win the day might actually be your undoing." He gave his beer a bitter stare. "So you see, it's safer not to say anything."

"But you've told us things before. You... You alts told me, under the MasterMage's Palais, that the Lonely Man and the Spirit Shaper always meet. That they are drawn to one another."

"Ah, destiny. Of a sort." He lifted his glass. "This gets better the more I drink."

I shuffled forward. "Tell me about that."

"Didn't you listen when I described how me telling you things could change them?"

"You're really frustrating."

He beamed. "Why, thank you."

I wouldn't get much useful information from him. He was either unwilling or unable to divulge anything to me, and he seemed to enjoy holding back. All his prodding served to raise my ire.

He seemed to sense that. "Look, all the Aubins are different, but we're all broken. The Spirit Shaper can help with that, or at least, she can *if* we let her in. However, it's up to us to let her in. You can't break down those walls for us, Thorrn. We get to decide when and even if." He placed his glass down. "Our special power," he said bitterly.

"A special power? You have a special power?"

Now it was his cheeks that flamed, to an irate puce in this dim light. "Gods, that beer really did go to my head. Forget I said anything. I mean it."

It stood to reason that people who could cross worlds and time as though they were nothing had other abilities as well. My hand sought my father's sword. "Who exactly are you? Or... what are you?"

His eyes glittered in the dim light. "I'm a traveller, Thorrn. My wife and I adventure with our soul companions, we just happen to cross portals rather than seas. Right now, I'm a grieving man. The woman I love is stuck somewhere just out of reach, and I'm in a bar trying to hold myself together." The deep breath he took shuddered his chest. "As soon as I know where she is, I'll be a man of action, and I'll do anything it takes to see her safe and well. I'll lie for her, kill for her, steal for her. I'd die for her." His gaze dropped to his hands. "But right now dying isn't called for, so I'll have to pass the time until I can do something useful."

My chest welled with sadness and the glass slid out of my hand. I had to catch it before it tipped. "My deepest apologies. I only sought to understand. I will help, of course I will—"

The Assassin held up a hand. "That bit about wanting to understand... hm. That might be enough for an Aubin." Tossing his drink down his throat, he jerked his head toward the door.

I took the hint, draining my drink of its dregs and putting more rubles on the table than the beer was worth as payment.

The night was a cold one. The soothing slap of the canal water underneath the bridge we tramped across was as much a melody of the night here to me as the music floating from the Dinahen quarter.

The Assassin peered around, hands under his armpits. "What a difference the right ruler makes," he muttered.

"Hm?" I asked.

He started walking back toward the castle. "Just that this world is much safer. Look at that, a young couple waltzing along the side of the canal with no bodyguard."

I tried to see the streets surrounding the castle courtyard with fresh eyes. "The lords and ladies of Oberrot keep homes here, for when the king is in residence. There are Upholders to maintain the law, see, and they are well paid to maintain these streets in particular." I pointed out a man in dull brown, patrolling the streets with a bored air. The couple the Assassin had pointed out earlier were canoodling in a corner. Although I wouldn't perhaps particularly want to kiss my lover in public, the fact that I could not stung a little, like an old burn.

He shot me an unsteady look. "Ah, but these are Upholders for the law and *justice*." He hissed the word. "We have those as well, and they maintain the laws that suit them."

I turned that over in my mind. "So did you save us, or save Gough?"

"Too many questions," the Assassin mumbled.

"Ah." I flashed him a grin. Saving the king was something I could support. "Alright then. I'm desperate to understand what it is you're doing here. A few visits was interesting, but this seems to be developing into something else. But Evyn says something like 'I'm dying to know' and I am not sure I would be that desperate to discover the truth."

He laughed so loudly it rang from the high walls of the lords' city homes. "You know, it's interesting seeing my friend walk around so forthright and talkative. It goes to show what a difference life chances make to a person."

I matched my steps to his as we crossed the plaza in front of the gates. "Will Shoulders do well enough to come to Skien? It can be a bit overwhelming anyway."

The Assassin shrugged, moving into the complete darkness underneath the gates. There was not even a guard posted here, and the doors had fused open as far as I was aware; anyone could come freely onto the castle grounds, it was only the castle courtyard that was monitored. In the shadows his voice seemed quieter. "Who's to say? He keeps himself together but it costs him. All this newness and strangeness, and meanwhile he's bereft without his Evyn. Remember that he grew up isolated and trapped, the same thing day after day, sennight after sennight, turn after turn. He takes it all in, but he cannot cope with a lot of new things.

"I would suggest leaving him somewhere safe, but where is safe, truly? Better that he's with me. And if you don't mind lending out your soul companion, having her with him will help him greatly."

I tamped down the upswing of jealousy. My hand itched to hold hers, but he did need her more at this moment. "Well. Yes. That's good." He had looked listless, but the Assassin was nearing the same in the ghoulish green light of the one rising moon.

I turned over his approach in my mind. The Assassin wasn't pressuring or hurrying his Thorrn into accepting the situation; he was helping him cope, supporting him to find a way through.

Had I done that for Aubin? Had I helped him, or had I pressed him? I pondered that as we maintained silence all the way up to the apartment and parted for the night, not much liking the answers I could honestly present to myself.

# CHAPTER 17

I woke early, with Evyn still deeply asleep across from me. Padding downstairs, I twitched the curtains open. The green moon still hung on the horizon, the navy sky sprinkled with the stars we would shortly be using to navigate. Vigour coursed through my veins, sleep banished, for today would be long and full, and I was eager to throw myself into it.

First, I would check on Tuniel, to see how she fared and what she had been able to achieve with Gavain.

The infirmary atrium was colder and quiet. Zelora sat tucked into one of the chairs, a blanket slipped from her shoulders to pool on the floor. I laid it back onto her as a door slid open opposite.

"Oh, Ranger." Tuniel MasterMage stood framed, the sickroom beyond. She closed the door behind her. In the shadows she looked pale as a spirit floating across the stone floor.

I stepped close to her, keeping my footsteps quiet. "Are you hale and well? What's the situation?"

She swallowed hard, tired, her lifebeat fluttering in her delicate throat. "We have successfully merged the living metal with his heart, the sheets overlapping damaged tissue. We had hoped to keep it away from the healthy parts, which Hepzibah found were few." Tangling her fingers in her hair, she met my eyes. Her ice-blue eyes were drained by exhaustion, yes, but alight with purpose. "There is metal in that man's body, and it's keeping him alive. It's... indescribable, Thorrn."

"Oh, you'll find words to describe it, when you write your papers on it." I traced my finger over her cheekbone, pushing a strand of hair behind her ear. "I am proud of you, of what you have been able to accomplish."

"It's the start of something so very, very exciting, if we can get it to work." Glancing back over her shoulder, she wrapped her fingers around mine, cold and trembling. "I think it will work, Thorrn. We were slow and careful, and we discovered an amazing way to link the signals between living flesh and metal, but I had to embed a small chip of a lodestone close by to ensure that it worked."

"So then you're telling me... his heart will glow when you're near?" I beamed at her.

"Inside his chest, obviously." Yawning, she stumbled back a pace, and I took her shoulders, wrapping my arms around her. She rested her forehead against my chest for half a heartbeat, then gently pushed me away. "We should not be seen together," she said, as if she were reminding herself.

"Yes." I stepped back smartly, smiling at her. "Congratulations, MasterMage."

She covered her mouth as she gave another yawn. "Hepzibah says I can rest for a few turns of the glass to shore up for the next stage. Are you leaving for Skien today?"

"Yes. We'll need a travel mage or mancer to get us to the border."

"Done."

"My thanks, MasterMage." I saluted, but instead of a double tap of my fist, I pressed my palm flat to my chest.

She frowned slightly, lips parted, and dropped her gaze as a shy smile spread across her face.

Seeing her cheeks flush made my own heart ache and soar in

equal measure. "I'd escort you to your rooms, MasterMage, but that might delay your rest."

Smoothing her skirts, she lifted her chin, a smirk on her lips. "Indeed, Ranger. Go well."

I left first, shaking out my hands and trembling inside. *Gavain will live.* I could crow to the heavens about that. After Skien, we would navigate this new truth between us; not a false friendship, but something akin to professional respect. For now, he would rest to one side in my mind as I focused on Skien.

Training was well underway for Special Forces, Barlay stood at one end of the field and the troops marshalling themselves into groups. In passing I saw Kari stepping up to take a leadership position as the contingent leader, but Aleric was in her group rather than putting himself forward. Perhaps he had been unable to; he had been part of the group that had attempted to intimidate Gavain, although he had sent me that message so I would be around to intervene, but perhaps Barlay did not know that.

I leapt over the fence and jogged lightly to Barlay. "Captain, sir, quick bit of intel."

"Yes, Ranger?" Barlay turned to me, hands behind his back.

"Swordsman Aleric sent me a message to meet him last night, so I would be nearby to assist Gomoresson. He also stepped beside me to guard my left side in the pending altercation, which thankfully never escalated."

"Sounds like Aleric. Why the need to pass this information on, Ranger?"

"Only to keep you informed, sir, in case his involvement last night wasn't clear."

Barlay studied my eyes. "Ah, you think I'm not letting him step forward to lead a team in Skien. Ranger, I spoke to him and his story chimes with yours, and I believed him when he told me this morning. He's not wanting to step up of his own accord." Barlay shrugged. "Some people lead, some people follow. Each are useful in their own way."

"Oh." Aleric was a natural follower, turning with the tide of favour.

Barlay nodded, watching the corps at their exercise. "Hopefully he'll start following a better model. Some people blaze the trail; others need to see someone do it first. It gives them permission, almost, and especially in the corps, where a wrong move can mean review or worse. It's not bad or good, it just is." He clasped his hands in front of him. "Was there anything else?"

"No sir." I saluted, storing his words for later to turn over what they awakened in me.

My next stop was stores, where I flashed my tattoos at the quartermistress. "Ah, Ranger. The researcher dropped off her notes yesterday, so we've been preparing the supplies for Special Forces. You want one the same?"

"What do they have?" I asked.

"Big items are warm furs, tents and materials to make a cordon. Axes to chop wood. Usual trail rations and medical packs."

"Give me the furs and one tent." In a snowstorm, I would want to be able to shelter us, even if we were all huddled together. "Medical supplies yes, but no bruswurt at all."

Stores looked up a sheet of paper. "We don't have many medicines anyway, so the medical supplies are just lyneal paste and some bandages." She frowned over her shoulder at her colleague, who was sweating rubbing wax over a stretched piece of canvas. "Where did the king's apothecarist go? Didn't we have one to call on?"

The man grunted, barely looking up from his canvas. "Didn't know the king had an apothecarist."

"Yes, he did! Used to bring round the tinctures and things."

I leant back slightly. Aubin had been bereft that no one remembered him. "What did he look like, this apothecarist?"

The quartermistress frowned. "I dunno. You know, I couldn't tell you even if you put me on the rack."

Her colleague snorted. "Memorable, then."

"Hm, maybe we didn't have an apothecarist." The quarter-mistress shook her head.

That hurt, a pain on behalf of Aubin. He really had disappeared, and no one knew or cared. Imagining myself in his place, walking in disguise among people who didn't even miss you when you were gone, turned my stomach. I would feel like a spirit, haunting the halls but with no one recognising I was there.

"Need anything else, Ranger?" The quartermistress peered at me.

I brought myself back to my task. "Food stocks that can be eaten uncooked, for four people for a sennight." Hopefully we would be able to find a town in that time. "Rubles for trade."

"Right." She rubbed her chin. "You know you'll need a woman to trade in Skien, yes?"

I sighed. "Yes, I'm taking one."

"Good." Her eyes sparkled over the rim of her glasses. "Come back in three turns of the glass. Captain mentioned you'd be going first, so I'll prioritise your load out. Gods' luck on the mission, Ranger."

"My thanks." I tapped my fist to my heart in a salute. The castle functioned like the corps itself, each piece lending its elements to work efficiently and effectively.

Jogging up the stairs to our apartment, I had to dodge around the healthy metabolism of the castle: the messengers all flowing up and down, the servants keeping the ways clear and clean, the cooks and chefs feeding and fuelling us. There were more intangible elements too, as while the researchers dredged up knowledge that most would not see, it helped to fine-tune the rest. The castle moved in one direction, headed by the king, and right now he was pointing firmly at Skien. It pleased me no end that we were aligned, that he saw what I saw and wanted to address it, helping those people to escape, their only crime being able to tap into magical forces that apparently surrounded us all.

Hopefully Special Forces could see that as well. Yes, we were deployed to protect the mundanes and others from rogue magic users, to take down those who posed a threat to peaceful life, but the ones who wanted only a fulfilling life, who would use their magic for others as a tradesman would their skills or a merchant their wares, deserved our protection as well. They were people at the heart of it. We all were.

*This must be coming from Evyn.* Her open compassion for others was a wonderful perspective to have. I wondered what she was feeling, how this was being balanced for her. I had enough self-awareness to recognise my previously closed mind, focused only on the next task and the next promotion, hardly stopping to think about what my actions meant. Since meeting Evyn, that had started to change in a rush. Evyn... and Aubin.

What tack would I take to convince him to come back and return with us? Perhaps I could talk it over with the Assassin and Layloree as we went. Maybe Evyn had a few ideas, but she wasn't looking forward to seeing him, that came across clear as orders shouted across a field. Was that trepidation over our initial reunion? Would it fade after that, or would it only grow, as it seemed to around the Assassin?

What would she be like around the real Aubin?

In our apartment, three small rucksacks sat by the door. Evyn pored over a pile of papers, scribbling something. On the sofa sat Shoulders, head down again, those impressive wide shoulders less imposing when he quivered with grief.

I put my hand on his back. "We're heading there today."

He couldn't speak, wringing his hands between his knees. He looked so exhausted that I wondered if he would be fit to come at all, but I also knew there would be no stopping him.

"Nearly done here, then I can send this report on dhampir to Barlay," Evyn murmured.

"Yes. Find anything?" I asked, mainly to help Shoulders focus on something else.

Evyn talked while she wrote. "Well, they are definitely part of your folklore. There's lots of stories of beings who can perform feats of strength. They also feast on the blood of the innocent and the not-so-innocent." She ruffled her papers into alignment, muttering, "It's all about blood here."

"What do they look like?"

"Accounts differ only slightly in that, actually. They're usually very, very pale-skinned, some say their touch is like that of the dead, so I'd say they are cold, and others say they are actually dead and walking around."

I shuddered. The idea of the dead walking rather than resting made my skin prickle, even though Daronians, my mother included, believed that would happen before the end of days. "So they are real?"

Evyn wrapped her papers in wax paper, then cast about on the table for something. I picked up the leather straps hanging off the back of a dining chair and passed them to her. She smiled in thanks, a brief flicker that barely visited her face before it became stern again. "It has as much evidence for it as Earthians, so read into that what you will."

"I don't read anything, I can ask you to assist with that."

She sighed. "I meant, although there's only folklore evidence for dhampir, the same is true of Earthians, so..." She gestured to herself. "I guess sometimes there's a grain of truth to every legend, but your Earthian stories are wild. Not only do you have a drop of blood giving everyone within a twenty-mile radius unlimited magic, but it does kooky things to mages – I reckon those particular myths were written by certain kinks rather than reality – and everyone's supposed to fall instantly in love with them." She snorted. "That last one makes me laugh."

A cool feeling spread over my core, sour and bitter. She didn't find that element of the legends surrounding her world amusing at all.

"It's true," Shoulders said from the sofa. He stood up, shuffling around the furniture like an old man, bent and bowed.

"Of course." I added my voice to his.

Evyn scowled at me. "No one instantly falls in love with anyone. That's just lust or something, and believe you me, I know I'm not first prize at the fair."

As her soul companion I couldn't and wouldn't feel attraction as a man would his preference in partner, but I could decry her self-deprecation. "You are evidently attractive enough to have someone commit treason and risk a horrible death to rescue you."

Evyn rolled her eyes.

Shoulders looked between us. "What's this?" he croaked.

"Recall that Aubin went from talking to her to administering my test to enter Special Forces." My chest tightened, as if we were back in that horrible steam-filled room and Torgund was watching me try to hold my stance as Evyn drowned at my feet. "He came straight to find me and offered to support a break-out."

Evyn tied a strangling-tight bow on the papers for Barlay. "That would be for some other reason."

I shook my head. "He didn't want your blood," I whispered, careful not to say anything that might be overheard.

"He's doing it again in Skien, helping the helpless or whatever. Maybe he's got a secret hero complex." Her nose wrinkled.

"The good he is doing in Skien is saving lives," I pointed out, careful not to sound too stiff.

"Yeah, I know." Toying with the knot, she sighed. "It just means I didn't drive him out of his mind with love or something, it's his own thing to rescue someone. I read into that, I guess. Like I always do."

I opened my mouth to refute, but it was Shoulders who spoke. "The Lonely Man falls immediately in love with the Spirit Shaper," he said. "I've seen it many, many times, over so many worlds I've lost count. Each time it's like something opens up in him and, for once, he doesn't run away from it." He sighed happily. "It's lovely to see."

"So... they are a fated match?" That intrigued me. "Are we fated to meet and love Tuniel?"

Red-rimmed eyes darting to the side, Shoulders shrugged. "I've probably said too much and Evie will be cross with me, but yes, our complete spirit belongs with theirs."

That simple answer was enough to fill my chest to bursting with a swell of love. Across all the worlds and all the universes, all the different permutations and tessellations of our lives, we formed a partnership and we fell in love.

Evyn hefted up the papers into her arms. "I need to deliver these, leave you guys to keep talking about fairy stories if you want."

"It's not a story. It happens." Eyes widening, Shoulders stared off into the distance. "Again and again it happens..." His brow dropped, as though he were thinking through a difficult problem.

Someone rapped at the door. I turned to answer it, calling over my shoulder, "If that's a messenger they can take the papers for you." I tilted my head down and opened the door expecting a young boy or girl, so my gaze had to track up a set of green skirts, rounded hips and a magnificent cleavage before resting on the face of my beloved, the love of my life and my match across all the worlds.

It was everything I could do not to pull her into my arms. "MasterMage," I said, in a strangled cry.

A few turns of the glass of rest had restored some colour to her cheeks, or she was equally pleased to see me. "Ranger."

Behind her loomed Carreelee in her male form, and Layloree stood with a hip cocked to the side, gap-toothed grin fixed firmly on me and holding some kind of wrapped parcel.

I straightened. "Won't you come in?"

"Why, thank you." Tuniel kept a handspan away from me as she passed by, but her eyes slid toward me.

Distracted, I nearly shut the door in Carreelee's face. "Oh, my apologies."

Her craggy weathered face was glum. "That's to be expected. Don't apologise. Sorry for being an inconvenience."

Layloree hooted with laughter. "Carreelee, your lower-tier man is perfect. Even I cannot tell the difference."

Her behaviour made my stomach crawl. Had there really been a time when I wanted people to act like that toward me? "Come in, and you don't have to act so deferent around me."

Carreelee nodded, steps slow, while Layloree slid past her and through, sauntering through our corridor and taking everything in. "Nice windows! Bad for heat escaping in the winter."

"We don't have that problem in the city," Tuniel said.

A spiral of panic twanged against the bond, tight as a drawn bowstring, and Evyn sidled up to me. "You didn't mention we were expecting guests," she said out of the corner of her smiling mouth.

"I did not know either. I'll help you with refreshments."

"We won't be long, Ranger, Lady Evyn," Tuniel said. "I wanted to make sure the party was properly introduced and to deliver Lady Evyn's gift personally."

Evyn perked up. "Gift?"

I straightened up as if on parade. "Introductions, then, although the Assassin is not here."

"I am." The door to Aubin's room cracked open, the Assassin standing there, shirt hastily buttoned and collar open. "This is rather early for a party."

Layloree sucked a breath between her teeth. "A *fordubbla*! Ah, wonderful."

The Assassin inclined his head, amber gaze sweeping up to me. "Well, then. Introduce away."

I cleared my throat. "MasterMage Tuniel, Mage Carreelee the beastshifter, Layloree of North Hold, please may I introduce my soul companion Lady Evyn from my world, and the Assassin and Shoulders from another." I gestured to each. Evyn gave a small wave, tucking her hand into mine.

"Which world?" Layloree asked the Assassin.

He gave her a small smile back and a shake of his head.

Layloree snorted. "Then we will have much to talk about."

Carreelee tugged at her beard, looking at Shoulders and the Assassin. "I wager I'll beat both of them," she murmured in Skienien. "I won't be at the bottom for long."

Shoulders frowned, and the Assassin studied his nails. "I wouldn't wager on that," he returned in the same language.

Layloree clapped her hands. "Wait to settle the hierarchy when we're on our way. We cannot cost more delay." She nodded to Tuniel, a serious expression drawing her face tight for once.

Tuniel's lips were thin. She held herself stiff, tenser than usual. "He was hurt again. The pain disturbed my rest." She made it sound as if she were put out by the inconvenience, but I knew her well enough to understand now: she was desperately worried.

*Aubin might be caught.* He could even now be facing mob justice. The Hudau saw him purely as an enemy; they wouldn't appreciate the depths to him, the quirks and foibles that made him who he was. I gripped the pommel of my father's sword, trying to shove out my dark imaginings of what a faceless enemy would do to him.

I focused on the here and now, channelling my despair toward action. *He is still alive.* I could do something to help as long as he remained so.

Carreelee grunted at Layloree's request. "Fine, but you're not the matriarch." Carreelee turned to me. "How should we address the matriarch?"

I shrugged a shoulder. "We're all friendly so... Evyn?"

"Mm?" She looked up at me.

"We can just call you Evyn, right?"

"What, me? I'm the... what?" Her eyes widened.

"We can't be wandering around without a woman making sure we stay in line," I pointed out. "That's how our Aubin and I got into trouble in the first place."

"Ah. So you have been there before?" the Assassin asked, a smile playing on his lips.

"Nevermind, it won't affect us." I cleared my throat, hoping I cleared my cheeks of any red at the same time. "And don't worry, Evyn. Having a woman escort us will make others feel comfortable, but we'll do all the work. You can order the Assassin to speak on your behalf, for example."

He shot me a glare. "Just because you're nominally in charge here doesn't mean you can order *me* around," the Assassin said.

Layloree tutted. "They must set their hierarchy too, eh?" She nodded to Evyn, braids swinging. "I can help advise. Many of the normal people of Skien will be understanding that you don't know the culture as long as you're trying to understand it."

"Are there any normal people in Skien?" the Assassin muttered, echoing my thoughts.

Tuniel took the parcel from Layloree and held it out to Evyn. "These are for you."

"Me?" Evyn took the package, placing it on the table to pull the bow free, unwrapping beautiful silvrine bracers filigreed with an intricate swooping design.

"These look like lace." She turned them over in her hands. "What are they, some kind of bracelet?"

"These are bracers, like mine." I held up one and she slid her arm into it. It flowed into place along her forearm like Amare did on me, protecting her wrist all the way up to her elbow.

"For now, they use the same activation words that Thorrn's have," Tuniel said.

"You mean Secare?" she whispered, and deadly sharp fins slid out from the far edge. "Nice. Unsecare." They slid back.

"How are they doing that?" The Assassin lifted a hand to touch her arm.

Evyn turned away sharply, then sighed and faced him, holding up her arm for him to see.

Tuniel took the other bracer into her hands. Her tiredness receded a little, replaced with eagerness to explain. "I have stored magic in these soul jewels, but without Aubin nearby, I have to store a lot more in them, so each stone is good for one movement out and one in." She tapped a panel in the unworn bracer and slid out a small jewel from the inside. "I will give you a veritable pile. You will need some for your armour as well, Ranger."

"Thank you, Tuniel, these are lovely." Evyn stroked the bracer on her arm.

"It was the swordsman Gomoresson's idea, and he paid handsomely for it." Tuniel met my eyes.

*Gavain wants her to have these?* "My thanks, MasterMage, for making it, and my thanks to him as well. This will help keep her safe. I wish you well in your endeavours here; and fret not: we will find and meet with your soul companion to hand over the rescue effort to Layloree and Carreelee." I left the rest unvoiced, because while most of the room wanted Aubin back, Evyn would struggle to see him again.

Evyn gave her bracers a contemplative look, sliding them on and putting her hands up in a passable guard. "Yes. If he's hurting, we have to go find him." The glint in her eye spoke of some kind of eagerness.

"Spoken like a true matriarch," Layloree said proudly, before cackling.

# CHAPTER 18

STRAIGHT AFTER MIDSUN MEAL, EATEN HASTILY IN OUR KITCHEN, A TRAVEL mancer took us all to Dretan, an Oberrotian settlement a few miles from Skien over sparse terrain. It was unguarded given that there were no roads directly across the border here, and according to the map there was a hot river only the other side of the hill.

As soon as the winds of travel faded, grass whipping at our heels, I scanned the immediate surrounds. Dretan was little more than a mining village with a tavern, situated to the north-west of Oberrot City, and the temperature had dropped significantly to prove it.

"Ack, that's cold." Evyn burrowed into the rim of her furs. "This is awful."

The Assassin rubbed his arms. "We aren't even in Skien yet. Hold your adjectives."

Evyn turned away from him and held Shoulders's hand as we crunched down the icy road away from the town, thickly-needled trees blasted nearly horizontal alongside us and either grey mountains or ominous snow clouds confounding the horizon. "It's got a beauty to it, for sure. A sort of hostile beauty."

"Hostile beauty is a good description for all Battlemistresses too," Layloree said with a hint of pride. "Now then, man mountain, I suggest that me and the *fordubbla hellione* scout ahead for easier paths."

"Why me?" the Assassin grumbled, but he picked his way forward even so and joined alongside Layloree.

"Can I go?" Carreelee asked me.

"If you want. I trust you understand and can adapt to the landscape here better than I."

"I can definitely adapt." She widened her feet so she would have better traction and cantered after Layloree up the slope. The landscape wouldn't change immediately when we crossed the border, but it was certainly stonier here, brown and grey grasses clinging to the sides of crags, wrinkles in the hills signs of land slippage, and those ever-present clouds hanging low to the ground.

Evyn shaded her eyes, watching after Carreelee. "That's quite the skill she has there. There isn't a single person who wouldn't want to change their appearance now and again, except maybe you." She nudged my elbow.

I picked my way over the rocky trail alongside her. The barely-there path Layloree had taken skirted round the mound, a steep slope on my offside. "I can safely say I've never wished for that, although I would like the ability to blend in every now and again. I stand out too easily."

"Yes, yes, show-off." She grinned at me, adjusting the straps of her backpack.

Following directly in her shadow, Shoulders tugged at her burden. "I can carry that."

"So can I," she said. "It's not that heavy yet, but thank you for the offer."

"Doesn't it have at least three books in it?" I teased.

"One, but it's a small one."

The scree underneath her feet slipped. I twisted around to grab her arm, but she was snatched from me by Shoulders pulling her up over his head.

"Er... hi." Evyn dangled over him.

He blinked slowly at her, then lowered her to her feet. "I thought we were both slipping. He could grab you if we were."

She patted him on the forearm. "Thank you."

"Of course," he mumbled.

I gave his shoulder a more vigorous hug. "My thanks as well." He had reacted fast.

"You must be really strong to lift me that high," Evyn marvelled.

"Those shoulders are wide for a reason, Evyn," I said.

His gaze dropped. "I got scared, pulled some berserker strength." He trembled all over, a shudder that rattled his jaw.

He was truly on edge if he felt a small slip down a hillside to be a major threat. No doubt his nerves were worn thin by the uncertainty around his Evie. "We will get her back."

"For that we need your Aubin, and all this time you've been saying he won't come back easily." The words tumbled out of him. "What if he won't? Evie mentioned he was suspicious of her. What if he won't help her?"

"He will," I said firmly just as Evyn said at the same time, "He might not."

I had to stop walking to face her, because walking forward with an incredulous look turned toward her was unwise in the event more scree decided to slide out from under us. "Of course he will help, and at the very least we will convince him to help."

Evyn shrugged. "We should prepare for the eventuality that he doesn't, though. Even he would say that: prepare for the worst, then be pleasantly surprised if the worst doesn't appear."

"I wish that attitude hadn't rubbed off on you." I resumed pacing. Surely he would help, and Evyn had been previously sure that he would, when the alts had first asked for our help.

The hillside twisted, the livestock trail petering out against the stone. Ahead of us lay a more impressive hill, plumes of steam billowing out of cracks along its ridges.

Evyn drew to a halt, staring. "Uh... is that safe?"

I shrugged my pack up higher. "Probably not. Don't go near any vents, that's steam, and you'll be burnt."

"Why is there steam coming off a hill?"

"The water is hot."

"Yes. Why is the water hot?" she pressed.

"Probably from the lava underneath it?"

"Oh. Oh good. Is this an active volcanic area?" Her voice sounded a little higher than usual.

"Yes. Didn't I mention that before? That's why it's sparsely populated, so we're unlikely to see very many people. It will also be warmer and more comfortable to travel along the hot rivers, the *heta koller.*"

"So this was actually in the plan?" Evyn's hands squeezed her pack straps.

I steered her onwards. "Fret not, Evyn. While I haven't been along this exact one, tracking along the rivers is usually safe."

"Usually." She gulped. "Well, okay. You say it's unpopulated but other people travel like this, right?"

I scanned the horizon. "Other people use the main roads. What I am on the lookout for is bands of rogue men, but they usually travel in groups of less than half a score."

"Oh, so it'll be just a lazy-day workout for you."

I grinned at her. "Precisely."

Both Evyn and Shoulders exchanged a look. A bead of sweat trickled down Shoulders's temple. "I'll keep a lookout too."

I shook my head. "We'll take it in turns. It's tiring to always be on the edge and plan for every eventuality."

He frowned at me. "Yes."

What was that look for? He stared for a handful of heartbeats before looking back behind us.

Evyn navigated around a smattering of rubble. She peered up at him. "Is that what you do, then?"

*Good thing Evyn is here to see it too.* The alts being secretive was one thing, but of them all, Shoulders was the one most likely to talk.

He wrung his hands in his coat. "They do all of that. They ask me to stay out of it," he said. "Arian is busy with her work as the Master-Mage, so she hardly ever asks."

"They? You mean your Evie and the Assassin? Or someone else?"

He looked away. "Them and someone else as well. But I really cannot tell you about them." His pained look made my heart hurt.

"It's alright." Evyn squeezed his hand. "We're just really curious. It's not every day you meet yourself."

"One day it would be useful to know what your purpose is, so we can help," I tried. Evyn shot me a level look – had I been too forward?

Yes, because Shoulders's face immediately dropped. "All the alts want to know that, as if they have their purpose that they're aware of at all times. We are just people who happen to wander across time-lines. Does that mean we have to have some special design, some big thing that we're herding everyone toward?" He met my eyes with a welcome spark of challenge. "What's your purpose, then?"

I ticked off on my fingers, the way Evyn did. "Serve the king and Oberrot, keep Evyn safe and happy, marry the love of my life – all my lives, actually – and assist allies. Travel the world defeating evil no matter where or when it might arise, and continually better myself." I lifted my chin. "I think that keeps me plenty busy."

"There's room for some rest and relaxation in there," Evyn said with a smile.

"Did you not hear the part where I marry the love of my life?"

She giggled, cheeks flushing. The warm burgeoning bubble in my solar plexus was back, and I rubbed at it, smiling back at her.

It flickered and vanished. Evyn's smile faded, and she bared her face to the cold winds. Her hair tangled over her forehead, hiding her eyes from me.

She must be thinking about Aubin again. I tried to relax, to let myself feel what she felt. Such a blend of feelings, each on a spectrum so wide they were almost opposites at the same time: love and hate, anger and acceptance, fear and eagerness.

Shoulders stomped forward. "I'm going to check ahead."

"Fine," I said. He might need distance to manage the rage that could tip into both me and him, especially without Evie to help him smooth it out. "Don't get too far in front of us."

He gave a jerky nod of his head as he doubled his pace, thumping along the track.

Evyn stared after him. "Is he okay?"

I shook my head. "He's struggling with something I would be hard-pressed to bear under. Evie missing, and being doubted. Why does everyone reflexively think the alts are up to no good?"

She flushed. "It's just new for everyone. It's new for us, too." She waved at me. "I mean, in the castle, there's that security dimension. What would you think if a new Barlay suddenly appeared, looking and acting exactly like ours?"

I tried to turn that over. "Hm. It would be an immediate security risk. I suppose we'd put sanctions in place to prevent the other one from issuing orders."

"Right, and here we have another you, so Barlay's immediately on edge. You have access to some pretty sensitive stuff as a Ranger. Add another me, who's a risk because I can get right to the king no problem because of Mum. And then an Aubin, and they're just hazards in their own right."

I scanned the track ahead and Shoulders's receding back. "Alright, you've convinced me. But we know the alts are just here for help."

"Do we?" She nibbled the edge of her fingernail, eyes unfocusing past my double.

I groaned. "Not you too." A flicker of frustration flared across the bond, mine and hers clashing in the middle.

She felt it too, folding her arms tight. "Thorrn, I cannot do any research about the multiverses because someone's hidden all my books," she snapped. "It's like being blind and deaf to the past. Any previous experience this world has with multiverses is just... gone. It's criminal."

Our pain opened up in my chest, no doubt an echo of hers.

"That's the past, Evyn, and someone else's experience," I said gently. "We go by who we know them to be, their patterns of behaviour over time. They have been nothing but help for us." I nodded to Shoulders. "He saved your life. It's unkind to treat him like a criminal and always question him now." I slowed to tackle an outcropping of rocks, picking my way through. "You just don't want to be anywhere near the Assassin."

She rocketed up next to me, little fists bristling. "And you just don't want to believe people you reward with your friendship are capable of hurting us, but they are, Thorrn."

I kept one hand raised in case she should fall and let her words percolate in, seeing how it blended with my truth and hers. *Yes, it is true. People we love and trust have hurt us.* I turned my face away from hers, gaze roving over the jagged hillside, all benign in their own right but potentially hiding hazards. "Yes, Evyn, I'll accept that, but we can only judge people by their actions, and their explanations for why they behaved the way they are behaving." I faced her head on, helping her over a boulder. "There is room for nuance, surely you can see that? Maybe they *are* using us, maybe they need us for something that they aren't telling us about, but so far that hasn't hurt us. For all we know, it's their pet project to go around making sure all the versions of themselves are happy. Wouldn't we do that, if we had the kind of power that they do?"

Her lips quirked as she dropped down next to me. "Are you saying that if you had the power to change the trajectories of whole worlds, you'd spend it just toddling around making four people happy?"

"Well, when you put it like that." I rubbed my hands over my face, scrubbing hard at my embarrassment.

Evyn gently touched my arm, and I lowered my hands to bare myself to her. She smiled up at me. "There's this kind of innocence about you that's really cute. You always believe the best of someone and think they are constantly striving to improve themselves, because you aspire to that." She wrapped her cold fingers around mine. "I like to think we share that belief that people just need a chance, but we've been bitten by that, Thorrn. I only want to make sure you're not going into any situation with rose-tinted glasses."

I could gather her sentiment if not understand her exact phrasing, and her protectiveness heartened me. "I know you think because we've misjudged our allies before, we could do so again. In that I suppose you are correct, but it can also go the other way, Evyn. The more complete a picture of a person we have across multiple different encounters, the more we can understand a person, or even a group of people." I walked on, side by side with her. "Special Forces is taught to assess quickly, to judge all relative threats within heartbeats, and draw conclusions on how to defeat someone based on previous experience with similar encounters. I want to break away from that and do something different. I want to allow for second chances, for explanations to be given and for people to make mistakes. As long as we all are willing to work together on that, I think that could really make something special."

Evyn frowned at Shoulders ahead. "Are you talking about Shoulders again?"

I hadn't, not really. "I suppose that could apply to both Gavain and... Aubin. He's on my mind a lot more now."

She shook her head angrily, hair flying. "Giving people chances and the grace to explain themselves? That's just asking to be kicked in the family jewels."

"The... what?"

"The, uh, oh, never mind." Her face flushed. "Point is, you're starting to sound naive."

I resisted the instinct to put up a guard against her verbal jab. "I'm trying to think it through, Evyn. I don't have all the answers right now."

She blew out a long breath, pulling her plait over her shoulder and picking at the ends with savage intensity. "No, I'm sorry. If I wasn't so wound-up, I'd be interested in pursuing what's behind this line of thought of yours, but right now I'm too on edge to even *think* about letting someone get close enough to hurt us."

I nodded. An angry Evyn was a strange sight to behold, given that she vibrated with righteous fury. Even her hair seemed to frizz with an energy like that of her world, a spark that lit instantly. She seldom displayed anything other than quiet and calm, thinking and turning issues over in her mind before speaking, except when situations riled her beyond reason. Usually, I was the root of her displeasure, and a view from the flanks for this occasion was welcome.

Her anger had a singular focus that narrowed her viewpoint, squeezing her compassion to thin dregs. Her attention would not be swayed from the subject of her high dudgeon. *Is this what I'm like most of the time?*

She raised her chin, her glare a challenge. "Does this new softly-softly approach apply to Liara?"

Immediately I felt tripped, wrong-footed and left stumbling. "No," I croaked, voice robbed of any conviction.

She flung her arms around me, burying her face in my leathers and a deluge of comfort crossing the bond. "I'm sorry, I really am, I'm so sorry. I didn't mean to blindside you with her."

But she was correct. I patted her back, trying to reconcile the nascent budding of my thoughts with my experience of harsh uprooting. How could I approach Liara's attack or the bigotry of the Skienien mob justice with any openness?

I couldn't, and the failure galled me. "Let's continue," I said. "We have to set up camp on some kind of level ground."

I walked with Evyn through the hills alongside a combination of Evyn's compassion and my desire to understand motive or driving force. A small fear crawled up my throat; was I going soft on our enemies? Would I want to understand Liara's intent rather than end her before she could end me?

Liara had seemed bereft, desperate enough to storm the Sultanate's Palace in Rush to obtain the tangles she needed to fuel her plans. As to what her goals were, that was almost immaterial.

Her methods were in opposition to what we stood for. The same was true of the Skienien mobs.

Before we reached where Shoulders had paused to let us catch up, I spoke. "We might not be able to understand Liara or the Skieniens that are driving out their own people by talking to them, but we can observe her actions and react accordingly."

Evyn nodded slowly. "Right." But her gaze flicked to Shoulders, and her nerves ratcheted tighter.

# CHAPTER 19

We walked on, the grey deepening to full night-time. Just as I was about to stop and wait for our scouts to circle back, we turned a corner and found all three of them in the lee of the hill, a wide scrub area leading down to a pool as blue as the Dinahen Defence Force's uniform. Steam roiled and rolled close to the valley edges, but the wind direction meant that it only occasionally wafted toward us, carrying a foul stench of sulphur.

"How's this for the perfect place to stop and picnic?" Layloree lay stretched out, head on her pack.

Carreelee and the Assassin sat with their legs out in front of them. Were they not freezing? Bending to touch the ground, I got my answer.

"The ground is warm here." Evyn stroked the soil.

"There must be a spring underneath." Carreelee's eyes were lidded, voice languid from tiredness.

I straightened up. "We'll sleep here tonight. Let's set up camp, agree a watch rota, and see to dinner."

Layloree waved her hand. "Dinner is cooking, and you and I will take first watch, man mountain. We can do some training." She smiled, eyes still closed.

The Assassin shuddered. "You enjoy that. I can take second watch with Carreelee."

"Leaving me and Shoulders in the morning. Nice." Evyn brushed off her hands. "Let's get that tent set up."

We had the large lean-to set up just in time, as darkness fully descended and made trying to discern anything even an arm's length away difficult. The red and yellow moons cast a sick and ominous light on the silent haze drifting below us.

"It looks like a river of ghosts," Evyn said, hugging her knees.

Layloree went down into it to the edge of the river and brought back a dripping bag. She must have submerged it earlier, and I wrinkled my nose as she brought the stench into the camp.

She shook the bag open, dropping small rocks into her palm. "*Heta* eggs." She held out the first to Evyn. "Matriarch, please take."

"Um, thanks." Evyn picked it up between forefinger and thumb, dancing her fingertips across it. "It's hot."

"Good, cooked all the way through." Layloree passed the bag around. Reaching in, I pulled out my own egg, almost too hot to hold. We cracked and peeled the shells, but the smell of sulphur combined with the taste of the eggs turned my stomach.

"Tomorrow I'll hunt some meat," I promised.

"Good luck finding anything out here," the Assassin said, picking at his meal. "There's only scraggly sheep."

Shoulders choked down his eggs in the same way I had; grudgingly accepting that nourishment was nourishment.

I looked up at the sky, recalling Barlay's charts of stars. "We will probably be close to a town tomorrow. We can have a proper meal at an inn."

Layloree snorted. "My cooking is that bad, you can't stand it for more than one day? You can cook for yourself from now on."

"Thank you for the meal, Layloree," Evyn said.

Layloree inclined her head. "You are welcome, matriarch."

Soon everyone wanted to turn in. Evyn and Shoulders went into the lean-to, where he lay along her back. Carreelee and the Assassin rolled into sheets close to the entrance, and Layloree and I waited in silence for their breathing to turn even.

"Now then, it's our time." Layloree was a dark outline against the fetid mist behind her.

"How are we going to train in the dark?"

"You need to see your opponent to land a strike? Oh my, man mountain, you are more stunted than I thought." She came into my guard.

I tensed, lifting my hands.

"It's not about hitting. The fight is in your head first. The exercises are to strengthen, to ease your body into new grooves of movements, but as you know from your own training, they are only the foundation. There are patterns, movements in response to how your foe reacts. You have to be like a pendulum, swinging up and back, taking their energy and turning it on them." She touched one of my arms, lifting it up by my forearm. Her other hand circled around my wrist and she twisted it slowly, stopping before my natural range of motion, pushing my hand away. At speed, that would be a deflection, only with her hand rather than a sword or the blades.

"Aubin has a... flowing, dancing movement when he fights," I said.

"Yes. You are water, you are everywhere and then you come together to bring your force into one powerful strike. You cannot be hit, for you are fast, but if you are, your energy spreads so that you tilt and recover."

That fitted him exactly, and not just his fighting style. "Aubin is like water. You don't see he's there, trickling by, not really noticeable, until he determines something. Then he's unstoppable."

Layloree's outline in the darkness nodded as she sat. "He tries to vanish like water too, pretending he had no impact. Cheeky water, draining off after a flood like it did nothing."

I hunkered down next to her, resting my forearms on my knees. "Do you think we will get him back?"

"If we are fast and smart, we can catch him." She leant back. "In all seriousness, I don't know the reason why he's gone. What drove him to leave?"

"Oh." My throat tightened. "He killed me. A mancer brought me back, I didn't die for long."

"Uh huh." Layloree tilted her head. "I wasn't expecting that. I thought you'd say, hm, someone like that delicious captain had tried to push him into your red uniform man mould. Water, see, it takes shapes for a short time, but it cannot hold them."

I cleared my throat, wondering if I would ever be able to look Barlay in the eye without thinking of Layloree's descriptor. "It wasn't him but me. I tried to push Aubin to be who I thought he could be."

"Could be, or should be?" Layloree's words drifted up over the stench-filled smog.

That threw me. "Should be," I admitted.

"Mm. And now you realise that, but will he realise you realise that? Tricky." She tipped her head. "How will you do things differently?"

"What do you mean?"

"You say you know you pushed now. You know water won't be pushed, won't be shaped, won't be moulded. Will you do the same, and keep pushing? Or will you do something differently?"

"Differently, of course, but I'm not sure what yet." This was the sort of thing I would talk over with Evyn, but her hurt and the brittle way she seemed determined to help him but not understand him made me wonder if she would even entertain the conversation.

"Better think, mountain man. We could see him tomorrow, you know. Keltskarr is two days away but he may be moving, roving around keeping ahead of the Hudau."

Claws of apprehension sank into my gut at both elements: the idea of seeing him and the idea of him being in danger both battling for consideration as the worse threat. Of course the danger should be my first consideration, but as for that first reunion…

Would I say well met? Ask if he were hale and well? Say something funny? Say anything at all?

Perhaps he would be grateful to see me. *Especially if a mob has him cornered somewhere.* Maybe we would join the battle and suddenly we would be alongside one another and I would say…

What?

Layloree stood, arching her back and scanning the hills looming dark against the purple sky. "This is the first time I've been back here. The mountains do not change, but I have. I see them differently."

"Is it hard for you to come back?" I asked.

She turned slowly, making a sucking noise. "No," she said finally. "It's just a place. It's the people that made it hard here, and easy to stay elsewhere. People make a home."

I sat for a while, the warmth from the ground below welcome. When Aubin and I had come to Skien, we had been able to keep to the proper roads between the towns, sleeping rough where needed. There weren't large hot rivers near the Skienien settlements; something sensible at least. "If I remember the map correctly, we'll need to cut straight down the valley tomorrow."

"When we get further in, it will get colder. I knew of one inn, which might still be good."

"We'll aim for that. My thanks, Layloree."

"It might have changed. I haven't seen all the changes yet, but it sounds much the same." She stretched, hands framing the moons.

The rest of the first watch passed with no issue. Just past the top of the night I woke the Assassin and Carreelee. Carreelee rolled out of bed, her edges blurring in the darkness as she changed shape. "There. Now I can see," she whispered.

I wondered what she had made her eyes to be but I was also too tired to ask. The day had worn long and with a watch on top of it, I was ready to rest. I ducked inside the warm tent, lying down on the ground on the other side of Evyn. She sleepily put one hand on my shoulder, and I fell into a light rest.

I woke when Evyn moved, getting up to do her watch. "Go back to sleep," she said, and I did as soon as I turned over, but it seemed only heartbeats when she called into the tent, "Morning! Rise and shine."

"Someone's had their tea." Sleepiness fell quickly off me, adrenaline surging. We were in enemy territory; I had to be focused when on duty. "I'll help make breakfast."

"Already done," Layloree said. She must have woken up even earlier. "Hot river eggs soon be ready."

Not again. I suppressed a sigh.

Stepping over the Assassin and Carreelee, who were shifting and waking, I made my morning ablutions away from the camp. This side of the hill was scree and grey grass, but it was rolling and pleasant compared to the hill on the other side of the valley. That hill was scraped bare by winter winds, thin tortured trees reaching out from what meagre anchor points they had been able to secure.

It was Skienien territory, and today we would interact with Skieniens in some way. *And we might see Aubin.*

I had to think about what I was going to say, and that was alongside the worry of whether he was even open to hearing it, but the first priority was getting there safely. There were a lot of obstacles between us and Aubin still.

Footsteps padded behind me. "Thorrn." The Assassin glared at the hillside as though it had personally offended him.

He had deliberately made noise so I wouldn't startle. "Well met."

"I need to talk to you." He kept his attention on the hillside. "My Thorrn's nerves are running high and, if we run into trouble, he might not be able to control himself and he could go berserk. We need to get him out of the way or he will be a liability to himself and others."

I rocked on my heels. Shoulders had seemed close to an edge yesterday and I could well imagine the heat of a real fight snapping his control. He might hurt allies as well as enemies. "Leave it to me. I have an idea."

We scraped and slid back to the camp. Carreelee was not yet up and around, but we could leave her abed until we served breakfast.

Evyn smiled a welcome. "Did you sleep well?"

"Yes, and you seem in good spirits."

She grinned. "Something about fresh air and exercise, maybe, but I always feel really rested sleeping next to you."

"Same." Our spirit recovered when we were close, bestowing a greater form of relaxation. Currently physical proximity was necessary to our bond, but I had hopes that one day we would be aligned on other levels as well. Aubin and Tuniel's bond was strengthened by their alignment of purpose.

With a soft sigh, Shoulders stood up. I wondered what Shoulders's and Evie's bond was based on, because if it was physical proximity, this forced separation added to the agony.

As Layloree went to get the horrendous eggs from the hot river, I beckoned Evyn and Shoulders closer. "I need to talk to you both," I said. "Today we're travelling toward Keltskarr. As we travel and when we get there, anyone we meet will recognise us as foreigners. They will be put more at ease if we're seen to be adhering to their customs, and that means putting Evyn out front to be seen. Remember, a man cannot be walking around without a woman beside him. We might run into a challenge, but I'll handle those."

"A challenge? You mean something more than an obstacle," Evyn said.

I nodded. "Each group of men has a hierarchy. It's really tiring meeting lots of new people at once and having to set your place with them. If you aren't good at fighting, you're at the bottom and no one will listen to a word you have to say. If we want to barter for a meal, we're going to have to do that little dance first."

"What do I do?" Evyn asked.

"Well, the women's hierarchy is more subtle. Their place is determined by how their men do. That's why they'll look after them and get them training and the like, and their men will look to their women to make decisions for them, so they have to be aware of what's going on at any one time." I tilted my head. "I wonder if they'll be impressed that you have three men plus Carreelee looking like a man at your beck and call."

Evyn flushed. "I don't really."

"For now you do." I scanned the hills again. "Skien can be a lawless place and those rogue bands of men I mentioned prowl for easy pickings. While Layloree or I talk, I want you two to watch our backs. Particularly you, Shoulders. I want you to be Evyn's bodyguard."

"Of course," he said, putting his hand on her shoulder.

"And you, Evyn, ping yourself and him out if there's a fight."

"Okay." She held her thumb up to me, her signal of assent.

"Wonderful. Evyn, will you help me wake a sleeping mage?" As we walked to the tent I whispered to Evyn, "Thanks for agreeing quietly to take care of Shoulders. His pride would have been damaged if I had suggested he stay back, but now he has a role in defending you."

"That's fine. I could see what you were trying to do. He's struggling a lot. I'm on it." She put her thumb up and ducked into the tents to wake Carreelee.

"All sorted." I grinned at the Assassin.

He smiled back. Of course he looked very much like my Aubin, but the warmth in his amber eyes rocked me back. When had Aubin last looked pleased to see me? "Very smooth," the Assassin said, breaking through my reverie. "Let's be off."

Once Carreelee was up we broke down the shelter, and we ate the eggs as we walked. Getting away from the sulphurous steam helped, but I still found it hard to choke down yet more eggs.

I went ahead with Layloree, leaving Evyn and Shoulders with Carreelee and the Assassin. Layloree seemed to be scenting the air, lifting her nose every score of paces or so.

"What is it?" I asked.

"Trying to find the fresher air paths, you look like you turn green every time wind blows across to us." She cackled.

She led us unerringly toward a road, and I was grateful to find a level path. "We weren't bothered by bands of rogue men along the *heta koller*, though," I pointed out.

"There's always more time in the day, man mountain. The gods hear your boasting and make you regret it."

"I boast a great deal and hardly ever regret it."

We regrouped, waiting for the others to follow down from the hills, and then walked on along the road in a loose group. Away from the hot rivers, the temperature plummeted even further. My core tensed every time the icy wind found its way across my face, my hands thrust firmly under my armpits as we walked through a small forest.

"Warm little city boy," Layloree teased. She had her coat open, her nose and forehead rubbed red by the cold.

"I don't know how you stand this."

"Gets much colder, and the next training uses it to good effect." She halted. "Smell has changed. People!"

"Back," I hissed at the others.

Too late. Men came out from the trees and vaulted over fallen trunks. One spat on the ground, the spittle lacing his matted beard, wiping his hand on his filthy furs.

They surrounded us quickly as I appraised them; nearly a score in all that I could see and others perhaps still lurking. They held spears, hefted hammers and sported a frightening amount of crossbows.

They snickered. "Three women. Your lives must be hell."

"Excuse me," the Assassin huffed, coming up by my elbow. "We're surrounded," he reported.

*Damn and blast.*

A rogue pointed at the Assassin. "Hey, that's the man with the huge bounty! The Hudau said dead or alive, and Brudamere said free men could claim it!"

Even more damn and blast.

232

"Lay down your arms and we'll make it fast for you," one of them said, as tall as me and hefting his heavy hammer as easily as I would lift my pack. Others lifted their crossbows, picking their targets. Three aimed at me, but two were angled to get at Shoulders and Evyn behind me.

I gripped my father's sword, calling the calm of battle down. "Evyn, ping out." We would deal with Carreelee and Layloree later, telling them Evyn was a secret mage or similar.

"Will do." She opened a portal. Immediately a huge deluge of water slammed us to the ground, washing us and the rogues down the path.

I spat, tasting salt, as Evyn closed the portal hurriedly. "We're in the middle of the Irish Sea!" she said.

"She's a mage, kill her," the rogues cried.

Scrambling up and drawing my sword, I attacked, resolving to kill, stabbing and swinging with fatal blows. Three men went down before me, one other slain by the Assassin's whirling Battlemistress blades as he supported me.

"They got a Battlemistress!" a man shrieked. "You won't take me alive!"

"Suits me," the Assassin snarled.

He gasped. "A man? It's so short!"

"I hate Skien," the Assassin grated.

"He's not a Battlemistress, but I am." Layloree drew her blades. "You will submit or die!"

"Hit the Battlemistress and the mage!" one barked.

No! "Fall back, protect Evyn. Amare!" My armour deployed as I stepped in the way of two crossbow bolts. They pinged off me, each as solid as a punch.

"I'll protect her." Shoulders turned his back to us and bent over Evyn.

"He might go berserk, I need to get to him. Hold on!" the Assassin shouted to his friend, Battlemistress blades flashing next to me.

"We're in a fight!"

"No! Are we?"

We wouldn't last long being picked off by crossbows. "Stay here and whittle them down, I'll charge in and cut them up."

A flash of shining black burst behind me, a roar shaking the trees and screams and yells from the rogue men filling the air. I spun in a panic, heart yanking out of my chest and reaching for Evyn, safely in Shoulders's arms.

Carreelee unwound in the air, hissing and snarling. A crossbow bolt passed straight through her as she warped and reformed around it. "Flee, mortals!" she bellowed. Many did, the others too frozen to move.

I charged into the line of crossbowmen, bolts slamming into my chest and bouncing off. One glanced my left arm and it went numb, so I gritted my teeth and swung my sword. Someone raised their crossbow. My blade sunk into the hard wood and stuck. I kicked him backwards but he took both weapons with him, the blade wrenched from my hand.

Unarmed, I fell on him. "Secare!" My bracers deployed and I slashed.

"This is bad!" Layloree was surrounded, whirling but tiring. "Kill faster, get over here!"

I darted for the second group of men circling Layloree, punching and slashing into them from behind, little finesse now, only violence.

One filthy man lifted his club right into my head. Momentum spun me, ears ringing. I felt hardness all along one side; the ground. Another blow slammed down onto my shoulder, pinning me down, Amare spent. I couldn't focus. I panted, staring at the bloodstained hard-packed road. Evyn, my heart cried. I failed.

Panicked shouting. The Assassin yelling something. I wasn't dead yet somehow. I rolled onto my back. The sky spun around and around but slowly it came back into focus.

Evyn's face appeared above me. "Thorrn! Thorrn, are you okay?"

"I... uh...."

"How many fingers am I holding up?"

I closed one eye. "Many?"

"Oh no." She gently touched my head.

"What's happening?"

"They ran off, Layloree and the Assassin killed the one who attacked you and picked a few more off when you fell."

I rolled back onto my front and eased myself up. My head hurt, but not as much as my shoulder.

She pushed me back. "You might have a cracked skull or a concussion, stay down."

"Help me up," I said instead.

She nodded once and held out her hand.

I leant on her a little as I eased upright. "They recognised him. Thought he was Aubin. He's a wanted man, with a bounty on his head." A smile spread across my face.

Evyn frowned. "I know we're in limbo with him right now, but why are you *happy* about that?"

"It means he's still out there, at large, and being a nuisance." A laugh bubbled out of me, ringing around the trees. "He's alright."

# CHAPTER 20



We hobbled out of the forest and down the path, leaving the bodies lined up along the road for now until we could get to a town and the Skienien equivalent of Upholders there. I felt largely clearheaded, just sore. Carreelee swaggered in front, grinning in her man form and saying, "Merely shock tactics, eh?" every now and again.

The Assassin's voice faded in and out of my hearing. He explained that Evyn had a weaker magic, a limited command over water, his lie blithe with its simplicity.

Evyn walked beside me hanging on my arm, Shoulders on the other. She seemed to be coping better with the aftershock of battle, her feelings more wrapped up with worry about me.

I touched her hand, the bond renewing with a wave of warmth. "I'm fine, Evyn. I'm just glad no one was hurt."

"You were hurt. You got hit in the head and the shoulder. Remember?" She touched her own forehead, a transposition of where I had been struck.

"And you felt it. I'm so sorry, Evyn." I would have to learn to shield when I was in battle, to pull myself back from the bond, especially when we were so physically close to one another. "I didn't even think, I'm sorry."

"Don't panic, *I'm* okay, you're the one who was hit."

A warm feeling flowed over me. *We survived, Evyn is worried about me, Aubin is alive and well.* Now to get out of the weather. It was turning darker earlier, the clouds potent with the promise of cold wet misery for us if we didn't get out of it soon.

Flurries of snow hastened the dim day toward darkness, but fortunately we came to a crossroads and an inn. I knocked on the door, my knuckles pink with the crevasses in them prominent, and clapped my hands to get warm.

The proprietor looked pained until he saw Evyn and Layloree nestled among us, then he relaxed. He greeted them cordially, looking to one of us to make arrangements on her behalf. The Assassin stepped up and negotiated us rooms while Evyn kept her hand in mine and Shoulders's.

The rooms were serviceable enough, but it was the baths that attracted my interest. The ones here were outside for men, inside for women, but shared the same pool, the inn built right on top to take advantage of the heat from the water.

I bathed with the Assassin and Shoulders, the former sliding in next to me. "Let's take a look at your head."

"It's fine."

"Let me check anyway."

I sighed and endured being poked and prodded.

"How many fingers?"

I looked up at his hand, then beyond to the face above me. For half a heartbeat I imagined it to be my Aubin, that we had faced down the threat together. *He is alive and he is still causing trouble.* That made me smile, but the wrong kind of attention was on him now. He might argue all kinds of attention was unwelcome, but if rogue men could identify him, his enemies were doing a lot to hamper his movements.

"Hello? Gods, this *is* bad." The Assassin's lips quirked.

"I'm hale and well, I'll get some rest and be back to normal tomorrow."

The Assassin inclined his head to my chest. "Don't you have to rest the armour as well?"

I looked down at the silvrine second skin glittering under the water. "Oh, yes." I reached back for a lodestone from my folded uniform, swaying a little from the heat in the baths.

Shoulders grabbed my torso, and Amare gave only a weak pulse in return.

I cleared my throat. "If someone grabs me in the baths, I usually issue a challenge."

"Are you usually acting drunk when you're in the baths, though?" the Assassin snorted, flicking some water at me.

I ignored him to touch the lodestone. White filled my vision as the connection to Tuniel came through. *"Thorrn."* The softness in her voice undid me.

*"My love across all the worlds and all times and places."*

*"What can I do for you?"* She sounded tired and... amused?

*"I just like hearing your voice. Thoughts. Whatever, in a lodestone."*

*"And it is nice to hear yours, I have had rather a long and trying day. So have you, it seems."* Amare warmed briefly, then started trickling up to my shoulder. *"The armour is completely spent, what happened?"* Her voice sharpened.

*"Attacked by rogues, but we saw them off. All of us, working in concert."* I was particularly proud about that. Special Forces worked alongside other members of Special Forces, all in harmony because of predictability and the ingrained patterns. But one sword fighter with two Battlemistress blades users and a beastshifter? It was not anything I had ever trained for, and yet it felt natural, blending disparate skills and personalities both.

*"You'll need to swap out the soul jewel, this one is nearly empty,"* Tuniel said.

*"Very well. I cannot wait to get Aubin back, then I will not go through*

*these soul jewels so quickly. Oh! The rogues recognised him. There is a huge bounty on Aubin's head."*

*"Hm. How big?"*

*"Massive. Maybe a life-changing amount."* In this I could tell we were both proud and amused. *"He's alive, Tuniel, and he's working hard to make himself a menace."*

*"Well, I knew he was alive. The bounty is new information. It's just as well you are on your way."*

That last was an Evyn phrase. Thinking of her ways of speech being adopted by Tuniel made me smile.

*"Rest, Thorrn. You need it."*

*"So do you. I hope all is well there."*

*"Don't worry about us here. Captain Barlay asked me to relay that Special Forces are deploying. By the time you find Aubin they should be in place, and Layloree and Carreelee can lead the remaining refugees straight to the cordon and safety."* Her thoughts turned resolute. *"Then the real work will begin, settling and reassuring them."*

Assuring them they had a home, no matter where they came from or what they could do. Welcoming the new abilities, the new perspectives. Not trying to force them to adopt my ways, telling them everything was fine but through my actions showing that I expected something different, something more that not even I could define. Just *better.*

My heart hurt in my chest. *"I did it all wrong. No wonder Aubin felt he couldn't stay. He couldn't give me what he thought I wanted from him, when what I needed was* him, *the way he is."*

Tuniel's voice definitely tilted toward amused now. *"Bed, Thorrn."*

*"Is that an invitation?"*

*"An order. We are currently hundreds of miles away from one another."*

*"Yes."* I gave a throaty huff of longing. *"Goodnight."*

*"Goodnight."* She broke the connection and the hot baths filled my awareness once again. The armour wouldn't move or squeeze

me, that would use energy from the soul jewels and we only had so many with us, but I wanted it to.

The Assassin poked my shoulder. "Well, that put it back, but the soul jewel stopped glowing."

"It's out of energy." I fumbled trying to pull the stone out of its cradle in the armour, but the damn thing evaded my prying fingertips.

The Assassin levered it out, handing it to me. "There."

"My thanks." I lowered myself into the pool, the heat on the edge of bearable, soft fat flakes of snow tumbling above us, disappearing as soon as they touched the water. Little prickles of cold soothed my forehead when I tipped my face up to the sky.

Another dig from the Assassin. "Don't you dare fall asleep in here."

I sat up, sending a slosh of water ringing around the pool. "Ah yes, we need to set a watch."

The Assassin rolled his eyes. "Evyn and Shoulders first, me and Carreelee, then Layloree wants to see you first thing for training. Rest, Thorrn, Evyn has it all in hand."

"She does? I mean, of course she does, but it didn't take her long to step into her matriarch role." I knew one day she would feel able to step up and stand up for the causes she wanted to champion. This was a good start. "Maybe my confidence is balancing her out."

"Yes, a good dose knocked across when you got a blow to the head." The Assassin tugged at my arm. "Out. Bed. I'll give you some lyneal tea to help you sleep."

"My thanks, Aubin. I've missed you."

He stilled. "As long as I can be of use," he returned gruffly, slinging me a towel. "Shoulders, help me with this lump."

Between them they got me to the room we had secured, a row of beds for the men and a side room for Evyn where she, Layloree and Carreelee would sleep. Evyn came out as Shoulders toppled me into bed.

She sat by my side stroking my head, feeling her way around areas that didn't hurt and islands that did. "How are you feeling?"

I grinned at her. "You know."

She sighed. "Yes, I do, you've always been more open. Thorrn, you're getting excited. Is it about seeing Aubin again? I don't know whether you feel a bit safer here or whatever so you're less worried about different things, but don't get your hopes up." She busied herself straightening the pillows, yanking the covers up to my chin.

I pushed them down, taking her hands. "Maybe I am. Maybe it'll turn out badly but, you never know, maybe it will turn out well?"

"Plan for the worst," she muttered.

"But keep a lookout for the best," I countered. "Don't be shy about snatching the good or something worth having from any situation."

A small smile fluttered across her face. "Good night, Thorrn. Layloree will wake you for your watch."

"Good night, Evyn." I sent her a wave of love as I slipped into sleep.

❄ ❄ ❄

Layloree did indeed wake me with whispered words. "I scouted during the second watch, I found a perfect place for training."

That got me up and out of bed in a heartbeat. The room was sharply defined by the grey filtering in from the outside. It was after dawn! I nearly roused the whole room but everyone could do with a rest after yesterday.

At least I could see and think more clearly. Touching the side of my head, I found the sore area, feeling around it. Such a small bruise, but it had rattled me enough that Evyn had felt the need to let me rest and step up into command; the fact that she had and the others had listened to her was wonderful. We were working in concurrence, and that pleased me greatly.

Now we would have to align on the issue of Aubin. I turned that over as I made my way downstairs after Layloree, my steps light so as not to disturb others at the inn. Evyn seemed minded to doubt him, whereas I wanted to find ways to persuade him to come back. First we had to find him, yes, but then we had to listen, and really listen, the pair of us, without our wants colouring our response. It was going to be hard for me, and I needed her to help me, to do that thing where she listened without judgement. She didn't seem able to do that for him, but maybe when we were right in front of him her natural instincts would take over. It was hard to rely on that, but I had to trust her. She would be open to him. Wouldn't she?

I baulked as Layloree opened the door to a carpet of white cloaking all the stubby grey grass, road and rocks to be indistinguishable. "One moment, I don't have my furs on." I didn't even know where they were, I'd shed them at the baths last night. I looked down at myself, clad only in my smalls. "Or... anything else on." Maybe my head was more addled than I thought.

Layloree's gap-toothed smirk chilled me more than the cold cutting in from outside. "I know. Training begins now, man mountain."

"Out... Outside? In the cold?"

"Aw, is the big city boy put off by a little snow? You said you would do anything I say – this is the training." She pointed outside with a stern flourish.

"Did you make Aubin do this?" I asked. I couldn't imagine him being eager to run outside in the cold in his smalls.

She nodded, solemn. "And in snow much higher than this. Gets to your chest in winter, man mountain; North Hold isn't for soft southerners."

I squared my shoulders. If Aubin had done this and in worse conditions, then I could do it. "Lead on."

Layloree walked out, and I followed her, gasping at the cold. Immediately all warmth was stripped from me, and I wrapped my arms around my torso to try to preserve something. The snow under my bare feet was wet and cold, a double insult.

"Now over here." Layloree trotted to the side, pointing to an innocuous, perfectly white drift, too perfect to disturb. "Stand there."

We were in sight of the inn so we could keep our watch at least. I winced as my feet sank into the drift, more of my legs disappearing with each step. It was deeper than it looked, the snow seeming to bite where it touched my skin.

I had never, ever, *ever* been so cold in my life, in thigh-deep snow, with the wind cutting cleanly over the top of it and slicing like a blade across my skin.

"Hands on top of your head, no cheating." Layloree folded her own arms across her chest.

Biting my tongue, I laced my hands on top of my head. Soon I couldn't feel them, and I juddered and shuddered with uncontrollable muscle movements. I closed my eyes. When I opened them, Layloree was considering me.

"Hm... nearly."

I gasped. "This – is – killing – me!" I couldn't get the words out.

She shrugged. "Then move. I do not physically restrain you, man mountain."

*Oh thank the gods.* I went to take a step, then halted. "We won't ever try again if I stop?"

She shook her head. "This is the training."

*Some training.* This had to be a test of endurance.

I kept my spine straight. "Then I'll stay," I growled.

Her eyes narrowed. "You think I will praise you for this? It's stupidity. Are all Oberrotians stupidly stubborn, or just you?"

Now she was just confusing me on purpose. "Is this training or not?"

"It's how I do things. I spend heartbeats in the morning, in the cold, to align with discomfort, to teach my body it is not safe, to increase the good inside it and strip out the bad." She took a deep breath in through her nose and out through the mouth. "Freeing, yes?"

I was suffering so much I couldn't jest. I chose not to answer instead, lest I say something I would later regret.

"And done," she said happily, and turned on her heel to walk toward the inn.

I had to wade my way through, lifting my thigh over and collapsing banks behind me. I couldn't feel anything below my waist, which was probably a blessing as my upper body felt gripped in a serrated trap.

I did not dare to dream that she would let me back in, but she held open the door for me as I fell into the hallway. Immediately the relative warmth washed over me, eating away at the stiffness and soreness that held me down to my bones. My ribs seized as I gasped and shuddered uncontrollably.

"There, see? Isn't it freeing?" Layloree frowned. "You're supposed to make a joke now; 'That's the wrong word, Layloree, it's *freezing*.'" She grabbed a fur from beside the door, holding it out to me.

I tried to extend my arms to take it but they were fused to my violently juddering chest.

She ignored my attempts and threw it over me, vigorously rubbing me down through the fur. It helped wake my body.

"Is this hazing, or just a bit of fun for you?" I asked Layloree.

She sat back on her heels. "It's an important component to training. The cold teaches us many lessons: endurance, steadfastness, adherence and understanding of limitations. You have the first three in spades, but not the last one. It's interesting."

My mind felt liquid and calm. "It actually feels very good."

"Cold training releases good feelings. Afterwards," Layloree said.

"I could probably do that again."

"Not straight away," Layloree snorted. "Have a bath now, cook back up like an egg, but think about what the cold can teach you."

I did as she suggested, and this time going outside to get into a hot bath sounded wonderful. I sank into the water, the heat on the verge of being intolerable.

What would the cold teach me? If I did that every day, I could prove I had complete command over my body at least. Exposing it to physical discomfort was not new for me.

What had the cold taught Aubin? If that was a foundation in his formative turns of life, he had taken Layloree's stance to heart. *She said she did it to teach her body it is not safe.* Aubin never operated from a place of safety, always looking ahead for the next threat. He had to be exhausted all the time, never allowing himself to rest, and then looking out for me and Evyn as well. *Letting people in to care for them means that he cares about what happens to them.* No wonder he had found that too much to bear.

What could I do to show him we would take our share of the watch, and what could I say or do to convince him that we would guard his back as he guarded ours? I included Evyn and Tuniel as well, for the four of us formed an unbeatable partnership.

I dressed and found ways to occupy myself in checking our gear, but quietly. As expected, everyone slept late, including the family keeping the inn. Their matriarch was a rounded woman who walked around helping where needed as one man cooked our breakfast, another made restorative and the last scrubbed the hallway where I'd dripped all over the floor, all working as efficiently as a unit.

Evyn came down first, looking into both of my eyes and nodding firmly. "You look more with it than you did last night. I was worried about you going to sleep on it, but the Assassin assured me you would be fine."

So she spoke to him at least. That was progress. "Yes, it'll take more than a club to the head to down me, Evyn."

"At least two clubs." She winced. "Don't do that again."

"Noted." I took her hand. "Well done for taking over."

She flushed. "Everyone kind of organised themselves, they just needed a bit of reassurance that what they were doing was what we needed."

"That's probably the heart of it." I liked that as a perspective.

Now that Evyn was here, the family running the inn relaxed further. "I haven't seen Oberrotians here for a while," the woman running the inn said in Skienien, striking up a conversation with Layloree.

"No?"

"Too much unrest for them. I don't blame them for not coming here." She looked at me and Evyn. "So. Oberrotians like magic, eh?"

"They tolerate it well," Layloree replied evenly.

Evyn squeezed my hand. She couldn't understand them, but she could tell the proprietoress and Layloree were sounding each other out. Was the matriarch here a supporter of the Hudau?

The woman nodded. "I would hope that we could tolerate it as well."

My stomach relaxed. Evyn felt that, sitting back in her chair with a sigh of relief.

Layloree's hands dropped from her hips. "Good. We are merely passing through and we will not stay long."

The woman glanced out of the thick windows at the flurries of snow spiralling down outside. "If only I could speak to the Oberrotian helper, I would tell him he needs to leave."

"Oberrotian helper?" I asked.

The woman gave me a dirty look. I suppose listening in was rude in Skien as well, but it was probably compounded by the fact I was a man who hadn't been given leave to speak.

"Oberrotian helper?" Layloree asked mildly, ignoring my interjection.

"Yes, Oberrotian helper." The woman rubbed her finger on the lintel, inspecting it. "Others are looking for him. I haven't seen him, and certainly not in my own establishment." She looked up as the Assassin and Shoulders came down the stairs. Shoulders was grey-faced and slumped as though he had not slept a single heartbeat, but the Assassin looked invigorated, burning with that internal fire pushing him on.

The matriarch looked up at the ceiling. "No, I have not seen him," she muttered.

I stood. "Very well. We'll eat a quick breakfast and go."

The matriarch gave me another withering look.

I nudged Evyn. "Can you repeat what I just said?" I asked her.

Evyn frowned but did so, essaying the guttural sounds well enough to be understood.

The woman smiled widely. "At once, matriarch."

I glared at the table, counting slowly in Rushia.

The Assassin took everything in quickly. "Restorative for me, then." He pulled the Rushia headscarf out of his pocket. "Time to wear this."

"I should have thought of that." Evyn flushed. "Sorry."

He shook his head. "We were all rather concerned about the king's swordsman taking a hit to the face. I should have realised after those rogues were able to recognise me." His eyes squinted slightly from within the folds; perhaps he was smiling. "I wonder what headaches two Aubins can cause here."

Untold damage, no doubt. "Let's rouse Carreelee and be away."

We left soon after, a grumbling Carreelee shading her eyes against the sun bouncing off the snow. Layloree and the Assassin took the rear, while I scouted ahead through the oppressively cold morning. Leaves crunched in our path and snow came down in flurries, never sticking. We matched pace with Evyn as our slowest but sometimes I would go on ahead and come back to get warmer, pulling my hood tight and burying my neck in the deep fur lining.

At midmorning we came across a parcel of land being guarded by a formidable looking man with an axe and a huge beard. He got very excited when he saw me. "This is our road! Away with you!"

I waved. "My matriarch and group are passing through. Can we barter for lunch?"

The man bellowed back to the homestead. "Get Kaydee!"

I sighed and signalled back to the others. By the time they had reached me, another four men and a woman with long blond braids had come to the edge of the homestead. All of them relaxed when they saw Evyn.

"We're not a rogue band. We are trying to get to Keltskarr," I explained. "We won't be here long—"

"I want to fight him," the axeman bellowed, pointing at Shoulders. Neither Evyn nor Shoulders could understand him so all they saw was an angry man shouting and gesturing at him.

Shoulders put himself in front of Evyn and raised his fists.

I shook my head, standing firm in the path. "No, that's our matriarch's bodyguard. If you want to fight him you have to win against me first."

"If that is agreeable to your matriarch," one of the other men at Kaydee's side said.

She looked questioningly at Evyn, who peered out from behind Shoulders.

"Evyn, say 'Ja'," I called back to her.

"What am I agreeing to?" she asked suspiciously.

Layloree snorted.

I cracked my knuckles. "Big guy wants a fight. It's like a greeting here, it's how they take the measure of people. If I beat him, they'll give us favourable trade terms and let us pass."

"What sort of fight?"

"Unarmed. I think." I confirmed with Kaydee's spokesman. "Yes, unarmed, first one to hit the ground."

"And you're okay with that?"

"Evyn, when am I not happy about fighting someone?"

"Are you sure you aren't part Skienien?" the Assassin muttered.

"We accept. Let's get this done." I took off my jacket and rolled my shoulders, my muscles bunching, ready. How would this man fight? I looked forward to finding out.

The challenger threw off his fur coat to reveal a huge barrel of a chest and a meaty, hairy gut. He yelled and charged me.

*Disappointing.* I jumped to the side, grabbed one of his arms as he flew past, and twisted it back behind him. Shoving hard, I tripped him face first into the road, an easy win.

I dusted myself off and offered him my hand. He declined it, rolling to his feet and getting behind his fellows. I wasn't surprised: a defeat like that would put him straight to the bottom of his pack.

Kaydee's jaw was rather tight when she spoke. "Well, then. Oberrotians. I can give you information about the road ahead, depending on your destination?"

Layloree put her hand on Evyn's shoulder. "We're on the road north, we will be encountering Keltskarr next," the Battlemistress said carefully.

"Then I recommend you avoid it." Kaydee spat to the side, and her men followed her example. "This is a dark time, and all Skieniens will look back on it with shame. My advice is that you do not stop there. Reroute, go anywhere else."

Layloree bent closer to Evyn, translating the information. I paced back, rolling my shoulders. I wanted to know exactly what to expect in Keltskarr, but I would not be thanked for speaking up.

"My matriarch is grateful for the information," Layloree said. "Do you know Keltskarr well? What does the centre look like?"

Kaydee nodded once. "You can come in and take your lunch here, and I'll tell you."

While the Assassin negotiated a simple meal of bread and cooked chicken at their well-worn but pleasant enough household, Kaydee drew us a map, and Layloree asked where all the different districts were, marking each with small symbols as Kaydee went through the warehousing, entertainment and living sections. Truly Keltskarr had a mining focus with one main street as its spine, smaller streets breaking off like supporting ribs breathing life into the town. Kaydee talked readily enough but she seemed guarded, a stiffness to her posture especially when Evyn looked up at her.

After we took our leave, Evyn sidled next to me. "That was really generous of her, but she seemed a bit put out."

I snorted. "Of course she was. I beat her man so soundly that technically we could have requested him and she'd have given him to us."

"Mm. Well. I know you beat him fair and square, but... try not to flatten them so handily. Try to make it seem like a close thing. That way, they're more equal to you and their matriarch will just think it was luck of the day or something that meant her man lost. Then she won't be so upset that she was completely upstaged, because she'll save a bit of face."

"Your pardon, Evyn? In Skien, fighting skill is how everything is organised here," I reminded her.

"I think they are more subtle than that, and at least that there are nuances."

"Subtle and nuance are not words I would ever have thought would be applied to Skien. Evyn, do you know how hard it is to draw out a fight and appear to be losing and then suddenly win?"

She looked up at me with wide eyes. "It is probably really, really hard. I bet it takes more skill than just slamming them into the ground."

"Yes, it does."

"It would be more difficult. Needs careful handling and attention."

"Yes."

"It would be a real challenge."

"Mm."

"I bet even with your high level of skill, you would find it taxing," she mused. "You might lose. That's okay."

"Well, we'll see, shall we."

The Assassin started laughing a few paces ahead of us, the sound only slightly muffled by the headscarf. "Evyn, you're a fantastic matriarch. You've already got him marching to your tune."

"Thanks," she replied and smiled at him, a tinge of pride zinging through her. That boded well for her seeing Aubin again, if she could take a compliment from the Assassin without getting defensive, and my heart rose further.

This was going smoothly, even the rogue attack yesterday which had only really hurt me. Only the final obstacle to go, the one that I really had no plan in place to tackle. I steeled myself and marched onwards. *It will go well.*

It had to.

# CHAPTER 21

Carreelee joined me at the front, walking in lockstep with me as the path turned more beaten and hardened by constant use. We had passed no other groups, the traffic to and from Keltskarr strangled for now.

She was in her male form, towering over me. "Do you mind if I walk here, sir?"

"Not at all. You don't have to defer to me when we're in the group either," I reminded her.

Her moustaches bristled. "You're leading us, though."

"That's true, but you can speak your mind around me."

She cocked her head at me.

I continued, "Do you fare well? How do you feel, being back here?"

Waving dismissively at the landscape, she lowered her voice. "I am somewhat nervous, but I am also satisfied. I am bringing back a group of people ready to assist those who cannot assist themselves, thwarting the Hudau and Brudamere's lust for violence."

"Good." That was a satisfying emotion; to be condemned as a criminal and hounded, and then return triumphant with the rightful ruler still gave me a frisson of fulfilment and more than a little pleasure in that huge, *"I told you so."*

Emotions that were probably not what Special Forces, battered as it was, wanted or needed from me. I rubbed my sore nose, the ache from exposure to the biting cold. "Carreelee, can I ask you something?"

"Technically, anything." Her pace slowed slightly.

"How am I as a leader? You're outside of my usual chain of command, so I am hoping for that outsider's perspective." And she did not have experience of the last turn's worth of events to colour her opinion.

Carreelee rubbed her beard. "That's quite a vulnerability you've exposed to me. Thank you." Before I could explore that, she went on, "I've been trying out listening to a leader and it really isn't all that bad, as long as the person leading you isn't malicious. It's something of a relief to have someone helping make decisions. I have always been expected to want to collect as many men as possible, but it seems to me that you work to inspire loyalty rather than impose your will on us. You're willing to work with my powers rather than tell me how to use them."

I frowned. "Well... of course. I don't know everything you can do with them. An outsider can help identify things you haven't even thought of before, but as for everything you know, well, it would take me a literal lifetime to learn the same."

She clapped me on the back. "Wonderful. Now then, Keltskarr is over the hill. We will see it shortly and be there within a turn of the glass. Is there anything we need to go over?"

"Yes. Let's wait for the others."

We halted at the side of the hard-packed road and let the others catch up. Evyn took out her water skin from her pack, fingers too stiff to work the stopper. Shoulders looked like he was on the verge of ripping it apart to release the water for her, but the Assassin took it before I could and popped it open for her with the edge of his blades. Layloree looked scandalised, possibly at such misuse of the blades.

I greeted them. "Well met. Carreelee informs me that we'll soon be in the town."

Layloree nodded. "What's your plan, then?"

"I think we should split up," I said carefully.

"I'm not leaving Evyn," Shoulders protested.

"And I have to stay with Shoulders." The Assassin nodded to his friend.

I raised my hands in placation. "Then we will stay together. Layloree, Carreelee, do you need a man with you?"

Layloree snorted. "We are a perfect team, and Carreelee adapts to any situation anyways. Two women can go places, and two Skieniens together will not be noteworthy, whereas all the Oberrotians will attract questions. It's clear you're foreigners, which..." She tapped her cheek. "Actually makes sense. If there are Skieniens with you, it's slightly suspicious, because why would we have brought you here? Stupid stumbling soft Oberrotians coming here all oblivious, that's normal." She nodded firmly.

"Should we separate now, then? And how will we stay in contact?"

Layloree gave me a withering look. "Mistress Tuniel gave me lodestones. You take the partner of mine, and we'll stay in contact. We should probably separate now, so me and Carreelee can come in later." She leant backward, completely one with the hostile surroundings, comfortable in the discomforts it offered.

Carreelee made a show of looking about us, twisting her head right around on her neck to do so. My stomach pitched, the lack of contents the only barrier preventing me from dishonouring myself. Satisfied we were alone, she shivered and melted into the squat mage, her long red braid twining around her head. "Be off with you," she ordered, folding her arms to match Layloree.

"If you're sure. If you get into difficulties, tell us, we will come to your aid."

Her lips twitched. "First one to find Tabreksson will get their beers bought for them by the other group."

I grinned. "Done."

Layloree drew one of her Battlemistress blades and held it out to Evyn. "Take this."

Evyn glanced at me, then shook her head. "What for, Layloree? This is your weapon. Half of it, anyway, and I cannot use it."

I agreed. "It's not sized for her." Looking at the length of the blade that curved backwards over the wielder's arm, I could see immediately that Evyn's shorter forearm meant the tip of the blade would interfere with the bend of her arm.

Layloree smiled. "You are right that a weapon for you would be forged to your arm; the length, the strength, the angle, the wrist. All blades are unique, and all have names, a history. A Battlemistress sings their glorious stories as she fights, bringing the previous victories onward, adding to them in an unbreaking chain." She paused, running a finger down the bloodletting patterns. "Oberrotians may not know, the blades are never defeated. Should a blade be turned aside, be cast down, should its wielder fall.... Then it has retired itself. No matter its pedigree, a retired blade must be sheathed forever." She held it out to Evyn. "It will stay with you to ensure the success of your goal. You will not fail with this at your side."

Evyn took it by the patterned grip on the hilt, which was so old it was nearly worn down to the metal. "I'll give this back to you when we regroup, if you're certain about this."

Layloree inclined her head. "Of course I'm certain, I would not say anything otherwise. Now go, we are parting for a day at most, it's not like we will never see each other again."

Saluting, I picked up my gear and helped Evyn situate her blade with a strap on her forearm. We walked down the road, the Assassin in front, Evyn, Shoulders and I walking in tandem. "Well, look at that. Now Evyn is a Battlemistress matriarch."

Evyn nudged me. "This isn't a jolly, Thorrn, we are trying to find Aubin so he can hand over being a conduit for the refugees to Oberrot and we can check he's alright." Her wind-slapped face was already red on the edges I could see, so I wasn't sure whether she was blushing at all, but that pendulum swing between anger and pining set up again.

I touched the soreness on my head. "I am taking this seriously. I'm relieved he is alive and apparently at large."

"So am I. I just don't know how on board I am with dragging him back by his ears if he won't come with us of his own free will," she said.

"Never fear, I will drag him by his ears or otherwise into another world to help my Evie," the Assassin said, his tone light, but there was a jerkiness to his motions.

The town quickly appeared, nestled in the dip of a valley with scores of homes tracking up along the swell of the hill beyond. The mine would have been the seed that started the town, winning ore that Skienien merchants traded to Oberrot for food and Skienien artisans turned into weapons. Beautiful weapons, really; even the axes and hammers had carvings and insignias in them.

"I should have asked Layloree if the weapons here act like our tattoos, identifying the person who holds them."

"Or at least the current holder, it sounded like," Evyn mused, touching the hilt of the blade. "I can barely use bracers, I'm not ready for blades."

I nodded at the fair, if downhearted, assessment. I was a novice with the blades myself, and Aubin had not had time to give lessons. We had been busy tracking down Liara and helping free Evyn from the Rushia spirits, and I had hoped to learn over the last sennights while we worked to track her down.

A missed opportunity, one that would not happen again.

We reached Keltskarr at quarterday. Already the sun was setting and icy winds started to blast up, so I was eager to enter the walls to get out of the path of the weather at least. That proved futile, as the streets seemed to encourage the wind to blow harder and in concentrated straight lines. In Rush they had done the same, but there it served a purpose for cooling; here, perhaps it served the purpose of raising hardy men and women who could withstand to walk against such a gale every day.

The guard posts were manned, literally, with three men in grey glowering over us, fearsome axes in hand. Up on the walls I caught a flash of green, a lighter shade to the green of the Regs in Oberrot, and met the eyes of a Battlemistress with brown braids either side of her hard face.

The men glanced up at her as well. They would be the Footsoldiers, their version of the Regulars, with the Battlemistress their commander and an elite fighter in her own right.

She looked to Evyn and the blade at her belt, gaze still raking hard over me and Shoulders especially, and held up a hand. My heartrate accelerated. The men barred our path, hefting their axes, and we waited in silence while the Battlemistress came down from the battlements.

I put my hand on Evyn's shoulder. "It's going to be alright—"

"No talking!" one of the men said.

Evyn patted my hand, then deliberately slid it off. She took a step forward as the Battlemistress emerged from the gates.

The woman looked her up and down, then beckoned one of her men to stand next to her, tapping her foot while he jogged up to her.

He turned and raised his voice. "Battlemistress Urodee wants you to state your business."

*We couldn't just be asked a simple question like that?*

The Assassin stepped next to Evyn. "We're traders from Oberrot. We're looking for new suppliers, and now is the time. No other Oberrotian merchants around to compete with."

*Yes, because they are scared away by the unrest.* I shifted my weight.

The Battlemistress folded her arms, murmuring to her man, her eyes growing harder.

The man slammed the hilt of his axe into the frozen ground. "Oberrotian trader with a Battlemistress blade, a Rushia and two men who walk like Oberrotian soldiers." The woman hissed something. The man's glare turned to me. "An Oberrotian soldier with an Oberrotian officer blade."

I wrapped my hand around the hilt of my father's sword. Not only Skienien blades had a history to proclaim, it seemed.

Evyn caught the exchange, and that it centred on me. "Assassin, what's she saying?"

"She's suspicious that you have a medley, and of Thorrn's sword in particular."

She nodded, lips firm. "What if we tell her I trade in rare gems and can afford the best?" She motioned to her backpack, being carried by Shoulders. "We've got all those charging jewels in there as proof."

The Assassin pulled an ingratiating smile into place to speak to the Battlemistress's spokesman. "My mistress is a trader with an eye for the rare and exceptional. We are her bodyguards, and we each have different skills drawn from our various backgrounds to be able to cope with any challenge we might encounter on our travels."

The Battlemistress's eyes narrowed. "Did you buy that?" she barked, thrusting her chin at Layloree's blade.

I had a feeling she would take offence if Evyn said yes, but I couldn't communicate that to her. The Assassin had stepped forward as spokesman, and I had to stand here like a good man.

Evyn had that translated, then replied, "No, it was lent by a good friend."

"Lent?" The woman chewed her torn and bloodied lips. "Then you have the favour of at least one Battlemistress on your travels. Can any of you wield magic?"

"No," the Assassin answered.

"Good. I cannot tell, but there are magic sniffers in town who will find you out if you are lying, and that will go poorly for you. Come in then, exceptional Oberrotian. If your men cause trouble we will look to you for reparation."

Evyn swept past, as regal as the queen if Ellesmere had ever worn so many furs and waddled as a result. I increased my pace to draw up next to her. "Very well done."

"Thanks." She smiled up at me. "I drew a lot on thinking that we would be able to adapt to get through it somehow. That was kind of... fun, in a heart-pounding, 'I might get found out any second' kind of way." Excitement and pride fizzled through her.

"Any heartbeat here, Evyn," I reminded her gently. "Now, then, let's be on our guard. We have to survey the merchant quarter now, but that'll be where the warehouses are, and I wager that if there's a hiding place for a group of people that do not want to be found, that's where they'll be."

"Too obvious," the Assassin said. "Let's look there, but I doubt another me would overlook the fact that it's the most logical place to hide people."

"Very well," I returned, a little stiffly, but Evyn put a soothing hand on my arm.

The merchant and warehousing district were empty, the stores boarded up and bands of Footsoldiers marching in between the rows, scuffing up the snow to be as miserable a grey as their uniforms.

"Everyone's fled." Evyn touched the edges of my furs so I would know where she was. "It must be really bad."

"Yes. We need to get to the other areas of the town, before we look suspicious out here on the outskirts. We need to pretend to look for accommodation and then entertainment, so we'll head for the town square."

The Assassin drew level with me. "Be careful," he said in Skienien. "The town square is where hangings will be held."

My breath caught in my throat. We couldn't separate from Evyn; not only did I want her near to protect her, but I couldn't wander around on my own.

I could with another man, though.

"Well?" The Assassin sidled closer.

"Damn and blast, not again," I muttered. "Let's see if we can observe anything distressing from a distance. If there is, we'll leave Evyn and Shoulders at a halfway decent inn and do some reconnaissance ourselves."

"Because that isn't rude," Evyn said, scowling at me. "What were you talking about? I definitely heard my name."

My steps slowed as we reached the concourse to the town square. "There might be executions here, Evyn. We didn't want to subject you to that without warning."

"Oh." Her eyes pinched. "That's considerate of you, but please don't make any plans without consulting me. We need to stick together."

"Yes, matriarch," the Assassin said with a laugh. He scanned the streets ahead. "I can't see anything in the square." Jolting, he turned to face an alleyway, completely still with shock.

"What is it?" I said, drawing my father's sword and coming beside him. I had never seen him act like that before.

In the alleyway was a grubby boy, black hair drawn back in a braid. Pale blue eyes stared balefully out from his dirty face.

"Oh, nothing. He startled me, that's all." The Assassin took another step back. "We... I..." He took hold of Evyn's arm.

She shrugged him off. "What's the matter?"

"I... nothing."

I looked between them. "Do you know this boy?"

"Never met a Rushia in my life," the boy volunteered in Skienien. He could understand some Oberrotian at least. He crept a little closer to the opening of the alleyway. "What's a Rushia and some 'Rotians doing out here, hm?"

I sheathed my father's sword. The boy wasn't a threat. "None of your business."

"Oh, how about I make it my business? I know everything and everyone in Keltskarr, even with all the changes what have turned it all around. Breathed a bit of energy into Keltskarr, I reckon. The Hudau moving in has been good in some ways, not so good in others." The boy spoke fast, one foot turned to run back deeper into the alley but a wide smile for us. "So, what are you looking for?"

"What's in it for you?" I asked.

The boy shrugged. "You give me a few rubles for saving you some trouble, and if you were looking for recommendations, the places I recommend might give me a ruble or two in thanks. It's the normal way of doing business, right?" He hooked his thumbs in his threadbare waistband. His boots were mismatched, one brown and one black, and looked to be different sizes.

I put my hand on our pouch of rubles in my pocket. "Are you looked after?"

Eyes narrowed slightly, his gaze darted to Evyn. "What, like, a matriarch? No thanks, I am my own man." He rapped his chest with a hollow sound.

"It's not time for this. I mean, we don't have time for this," the Assassin hissed in Oberrotian.

I shook my head at him. I was the spokesman now, even if it was for some poor waif. "I hesitate to ask this of you, but are there any executions on display in the town square, or anywhere in Keltskarr?"

His face dropped. "No, no, nothing like that. Just the rope waiting for the Oberrotian helper." He frowned at the Assassin's head covering.

I fought the urge to grab the boy by the shirt. "What do you mean, waiting for him?" My heart surged in my chest. Had Aubin been apprehended? Was he on his way to the gallows?

"Yeah, the leader of the Hudau, Brudamere, he made a big show of offering rubles for information leading to the capture of the Oberrotian nuisance spiriting away all the magic users. There's a rope up there ready to snap his neck as soon as Brudamere gets his hands on him." The boy tilted his head. "If it is a he. Some say the helper is a woman." He tilted his head the other way. "What do you think?"

His big blue eyes were earnest. "I think... that we're looking for a certain Oberrotian. Do you really know everyone in Keltskarr?"

The boy nodded firmly. "And everyone knows me. I've got nicknames from everyone in town, some are just kinder than others." He flashed his teeth in a grin. "First I'll need some rubles to help jog my memory of all the 'Rotians I know that haven't fled yet."

I dug out several, dropping them into his hand one by one. "He has tawny hair, light eyes, might fight using Battlemistress blades—"

"Oh, yeah, I know that gent." The boy stared at the three rubles in his hand. Back at the castle I didn't even need to carry rubles around, my tattoos were enough to requisition supplies and receive a meal as well as move around freely. Three rubles was worth a meal in the city, but the boy cradled the coins as though I'd handed him a largesse.

The boy shoved the rubles into his pockets and walked with a swagger up the road. "You want to come this way. Follow me."

"Say goodbye to your rubles," the Assassin murmured as I passed him.

"Even if that does happen, he needs them more than me."

We kept together, Shoulders and Evyn walking in lockstep, the Assassin and I on alert. The boy seemed comfortable enough, walking at a fast clip even in the snow, but he slowed at corners and junctions to wait for us.

Now there were more people, groups of large men with a woman somewhere in their centre. We were not the biggest group by any means; I counted eight surrounding one woman, who all bristled as we passed, axes and hammers to hand. They all seemed to be heading in the same direction as we were.

"Where are we going?" I called to the boy.

"Best place in Keltskarr. Beer is good value, beef is plentiful and the view is the best, though I wouldn't know about that last bit." He grinned widely, showing the points of his white teeth.

We turned down another street to find it busy. Hawkers stood outside bars trying to get customers to come in out of the cold, convincing them to warm up with beer, bread, beef or breasts. Some places offered entertainment in the form of fighting: cage matches, bouts, arm wrestling, normal wrestling, naked wrestling, it could all be found in Skien.

The boy led us up several streets, stumbling into a district that looked a little more unkempt. Rats raided the rubbish heaps on the side of the street and the lank air stank of urine, sweat and blood.

I halted immediately. "No, we aren't going down there."

"It's just a little further." The boy headed straight for a hoarse man hawking the delights of the beaten-down bar he was beholden to.

The man's lip curled and he shooed the boy away, but then he leant down as the boy explained something.

Eyes sharp, the hawker beckoned to me. "You look like you can spot a bargain when you see one! Mistress Desoree's bar has good clean fun and bad nasty fights!"

I frowned at the boy. "We're not interested in that." Not right now, in any case, as a Skienien bar was fun in its own way. The name Desoree was familiar. Where had I heard it before?

The man stretched his gloved hands forward eagerly, addressing Evyn and the Assassin directly. "We have the special on tonight!"

"We said we are not interested," the Assassin said.

The man stared at his headscarf. "Ah, wait, you're Oberrotian! You're so tiny, I thought you were a woman."

The Assassin folded his arms. "Yep, thanks, definitely a man, goodbye now." He waved at me to lead the way.

The hawker stood. "Wait, what are you looking for? Maybe I can help you." The man's voice changed from loud and brash to quiet. "You want a death bar?"

I glared at him. "No." Death bars were illegal in Skien as in Oberrot, the participants battling to kill each other for the enjoyment of the bloodthirsty patrons.

The man smiled widely. "Good, because Desoree doesn't hold with that either. Tell me, friend, what are you after?" His gaze held mine, teary in the cold.

Why were we here? The boy had led us here for a reason, and

now he stood at my side, hand in his pocket and shifting from foot to foot, looking between me and the hawker. Could Aubin be inside?

How could I ask without giving him away? "I'm looking for my friend. He's an Oberrotian, about the same height as him." I pointed to the Assassin. "Tawny hair, light eyes."

The man's face cracked into a laugh. "That sounds exactly like our special. He's an Oberrotian like you, he fights in the cage and he's good for the whole night! Takes on bout after bout, you've never seen anything like this! Come inside! Come and watch!" He looked at the blade at Evyn's forearm. "Tell your matriarch this, it's hilarious: the Oberrotian fancies himself a Battlemistress Blade Master!"

"Your pardon?" My heartrate accelerated.

"I know! He fights with them all night, never letting up. It's a good show, I promise you!"

"It's him," I hissed to the others. "An Oberrotian with Battlemistress blades, it has to be. He's in here."

# CHAPTER 22

"Wʜᴀᴛ's ʜᴇ ᴅᴏɪɴɢ ɪɴ ᴀ ʙᴀᴛᴛʟᴇ ʙᴀʀ?" ᴛʜᴇ Aꜱꜱᴀꜱꜱɪɴ ꜱᴀɪᴅ ɪɴ ᴅɪꜱɢᴜꜱᴛ.

"Battling, apparently. Come on!" I marched forward, flipping another ruble to the boy. "My thanks!"

He snatched the ruble out of the air and ran. The hawker stared after him, smile fixed as he waved us all in.

Two guards at the door gave each of us a searching stare but made no move to pat us down. Roars and cheering surged from behind a curtain at their backs, and I craned my head to catch a glimpse through a gap. What was Aubin doing, letting everyone know he fought using the blades? People were advertising it outside! It was a wonder the Hudau hadn't caught up with him already.

A woman sat behind the desk, riffling her long fingernails through stacks of rubles. "A score each," she grunted in Oberrotian.

"Each?" I gaped.

She squinted up at me. "Each. You want in or not?"

The men barring the door shifted their weight, hands straying toward the short hammers at their belts.

"In, then." I hefted my rubles bag, significantly slacker than before. "Damn and blast, that boy robbed me!"

"Do you have enough?" Evyn asked. "Let's just get in there." Her impatience and mine fused together into an almost unbearable ache radiating up from my chest to my jaw.

"Fine," I grumbled. "But if I see that lad again..."

"Doesn't he need it more than you?" Shoulders asked, hunkering lower next to Evyn.

Usually I would swear at someone throwing that back in my face, but Shoulders spoke so infrequently that instead I patted his back. "You're right, of course."

The woman took an excruciatingly long time to count the rubles, during which the hawker slid past us and into the main room, a resounding cheer managing to get through. It was going to be loud inside. I shucked off my furs and helped Evyn with hers, her arms shaking as she pulled them free.

"It's going to be alright," I said.

She rubbed her arms, her silvrine bracers shining in the dim light. "Sure, yes, let's get in there."

The woman gave us a jerk of her head. "Go through. If any of them cause any issues, we'll be after you, matriarch."

"Got it. You guys behave," Evyn said, taking the lead.

We hustled into a three-storey room, immediately blasted with hot air, a scrum of men hooting and hollering, and bare-breasted women serving drinks and food.

"What. The Hell," Evyn said.

I scrubbed my hair. How to explain. "Ah, yes, so, this is a battle bar and it's... it's not a place for Oberrotian ladies." I tried to control the rising heat of my face and failed.

Evyn turned a disgusted look onto me. She looked very much like her mother. "Why are they topless?" she ground out between her teeth.

"Battle bars are run by real retired Battlemistresses. She will be at the top somewhere... There she is, see?" I pointed at the top level where a grey-haired woman prowled the top deck. "She has nasty blades in her holsters, the Twell blades, all serrated edges which hurt more coming out than they do going in. All the women working here *want* to work for her, and they can choose to go topless. It entertains, it's seen as harmless fun, but if anyone touches, those Twell blades will come out and cut off the offender's hand and... well, other parts." I resisted the urge to slip into a defensive stance at the thought.

"The fight cage is in the centre," the Assassin yelled in my ear. "Also, I don't like the way the hawker and guards were acting. Something is very wrong here."

Apart from Aubin being in a battle bar? This noisy crush of an environment was the very last place I ever expected to find Aubin. "Right. Let's get to it."

We had to wade through a forest of giants, each as wide and tall as me if not more so, all festooned in furs and talking, shouting, laughing, betting and drinking. Evyn tried to move through first, tentatively touching furry backs and saying, "Excuse me." I bulled forward, moving men out of her way, and no one seemed to care when I pushed or eased them to one side to let Evyn pass.

Behind her, Shoulders clung onto Evyn's arms and guarded the rear. He was on extreme alert, red faced and swallowing rapidly. A man staggered into Evyn's path, earning himself glares and growls.

"Peace," I shouted to Shoulders over the noise. "Just make sure they don't accidentally jostle her."

"What's going on?" Being at the level of everyone's chest, Evyn couldn't see.

I waved over the jumping crowd ahead. "There's a cage in the middle of the bar and that's where the fights are taking place. The cage is open at the top, see, so it's actually to keep the audience out rather than trap participants in."

"And they're, what, fighting?"

"Yes."

"Unarmed?"

"Depends on the battle bar," the Assassin supplied. "There are blood battle bars around."

Evyn's eyes darted to me, then away. "Well, come on then, time's wasting." Underneath my chest I felt an unmanageable twisting, the angle of how I wanted to react to him changing. Would I greet him cordially or smash him across the mouth? I didn't know.

I took hold of Evyn's other hand, holding on tight. If I didn't know then she wouldn't either, but only together would we weather this encounter.

Our group slowly made its way toward the cage through the loud oppressive crowd. Surveying it, the bottom of the cage was on a lower level with metal bars reaching up to this level and beyond to the next. Everything smelled like booze and meat, furs pressing on all sides as men leant against the bars to see, rubles changing hands rapidly, bets being made and pundits shouting encouragement or condemnation.

I shoved my shoulders into a gap created when one man leant back to shout something in his friend's face, and I craned my neck to peer in.

We had arrived mid-bout, a girl with blades drawn circling her opponent. She looked to be a young Battlemistress, probably not fully blooded. This would be good practice for her to get used to the sounds of a crowd and battle.

Her opponent had his back to me; still and patient while she paced.

She darted forward, and his blades came up to meet hers with a clash. He shoved her, back muscles standing out, and the force set her staggering. Catching her balance, she whirled, hooking his leg with her foot and jerking it out from under him. He went down on one knee and she brought her blades down in a wide arc.

Raising his forearm to block, he held on to his knife only with the strength of his white-knuckled fingers, then shoved her away again with a powerful thrust.

She retreated, panting, and rapped on the side of the cage. The crowd cheered as she flipped her hair over her shoulder and left the arena.

Aubin turned in a slow circle, looking up at the supporters baying and booing at him.

"Is there another challenger for the Blade Master?" the announcer called. "Here's one: Battlemistress Baylee!"

Bellows and screams went up from the drunk men on either side of us as a blonde came into the cage, blowing kisses to all around her.

Aubin let her play to the crowd while he guzzled water, his chest heaving. He had gained muscle since I saw him last, his chest and shoulders prominent and marked with red slashes, bruises and scrapes turning parts of his olive skin shades of black, brown and blue. He moved carefully, every step balanced and ready.

"Well?" Evyn asked me in a yell.

I shouted back, "It's him. And he is *hot*."

"What?"

"He's on fire!"

Evyn went white. "What?" A spike of fear lanced into my heart from her.

"Yes? No, I mean, my apologies, isn't that what you say when something is particularly spectacular?"

Evyn lunged up to grab hold of my collar. "Thorrn, is he on fire? Is he alive?"

"Yes, he's getting his ass kicked by trainee Battlemistresses." Turning, I held her up to see, and the Assassin and Shoulders elbowed and outright shoved their way over to huddle at the bars.

Evyn's eyes widened as we watched Aubin face off against a fresh Battlemistress. This one had maybe a turn of experience, so she toyed with him. The crowd screamed with delight as she spun, slashing out with her blades into a whirl of peril.

Aubin jumped back, the blades missing his stomach by a hair's breadth. He waited for an opening and then struck without hesitation, shoving the side of his blades into her guard and kicking her backwards.

She tumbled and laughed as she rolled, then collected her blades and rapped the side of the cage to be let out, to the roars and cheers of the men surrounding us.

"Well. Now I am feeling all sorts of strange things," the Assassin said.

Evyn curled her hands around the bars, pressing her face close against the metal. The fear earlier had swept all that uncomfortable uncertainty aside for now at least, leaving space for a kind of stillness. Relief pooled into me.

He was alive, he looked well, but while I would absolutely enjoy what he was doing, he did not seem to be. There was a savagery to his motions that had not been there before, and he was either tired or hurting, because he was holding himself too stiff.

I opened my arms to let Evyn slide back down to the floor. "Well, we've found him at least."

Evyn scowled. "Why is he here, where people are advertising him, when outside there's a noose waiting for his neck?"

"All Aubins have a death wish," the Assassin said readily. "Some are more prominent than others."

Shoulders wiped his sweaty forehead. "Let's get his attention and get him out of there."

I tapped the bars. "He's going to be there all night, the hawker said. I'll get his attention; I'll get in there with him." I rubbed my hands.

"I'll stay here to watch," the Assassin said. "Gods' luck getting back through that press."

Shoving our way through the heaving crowd back to the stairs took what felt like a quarter turn of the glass. Again and again new opponents were announced for the Blade Master, each of them taking him on to trade a few blows before tapping out, it seemed. I marked where each of the guards were – at least the men I assumed were guards, given that they had their backs to the wall and were not drinking and laughing. I caught their eyes more often than not; I had definitely attracted their attention. I steadied my breaths. *We have to get to him as fast as we can.*

Downstairs it was even noisier, filled with challengers laughing, talking, practising and cheering at the bars of the cage. At least it was mostly women warming up with a few of their attendant men, so I could see over their heads. The women cast their eyes over our group and then nodded to Evyn, who nodded back.

"The announcer is over there." I pointed to a tall and grizzled Skienien standing next to one of the entrances to the cage.

"Well, then? Go ask him," Evyn said.

I smiled. "Yes, matriarch."

I walked over and tapped the announcer on the shoulder. "I want in next."

He looked me up and down with a snort. "It's not ladies' night, no one wants to see man-on-man brawls here. You'll have to wait until that 'Rotian gets tired, and he don't leave until he gets blooded."

I bristled. "Is he coerced to stay in there?"

"What? No! He's having a great—"

Aubin's bare back slammed into the bars beside us.

Evyn shrieked, and I swore.

Aubin spat to the side and collected himself, darting back into the fight, not registering us at all.

"—time," the announcer finished. "Look, you can be on tomorrow, unless he's taken the freak slot then."

"Freak slot?"

"Out-of-town entertainment. Something new." He looked me up and down. "You're an Oberrotian soldier. What, they chasing you all out like we do to magic users here, only in reverse?"

I backed away. "Nevermind. I want to speak to him."

"You, or your matriarch?" The man tipped his head to Evyn. "If she's wanting to speak to him, he isn't interested. There have been a few ladies hoping to tame and claim him, feed him up and give him a warm home. He isn't looking for that." He jerked his head up at the very top deck.

I followed his gaze up through the bars of the ring. From her vantage point at the top level, the silvrine-haired Battlemistress stared down at me, tapping the tops of her Twell blades. Her gaze never wavered from me.

We had definitely caught her attention, but how? Was it just because we were Oberrotian?

I turned back to the announcer. "When does he usually stop and leave the ring?"

"Give it a few turns of the glass before he crashes out." The announcer grinned at me.

I took a few steps back from the ring with Evyn and Shoulders. "They are only letting ladies in to fight, and he will be here for a while. Perhaps we should—"

Aubin crashed into the bars again. He faced a big red-haired woman swinging a huge hammer.

"Watch it! Stop throwing him around!" I yelled. "Is she trying to kill him?"

Aubin rubbed his head, scanning the crowd above him. For good or for ill, he didn't look over his shoulder to see me, and the woman swung at him, forcing him to focus on her.

Relief that he had reacted warred with irritation. Why was he letting himself be tossed around in a fighting ring? "I don't want to accidentally distract him and get him hammered into the ground. Let's go back to the Assassin and regroup."

I led us onward, pushing and shoving a way back toward the stairs. When I turned around, I saw only Shoulders following me.

He frowned.

"All hale and well?" I asked him.

He peered around me. "Where's Evyn?"

My stomach clenched. "She's with you!"

His eyes widened. "She said she wanted to walk with you!"

"No, I thought she was with you!" The floor heaved with people, and Evyn was short enough to be at their elbows. "I'll quarter this whole area, you guard the stairs, nothing in or out, got it?"

He nodded, lips white, but then the announcer cried, "Another new challenger for the Blade Master, and this one hails from the sunny shores of Tergue Hall. Two Oberrotians locked in a cell together! Who will come out on top? The Blade Master who fancies himself expert with the weapon of the women, or this Oberrotian Blade Bracer Mistress? Everyone give it up for... Evyn!"

I choked. "What?"

With a cry, Shoulders waded straight through to the bars, knocking Skieniens flying, but the cell door clanged shut as we got there.

I heaved at it. "Open this up! Open it up right now!" I screamed.

The announcer shook his head, and the other challengers pulled my arms back. I twisted round, blood surging ready to fight, when I caught sight of Evyn.

Evyn walked purposefully into the ring, her short sleeves baring the delicate bracers spreading all the way up her forearms to the elbows. Their wicked edge gleamed under the bright light of the glowstones. My heart thundered in my chest. A thrum of excitement hummed between us, a spark of sharp anticipation.

Aubin recovered at the other side of the cell, drinking in between harsh, laboured breaths. He put his waterskin down to face his next opponent, lifting his fists in preparation.

They lowered as he met Evyn's eyes. His jaw went slack, eyes widening and lips parting.

Evyn took a few steps into the centre of the cage where the light was brightest. She waved to him.

He did not return it. He stood rigid at the side of the ring, fixed in place as though she had rendered him into stone.

"Well? Come on then!" The crowd started baying and whistling.

Shoulders rattled the bars of the door, tugging at it, the muscles in his arms standing out like cords.

"Hi, Aubin," Evyn said. Over the noise I couldn't hear her clearly, but my mouth moved in tandem with hers. We were one in this moment. "How have you been?"

He pressed his lips closed. Bitter pain flashed across his face, lips curling in a sneer.

Drawing his blade along the skin of his forearm, he made a shallow cut. Turning his back to Evyn, he slammed the hilt of the blade against the opposite door. The assistant there opened it and Aubin strode out, and with every step our feelings flared into anger. Aubin did not even glance backwards.

Evyn turned her head to search me out. Tears threatened to spill over at the corners of her eyes. He was leaving her again, turning away without even giving her a chance to speak. Resentment surged through me, hers and mine.

I beckoned her closer to me, but the announcer shouted, "The Blade Master tags out! Who now will be the challenger for this girl from Tergue Hall? It's Maresmere the Magnificent!"

"Finally!" A huge lumbering man pushed through the open door, a monster of a man lifting his double-handed sword. "Have at it, my lady!" he yelled with delight.

"Evyn! Ping out now!" I ordered. She couldn't ping, she'd be run out of town, the entire bar would accuse us of being magic users and fight us, but it was better than facing this man alone.

Evyn took a step back from the huge man and then raised her small fists in front of her face.

I screamed. "No, don't! Don't hit her, don't, she doesn't know how to fight!"

With a huge yell, the man brought his sword up above his head and prepared to swing down. The blow would cleave her in two if she didn't move.

"Evyn!"

Someone dropped from the ceiling and landed on the man's shoulders. He overbalanced, toppling forward. The Assassin rode Maresmere to the ground and leapt off lightly in front of Evyn, hands raised to put her behind him.

With a huge scream, the cell door beside me ripped from its

hinges, Shoulders throwing it aside and charging in. Other challengers immediately spilled in behind him.

Maresmere laughed. "Now this is a fight!"

I shoved and punched my way in to Evyn and the Assassin. "Let's get out of here."

The Assassin grabbed Shoulders. My alt reared around, ready to punch, but desisted when he saw us. He gathered Evyn up, crushing her to his chest.

"It's Battle Royale time!" the announcer yelled happily as the cage filled with challengers streaming into the open door.

We shoved and pushed and hit our way against the tide, finally getting free and panting to one side of the cage.

"Are you alright? Are you alright?" Shoulders kept asking Evyn.

"She won't be shortly," I growled. "Evyn, of all the—"

"I knew he wouldn't hurt me. I wasn't expecting him to just leave. Again." The shock in her voice halted my tirade.

I touched her hand, feeling our bond renew in a moment of shared pain. *We are being rejected again.* Fury flared, grating against my nerves. *How dare he just walk away from her like that!*

She pushed her feelings to one side, the sensation of her emotions dimming akin to when she shielded, pulling away from the bond. *It's not my fault this time, Aubin's making her hurt, and she's trying to protect me.*

I worked to breathe through the anger rather than reach out to grab her, but it was too much, the edges of my vision dimming. "Evyn, this is hard for both of us. Please don't pull away from the bond, I want us to work together."

She scowled at me. "You're pulling away too, you know. It's like you're keeping our anger away from me when I really, really want to just be angry. Sometimes you need a bit of righteous rage, and this is definitely the time."

No, not rage, not here. My arms shook with the effort of keeping them still. "I might kill someone. Evyn, help me."

That seemed to wake her from her wrath, opening fully. "Oh, Thorrn, I'm sorry."

I nodded, wiping my face. "Let's calm down and get out of here. The proprietress will probably blame us for this riot." Once I could trust myself to walk, I took Evyn's hand.

The cage heaved with men, furs, weapons and delighted shouts. The sounds of glorious fighting faded only slightly as we ascended the stairs, the clashes and clangs, joyous yells and screams of delight ringing round the room.

"They are a bit wild, aren't they, Skieniens," Evyn said.

That was an understatement. "Yes. Yes they are." I headed for the exit.

The guards came in from outside, blocking our path with a glower. Behind us, three men obstructed the stairs, and the guards ringing the room stepped forward, axes and hammers in their hands.

I pulled Evyn behind me, Shoulders and the Assassin immediately turning to make a ring around her.

I tried a smile. "Oh. About the, uh, melee downstairs. We can pay for repairs." I'd have to ask Gough to send more rubles.

"I am not concerned about that." The Battlemistress's steps flowed down the stairs, silvrine hair in a tight coil around her head. She drew her Twell blades. "Get the woman. I have some questions for her."

My heartbeat accelerated as the men all took a deliberate step toward us. Nine, and all with hammers and axes, bludgeoning weapons that were hard for a swordsman to turn aside.

The Battlemistress's harsh gaze landed on me. "Kill the men."

# CHAPTER 23



The man closest to me raised his hammer and I drew my father's sword, swinging wide to keep him at bay. If he got close to me with that weapon, I would be hard-pressed to block, but if I dodged, he might hit Evyn or one of the alts. My heart beat steady and true, but my stomach clenched. We were in a very tight situation and I couldn't see any way out. I would have to take lives. I sank into an attack stance, ready to spring forward.

"Stop!" Aubin pushed the men at the stairs aside, moving unhindered through them to get to the Battlemistress.

She held up her hand. Her men paused, gaze darting to her for orders.

"What is this, Tabreksson?" she asked.

Aubin sucked in breaths, winded, words tumbling out of him. "They are allies, Battlemistress. I ask that you don't hurt them."

Desoree's lips pinched. "They were asking questions about you, trying to find you. I thought they worked for Brudamere. I did not know they were your friends." With a curt nod to her men, she said, "Leave them."

The men lowered their weapons, and I sheathed mine in turn. Sweat trickled down between my shoulder blades, tracking over my scars. That was close.

I grabbed Evyn's hand, glaring at Aubin. "You took your sweet time! Where did you go, off for a walk?"

He folded his arms across his bare chest. "I had to leave to intercept Battlemistress Desoree. She springs this trap on anyone who comes looking for me. I would have got here sooner but someone—" He gave me a withering look. "—started a riot."

"It wasn't actually me this time, it was Evyn," I grumbled.

Battlemistress Desoree set her hands on her hips. "Forgive me, friends," she said, speaking Oberrotian. She appraised us all briefly, but especially Evyn. "Are you their matriarch?"

Evyn shifted her feet. "In a way, yes."

The Assassin slid his blades home. "She keeps us in line and shows us how it's done, especially cage fighting."

The Battlemistress cocked her head at Evyn, glancing at Aubin beside her. A smile spread across her weathered face. "You defeated the Blade Master."

Aubin choked at that.

Evyn frowned. "No. He quit and left."

"He still lost to you." She nodded slowly. "I want you to take him away. He's been good for Keltskarr and my business, but I am not a death bar. He has the look of a man who needs a matriarch, or else he'll splinter himself on the rocks."

"I am standing right here." Aubin screwed his hands into fists.

Desoree waved him away. "You don't know what's best for you. Go with your friends, talk, eat, plan and call on my resources if you need them, but I want you gone by sunrise."

The tone of the order had Aubin nodding once, gaze skittering away from us. "Come on then." He jerked his head to the steps leading upstairs and led the way.

Desoree watched after him. "I didn't know he had friends."

"Yes, he does," I said as Evyn said, "Sort of."

We stared at each other.

I lowered my voice. "Evyn, we have to get him out of here. He's in danger."

Her cheeks flushed. "Yes, we will, no problem, but I'm still mad at him, and I'm still allowed to be mad at him." She tossed her hair back. "So come on, let's talk."

With that she turned on her heel and stomped up the stairs.

We walked past Desoree to follow. Shoulders slowed as he passed the formidable Battlemistress. "I... I'm sorry about your door."

"Hm? Oh, that's nothing. It usually gets ripped off once a night."

"Skieniens," I muttered.

We made our way to the upper level. It was quieter here above the noise, more exclusive. A few parties of women surrounded by their men ate and drank their fill, only paying minimal attention to the fight below. I saw both the blonde and the red-headed Battlemistresses ensconced with their men, huge heaping plates of meat in front of them, all eating with gusto.

Pressed back in a dingy corner sat a chipped circular table over-loaded with platters of meat and several dirty glass tankards of foaming beer. Aubin sat alone, still shirtless with his back to us, facing the wall. He ate with both hands, ripping meat directly from the bone.

We all filed past him and stood around the table. Gone was the fastidious eater, instead he seemed intent on gorging himself. The spectacle turned my stomach.

Evyn put her hands on her hips. "So everyone's been fretting and worrying over you, and you're in a bar."

Aubin swallowed and took a glug of beer, not looking up. "I highly doubt anyone was worried about me. This was the perfect disguise to explain why I'm here, to be seen by the right people and entice the wrong ones into Desoree's trap."

"How does that work?" I asked, moving to sit next to him.

He lashed out, kicking the chair out from under me.

I glared at him as I put it back upright. "That's enough of that." Moving it away from him, I settled myself, elbows on the table. "Well? How is this operation working?"

He kept his eyes on the meat. "I intercept the Hudau's targets and guide magic users to a safe staging area. Desoree stepped in when I struggled to find somewhere to put them. She provided the warehouse because she cannot act directly, and she hides me here. A few of Brudamere's men have tracked me down to this location, and they haven't returned to tell of it."

"Sounds comfortable, except that Desoree's telling you to get out now." I put my thumb over my shoulder, the way Evyn did sometimes. "Who is she? She must be a powerful Battlemistress to have so many resources."

He gave me a withering look, one that made me both grind my teeth and grin, for while I never exactly enjoyed being the brunt of one of his put-downs, I was so happy he was finally around to administer one. "She's the matriarch of Grendamere the Great, the current Chief of all Chiefs in Skien."

My eyes widened.

"The queen of Skien?" Evyn asked.

"In a way, I suppose," Aubin answered before I could. "Clan chiefs are men as figureheads, but they will have a matriarch to look to." He snapped his mouth shut, jaw working, clearly annoyed at something.

Maybe it was speaking to us.

The Assassin sat next to me, pulling off his headscarf. "Well met and all that, looks like you've stuck in and are having lots of fun, but I have a proposition for you."

*What is this?* "Aren't you here because you need his help? Evie is missing," I explained to Aubin.

Picking up a chicken thigh, Aubin's fingernails tore at the meat. "And that's my problem why?"

I tamped down the flare of anger. Maybe he was goading me, but it was certainly testing my patience.

The Assassin grinned, laying his hand flat on the table as if delivering a winning spread of cards. "I spent two turns of my life researching bruswurt for you. You owe me, and I'm here to collect."

Aubin swallowed his mouthful of half-chewed food hard. "Thanks for that. Greatly appreciated. Now go away, all of you."

He hunkered lower into himself, shutting us out. I had to find a way to talk him round. "We need to get you out of Skien," I reminded him.

"I'll get myself out. Tuniel said she was sending someone to help rescue the last refugees, I assume that's you."

"We need to do it together. You're the commander here, the first Ranger on the scene, and you won't be able to hand over to me all that quickly."

Snarling, he threw his half-empty tankard into the wall. Glass shattered, beer splashing and slopping across the table. His lips drew back from his teeth. "What do I have to do to get you to leave me alone?"

My heart thudded in my throat, spiked by the violence, but instead of anger, all I felt was pain. The pain of rejection, refusal. Even with his back against a wall, he wanted nothing to do with me.

"Aubin..." I didn't know what to say, what I could say. Reticence closed my throat. "We have to get you out, first." If nothing else, we had to see him safe.

Evyn wiped warm beer off her face. "Yuck."

Shoulders leapt to his feet, his chair crashing behind him, sweeping Evyn up in his arms.

"It's beer, not bruswurt. She won't die," Aubin sneered.

Shoulders snapped, "Glass could have hit her eye! No. You don't get to come near her anymore. Evyn, we're leaving, let's go."

"We need him to get Evie," the Assassin said in a low voice. "Sit back down."

Looking between Evyn and the Assassin, Shoulders sat slowly.

Aubin's gaze darted between them, watching them warily but then fixing on the Assassin. They were mirror images in appearance but their aspects were completely different; Aubin holding himself tense, barricaded behind a mound of meat, and the Assassin completely relaxed, smiling as though this were a pleasant night out with friends.

The Assassin leant forward, addressing Aubin directly. "I'll be blunt and brusque, because you're clearly busy here. As I've explained to your ex-colleague, we need you three to help find and potentially liberate our Evie from whatever situation she's found herself in. Now, I don't actually care how you come along." He smiled widely. "Kicking, screaming, whatever, it's all the same to me, but it seems like you have a death wish, so you might welcome that. Instead, I'm going to offer something else."

Evyn and I listened, rapt.

Aubin's eyes smouldered with fury. "Whatever *you* have to offer, I don't want it. Who knows why you're here, messing with our timeline for your own ends."

The Assassin smirked, laying a finger on the sticky table. "I can mess with it some more."

"Is that a threat?"

"A promise." The Assassin threw his arms wide, encompassing not only the bar, but our tableaux around the table. "How would you like all of this to just go away? Even better; never have been."

Shoulders rumbled something, but the Assassin cut him off. "I know Evie will go ballistic when she realises I've told you this, but I'm tired of waiting. There's something you should know about the Lonely Man. By which I mean me, as I'm the original and best."

We frowned at him.

He laced his hands behind his head with a relaxed smile, smug in his superior knowledge. "You'll know our Evie is what we call a travelling mage. She travels across worlds."

Aubin tore into the meat, fingers slippery with grease. "So we have seen. How are you here without her now?"

The Assassin's face fixed. "That'll become apparent, and that is something we really do not tell alts about. You'll see soon enough when you agree to come along; don't panic, and don't interrupt."

The Assassin walked his fingers along the table grain, following a single plank of wood. "She travels across time as well as across worlds. She's the only person we know of that can do that." He skipped his fingers backwards. "As far as we have tested, she can only travel in her lifespan, so from the time she was born onwards."

Evyn craned forward. "That's amazing."

The Assassin smiled at her, a genuine softness stealing across his face. "That's what I like to hear."

"That must be... wow. Fun and dangerous at the same time."

He buffed his nails on his shirt. "Very much like me."

"Enough." Aubin banged his fist on the table. This was very much unlike him, as if living in Skien had stained him with its coarse nature. "This is ridiculous."

"There's more, so shut up and listen." The Assassin walked his fingers back along the grain. "Evyn can travel, but she can't influence events. She's powerless to change anything and can only watch while they unfold, and no matter what she does in any timeline, it still turns out the way it did before. But the Lonely Man—us—we can change things." He jumped his fingers to another plank in the table. "We can influence events through our choices and make things turn out differently. We don't create different timelines; we change what's gone on before."

Evyn gasped. "That's what I was reading about in the library! It's you?"

He bowed his head. "Autographs later."

Evyn grabbed hold of my hand hard. "It sounds incredible but, I mean, there's alternative histories littering the place." She frowned at the Assassin. "Wait a sec, why haven't you changed time so your Evyn doesn't disappear?"

"Because it does need both of us. Without her, well, I'm less than I could be." He winked at her.

My head swam, trying to shift and grab hold of the possibilities the Assassin talked about, assuming he told the truth about the depth of his ability. Evyn seemed to believe him, and that was enough for me. My stomach twisted. "Could you change whether Torgund takes over? Could you bring... bring my father back?"

The Assassin's face turned sober. "No. The Lonely Man can only change his own choices, and from what I understand, he had nothing to do with Torgund taking power."

"Oh." My stomach settled back down, lower than before.

"'*Oh*', as if it's not actually that amazing an ability." The Assassin rolled his eyes.

Aubin had gone very, very still, his glare disgusted. "You want me to believe that I can change how things play out? You're really desperate, aren't you?"

"Yes. I am." The Assassin drummed his fingers on the table. "Well? How about it? You do this for me, and we'll give you one opportunity to change the course of events here, to do whatever you like with the chance."

The Assassin's words were light, but an undercurrent ran through them. He was bending all his self-imposed rules to do this, to find his Evyn and retrieve her. What he offered Aubin also filled me with dread, for what would Aubin do with such a chance right now? If he could rewrite history, where would he start?

First, there was a more pressing issue. We had to set time travel aside for now. "We've got to get out of Keltskarr. Aubin, if you say you need to leave immediately, that it's too perilous here for you to remain any longer, then let's get you out straight away. Give me a contact or a place to go afterwards, and I'll pick up what I can once the rest of our group gets here. Now then, do you have enough supplies?" I waved at his shirtless mien.

Aubin stared at me as if he had never met me before. "You're just going to, what, help me escape over the walls?"

"Yes? Or whatever the best alternative is. If you say it's over the walls, then over the walls it is, I don't have enough grounding and intel here. I can make suggestions." I pointed at the Assassin. "He walked in without any trouble as a Rushia, so if you have that as a disguise, I highly recommend it."

He continued to stare at me, jaw working, and his amber eyes softened. That made my heart leap with hope. What had I said that made him relax a little?

"*Or*," the Assassin said loudly. "You can just make one small little change in your history, and everything will be completely different. What could that be, I wonder? When did it all start to collapse for you?"

I scowled at the Assassin. "We don't have time for this."

He laughed. "Time is exactly what I have, in great heaps. It's rather inconvenient."

I swung back to face Aubin, but the moment had passed and he was all hard edges again, eyes dark. The inciting incident leading to his departure was when he found himself able to smother me, but he might have left because he felt I was pushing him toward being one thing, one type of person that I wanted, rather than letting him find himself in his own time.

Evyn set her elbows on the filthy table. "I think it was storming the Tower to get me. Right?"

I flinched. "Evyn?" What was she doing?

She waved me down. "I'm thinking this through. If Aubin doesn't choose to do that, what does that change?"

Aubin dropped the bones to rattle on his plate, face dark with pain. "You're right. My life imploded when that happened."

"You... I mean, you *chose* to come with me and do that!" I said.

"Exactly," Evyn murmured. "If he makes a different choice, then he won't be involved."

My stomach turned. "Evyn, what are you doing?"

She met my eyes, all efficiency, as if this was a bookcase she had taken upon herself to put in order. "I'm sorting this out. He has an opportunity to make it so all that horrible stuff never happened to him, and all that trauma and heartache will be lifted, poof, gone." Evyn counted on her fingers, speaking softly. "You wouldn't have been captured by Waker MasterMage and driven nearly insane..."

"I wouldn't have stabbed Gavain, so I wouldn't have been executed on paper, and I wouldn't have been a Ranger," Aubin finished, now rendered breathless with the possibilities.

"Evyn, this is... I can't..."

She patted my arm. "Don't worry, I'll handle this." She turned to the Assassin. "What happens to us, our memories?"

The Assassin's lips were tipped up in amusement, dropping down to address her question. "You will not have had any of those experiences. You and I would meet at some point, probably in Waker's dreamlands as before, but you won't have any knowledge of your Aubin. I can finally be called by my real name instead of a moniker."

Evyn's smile became grim. "Great. That works for me."

"Evyn!" I felt as though the world tipped sideways. "I need to talk to you." I stood and walked off a handful of paces.

She followed, leaving Aubin hunched in his seat, hands pressing against his knees, with the Assassin smiling on one side and Shoulders gaping open-mouthed on the other.

I took a deep breath, trying to find her calm compassion, but her feelings tumbled with turmoil. The bond between us pulsed with a mixture of heartbreak, protective fear and indignation. I could all too easily align with that, and then our course would be set, and this mad plan set in motion.

I wouldn't be able to pierce through it without her helping me, but it was Evyn I had to convince. "What about taking the good from a relationship, no matter how it ends?" I tried.

Her face softened, guard lowering. "I can only take so many blows, Thorrn. It's wearing away my self-esteem and eating into me. The constant reinforcement of people I love leaving me is... it's just too much, and I can't expect you to even begin to balance that out. It will be like a bucket with a hole in it. A great big gaping hole, one you can't fill no matter how hard you try." She squeezed my hand. "It's not your fault or your shortcoming, please don't think that."

"Evyn..." What could I say against that? "We will make it through together. You don't have to do *this*. It is an extreme solution to heartache."

"I think it fixes a lot of problems, so why not?" Her encouraging smile was brittle. "It helps Aubin, it helps us. Everyone wins, and you've got to like a situation with an outcome like that." She led me back to the table, cutting off the conversation, and I stumbled in her wake.

I looked up at Aubin to see if I could expect assistance from that quarter, but he kept his attention on his plate. The bruises and scrapes on his back and shoulders spoke of a brutal battle every night, his golden skin pale against the blacks and purples. I would throw myself into such training, but this wasn't training to improve himself.

This was something else.

Evyn halted opposite Aubin, the dirty table between them, and planted her feet. "Do you want this?" she asked him directly.

His gaze flicked up to meet hers, a twist of anger and grief in his face. "Want what?"

"Do you want this life, or do you want to choose this clean slate the Assassin is offering?" Evyn raised an eyebrow at him.

Aubin was still, studying Evyn's face as though he was memorising her, although I knew he could recall every single detail. "I want a new start," he said.

"Fab." Evyn turned to the Assassin. "It's a done deal."

The Assassin inclined his head.

This was madness. "I cannot believe you are convincing me to do this," I hissed at Evyn.

Aubin glared up at me. "Then let me help you," he said. "I wish I'd never met you."

"I wish you'd... argh." I balled my fists, relaxing them with an effort, pushing back our umbrage at such a statement. "I know you're pushing us away. I wish you'd stayed with us, talked to us. We can sort this out. I'll listen, I swear, and—"

"You know what I really wish?" He placed his hands flat on the table, eyes burning into mine. "I really do wish I'd never scaled that damned tower. I should have kept my head down, as I had been doing for my whole life." He breathed hard, as if he's been running or fighting, wrestling with something I couldn't see and never would. "I wish I'd done that. I wish I still had my life, my shop, my clients. I wish I'd just done what I was told."

"Then Evyn would be—" I clamped my lips together. *No.* Thinking back to obediently giving Evyn over to Torgund, in a state of shock after my father's death and then handed orders that I needed to adhere to, dread curdled in my throat. "Do you really wish you hadn't saved Evyn?"

Aubin said nothing in response.

"But... But that means..." My hands shook. Would I have stormed that tower alone? Would I have known I needed to? I only disobeyed when I learnt that Torgund meant to keep her locked away; by the time it became apparent that I wasn't seeing her around the castle, it would be too late. Perhaps Evyn would ping herself out but she would have been caught, we encountered far too many regulars for her not to be. I stilled my hands with an effort, locking them together and putting them between my knees, the shudder making its way up my arms.

Aubin took deep breaths as if his throat had suddenly loosened and he could take in air again. "You would go up there alone to get her, you know you would. We didn't encounter all that many obstacles, you would have been able to defeat those on your own."

My stomach rolled. Would I? I had needed the intel and the push from Aubin. I shoved that away for a different tactic. "You can't really want things to go back to the way they were before. Do you?" Did he really wish to erase everything? Yes, there was heartbreak enough for a lifetime, trials and tests beyond what I ever realised I had the capacity to endure, but endure it I had. I had weathered it with my soul companion, my promised and the man before me at my side.

*He hasn't been able to bear it alone.* The realisation hit me as surely as it had when he had asked me what I meant to do now that I knew Evyn would be locked in that tower for life. "Aubin, you aren't alone. You have us."

Aubin met my eyes. "Not everyone wants a thrilling life, Shardsson. It was exciting enough as the soul companion of a mage, and I deliberately worked hard to be unobtrusive." He sneered at the Assassin. "This is all academic anyway, and assumes that this power is even real to begin with."

Lacing his fingers together, the Assassin levelled a look at his counterpart. "If you are serious about not wanting to go up that tower, you would be able to follow Evie and change it. Once we find her, of course."

"And then you'll, what, forget us entirely?" My voice cracked.

Both Aubins looked at me. The Assassin looked sad but determined but my Aubin looked grimly satisfied.

"Thorrn," the Assassin said gently. "It's not that you're not great."

"You're just not conducive to a peaceful life." Aubin nodded slowly, lips set in determination. "Thorrn, when I left the city, you said you would not stop me because you both loved me. Does that still apply?"

My mouth opened and closed. Was this truly what he wanted? Did what I want matter?

Evyn coloured. "Yeah. I did love you. This will probably be for the best for all of us." She took a deep breath, taking my hand. "Can we make sure this doesn't affect me and Thorrn? As long as I have him, I know it'll be alright."

That was true, but events were rapidly spiralling out of my control. "Evyn, stop." If she was content with this, pushing for it even, then where did my opinion figure? Was I being overruled, outnumbered and ousted?

Evyn turned to me sadly. "Come on, Thorrn. It really is for the best." She raised her chin at the Assassin. "Well?"

He grinned, entirely self-satisfied. "He'll be able to choose from a smorgasbord of timelines."

Aubin said, "I will make sure that you meeting Thorrn is not affected."

"Great. Then that's settled." Evyn held out her hand as if to seal a bargain the Rushia way, a clap palm to palm. "Let's do it."

"No, stop, no!" I grabbed onto the edge of the table, sucking in breaths.

Someone touched my back. Shoulders lowered himself next to me. "Thorrn, it's not an immediate thing. First we have to find Evie, and we'll need to travel around to do that, because we don't know where she is."

The Assassin nodded. "That's right. I change time but I need Evyn to take me there. My Evie, I mean."

"How long will it take?" Aubin asked, every muscle tense, as though he would spring up and seize the opportunity.

"How long is a piece of string? We'll find her when we find her, but the beauty of world-hopping with Evie is that time doesn't need to pass here. We can be there and back in mere turns of the glass, or even shorter if we need to. It could take us sennights or mooncycles to find and help Evie, but very little time could pass here."

"The spirits really can do it all in one night," Evyn murmured to herself, chuckling.

"Spirits? What? And how can you find any of this funny!" I put my head in my hands.

Evyn shifted toward me, pushing her hand up between mine to stroke my head. "You'll have time to come to terms with it, and I'll help you. We'll be fine, because we'll be together." She beamed at me.

That heartened me even as loss cut at me. Rather than separated by circumstance it would be by choice, which was one type of pain, but then everything between us utterly erased on top of that. What would that do to me? I had grown and changed greatly, taking huge strides and gaining new strengths. Would I have done that without our time together?

What would that do to Aubin? He had found something with us, I knew he had, but he seemed determined to push it away. Or maybe he felt it had been withdrawn or, worse, wasn't there to begin with?

Looking at him now, at his unbending posture, I knew from previous experience that pushing him to accept us would not win through. He would put his shields up and wait me out.

What *had* he found with us? What had made him want to storm the Tower, support me when no one else would, and drive him to stab Gavain even knowing it would end with his execution?

As Evyn said, we had time. The two of them were aligned at least, it seemed, on making this happen, but I would have opportunity to listen to him, as I had Gavain. *If I can do it for Gavain, I can do it for Aubin.* I had to show him through actions and words what he meant to us, showing him why he would want to remember us rather than forget us.

I took a deep breath to shore my reserves. "I'm not happy with this at all, but I do want to find Evie and make sure she's hale and well. That's priority one, if we really can just leave this mess here in Skien to pick up later."

The Assassin nodded eagerly. "It won't even be that much later. We'll go and come back in heartbeats."

My heart stung. "Very well."

Aubin stood, full of dire purpose. "Then what are we waiting for?"

# CHAPTER 24

Aubin went to a further attic level to retrieve his pack, and I went with Shoulders to grab our effects from the doorwoman. He was very silent, avoiding looking into my eyes.

"So this is what he can do," I said, to break the heavy silence.

"Yes. I'm sorry, I didn't know how to tell you before."

Anger kindled against my heart, but lashing out at Shoulders would not make me feel any better. "What can we do? Anything?"

"You mean if we have special abilities?" he asked. I had not meant that, but I waited anyway. He glanced up at me before returning to study his steps on the stairs. "Unless the ability to endure is special, then no."

"Nevermind then. I meant, what can we do to stop them from changing time?"

Shoulders hunched lower. "There's a lot we need to do before we get to that point. We need to find Evie, and we're going at last." He shut his eyes. "I still cannot Find her. I know she's unhurt at least, but I..." He trailed off, hands opening and closing on nothing.

"We will find her and Liara, and defeat her if it is she who stands in Evie's way of returning." The enchantress might have Evie even now. As Earthians, Evie and Evyn were both immune to magic, but Liara was desperate, and people pushed to the edge of what they could endure often made the most vicious fighters.

We hurried back upstairs to rejoin Evyn and the Assassin. Desoree had given us a private room, piling that table high with fresh meat and beer. The smell turned my stomach.

Far from my dour resolve, Evyn seemed to shiver with excitement at the table. "We're going to another world! How wild is that?"

"Not very," I pointed out gently.

She gave me a searching look. "Don't be sad, Thorrn. Soon you'll be over him."

I set the packs down and cast an eye over the meat, ripe with juices, and the copious glasses of warm beer lined up on the table. Picking one up, I contemplated whether downing it in one would be better than tasting it, but placed it back firmly. I couldn't afford to be blunted by alcohol, no matter that it might take the edge off my heartache.

"Thorrn?" Evyn touched my elbow.

Her touch sent warmth to my core, loosening my throat. "What did I do? What have I done that makes him want to forget me?" The glass squeaked in my hand.

She took the glass I was in danger of cracking into her hands. "You didn't do anything wrong. He just wishes his life was different and unfortunately it all changed when I came into the picture."

"That wasn't your fault, Evyn. He chose to help me rescue you, and it was his choice to make!"

"Thorrn, inside voice." She winced. She sat on the edge of the table, staring into the murky depths of the beer. "Look. He made that choice, but now he wishes he had made another one. He wants to go back to having things nice and ordered and simple. Life doesn't ordinarily work like that but, apparently, he's special, so he can have it." Setting the glass down, she whispered, "Aren't there any mistakes you would like to go back and erase?"

"We aren't mistakes."

"Okay, yes, fine. Events, then. Like... what about your father?"

I leant against the counter, my father's sword heavy at my hip. "Well... if we had never gone to Earth, would that have changed anything? Or made it worse? Maybe Torgund would have ended me at the same time."

"You're probably right, but we can't know that." She looked hopefully at the Assassin.

"I'm saying nothing, you've had a lifetime's worth of secrets from me," he said.

"You can shut up." I heaved the pack up and onto my back, tugging the straps down with firm jerks. "It's your fault he even has this idea in the first place."

"Oh, gods above, whipped for telling you, whipped for keeping secrets. I can't win." He rubbed the bridge of his nose.

"Well, I have some things I would want to change," Evyn whispered.

I could guess a few. Her father, her friend Ben, both losses that hurt her in her early turns of life. "I'm sorry, Evyn."

"Not just the ones we've lost, though. I wish I hadn't been stupid and scared Mum. That's a choice I would redo if I could." She wiped her face, her eyes watery with tears but firm with resolve. "I can't. Aubin can, and we should let him try."

"But Evyn, we'll forget him too. We'll forget what he means to us."

She nodded.

My stomach fell. "You want that to happen?"

That gyre of push and pull, longing and disdain, tugged at my chest. "I do. I want to flip a switch and not feel like this, that would be great. This is the next best thing, and the best part is, everyone will be happy." She said it with a smile, but inside I felt her dread and mine.

Bile rose in my throat. My first reaction was to fight it. I didn't want to lose him and I knew Evyn really did not truly want to either.

Aubin returned wearing a shirt that had gone murky around the cuffs and collar with the buttons straining at the chest. Based on what I saw earlier, it hadn't shrunk being washed.

His gaze landed straight on Evyn and stayed there, his face unreadable. He had closed himself off to us, perhaps intending to be the bland apothecarist on this trip, fading into the surroundings. He looked up at me briefly, then tore his gaze away.

How did he expect me to react? Previously I would have shown my anger and demanded that he talk to me, refusing to be scorned, but that would make his choice natural. I needed to at least be approachable, and we needed to be able to work together for this mission.

I reached into my pack. "I have a spare shirt. Here, let me find it."

Aubin glanced at the others, as if trying to ascertain who I was speaking to. His eyebrows dipped when I held out the folded shirt for him. "No, that's not necessary."

"That one's ill fitting and too well-worn."

His lips twisted. "Apologies for being too busy with refugees to tend to my wardrobe, *sir*."

The drawn out "r" rang between us, exactly as it had when he had been an apothecary. *Damn and blast.* "I didn't mean it in that way, Aubin."

Evyn scowled at Aubin. "He's trying to be nice and you're slapping his hand away."

"Evyn, you don't need to—"

Aubin's face coloured. He snatched the shirt and strode off.

"I think that's the best you can expect for thanks," Evyn said.

Turning my gaze up to the ceiling, I counted slowly in Rushia. *Off to a splendid start.*

The Assassin was smiling as though this were the midsommer play and the highlight of the season's calendar.

When Aubin returned, Evyn took charge yet again. She turned to the Assassin. "Now what?"

"Now… we do something a bit awkward." He slid the bolts home on the door. Lit by the orange glowstones, his face took on a grim visage. "This is our failsafe, an emergency procedure we put in place for when our Evyn gets lost in time. I'm going to open what I call a bad portal. It won't look normal, because it isn't. It will open to the space between worlds. It's very dangerous for us to be in there and it will kill you if you're in there too long.

"In there we're going to meet someone. I don't know how he knows to meet us there, and I am not allowed to ask. He will take us back to our world, but he won't help us any further." The Assassin looked at each of us in turn, Shoulders nodding and girding himself, Evyn eagerly breathless, Aubin leaning against the wall and scowling, and myself. He stared at me the longest. "Listen carefully. No one else says a word. Do not turn back. Do not stop going forward. Now, do you understand?"

"Yes," Shoulders and Evyn chorused.

"Yes," I said, saluting.

Aubin inclined his head. "I understand."

"Good. Stand together."

I grabbed hold of Evyn's hand. She clung onto me as hard as I clung onto her.

The Assassin made signs and shapes that looked to me to be the same as Evyn's. She frowned, then gasped as he opened a way between the worlds. A big black sucking hole blasted out hot air just in front of the table. Evyn's portals through realities were unnoticeable unless you happened to be standing in the right place, but this was truly a tear, ragged edges flapping in the awful wind.

"You've made a complete mess of that." Aubin strode forward.

"*I* don't make portals." The Assassin flashed white teeth at him. His hands were shaking. "Come along."

*He is terrified.* I put my hand on my father's sword. Shoulders followed readily enough and Evyn tugged me to go too. I glanced over at Aubin to find him looking at me at the same time. We exchanged a look, faces grim; he lifted his arms to show his

Battlemistress blades in their holsters at his hips, and I squeezed my knuckles around the hilt of my father's sword. When Aubin fell in behind Evyn, grim satisfaction trickled across my trepidation. *He'll help protect her if something happens in there.* Shading my face from the wind, I pushed forward.

As soon as we took a step inside, the portal behind us sealed and the wind cut out immediately. We drew up behind Shoulders and the Assassin, who stared straight forward.

A young man appeared before us with no winds of travel from a mancer; he simply was not there one heartbeat and there the next.

I swore loudly and drew my sword.

The new arrival frowned at me. Of Aubin's height and thin in the way that young men are when they fill out their bodies, he slouched with his hands in his pockets. His tawny hair was stuck up, mussed and in desperate need of a brush. "Wow. Bit of a mixed bag."

"Stand up straight, at least," the Assassin said.

"Make me," the youth scowled.

Was this person who the Assassin was afraid of? They looked a little at odds with one another but not ill-disposed toward one another. Moreover the boy would not pose much of a challenge to me if it came to a fight. He didn't even hold any weapons that I could see.

Still, Evyn had taught me that first impressions were worthless if I approached a meeting with a closed mind. "Well met—" I began, but Shoulders shushed me.

My greeting was ignored entirely. "Where to?" the youth asked the Assassin.

But it was my Aubin who spoke. "I want to go to a world where I have never met Evyn or Thorrn."

I flinched, turning to look around in disgust, but Evyn grabbed my arm. "You cannot turn here," she hissed. "Remember what the Assassin said!"

I let her hold me, anger burning hot, feeding from the pain of rejection. Evyn's was the same and fine kindling for a roaring fire of rage, if I let it. I cut off the anger, choosing instead to feel that pain.

The youth furrowed his brow at Aubin's request. "That's a hard one. I'll get it as close as I can."

The Assassin said, "No, wait, that's wrong, he's not the right Aubin, *I'm* the real Aubin!"

The boy ignored him. "Come on, let's go." Turning around in place, he led us deeper into the oppressive heat. The wind had gone but now complete silence swallowed up the sound of our steps and breaths. There was a lack of lightsource in the surrounding darkness, yet I was able to see my companions.

This place wasn't real, or it was functioning from principles I didn't understand.

"This is fascinating," Evyn whispered. "I can see why the alts do what they do if they get to explore places like this."

"I really don't like it." I could barely see a length ahead, where the darkness was absolute and anything could be hiding within, watching me. I had no doubt that it would swallow me forever if I were to stray away from the group. "Do you think Liara came here?"

"She probably did, that portal she made was very similar to the Assassin's, wasn't it?"

"Excuse me," I called to the boy. "Have you seen an enchantress around here?"

The boy pulled a device out of his pocket. It was similar to Evyn's hand held box, with a bright screen that he swept with his fingers. "You're going to need to be more specific, swordsman. Who are you looking for?"

"Sinjorina Majestica Liara, from Dinahe." I ground her name out of my throat.

"And which timeline?"

That threw me. "Uh... mine."

The boy nodded. "She came through here." He put his device away.

"But where did she go?"

"That's the wrong question. Try *when* did she go. But I can only do one timeline at a time, you know. Well. I can do multiple, but, I think you might actually die, so..." He shrugged. "I'm up for experimenting with it."

"I'm not," the Assassin said. "Take us to the place and time where Evie is lost."

"Oh my goodness, get in the queue..." The boy halted. "Oh! Actually, it's okay. Here's the timeline where Aubin never meets Evyn and Thorrn. Say hi to her when you see her for me."

"Who? Liara?" I snapped.

The Assassin said, "Do you mean Evie? Is she here?"

The boy nodded. "Two for one in this timeline."

My heart surged. Evie was here, in a reality where we had never met Aubin, no less. *At least we know where she is.*

Shoulders beside me let out a muffled cry. "Where?"

The boy rolled his eyes. "You know I can't tell you. All these rules, eh?"

"Yes, but she's not here to mind us right now," the Assassin said in a reasonable tone.

"Oh, she'll know, though. I want my dinner tonight."

Who was this she they referenced? Before I could ask, the boy opened a portal and sauntered off, back into that all-consuming darkness. If he could walk here without fear, what kind of magic did he wield?

The Assassin muttered swearwords under his breath as we all walked through into a hallway, the air warmer than it had been in Skien but thankfully not as hot as that between place.

"Who was that?" I whispered to Evyn.

"Can't you tell?" She grinned at me.

"No, hence the question." I scoured the corridor. I would know those stones anywhere across worlds. "We're back at the castle. We travelled geographically as well as, er..." I fumbled for a word.

Evyn touched the sides of the corridor. On our world Rose and

Evyn used this little-used area to travel back and forth between Earth and Oberrot. "Multiversally?" she suggested.

"Sideways," I tried.

Evyn grinned, putting her thumb up. "I like it."

The Assassin took the lead. "Well fantastic. Rather than going directly to save our Evyn, we're now on a sightseeing tour," he snapped at Aubin.

"You can leave me here." Aubin folded his arms tight.

"I am tempted by that, believe me." The Assassin looked to Shoulders. "But the Waykeeper did hint that our Evyn might actually be here—"

Shoulders gasped. "I can Find her! There!" He pointed directly up.

On our world, above us would be the service areas, living areas, the accommodation and...

"Oh shoot," I said. "The Last Tower is directly above here."

"The Last Tower? The bolthole of the royal family?" The Assassin's hands roved over his holsters at his hips. "We need to get out of sight and get out of the castle until we can find out who the ruler is. We need to do some reconnaissance: who's the king or queen here, who's allied to whom, what versions of ourselves and others we are dealing with."

"City or Academy?" Shoulders asked him, flexing and relaxing his hands as I did to calm myself. Clearly they had done this many, many times.

The Assassin clicked his fingers. "Academy, let's go."

We followed him, the worn stones of the castle exactly as I remembered them. "What do you mean, who the ruler is?"

"It's usually either Gough or Torgund, with a few outliers. The difference is rather stark." The Assassin craned his head around the corner. "Alright, it's deserted, go."

We walked at pace across the main atrium to the doors opening onto the castle courtyard. It certainly felt quieter, but everything looked the same: the large mosaic map on the far wall was still present, the drapes on the tall windows the same colour. Everything, until we got to the door.

Outside, the usually bustling castle courtyard was vacant of anyone living, but festooned with plenty of corpses.

"Evyn, don't look." I bundled her close to my chest.

"Oh, god." She clung onto me.

"We're in a Torgund timeline. How lovely," the Assassin drawled.

I pressed Evyn against my rapidly beating heart, trying to take a cold inventory. Men in the greens mainly, but some in the white livery of the castle service.

"This looks to have taken place this morning," Aubin said quietly. He looked up at the hanged men, hands wrapped around his Battlemistress blades, his experience with the living and the dead wider than mine for telling how soon someone's half-spirit had departed their body.

"No wonder everyone is avoiding the courtyard." The Assassin pushed forward. "Come on. We have no idea whether the versions of us here are around or what their position is in the world, but if they are wanted for any reason, at least we know what the consequence for that would be."

We left the grisly display in the dire courtyard, hurrying past the empty guard post and stopping at the track toward the city gates. It was coming on to quarterday and training would be over on our world, but men and women in the reds and the greens practised separately in long rows.

"Don't dawdle, don't rush, stay in the group," I said. The gravelled track to the city gates had never looked so long.

"We need disguises, they obviously know Evyn." Aubin pulled his Rushia headscarf from his pack as he walked. "Evyn, keep your hair hidden and wear this."

She took it from him, weighing up the material. "How do I even put it on?"

Aubin hesitated only a heartbeat before stepping close. "Tuck your hair up please, Lady Evyn."

She gathered her long hair into a ball at the back of her head. Aubin held it in place and wound the fabric around her face, hands working quickly. Red trickled up Evyn's throat and a burr of nervousness bloomed in my solar plexus.

I rubbed at it as I marked the patterns the swordsmen and women were engaged with. They were utterly familiar to me, the clacks of the practice swords like chords in a musical refrain. "Their training is the same."

"Yes. Be careful, though; the similarities can be more disorientating than the differences," Shoulders said. He looked up at the Last Tower, hands bunching. "She's up there. I can't walk away from her," he said, voice pained.

"You have to." The Assassin reached over to touch his friend's arm. "You can do this."

The quiet reassurance served to settle me as well. I glanced back at Aubin and Evyn, nerves tangling my stomach.

Aubin had finished helping Evyn with the headscarf and stepped back. "She's ready."

Evyn bustled over to me, holding on to my forearm. Her heartbeat pounded through her chest, reverberating against my arm and echoing my own.

I nodded thanks to Aubin, who stood well back from us in the shadows, and turned back to squint at the lines. "If I'm correct, they'll break to gather and sort into exercise groups soon. That might be the best time to walk across."

The Assassin, rocked on the balls of his feet. "Very well."

We watched for a handful of heartbeats more before a sergeant's cry went up, exactly as I'd hoped. "Hoods up," I said. "We don't want to draw too much attention, and we're two sets of twins with a Rushia."

The Assassin frowned at me, looking over my shoulder. "One set of twins. Your Aubin has gone."

"Gone?" I turned around. The gatehouse was void of Aubin. "Well, damn and blast."

"Who could have predicted this?" Evyn muttered, in a tone that suggested it wasn't a question she expected to be answered.

"He'll be back or killed." The Assassin shrugged. "Come on, we cannot afford to look for him, and he knew that."

The Assassin was right, as remaining in the open in enemy territory was suicide, but leaving Aubin now felt wrong. Not only could I not convince Aubin to return with us if he wasn't there to talk to, but we were strangers in a foreign land, no matter how much it mirrored our home.

*He can handle himself.* Did I really need to see him in front of me to know he would be fine?

Evyn hung back.

"He will return," I reassured her.

The headscarf tilted. "How do you know?"

"I just know." Squeezing her hand, I focused on the task ahead of us.

The Assassin waited a handful of heartbeats more before saying, "Now, let's go." We walked in tandem, two by two, with me closer to the fence line and shielding Evyn from view. I held her upper arm, careful not to crush it in a tight grip as we crunched along the gravel to the city gates. Sweat trickled down my spine underneath my Ranger leathers.

The gates stood open and we spilled through them to the top of the city boulevard. The houses were as I expected them, the little bridges over the canals, and at last we saw civilians going about their daily lives in the street below. Standing stark between us and them was another set of gallows, mercifully unoccupied but throwing a long shadow up to our feet.

"He likes decorating his reign with those," the Assassin said. "Expect to see a few more."

"Is it like this in your timeline?" My mouth was too dry to let the question carry far. I cleared my throat and tried again. "Is this what you see every day?"

The Assassin tipped his head from side to side, lips moving as he surveyed the streets. "Small variations in numbers strung up, probably. It suggests that this is close to our history." He waved us forward. "We'll go to the Academy. Try to listen to conversation and gossip as we go. We need to work out how long Torgund has been in power and who the MasterMancer or Mage is, as that will give my colleague and I clues on how to get Evie out of the Last Tower."

I led the way alongside Evyn, past the winding streets of the lords' and ladies' city homes and down into the commerce districts. Instead of the warm smells of baking for the mid-afternoon luncheon that nobles insisted on, the stench of strong spirits wafted from the restaurants. The bar that Aleric and I had fought in and the Assassin and I had talked in was boarded up.

"This is making me feel strange," I admitted.

"Like it's a dream." Evyn made a low noise of distress. "This might upset Aubin more than we thought."

"Yes." If Aubin really did want to change our pasts, would he have to deal with this sense of dislocation all the time?

"He would get used to it. He'll have to," she said, her tone doubtful. She laced her fingers with mine, something that was tactically disadvantageous if we were suddenly surprised in an attack, but I couldn't bear to shake her off.

The heart of magical learning was deep under the mountain the city sprawled on, and the entrance to the Academy was a domed building which housed the top of the stairs down. We passed people puffing their way up or recovering from the climb in the cavities cut into the side of the stairs for this purpose. Traders eyed us with suspicion, holding onto their bags, and mothers tucked their children closer.

"They don't like groups of men," the Assassin said, frowning.

I sighed, resigned. "No one does recently."

Evyn squeezed my hand as we entered the well-lit underground cavern housing the Academy and the town that serviced it. Aubin's old shop was along the back row underneath some wooden apartments. Canals had been carved alongside the streets, ferrying goods and passengers, and sounds of water filled the air.

"I'll have to check out the Academy to see the portrait of the incumbent Master of all Masters." The Assassin talked in a low voice, as if to himself, leading the way along the main canal. He came to a grinding halt. "Another gallows up ahead. Turn around, get to the inn."

"The inn. Right." Shoulders headed off down a side street.

I made sure Evyn went ahead of me, keeping my attention behind us and becoming the rear-guard. "Somewhere you frequent regularly?"

"That place never changes," the Assassin explained, keeping his voice low. "Inns are the best places to overhear conversations, because the patrons are often talkative and louder than they realise."

We went down a few more winding side streets. I saw no mancers or mages but many more empty shops, the glass dusty with neglect. "Gough really is better for Oberrot," I said with pride to Evyn.

"Be very careful." The Assassin looked both ways up the street before stepping out. "A statement like that could be a treasonous offence here."

"I'll keep my allegiance close to my chest, then."

The inn slumped between a stone edifice likely used for teaching and what looked like a soul swapper's store with its red-and-white pinstripe banner hanging limp above the lintel. I tucked Evyn behind me, scowling at the blacked-out windows. Inside were mages or mancers able to sense out the soul bond and, worse, cut it, sundering our spirit and rendering us both separate.

The Assassin and Shoulders gave it a wide berth, and I steered Evyn away from it into the inn.

Inside it was clean and well-stocked, the tables full and the patrons well into their cups. The Assassin darted toward a booth, a painting of Torgund's smug face glowering over us as we settled.

"I'll get the beers." It would be suspicious to enter a bar and not order a drink or food. Hailing the barman, I ordered four beers, a pang sliding through me for the fifth member of our group. Hopefully he was still hale and well, investigating this new reality as safely as we had.

I handed over rubles to the barkeep.

He frowned, turning one over and holding it up to the glowstone. "*Gough?* Sorry, friend, this currency has been out of circulation for turns. Where did you find this?"

Before I could answer, the Assassin slid next to me. "A bequest from a recently deceased relative. Must be old coins."

"Very old coins," the barkeep agreed, turning my shiny ruble over in his palm. "King Torgund changed the coinage soon after he inherited the throne. This must be a score old! Looks freshly minted." He handed it back to me, pressing it into my palm. "Can't take it, though. You'd best melt those down, and quick. I know a metal mage who'll do it, no questions asked."

Before I could speak, the Assassin reached forward, handing grubby rubles over to the barkeep. "Our thanks, and here."

The man looked up at his face and choked. "My lord, I... I had no idea you were in my... welcome, and..." He gripped the bar top with white knuckles. "Drinks are on the house, my lord!" He bowed his head.

The Assassin said nothing in return, keeping his face flat as he grabbed the drinks, weaving back between the tables. Conversations petered out and died as patrons glanced up at him, their eyes widening.

Uh oh.

The Assassin set the drinks on the table with a clink. "Well, I'm finally feared, but famous as well. I'll have to wear a disguise." He pulled his hood up over his head as he sat, facing Evyn. "We're all looking awfully shady over here."

"Famous?" Evyn asked.

I put myself between her and the patrons, sitting on the edge of the wooden bench of the booth. "Yes, the barkeep was terrified of him. What does that mean?"

"Anything at this point, but also that we should drink up and move on." The Assassin took a sip of his drink as though everything was normal. By some kind of magic, the bar also started to settle, the drone of quiet conversation starting up again.

I had a few questions of my own. I held out my hand. "You have the right rubles?"

Digging slowly in his pocket, the Assassin passed me three coins. "A few of each sets of currency."

They were thin, the edges uneven, Torgund's handsome but cruel profile gracing one side. I compared it to my brighter, sturdy coin, Gough's neutral face stamped clear on it, before showing Evyn.

"Wow." Evyn cradled them.

"Keep those rubles, you might need some."

Around us, the room returned to normal, and the Assassin and I both took our hands from our weapons. The Assassin beckoned Shoulders closer, lowering his voice. "We're in a place similar to ours. Torgund came into power a score of turns ago. Gough must be dead or presumed dead."

"I wonder if he is really dead," Shoulders murmured back.

The Assassin drummed his fingers on the beer glass, making it sing out. "There's another clue I haven't appreciated yet. That other useless version of me asked for a world where he doesn't meet Evyn or Thorrn. How would the Lonely Man not meeting the Spirit Shaper or the Patient Slave change things?"

Shoulders's eyes dropped to the dirty table. "Our equivalents might still be in southern Oberrot. That's where I was a slave," he said roughly.

Evyn touched his arm, sorrow keen across the bond. "Maybe. I'm sorry."

Another version of me could be a slave here? My jaw tightened. "If we find him, we will help him," I promised him.

"One at a time," the Assassin murmured. His eyes half closed as though he were turning around a problem in his mind. "If this is my history and I don't meet you, then I'm wandering around assisting Tuniel somewhere."

*Tuniel!* My heart leapt in my chest. "We didn't even tell her we were leaving, let alone what Aubin is planning."

The Assassin waved his hand, irritation on his shadowed face. "It's too late now, and in any case, you'll be back before she even realises you're gone." His gaze slid away from me.

Sick dread crept up my throat. "Unless Aubin changes time and we never meet him. What does that do to my relationship with Tuniel?"

The Assassin had the good grace to flush up to his ears. "I don't know yet. In either case, first we have to find Evie. Can we deal with one reality at a time, please?"

Lose Tuniel as well as Aubin? I spun to face Evyn, gathering her hands. "Evyn, please, the only reason I let Tuniel come anywhere close was to help Aubin; she is a mage, I won't want a mage anywhere near you."

Evyn's eyes, shadowed by the headscarf, watered. "Oh, Thorrn, I didn't even think of that."

The Assassin tapped his fist on the table. "Remember what I said about people being talkative and far too loud here? Be careful you aren't overheard." He glared into each of my eyes, unblinking and unflinching while my heart broke in front of him. Choking sadness filled my chest, a pounding anger mixed with heartache.

His gaze softened slightly. He continued in a whisper, "It will turn out for the best. Trust me. The Lonely Man meets the Spirit Shaper and he changes, but the Cold Mage meets the Patient Slave, and *their* mettles fuse into something unbreakable."

That did indeed settle me, confidence spreading through my core. We were a fated match as well? "Good. My thanks." I blinked slowly, rubbing my eyes.

"That's nice." Evyn wiped her eyes in between the slits in the headscarf. The contented warmth cooled, tempered by a cold ache.

My cheer at finding out from the time travellers that Tuniel and I were destined to be lovers faded. Where was the person giving Evyn undying love and utterly devoted to her? Of course I would be that for her as the other half of the spirit we shared, but being chosen was also special in its own way. It cut me deeply that Aubin had thrown himself into bar brawls instead of a life with Evyn, but he had fallen into helping people who needed it along the way.

I had to set that aside for now, focusing on the mission at hand. I squeezed Evyn's fingers. "Why is Evie up in the Last Tower?"

The Assassin pulled at his hood to hide his face further from the bar patrons. "Same reason your Evyn was in there, because of where she comes from, most likely."

"So that means Torgund knows about her heritage," I said. A part of Evyn's headscarf slipped over her eyes. I helped hold it up while she tightened it at the back. "Sorry, but you're going to need to wear this."

"Sure thing." She sounded less than enthused.

"What could that mean for the Evyn here, and the Thorrn attached to her?" If my experience was any guide, could there be a Thorrn around here, desperate to storm the tower but without an Aubin to help?

"Maybe we don't exist, full stop, period," Evyn said. "Maybe that's what your son said, trying to get it close enough."

"Oh, Evyn, don't say that." The Assassin put his hand over his eyes.

"Son? What?" I looked between them.

Evyn chuckled quietly. "That's who that Waykeeper person was, Thorrn. He's their son."

I frowned. "But he was nearly a score old, I thought."

"And a *time traveller*," Evyn said, emphasising with her hands as well as her voice.

"You are a witness," the Assassin moaned to Shoulders in a pained voice. "She put two and two together herself."

"Yep. Witnessed." Shoulders smiled at Evyn.

"Goodness." I sat back in my seat. The Assassin had a son? He didn't look much older than us, but now I studied his hairline, it was a little more receded than our Aubin's, even though there were no silvrine strands that I could see.

He met my eyes with a challenging glare.

"Yeah. Wow." Evyn's face fell. "So maybe we don't exist."

My hand curled around my father's sword. This time travel stuff was dizzying, but I had a mission to focus on. "We know evil is in charge. What are we going to do about getting your Evyn out of the Tower?"

"Do you know the layout and the defences?" Shoulders asked.

I nodded. "Intimately. If it is fully guarded there is no assailing it."

"No assailing it if you don't have a pinger," Evyn pointed out.

Fear jerked at me. "Oh no, I'm not having you storm up the Tower with me."

Her eyes brightened. "Ooh, I've had a better idea. What if I give myself up? They know Evyn is special, so they've got her locked up. They lock me up too and I ping us both out and we make our careful way down."

My mouth opened and closed. No, I wanted to scream, but she had a point.

"Or, because they know you're special, they hit you with perdure and never let you wake up again," the Assassin said severely.

She deflated against the wooden bench. "Ah. Right." Her disappointment mingled with my relief.

The Assassin drummed his fingers on the table. "We need to spend a few more days in reconnaissance, and I need to stay out of sight. I will need you three to understand where the other versions of us are and what they are doing, friend or foe."

"Most definitely foe."

We startled. Aubin stood at our table, his eyes wide.

He looked the same as when he had left us, down to the white shirt I had given him, but it still behoved me to be careful. "Are you our Aubin?" I asked tentatively.

He did not even make a smart remark. "Yes, I am. I've heard what the Aubin that lives here does."

"And?" I asked.

He swallowed hard. "Chief Executioner."

# CHAPTER 25



I whistled with shock.

"Keep quiet," the Assassin hissed.

I ignored him. "So without us, you go full-on legal killer."

"Shut up," Aubin snapped.

"No one wants to listen to me, Evyn," I complained.

"Dear, shh. Not helping."

I held my tongue.

"So the Aubin here works for Torgund, and in a trusted position too." The Assassin sat back. "No wonder the barkeep became bathed in sweat when he saw me."

I frowned, looking between the two tawny-haired men. "Is the Executioner the new Assassin? Is he Aubin and you're Aubins One and Two?"

The Assassin gave me a withering look. "He's technically the real Aubin here, but I'll stay as the Assassin, he—" he indicated Aubin with a tip of his head "—can be Aubin so it doesn't snap your fragile mind in two, and we'll call the other one Evil Aubin."

Evyn raised her hand. "We haven't met him yet, though."

I ducked my head to hers. "A Chief Executioner is going to be just a little bit evil, Evyn."

"Not necessarily!" she whispered back. "He's kind of performing a function for the public. Ish."

"Chief Executioner is also head of torture."

Evyn flushed. "Ah. Well. Um."

"Let's call him the Executioner." The Assassin nodded once. "Sorted."

I beckoned to Aubin. "Where are the other versions of us here?"

He stood at the end of our table, awfully exposed without a hood on hiding his features. I had a strong urge to reach up and tug him down next to me. He kept his voice low. "I haven't found out yet, I just thought you'd want to know about this Aubin straight away."

"Thanks," the Assassin said brightly. "Now you go enjoy this version of reality you wanted, and we'll take care of getting Evie out of the Tower."

"Yes, of course." Aubin ran his hands over his jerkin. "Well. I..." His searching gaze found me and Evyn.

Evyn looked away. "Look after yourself, Aubin."

His mouth twitched, arms sliding up and around his chest, holding himself together. His gaze met mine.

I held it, willing him to see my sincerity.

He said, "You could use my help."

My heart ached even as it leapt. "Indeed, no question there." I shifted over to give him room, pressing against Evyn. She scooted away.

Aubin slowly sat next to me, facing the Assassin. "I've been inside the Last Tower as well, and I remember more details than he does."

I nodded. It wasn't a dig, it was the truth, and he said it neutrally enough.

The Assassin steepled his fingers. "Ah, yes, was that when you rescued your Evyn? Isn't this repeating that, though? You didn't want to scale the tower, as I recall. You're excused and exonerated from any expectations here." His lips turned up. "This is the reality you asked for, after all."

I could definitely imagine the Assassin as a torturer, given that he seemed to be enjoying twisting the knife with a contented smile in place.

Evyn threaded her arm around my elbow as though we were out for a walk. I touched her hand. The pair of us were still, our churn of emotions quiet, waiting for what words Aubin would drop into us and ripple away.

Aubin's jaw twitched. "I still don't have a place here, this isn't my reality. I wanted to change my actions in my world and change my history. When does that happen?"

A flash of pain became hard determination. I bowed my head, latching on to my resolve. *I have to stay open.*

"We can't do that without the Spirit Shaper. She does the jump, we make the changes. Evie," the Assassin amended, sitting forward. "She's the only travelling mage version."

Aubin looked around at us all, gaze jumping over Evyn. "Then let's get her."

"Fine." The Assassin's face turned hard. "But I need you whole-heartedly in this endeavour. You cannot be partly committed; you must see this through. We will rescue Evyn or die trying." He put his hand palm up on the table.

"Yes," Shoulders said, putting his hand on his Aubin's.

"And me." I slapped my hand down.

"I'm in," my Evyn said. All three of us looked at each other to confirm; we would die before she even got a scratch.

Aubin sighed. "Yes. I'm in." He put his hand on mine. A flash of satisfaction warmed my chest. *At last.* Or, at least, for the time being.

Evyn put her hand up in the air. We stared at it. She lowered it again. "So, I've had an idea. What if I ping to where I'm from and see what happened to my family? That might give us some clues as to where the other versions of us are in this timeline."

The Assassin leant over his untouched beer. "That is a good idea, but how will you gather the information?"

"The internet is a hell of a drug," she said. "I can go to the library and be back in a jiffy."

I tried to parse that out.

"Are all of those words?" Shoulders asked.

She flashed him a small smile. "I can be there and back quickly."

The Assassin nodded. "Very well. One or two of us should go with you, of course." He lifted his drink and gestured to Shoulders. "He and I will try to create a safe base here. We've jumped to different timelines before and we know the drill."

"If you don't need me, I'll go with Evyn," I said.

She squeezed my hand. I too was grateful we would be together.

Aubin looked between the Assassin and us.

The Assassin took a slurp of beer, noisy in our silence. "Two Aubins together is noteworthy, especially if we have a famous counterpart."

"Then I suppose I have to go with you." Aubin's hard eyes dared me to challenge him.

I picked up my beer. "Good." It tasted watery, the foam sparse flecks rather than thick and heady. I put it down after a sip, trying to keep my face neutral so Aubin wouldn't think my grimace at the taste was for him. "Evyn? Is that alright with you?"

"Fine by me." Evyn held herself still, but her stomach churned with a mixture of the tremulous bubble in my solar plexus and a sour dread. "It's the gang back together."

The Assassin lifted his beer as if to clink it against mine. "Go well and be content that if there are any disagreements, it will all be fixed by that trip through time." His smile widened, showing a flash of his incisors.

*He definitely has the right characteristics for a torturer.* Shoving back my foreboding, I stood. "Let's go. No time like the present."

The Assassin chuckled with a cruel smirk. "Indeed." He handed me a lodestone. "Contact me when you get back. They won't work over a long distance, of course."

He meant across worlds into Earth. I tucked it into my jacket. "My thanks. Gods' luck here."

He inclined his head, and Shoulders lifted his hand in farewell as we three left the bar.

The high cavern roof was always disorientating after being inside. "I expect to see the sky when I come out of a building," I murmured to Evyn.

"Yeah." Her reedy voice barely reached my ears, not just because of the headscarf she wore.

Aubin walked three steps behind us, close enough that we were walking together but far enough to be out of my reach.

The silence between them was almost a fourth person in our group, an element of its own.

"Who do you think the MasterMancer or Mage is?" I asked for something useful to say.

Evyn shrugged. "I have no idea, Thorrn. Playing guessing games isn't going to be helpful." She squeezed my hand in remorse. "Sorry. I shouldn't snap at you."

"No, but you're right." I slowed my pace to match hers rather than march off dragging her along.

We climbed the stairs to get up and out of the Academy. We needed to get to the level of the castle at least in order to ping through to Earth, otherwise we would end up underground. To my knowledge, Evyn had not ever tried entering or leaving the worlds at the city gates, so it was unclear where we would ping through if we tried. "How close do you need to get to the castle?"

Evyn's grip on me tightened. "I don't want to go back there, and I don't need to," she whispered.

"Of course." Relief spread through me at the same time as I tried to think through every eventuality. Would we ping through into a car beast's path if we tried pinging from somewhere else? What if someone in the city saw us on this side?

Evyn's hard breathing convinced me to pull into a rest area. I sat next to her, tapping my fingertips on my Ranger leathers. The darker reds might not be recognised here as part of the castle forces. I needed a set of Special Forces reds to try and blend in when we did assail the tower.

Aubin came round the corner from below, gaze fixed on the steps ahead of him. He glanced up at us then tore his attention away, coming to a stop at the mouth of the cavern. Leaning against the wall, he looked up and down the stairs, like some kind of sentinel.

Evyn dug her nails into her palms while looking at his back, and I felt every little pinprick of pain, sharp against the deeper ache rolling inside her.

I took her hand and unrolled it, smoothing out each of her fingers. Her little hands were soft, not work-worn and callused like mine.

She stared off to one side before her eyes slid shut. She was tired, and not merely physically. Her tiredness extended to the swing and swirl of our emotions, hers and mine. Should I pull back to give her a break from my influence at least? That would not help her balance her own emotions, and the thought of leaving her to face heartbreak alone distressed me. No, I would try to be the calm direction she needed.

Her eyelids fluttered open. "Okay, I can go again. These stairs are a killer."

"This is another reason why I don't go to the Academy very often."

She dusted off her trousers from the grainy stone bench. "I would have thought you'd be up and down these twenty times a day, getting a sweat on."

"That *would* be a challenging exercise." I walked her toward where the rest area rejoined the stairs.

Aubin shifted aside, turning his face away from us.

I hesitated at the steps upwards. We had to get talking somehow.

"How many times a day did you have to climb up and down these, Aubin?"

He did not turn toward me. "Depends what was needed at the castle."

I licked my lips. I had to draw him out. "Give me an average. Half a score? Five?"

He shook his head. "I tried to bring everything I thought I would need, but there would be odd ailments needing a specific tincture or times when I needed to resupply. I organised it so I saw cases in the morning, took midsun down here gathering what I needed, then treating all the way up to the evenings."

"Oh. I was thinking this staircase was the reason why you are in trim condition." I waved him alongside us to carry on tackling the stairs up.

He hung back, but at least he was following at only a step behind us. "I trained every morning, at midsun and at night before bed."

The fact that he volunteered the information made my heart swell. "That's a punishing regimen. I like it." I settled into a rhythm of walking up the stairs, wondering what to try next. "Layloree showed me some of the training."

"Layloree?" He stumbled a step.

I spun around to grab him, but he had already regained his balance. He rolled his eyes at me, and I grinned back.

He didn't smile but he stepped up next to me, and my heart lifted further. I kept my gaze forward. If I reacted to him getting closer, he might pull back.

He asked, "You were saying something about someone called Layloree?"

"Yes, the Layloree who taught you Battlemistress blades. She took me through the cold training and some of the stances."

"Of course she subjected you to the cold training."

"It was heavily taxing despite not doing anything." I grinned, unable to keep the excitement from my voice.

"And of course you delighted in it." He sounded amused. If I looked at him, I might see a smile on his face. Would it vanish if I showed I'd noticed it, like some kind of animal that would only approach when no one was looking and flee if it sensed any attention?

His steps matched mine. "When did you encounter Layloree? Did you meet her through Tuniel?"

"Layloree came with us to find you. She's in Skien, ready to help take over the rescue operation if you needed us to remove you immediately."

His steps slowed. I slackened my pace, but Evyn pushed forward. I sped up again to keep up with her and Aubin followed behind, silence draping over us once more.

Sunlight warned me we had nearly gained the entrance. We emerged blinking, moving off to one side to let Evyn catch her breath. Wearing the headscarf and being breathless beneath it caused little spikes of panic in her chest. I rubbed her back. "Let's think of a better disguise for you, and you need a hood," I told Aubin.

"Yes." He put his hand over one side of his face, keeping the other half turned away from the opening to the street. Not that anyone was passing by, the city eerily quiet for how I knew it to be. Aubin faced the frieze of the five moons on the back wall. "The Rushia headscarf works well. We could get a colourful woman's one to hide your hair, and Rushia women veil their faces in between being betrothed and married."

Evyn's anger flared. "Oh, yeah, great, swan around pretending to be engaged to you. Lovely."

His shoulders flinched. "It would be a viable disguise."

Despite the pain, it was the best we had. "It's a good idea, Evyn."

"Don't," she hissed at me. "Whose side are you on?"

"Yours, always," I said without hesitation. "In order to travel safely, we need to hide your features."

She would listen to reason, or at least not be able to battle it without compromising too much of herself. Sure enough, I felt her relenting. "Fine, but I'm not happy about it."

"Yes, I can tell," I said.

We made our way to the Rushia district through desolate streets. The buildings around here were in disrepair just as in our world, something Gough tried to address but the Rushia settlers refused. They seemed to like the crumbling buildings, tacking their colourful tents around them and slowly replacing fallen stone walls with thin fabric, just the way they liked it. The Rushia did not build with stone very often, preferring to be able to roll up their lives and leave if need be.

On this world, it seemed they had done just that. Broken buildings lay crumbled in our path, the few tents threadbare and weather-worn, not loved and cared for.

"Maybe Rushia are rare in the city." I kept within an arm's length of Evyn as she peered down a side street.

"We cannot keep making assumptions based on how things are on our world," Aubin said, scanning up and down the shadowed streets.

Evyn tugged my arm. "There, that looks like a shop."

A woman sat smoking a pipe behind bolts of fabric lined up in an alleyway. Her eyes narrowed as Evyn and I approached.

"Well met, and the blessings of the gods be upon you," I said, the language flowing easily from me.

Her eyes flickered from me to Evyn and back. "How may this one be of service?"

Using Aglo's Rushia, I bartered for a golden headscarf and thin bronze veil for Evyn. "My thanks." I bowed and handed her the rubles the Assassin had given me.

As expected she spat in her hand and clapped her palms together before taking the coins. "May the gods smile on you."

I led Evyn back to where Aubin waited in a side street. "Some things are the same at least. Maybe the Rushia never change." I held the headscarf for Evyn.

She pulled the man's black one off, her long hair tumbling free.

"It's pretty fascinating, if a bit scary too. This is like some form of culture shock."

"Time shock?" I smiled at her. Turning the headscarf over, I tried wrapping it around her hair and succeeded in trapping her hand to her head. "Hm. This is harder than it looks."

"May I?" Aubin came up beside my elbow.

Evyn's anger twisted my stomach into knots. I breathed through it, trying to mitigate it, riding over the wave of fury as it swept across me.

It settled. "Fine," she snapped. "Be quick about it."

He took the golden fabric from me, unwinding it and carefully pulling her hair free.

Evyn looked to the floor but then raised her eyes, challenging him to look at her.

His face stayed composed, whatever he felt hidden and locked away from us. He focused on the task, but it did not escape me that his breathing had quickened.

With the headscarf secure in place he took the thinner veil from me. Little clips secured it to the headscarf, letting it flow down over her face. His long fingers brushed her temple with a tremble.

"All done." His tones came out husky and low.

Evyn twisted away from him, pounding up the street toward the castle.

I followed, long strides catching up to her. I looked over my shoulder at Aubin, pressing the man's headscarf Evyn had been wearing to his chest. "We need to wait for Aubin to put his headscarf in place."

"He will catch us up." Evyn rubbed her cheeks underneath the veil, her movements jerky. "I cannot wait for this stupid mess to be behind us."

"Me either." I looked up the wide boulevard up to the space in front of the gates between the city and the castle. The wooden gallows stood stark against the castle walls, the Last Tower prominent behind that. Loops of rope dangled, swaying in the heat, the price of failure and our future should we storm the tower and be defeated.

Evyn frowned. "You mean you're coming around to the idea at last?"

I had to think what she meant for a heartbeat. We were consumed with our own thoughts and worries. I tried to tune into her. "You're still the sole supporter of this change-time thing between us. I'm not, but I won't let that stand in the way of rescuing Evie from the tower."

Evyn huffed. "Yeah, I suppose it makes sense that you are the cool-headed one here. You have the love of your life and get to skip off into the sunset. What do I get? I get to change a man, and then he's so ruined by it that he wants to change it back and forget me entirely." Her voice hitched.

Something cracked inside me. "Oh, Evyn." Pain akin to Gavain choosing to follow orders rather than follow me, a path that conflicted with mine, swelled into the cracks, but infinitely sharper.

Her steps faltered. "It hurts, Thorrn. The one and only time I ask a guy out he decides to change time so he's never met me. I can't... I can't handle that kind of rejection."

"I'm here. I'm not going anywhere."

"I know, but... Dad couldn't stay, Aubin did a runner..." She bit back a sob. "What's wrong with me?"

The crack tore open into a pit. Like the bad portal, this clawed at me, dragging me toward the edge. Panic welled up inside me, inside us both.

"Nothing is wrong with you." Aubin had caught up to us, head-scarf in place at last. "Evyn—Lady Evyn, I mean, there's nothing wrong with you."

She shook her head against my chest, anger rallying her away from that dark despair. "Go away. I don't want your opinion, thanks but no thanks."

The intervention allowed me to regroup. "Evyn, listen to me." I tipped her chin upward. "You saved my life and burnt my pizza. Yes?"

Her smile lifted my heart, the sucking sadness that had threatened to overwhelm me abating. "Yes. I know. Alright, wobble over, let's focus." Turning away, she marched onward.

Aubin stood with his hands limp at his sides. He braced himself as I stepped close, but made no move to defend himself even though I was in his guard. If I were minded to, he wouldn't be able to block a punch to the gut at this distance.

"My thanks for helping her with the scarf." I paced away after Evyn, focusing on cataloguing what and who lined the streets. After a heartbeat, he followed me, and as natural as breathing I let him survey his side while I studied mine.

He had wanted to reassure Evyn. Seeing her in pain wasn't his aim, it hurt him deeply as well. Was this what his goal was, avoiding causing her pain?

He loved her, and he wanted to not love her. Why was that?

We slowed as we neared the outer walls, and I gestured down at my leathers. "I do have reds, but they are unusual. I can pretend to be escorting you, but if I'm challenged I'm not sure how I would fare trying to lie."

"Quite poorly," Aubin murmured.

Another accurate assessment. "Any other ideas?"

"We can ping through in the gardens." Evyn motioned toward the east. Between the castle and the wall, past the King's Lake, was a series of functional and decorative pleasure gardens.

"Where does that come out?" I asked.

"Close to the canal in a farmer's field. We can get across no problem."

"Then that's what we'll do." Steeling myself, I walked through the gates, trying to act as I always had. This castle was my home, the warp and weft that ran through me, making me. Torgund had twisted it, and from there his poison had made the city suffer. I recognised enough of the castle to make the dissonance resonate like a sour note inside me, homesick while walking through my home.

Evyn followed and Aubin brought up the rear. Keeping to an ambling pace, I scoured the training fields. They were still at it, endless drills that would exhaust the troops rather than replenish them. I saw no one I knew, but people that I felt I should recognise, as if they were close cousins. A sergeant stalked the rows with his head buried in a scroll of information, but I didn't recognise him at all. "Where are the other versions of my contingent? Gav and Al, Captain Barlay and the rest?"

"Torgund," Evyn murmured. That was all she needed to say.

My chest tightened. "Oh."

"This isn't our world." Aubin drew next to me, looking back at Special Forces, his expression hidden. "They are still alive in our reality."

"Yes, but it hurts to think of them dead and gone here, all that potential and all their lives just... wasted." I wrapped my hand around the pommel of my father's sword. If Aubin did change time, would that affect who survived Torgund's reign of terror on our world?

Aubin made a low noise, and as if he had heard my thoughts, promised, "I'll make sure they live."

"They are alive now. Will your choice change things?" The gravel changed into grey grass as we entered the formal gardens. Many of the beds sported low-lying flowers in a carpet of colour while a few were choked with weeds, something I knew our gardeners would have waged war over.

"Perhaps, but that other Assassin Aubin assured me I would be able to choose from a variety." His pace slackened, shaking his head at the state of the gardens.

"Let me find the right spot," Evyn said, moving forward.

I kept an eye on her, but when Aubin touched my arm, I turned toward him.

He held himself still. "This will be much easier on you as well. Think of all the friends you've lost since this time last turn."

I folded my arms slowly. He was speaking to me at last. I had to weigh my response carefully. "Those 'friends' didn't actually like me, if you're referring to my contingent." I ran a hand through my hair. "Gavain and Aleric explained their side of the events. I can see what it looked like to them."

"Gavain?" If I had thought he was still before, Aubin had gone very, very still now.

How to explain? "Yes, he returned, and—"

"And you decided to get back to making the same mistakes over again. When will you learn? Does he have to run Evyn through in front of you, or will you still explain away his actions?"

"He has changed. Really and truly changed. Aubin, listen. He has apologised and changed his behaviour. I saw the pain in his eyes when he realised he had really hurt Evyn." I kicked at a stray stone, embarrassment tight and hot. "I made mistakes too, it wasn't just his fault. I should have approached him when I became a sergeant, after we restored Gough. We would have slugged each other in the face a few times maybe, but I should have listened when he wanted to talk to me." I checked on Evyn, still walking around the beds muttering. "Aubin, I've changed. I want to listen to you—"

"No, you want to tell me to listen to you. You want me to come around to your point of view, because you don't want to budge from yours in the slightest." He bristled, as prickly as the overgrown briars surrounding us. "You've decided to let Gavain back into your life? Go to, it's no business of mine what company you keep."

"Aubin, he's part of the contingent. I have to work alongside him once he's back to active duty. If we're talking redoing choices then I think that, no matter how I phrased it, the Gavain back then would never choose to follow me as I was. He was ruthless and opportunistic, and I was arrogant and brash. He would not have changed sides to follow that, nor should I have expected him to."

Aubin's gaze locked onto mine, amber eyes unfathomable.

"I don't know if you saw something in me, or whether you just needed someone with the skills of Special Forces to help you, but once we rescued Evyn, I started to open up my mind and my heart, truly seeing what was around me. Maybe it was Evyn's influence and our bond, but I think a great deal of it was you, Aubin." I willed him to hear the sincerity in my voice, the earnest plea in my eyes.

He shook his head. "You had that spark, Thorrn, and Evyn would fan it with no help from me." Folding his arms tight, he stepped away from me.

*Is that an improvement, or have I made things worse?* At least I had gotten some honesty from him, seeing some of the raw turmoil he struggled with. I would have to unpick it slowly and when he opened to me, not keep digging and pulling things out when he wasn't ready to let me, and perhaps he would think over something I said.

"Got it." Evyn walked up to us. "Over here."

She led us to a quiet corner and, after a quick head turn to make sure no one was close enough to see, she pinged us through.

We appeared along the canal on the other side. "Very convenient."

"Not really," Evyn grumbled. "We have to walk to the nearest bridge. But look, it's not a farmer's field anymore." She pointed behind us at a tall set of houses. "Hopefully no one saw us just appear."

"Then let's depart, and quickly. Where is the library?"

Evyn fiddled with her veil. I helped her take it off. "It's in town. We'll take the bus from the park, just like old times." She scowled briefly, but it changed to a smile to look up at me. "Thanks for the help. We'll have to put our headscarves and your weapons away to walk into town."

I put the disguises in my pack and, although my father's sword protruded from the top, Evyn insisted that as long as it was cross guard down, it would look odd but not immediately like a banned weapon. Aubin's Battlemistress blades were well hidden on his back underneath his jacket.

We walked in silence along the canal to the road, where we were able to cross. "Just down here is what would be our house." Instead, we discovered a tall block of what they called "flats".

Evyn's mouth turned down as we passed. "Oh. That's a shame."

We continued to the park, except there was no park. More flats crowded the space it should have occupied.

"I did not imagine that the me here not meeting your equivalents would cause this much change," Aubin said, looking both ways up the street.

"Me neither." Evyn's face was pale. "Why would that affect town planning and building regulations on another world? This doesn't make sense."

"Maybe the situation that led to us not meeting has this wider effect, and not necessarily our meeting." Aubin sounded as though he was trying to convince himself.

Evyn led on, trying to navigate through the blocks of new homes to get to the road that had been on the other side of the park. I could feel her breaking heart, a twin to mine, shearing and splitting off shards that dug deep into me and her. It was no wonder she felt forgetting him was preferable to feeling this pain.

Talking about it often lessened it, or at least let it flow across the bond so it wasn't concentrated in one person. Evyn would open to me if I did so first. "I'm struggling, Evyn. It's hard to bear."

She glanced up at me. "I know. I feel the same way. It's not you, though, so don't think that. He's decided we're somehow to blame for all his problems so he's fixing it."

"And making it better for you two." Aubin had caught up, walking on the lower road next to us.

"Making what better?" Evyn snapped.

Aubin stared straight ahead. "Without me, you'd be married to the Prince of Dinahe sooner. I got in the way of that and I apologise."

Evyn snorted. "Sooner? I gave his jewel back to him after you left. So no, I don't think I'd be married to anyone."

Aubin's gaze snapped to her. "I heard he was promised to a person of importance in the castle... You gave it back to him?"

"Yeah. Not that you wish it to be your business."

"Why – you're right. It is none of my business." Aubin shoved his hands deep into his pockets. "I'll be sure to fix it so that Gerlay will give you the jewel and there will be no need for you to give it back."

"'Fix' who I'm married to? No thanks, I'll be in charge of that." Evyn rolled her eyes at me, mouthing, "Can you believe this?"

I rubbed the bridge of my nose. He thought he was helping. He was trying to improve her life by his measure: a solid husband incapable of giving her heartache.

"You wanted this too," Aubin reminded her.

I winced.

"Yes, well, why do I need it in the first place, hm?" She stomped off, and I jogged to catch up.

We arrived where the bus beast normally stopped, but there was no information about them that Evyn could see. Buses passed by, but they did not stop when Evyn hailed them.

"This traffic is quiet," I said, desperate to break the heated silence smothering us.

"Yeah." Evyn sniffed. "And the air smells better."

Eventually we had to give up and walk. The buildings of the town grew denser as we neared the heart of the market but there were a lot of glass buildings and huge signs flashing bright colours. The smell of strong restorative permeated the air.

"It's just advertising, coffee shops and offices. Shared spaces. Where's the shops?" Evyn flagged down a passer-by. "Excuse me? Where's the library?"

"Library? There hasn't been one of those for years. You must mean the archives, right?" The lady gave Evyn directions. "I can send these to you if you'd like..." She frowned. "Sorry, the network can't... can't see you." She raised an eyebrow. "Are you an anti?"

Evyn stared at her. "Uh, thanks for the directions. Hope you have a good day." She clung onto my arm. "No library? Network? Anti?" A wave of fear washed over me, that horrible feeling of the familiar tainted with the new rocking her as it had shaken me.

I had breathed through the feeling before, and I did it for her now. "This place is really very different from before, but we are navigating it admirably well." I marked some Earthians hovering around on small wheels, staring at them.

Evyn saw what I was looking at and smiled. "Those are roller skates. I recognise those at least." The relief from her at seeing something familiar that she could understand loosened the homesick feeling in my chest, and I could take a deep breath at last.

We walked to the archive place, but the doors would not open for us. Eventually a young man came to the entrance. "Sorry, it mustn't be working today, sometimes the scanner gets a bit dirty..." He wiped his sleeve on a box on top of the door.

"What's a scanner?" I asked.

"What's a – oh. Are you antis? Then you won't have chips. Wow. I haven't met antis before." He took a step back. "Are you immunised at least?"

"Yes," Evyn said firmly. "I'd like to access the internet please."

"An anti-networker asking to access the internet! Come in, let's get you started." He beamed and led the way down tall shelves stacked with books to a dusty box, using a cloth to wipe it down. "Sorry. Most people are networked nowadays so there's no need for terminals. Here. Let's log on... Right. So. The internet is—"

"I know what it is. I just want to do a quick search. Thanks." Evyn smiled.

"Alright. My mother is meeting me for lunch anyway... ah, here she is." The young man waved.

I followed his line of sight and nudged Evyn, perhaps a little too hard.

Her hand flew to her shoulder. "Ow! What?"

I gaped at the woman coming in through the door. She was older, but she still wore her hair pulled back from her face in severe fashion and great golden hoops in her ears.

"Mum! How was your lesson?" our docent greeted her.

Teresa grinned, the gaps in her mouth filled with white teeth. "Great, thank you, Jess. Ready to go?"

"Yes Mum, I'll just help these antis get settled."

Teresa frowned at Evyn, frozen beside me. "Do I know you from somewhere, love?"

She looked at me and her eyes widened. "It's you! The SAS man! But... no, can't be. You must be their kids. Wow."

My head swirled, but I could cope with the unexpected. She recognised us, so we must have helped her in this timeline!

Teresa cocked her hip. "So where did she and that hot pancake end up, eh?"

Evyn had been rendered a statue.

This did not deter Teresa. "Jess! Remember I said about what happened with your dad? Well these have to be their kids. Look exactly like them! What was her name... Evyn, that's it, used to call her Frog. Kind of cruel in hindsight but kids are cruel, eh. She did me an absolute favour, saved us both, darling, got me to rethink what I was doing and who I was with and why. So, what are they up to now then? Lost track of her, never saw her or him again after that, like you was my guardian angels or something." Teresa finally stopped talking, looking expectantly between myself and Evyn.

Evyn put on a wobbly smile on her face. "Oh. Uh. I'm sorry, I don't know who you are." The lie trembled on her tongue.

Teresa's delight dipped a little. "Well, I'm Teresa, and this is my son, Jess. Anti-networkers, eh. Always wanted to know what it's like off-grid. Must be hard, nothing works for you, right? Everything's all networked up, even doors in buildings, information, catching the bus, all just a thought and it happens. You must have to walk everywhere."

"I... yes."

The man checked his watch. "Come on, Mum. You're overwhelming them, this is probably their first time in a town!"

"Oh, Jess, it's not like there weren't towns before. Bet you think I grew up in black and white, eh?"

"Didn't you?"

"Cheeky!" She swatted his arm as she took it, and with a laugh he led her toward the doors as she talked at him in her rapid-fire fashion.

Evyn took in big breaths, the bond thrumming with prongs of panic. Her fingers flew across a small black bar, and she studied the words appearing on the box with a feverish intensity.

When she sat back, she rocked in her seat. "We're not just in a different timeline. We're in a different *time*. This is twenty years into the future, guys."

# CHAPTER 26

EVYN TURNED THE SCREEN TOWARD ME. BLACK LETTERS STOOD STARK against a white background, but all manner of images danced along the periphery. I had no hope of deciding what she was trying to show me. "What does it say?"

Evyn lowered her voice. "From what I can tell I was born here, right time, right place, and me and Mum used to live here. The blogs I wrote when I was in my 'poor me' phase are here, even. It's like... this is me, but then we just disappear."

She moved a small stone-like object on her right, changing the view on the screen. "There's a local news article about the house being abandoned, a bit of police presence trying to track us down, but we're just indefinitely missing persons. See, missing posters." She pointed at a picture on the screen.

I hunkered down next to my Evyn, staring at the image of her in a smart shirt with a tie, her mouth smiling but her eyes empty.

Evyn said, "That's me in my school uniform, probably the most recent picture they could lay their hands on, and that was eighteen years ago here."

My chest squeezed painfully, my vision darkening to the picture on the screen. "Where is this Evyn? Where are you, what happened?"

"Breathe, Thorrn." Evyn took my hand. "I'm right here."

They were all my soul companion, every single one of them across all the worlds. A terrible swell of foreboding knocked into me. "You wouldn't just disappear."

Aubin leant in on her other side to look at the image, his gaze darting across the screen. He could absorb the information and parse it much faster than I; I stepped back to let him move closer.

His ears flushed, sidling closer to Evyn, but he focused on the screen. Aubin pointed at something. Evyn bit her lip but manipulated the stone she held, and the image became bigger. "My thanks, Lady Evyn. Let's think. You were here and you saved Teresa, just as you did before. This could be our timeline, but why have we jumped forward in time?"

Evyn squeezed her lips shut, but then the mystery proved too strong a pull to resist helping Aubin. "The boy that guided us in said he would get us close enough. This must be the longest period without us meeting that he could find."

Aubin murmured, "That matches the intel we have that Torgund took over a score of years ago."

"We're, what... fortyish here? Teresa looked about that."

Aubin maintained his rigid stance. "What went wrong?" he whispered.

Nausea tipped into me, sudden fear for the girl in the screen seizing my limbs. "Something happened on Oberrot, and I think it has to do with the tower." I glared at Aubin. "You said you didn't want to scale the tower? Well, this is what happens when you don't."

Aubin flinched. "I asked not to meet you at all," he stated, voice quiet.

"Same outcome." I reined in my rage. It would not help find the lost girl, her pale image the only echo of her presence.

"I... I would never want you to be hurt. Neither of you. In any case, we cannot even be sure yet that something untoward has happened."

"Are you finally developing an optimistic outlook for once?" I stood, needing to move.

"Of a sort, I suppose." Aubin watched me warily. "When we catch up to this Evyn, she won't know who I am. You'll see first-hand what a blessing that is."

I wanted him to speak to me, but I didn't want him to express sentiments like that. My chest ached, wrenching the teeth out of my anger. *He has to be hurting badly if he believes that about himself.*

"Thorrn." Evyn touched my hand. "Are you alright? You... you feel different."

"Different how?" Aubin reached out toward Evyn's shoulders, ready to pull her away. "About to slip into a rage different?"

"No, I'm in command of myself." I breathed deeply, trying to unseat this pity. He wouldn't appreciate it, and it wouldn't help him.

I had to find something that would, but Evie was the priority. Looking at Evyn's picture on that cold screen made my heart howl. "Are we done here, Evyn? Let's go back. The alts might have worked out we've come forward as well as sideways."

❈ ❈ ❈

THE WALK back from the library to the canal was quiet, each of us consumed with our own thoughts. The tower was designed to be difficult to assault and it would not be easy under any circumstances, let alone if we ended up having to fight our way up. "We need disguises, uniforms," I muttered to myself. "Perhaps we can make the same ploy that Aubin and I managed to pull off."

Aubin hung back a step, falling into pace alongside me. "That only succeeded because the men guarding her called me up there, and there were no other guards in place along the tower defences."

I accepted that. "Instead, we'll figure out their rota and password of the day and relieve them at the appointed time."

"That would mean we need to infiltrate Special Forces. Applying, winning their trust, working for them for a while. How long before new recruits are posted to something as important as the Last Tower?"

"At least three turns." A knot of frustration tracked up my throat. "Any ideas?"

"I'm thinking."

I watched his face, the narrowing of his eyes, the twists of his lips, the working of his jaw. His mind rifled through information and leapt to conclusions far faster than mine. If there was a way I couldn't see, he would find it. I left him to it, trying to keep my own thoughts to myself so as not to break his concentration.

When we got to the ping-through place Evyn and Aubin pulled their headscarves into place. Evyn wound hers three times and then let her hands fall, defeated. "I give up. Can you help me with this please, Aubin?"

"Of course." He finished tucking his headscarf in, stepping close to help her.

Evyn gnawed at her lower lip while he wove the layers around her head and hair. She had bitten it raw and the cold winds of Skien had chapped the rest, so her teeth sparked pain across the bond. She did not seem to notice.

Aubin did. His hands fell. "Please don't do that," Aubin murmured.

"Mm?"

Aubin touched his own lips. Evyn raised her hand as a mirror, then winced when she felt her mouth. "Oh. Nerves. I didn't realise I was doing it."

He kept his hand raised. "I can give you something to soothe that when we get back."

"Maybe." Evyn spun away to pin the veil into place herself. Her feelings burnt hot, soldering a shield between us and him. Accepting something else from him was too much of a concession for her; she would help him and give readily enough, but receiving from him was a vulnerability she would not allow, as if it would make her beholden to him afterwards. She turned away, footsteps thumping up the canalside.

Aubin's hands fluttered down to his sides. He studied the surface of the canal, the ripples along the edges and the leaves floating, suspended, in the water column. He said nothing, and I reciprocated.

Once Evyn's anger simmered down, and after confirming we were ready, Evyn opened the way. I went first, stepping through into the heat, on edge to hear if there was an outcry at my sudden appearance, sweat standing on my forehead not only from the sudden change in climate but the sheer stress of standing still in potentially hostile territory. There was no hue and cry, no alarm and to arms, and I waved for Evyn and Aubin to join me.

The lodestone the Assassin had given me jangled in my pocket. I couldn't afford to be distracted here, so I didn't answer it immediately, waiting until we had walked along the walls and then out through the gates.

The sun was setting, red drenching the wisps of clouds above us and the gallows we stood behind. "The lodestone won't stop vibrating, the Assassin might need something urgently."

"Answer it then." Evyn shifted from foot to foot. "What's the matter?"

I put my hand on it and my awareness fled away, into the white stillness of a lodestone connection. The Assassin's thoughts flooded mine, terse and tense. *"Thorrn, there you are. We have a problem."*

*"What's happened?"*

*"While we were sorting out a secure place to stay, they must have cut the bond between Evie and Shoulders. Or, she's dead."*

*No.* Grief gripped me, tearing into my chest. How could his thoughts be so calm? All I sensed from him was cold tranquillity, no anger, no pain.

The Assassin carried on his report. *"Shoulders went berserk. He's been arrested and detained in the castle."*

The castle? *"Then he's in the dungeons."* We were in no way ready for any assault, but we could try something more covert. *"The dungeons are only on the second level. We will turn around and go back, Aubin and Evyn can ping, and we'll make our way there as quietly as we can to rescue him."*

*"He will be hard to handle."* Images of Shoulders in a full rage, tossing Regulars into the castle walls, flooded into me. The Assassin's memories. Shoulders was stronger than me by a wide margin, but what broke me were his wet cheeks. He had been sobbing in his rage.

*"Evyn... my Evyn can reach him. She did it once before, in these very cells, or ours, anyway."* I pulled my grief to the side. *"Our mission was fruitful and we learnt we are a score of years into the future."*

*"That accounts for a great deal."* He paused a heartbeat. *"We could be in your timeline."*

*"We have come to that conclusion as well."*

*"While you're rescuing him, I'll need to relocate. I'll also see if I can find out who the MasterMancer or Mage is."* He was collected, running through his list. How many times had he done this on other worlds, to fall back into this pattern when his wife could be dead?

Something touched my arm, outside of my awareness of this white space. *"I have to go. Go well."*

*"Gods' luck, swordsman."*

I broke off the contact, blinking at the sudden sunlight. I shaded my eyes. "What's amiss?"

"You are." Evyn hugged my arm, tears in her eyes. "You're Calling. What's wrong, what did he say?"

My sorrow had bled across the bond, but I could not pull away from Evyn, not when Shoulders was undergoing the most horrific experience. "Evie, Shoulders..." My voice cracked. "Their bond has been cut. They are sundered." *Or she's dead*, my heart screamed, but I refused to voice it.

Aubin knew the implications, the scenario I couldn't face. He put his hand on my shoulder.

I leant into it only for a heartbeat, bowing my head. It was too much, all this was overwhelming to begin with and now this...

I fortified myself on Evyn's and Aubin's strength, screwing my resolve down tight and trapping my sadness beneath it. "We are on a rescue mission. Shoulders went berserk and got arrested. We have to get him out of there."

Aubin put his hands on his hips. Like the Assassin, he locked his emotions down and focused on the task. "We need to wait until nightfall at least, we're less likely to be seen around the castle grounds. We will ping in and out of the cells tonight to rescue him."

"I agree. I don't like waiting, but it will be quieter then, and we need time to run through several iterations of a plan to account for unexpected events."

Aubin's amber eyes, lit ruddy by the sunset, widened slightly. "You aren't frothing at the mouth to charge in, expecting to over-come all obstacles by a combination of luck and skill?"

"No, that would be unwise."

Aubin leant back on his heels. "You *have* changed."

*Have I?* "It's the most logical thing to do, that's all. Come on, let's get out of the shadow of the gallows."

"We need something to eat, a bit of rest." Evyn trotted next to me as I strode toward the boulevard. "We haven't stopped since this morning," she reminded me gently.

"You're right, back in another world, time and place." I scrubbed my hair, pulling up the hood of my Ranger jacket. "I need to get away from here, Shoulders has been seen throwing Regulars at the city walls."

"Good for him," Evyn said, a touch of ferocity in her words as she glared at said walls.

I chuckled, surprised when Aubin also joined in. She grinned at me but her smile flickered out when her gaze passed over Aubin.

He did not react to that. "I know a place out of the way. Or, at least, I did."

"Then let's see what time and tide has done to it," Evyn said, putting her arm through mine.

I indicated that Aubin should proceed and he hesitated for a heartbeat, striding forward over the canal bridge and taking care to watch either side of the street carefully.

Watching his profile walk confidently down the boulevard, I knew he would be reliable as a forward scout. He said he wanted nothing more to do with us, but still I trusted him to protect us.

I touched Evyn's shoulder. "Are you hale and well, Evyn? How are you coping?"

She nodded, eyes surveying the grey glass of the storefronts we passed. "Skidding around on adrenaline but it's strangely okay. It's just been one thing after another. I suspect when I try to sleep tonight it'll all come crashing down on me." She looked up at me. "Changing time? Is that really real?"

"Your reaction was what convinced *me*, Evyn. I'm not sure if it is real." I nodded to Aubin's back, his tight shoulders belying his disquiet. "This must be hard on him as well."

"He's the one making it weird, don't feel sorry for him," Evyn muttered.

"He wants to fix all the perceived mistakes he's blaming himself for in both our lives. In a twisted way, he thinks he's helping us too."

"I know that. I know." Evyn's grip turned hard. "He still cares, he just wishes he didn't. When we exploded into his life he got to have a lot more experiences, I suppose, but now he doesn't want to live with the consequences and the memories that have been left in the wake. It has to be weighing on him a lot, Thorrn, for him to want to change it."

*At last.* Evyn's compassion resurfacing meant that hopefully her anger had abated for now and she would be able to think with her whole heart once more. I needed to speak to her about this, and finally she might be open to doing so. "He thinks I won't listen to him, that I will force him to be what I want him to be. It's just that I saw all that potential in him, Evyn, and I wanted him to use it, to trust in himself enough to see it."

Evyn frowned at me. "He didn't run because of that. He ran because you saw something he feels he's not. He's not an unstoppable force or an amazing fighter, and he can't move stones or melt metal. He isn't going to be able to save your life every single time, you know."

"He has so far, but I get the thrust of your point." That was even more pressure, preventing me from feeling the consequences of my choices, morphing my mistakes and missteps into a series of successes. "Gods. It's no wonder that I never had friends at all."

Evyn hugged my arm, a beat of reassurance racing up the bond. "He's also got that whole killing thing to reconcile with. I know you have tenets and things to decide what moral and ethical choices you want to make ahead of time, but he didn't, and then he added, 'Kill painlessly', which, okay, I suppose is an improvement somehow?"

"It's a good and noble tenet to carry." I checked behind us and refocused on Evyn. "He hates that he had it in himself to kill me. He cannot reconcile himself to that, the part of himself that can disconnect his emotions and complete the task."

"That very ability is one of the reasons you value him as a Ranger partner," Evyn said gently.

"Yes, but only one. If he wanted to change, I would try to change too. Anything but this."

"Mm." Evyn's pain simmered toward the surface again.

We passed more boarded shops. A man slumped in the doorway of one, wrapped in blankets. This city was dire compared to ours. I marked three more boarded-up shops, then a red-and-white pinstripe flag that made my heart contract. Another soul swap. My hand tightened around Evyn's. Their magic had been used to render Evie and Shoulders separate until they could get close enough to reinstate their bond. Having Evyn cut from me was my worst imagining, second only to her demise.

Evyn jiggled my arm. "Thorrn, are you okay?"

I shook my head. "No. I'm thinking about Evie, how we have to get her free from the Tower, but I'm also scared about afterwards. About what Aubin will choose."

Aubin slowed and stopped in the street.

I pulled up to him, hand on my father's sword. "What is it?"

"It's actually here." He pointed to a small Dinahen restaurant, a low bench set outside under a twisted tree.

Run by a small round woman who bustled back and forth making sure we were comfortable on the pillows and bringing out big bowls of hearty meat and rice, this was the most comfortable Evyn and I had felt since entering Keltskarr, despite sitting in silence across the table from Aubin, who also sat unbending and ate mechanically.

"Well, this isn't awkward," Evyn said.

Aubin put his plate down with a clink. "There's nothing we can do about that."

I cast about for something safe to say. I did not yet want to turn our attention to the mission ahead; a mental breather would do us great good.

Evyn gently poked her skewer at a morsel of meat. "What is or was this?" she asked me.

"Spiced chicken." I lifted my hands helplessly. "It tastes good."

She turned it over to expose the red side. "Spiced with what?"

Aubin leant in, frowning. "Let me try it."

I gripped the table, heart rate spiking. "Oh gods, it's not another type of herb that can hurt her?"

"No, not in a Dinahen restaurant." Aubin's skewer hovered over Evyn's plate. "May I?"

"Knock yourself out," she said.

He raised an eyebrow at her.

She flushed. "Go to, that's an invitation to proceed."

Aubin nodded, spearing the offending morsel. Taking a bite, he closed his eyes. "Oregano, tarragon, saltine, marjoram and garlic." He took a sip of water.

"I didn't know you could do that, that's cool." Evyn's eyes gleamed with curiosity, the curtains of anger parting slightly.

I said, "He uses it to identify what people have been poisoned with too."

Aubin turned a dark look onto me.

"What, by licking them?" Evyn scrunched up her nose.

I laughed quietly. "If they ate or drank it, Evyn, where would it be?"

"Ew, their mouths? You lick inside their mouths? Gross!" She slapped a hand to her face. A fizz of delight filled her chest, her sadness lifting in the moment.

I nudged her. "A kiss isn't gross, Evyn."

"Oh, a kiss. Well, that's okay then." She put a hand over her mouth, giggling. The sound made my heart lift. "I'm imagining you having to kiss patients now."

"A respectable method of diagnosis, I assure you." Aubin sat as straight as a Dinahen staff.

"Yes. Respectable." I smiled and pushed my plate aside, gratified to notice his ears going pink.

The moment had restored something, reminded me of what we were and what we could be again. Rather than point that out to him, I moved on. Aubin would have seen it, he was perceptive.

I set out little toothpicks in what I could remember the defences of the Last Tower looking like.

"They jutted out a bit more," Aubin commented, poking one of my picks.

I grunted. "You're sure? Of course you're sure." I groaned, sitting back on the cushions, the comfort far removed from the inevitable discomfort of assailing the Tower. "How are we ever going to overcome these?"

Aubin drummed his fingers on the table. "The Rushia Art would suggest we can fire into the kill slots at the men behind."

"Killing men doing their job. I'll keep that for when we've run out of other ideas."

Aubin pulled his hands to his chest. "I... Yes." His face fell.

I met his eyes. "You *aren't* a murderer. That's why you're having so much trouble with thinking you are."

He shook his head. "I can't help myself, evidently." He shut his eyes tight.

"Aubin, I kill when I need to. The last time were some Skienien rogues. Thinking through the tenets we want to swear to helps with—"

"You look a colourful specimen, but a few cosmetic additions only skin deep won't do anything for me."

"It's not about tattoos, Aubin." I stroked my forearm. "They just represent the words you swear in your heart, the truth you want to uphold. What's your truth?"

"I don't *know*, Thorrn." His voice rang with an edge of discomfort.

"I think you don't swear it, but you live it anyway. Why did you come with me to storm the Tower?"

The jump of my conversation seemed to upend him. He opened and closed his mouth, the headscarf fluttering, but no words emerged.

Had I pushed too hard? I refocused on my model. "I don't suppose you can ping upwards?" I asked Evyn.

She wrenched her attention from Aubin, looking down at the picks as though I'd caught her out. "I don't think so. We'd have to jump up, and quite far so that we weren't ever exposed to projectiles."

"The other alternative is to drive through with my armour." I hopped my finger along the defence lines. If only it were really that easy.

Aubin said, "Your armour won't be able to sustain that many hits."

"I know. This fortress was designed to withstand an attack from an entire army guarded by a handful of men." It was made of stone. Tuniel would probably disable the kill slots and trap the men inside, but she was back on our world, a score of turns in the past. "Tuniel wanted us to find you, you know."

Aubin threw up his hands. "Keep to one topic at a time, Thorrn."

I scrubbed my face. "My apologies, I have a lot to think about."

"Yes, well." Aubin's gaze fell back to his plate, the food barely touched.

The silence sank low between us, sullen and swollen.

I tried again. "She felt your pain. She said she wanted you to be closer."

He turned his head away. "That's not sensible in the least. The ruse is something we have practised for most of our lives, certainly all our adult lives." He let out a gruff sigh. "What is she up to?"

"She's combining her magic with a medimancer or mage. They've made a metal heart, a beautiful silvrine shape as big as her fist. It works, apparently. Well, so far."

A flicker of interest sparked in his eyes. "Sounds quite fascinating."

"It is. It's a shame I understand none of it." I waited for either of them to take the bait, forcing my tension through my fists under the table. *Please.*

"I do." Evyn pulled her veil back into place. "The hardest bit was getting the electrical signals from the brain to translate into something the metal could read. I helped out there, I studied human biology for a while."

"Electrical... you mean sparks?" Aubin's eyes brightened beneath his headscarf.

I could barely restrain my excitement. *Excellent.* I joined in. "We have sparks in our bodies?" I stared down at my chest. "In my chest?"

Evyn patted my hand. "Yes, a signal to go from your brain to your heart to tell it to beat."

"Like a message? Once a day?"

She laughed again, and my heart received the message that she was feeling leagues better. "Try every single beat."

"Gods. I had no idea." How did she know all these things? It was remarkable she could learn and retain so much.

"Has she tested it yet?" Aubin asked.

"Yes." Evyn glanced at me, tugging at her veil. "On Gavain."

He blinked slowly.

"Gavain came back in really bad shape," Evyn explained quietly. "He was going to die eventually. Tuniel offered to replace his heart."

"She undid what I did." His fingers curled in against his palms, his back rounding again.

Evyn nodded, her eagerness turning sour with sorrow. She had loved Aubin's interest in what she was working on, but now that was tainted.

I hastened to explain. "You can choose to look at it like that. Tuniel also said she would be able to affect his metal heart from afar just as she can move my armour."

"So it's a provision." Aubin sat straighter, eyes downcast again. "You know, I could change it so he never gets stabbed. You'll come to this sort of accord that you seem content with, and Evyn will never have been hurt."

That slowed me. If I had spoken to Gavain, would he have jumped on the hazing so hard? Would he have dragged Evyn into our disagreement?

"We made mistakes," I set out, for myself as much as him. "Learning from those mistakes was painful but vital. Gavain and I are both changing, but we needed to travel that road." I looked down at my hands. "Of course I would never want Evyn hurt. If there is a way that we can learn those lessons without her safety at risk, then I would be open to it." A world where all my mistakes would be erased, and I could be the perfect member of Special Forces again.

I grabbed the pommel of my father's sword. "But it's not real. It's chasing what we think we want, rather than what we need, and what type of man is the result of that?"

Aubin's gaze stared past my ear. "There are only so many lessons a man can take, Thorrn. Only so many truths he can confront about himself before it becomes too much."

"Then share them." I put my hand palm up on the table. "Come to me, tell me what they are, and we'll defeat them together. When Evyn was in that tower we worked together seamlessly, because we had a common goal despite being nearly complete strangers to one another."

Aubin gestured to my model. "We should focus on rescuing Shoulders."

I left my hand there. "We should, you're right." He would think about what I said, of that I was sure.

Night fell and deepened while we talked through a few scenarios of how to rescue Shoulders from the dungeons. Evyn would come as fast ping support and she was getting better at adapting to high-risk situations, so even though my heart rebelled at the idea of escorting her into danger, I knew she would be able to ping away.

We paid and walked back, projecting confidence with every step up the street as if we belonged here when truly this was not a home I recognised. The city was quieter than I had ever seen it or wished to see again, the Dinahen district subdued, the Rushia tents dark, the Daronians closing their doors firmly to the outside. The city cowered in the dark under Torgund's heavy rule. It jarred me to see my city so different, sickening me when I knew what was possible from the experience on our world.

The gates to the castle grounds were closed. "That's unusual," I whispered to the others. Ours had possibly rusted open, I had never in my life seen them closed.

"Probably par for the course here," Evyn whispered back. "I can ping us through when we're ready."

Aubin put his hands to the headscarf. "It's too dark here for me to see well. I need to take this off."

"Then do so. I suspect if we're spotted it won't make any difference anyway."

"I'll do the same." Evyn pulled her disguise off, and we shoved it into my pack. We left it behind a strut of the gallows; there was nothing valuable in it apart from the stones to reset Amare and

Evyn's bracers, but I couldn't carry all of them on a stealth mission. I put handfuls in my pockets along with the lodestone from the Assassin.

We signalled we were ready and Evyn pinged us through the gates, making a wide portal. It hovered just above ground level on Earth, and we had to jump a long stride. I went first, turning to catch Evyn and grabbing onto her forearms. Aubin landed lightly beside us, and Evyn closed the portals.

The grounds were empty and still, no messengers flowing and no patrols nearby. The lights in the castle were few and stuttering, tiny pinpricks in the looming edifice. Aubin took the lead as we made our way around the walls alongside the training grounds. The cells were on the second floor of the castle, and I knew from my own experience some windows overlooked the training grounds. Were they in the same location here? This was the first obstacle.

Aubin whispered, "I can see metal bars, the cells are where we expect them to be." Light flickered fitfully between the target windows, a candle or perhaps a brazier.

I sent him a Ranger signal, *lead on*, and Aubin took a step.

A howl of agony rang from the castle. My stomach contracted.

Evyn grabbed my arm. "It's him." She looked ready to storm the castle herself, despair and determination etched on her face.

"The servant's stair. Come on," I whispered to her.

Aubin led us to a passage between the barracks and the castle. He crouched by the lock and I took a guard stance, Evyn behind me. There was no possibility that no one else could hear those occasional but heart-ripping screams, and yet nothing stirred. No one dared to inquire.

Was this what it had been like under Torgund? My home changed, fear ruling as effectively as the monarch?

"We're in." Aubin prised the door open and stole inside, steps noiseless.

Ours were not, and it kept my senses strained for any sounds ahead of us. Sweat made tracks down my back and chest, but my hands remained dry and still, completely in my command. My heart-beat sang with apprehension, Evyn's and mine, shot through with a core of resolve. We would rescue Shoulders.

The screams were muffled while we were in the backstairs but rang out every hundred or so heartbeats. Aubin led us through twisting passageways and up narrow stairs before drawing to a halt. "This will open up near the upper atrium. We will turn left to get to the corridor for the cells. Go still if you see anything move."

Evyn and I nodded assent. The door creaked and we all locked into place, but I could not hear any movement in the atrium. Not that I blamed the castle denizens of this reality; perhaps there was a curfew, and the only crime the men outside had committed had been walking.

There was a guard on duty at the cells. We had planned for this: Evyn pinged me and Aubin behind him, and Aubin subdued him with somnus root. We travelled inside the cells, pinging through the walls from one to the next.

A low hiss started just before Shoulders's next scream. We were close enough now to hear his groans. "Evie!" he cried out. Then a regular *scrape, scrape* as he panted and moaned.

Evyn bit down on her knuckles.

I halted them. "Next cell. It has to be." I drew my sword and checked Aubin was armed. "Evyn, open the way but stay in here until we have secured the area. Once we've done that, you can come in and help him."

"Yes." Tears rolled down her cheeks.

"Count of three," I whispered. "One. Two. Three!"

She opened the two portals and left them there. I jumped across ready to fight.

There were only two people in the room. One was Shoulders, shirtless and dangling from chains in the ceiling, his torso smoking with angry red burns. He was sweating and shaking, blinking through tear-blurred eyes to see me.

Facing him, with a red-hot poker in hand, was Aubin.

# CHAPTER 27

*The Executioner*. He looked much the same as my Aubin except for the deeper frown lines on his face and his slightly receding hairline. His face maintained that regal look with his high cheekbones, and his light eyes were still cutting.

He raised one eyebrow slowly at me. "A twin?"

My Aubin jumped through. "Move over, Thorrn," he groused. When he came face to face with himself, he took a step back.

The Executioner's eyebrows shot up. "Who are you?"

"Introductions later. Drop that poker." I raised my sword.

"I don't think so." Swinging it up to flare red, he set it an inch from Shoulders's throat. Shoulders tried to push back from it, neck muscles straining. The Executioner watched with no emotion. "That will burn right through his jugular and kill him, by the way."

I ground my teeth, keeping my sword trained on the Executioner. A deadlock.

He sneered. "Now then. Who are you?"

"I... I'm..." Aubin looked him up and down, his calm deserting him.

"Hi, I'm Evyn." She came in through the portal to stand behind me.

"Evyn, get back in the other cell, now!" I ordered.

"I had a better idea. Trust me." She flashed me her smile. Her resolve was as firm as mine, and she was absolutely certain about whatever she was doing here.

"Evyn, a Dinahen man's name. And what are you doing here?" the Executioner asked.

Evyn pointed to Shoulders. "We're rescuing our friend. Will you let him go, please?"

The Executioner shook his head, eyes still on Evyn. "This is highly irregular but, sadly, I am far too curious in what he has to tell me." He lifted the poker slightly.

Shoulders made a choking noise in the back of his throat as the heat hit him. I jerked forward.

Evyn stopped me. "What is it you want to know?" she asked, her voice level and barely louder than the sizzle of coals in the brazier.

"I ask questions here usually, but I suppose this is something a little different." To my great relief, the Executioner put up the poker.

Shoulders gasped in relief, his head falling forward.

"This needs reheating anyway." The Executioner moved to the back wall and shoved it deep into the coals, grinding them together. I swallowed hard against the nausea stirred by the smell of smoke and burnt flesh. He selected another and while he lifted it, he didn't thrust it in Shoulders's direction. *Yet.*

"The King is... hiding something from me," the Executioner said. "There's someone up in the Last Tower that he's protecting. This lad was brought to the cells in somewhat of a state. When the guards here could get sense out of him they told me what he said. I like to collect information, and I reward it when it is passed to me with veracity and velocity.

"He's apparently trying to get to the Last Tower. He knows what is in there, and is willing to accept death to get to it." He shrugged.

"That's it? You're torturing him for that?" Evyn frowned.

"My dear girl, politics being politics, it behoves me to know everything that's going on in this castle. Especially things the king I am loyal to doesn't want me to find out."

"You're being awfully open with us," I said.

"I am, aren't I. That's because you aren't going anywhere."

"I can walk through walls," Evyn pointed out.

"A very neat trick. But can you get out of floors, I wonder?"

My feet sank into the stones. The Executioner took his hand from the side of the wall where a soul jewel glowed faintly. Stone magic no doubt, perhaps from the Tuniel of this world. A quick scan showed me that Aubin had been trapped as well, but Evyn was just unbalanced.

The Executioner's eyes narrowed.

"Evyn, run!" I said.

"No. Trust me." She plucked her feet out of the runny stone and picked her way toward Shoulders and the Executioner.

The torturer swung the poker toward her, red tip flaring in the air between them. "Stay right where you are." He seemed serene, his hands steady, but his jaw was tight.

Evyn said, "I'll make you a deal. If you let them all go, we'll have a chat, just me and you."

"Evyn!" I howled, reaching for her.

"I'll tell you what's up in the Last Tower, who we are and where we've come from, all that."

"D... Don't..." Shoulders groaned.

The Executioner's gaze burnt into Evyn's. "You are offering to stay here, with me?"

"Yep." She held out her hand.

"Me?" His mouth twitched upward. Was he amused?

Evyn kept her hands raised. "Yes, you. You've seen what I can do; if I don't like the hospitality, I'll go, so I trust you'll keep it civilised. But to start with, as a show of faith, I'd like to see my friends safe."

The Executioner blinked slowly several times.

I looked between them, Aubin doing the same. What was Evyn up to?

"Very well." He released the chains and unlocked Shoulders's manacles.

Shoulders swayed on his feet. I reached for him, holding onto his arm to keep him upright. He leant against me, utterly exhausted.

The Executioner brushed past us and pushed another jewel in the side of the cell. The floors shivered and returned to normal, disgorging my ankles and releasing Aubin.

The Executioner opened the door, jerking his head at us. "Well? Off with you."

My heart lurched in my chest. "Evyn..."

Shoulders coughed. "Don't... leave her... with him."

I wrapped my arm carefully around him, my gaze on Evyn.

She looked contented. Happy, even. "I'll be fine. Thorrn? Really." She felt certain, even a little smug, as if she had just found the solution to a puzzle.

She could ping out of the walls, she would be more able to escape than any of us, but the idea of her alone here, facing the Executioner, made my heart scream.

She frowned at me. "Go, Thorrn. I'll be fine."

I took a shuffling step toward the door, dragging Shoulders on top of me, when the poker whooshed past me again.

The Executioner levelled it at Aubin. "I want a little chat with him as well."

Aubin stayed still, gaze darting from the end of the poker and back to the eyes of his counterpart.

Evyn stepped in front of him, folding her arms. "We'll have ours first and then we'll see. Let them go."

The man looked from Aubin to her and back again. "Fine." He stepped aside. "Quickly now, I'm eager to do some questioning."

I staggered underneath Shoulders, trembling. "Evyn, I can't—"

"You can. I'll be back soon, promise." She smiled at me again.

I glared at the Executioner. "If you hurt her, I will kill you."

"I don't doubt you'll try," he said.

*Is there anything of my Aubin in this one?* The face was the same, his eyes quick, and he seemed outwardly unfazed by anything. His gaze was drawn to Evyn, the poker held lowered away from her.

"I'll stay with you," Aubin told Evyn, just as calm.

Relief surged over me.

Evyn turned in place, putting her back to the Executioner to face Aubin. "Why? I'll be fine here."

"I'm staying." Aubin stayed still, planting his stance, immove-able. "I'm not leaving you."

A prickle in my solar plexus turned to a surge of heat, so much so I staggered. A bubble of love pierced through my tension, my shoul-ders dropping.

*I would trust him with my life and with Evyn's. I would trust her beyond that.*

Pink-faced, Evyn waved to me. "You better get going. Look after Shoulders, and I'll see you soon, don't worry."

"I cannot swear I will not worry." Seeing them standing together shored up my resolve.

I dragged Shoulders out against his exhausted but vehement protests. "Don't leave her with him!"

"She will be fine. She is with Aubin," I said firmly.

Hopping, we made it to the servants' stairs and down, my head and heart disorientated but strangely composed. Evyn had been so sure that she could take command of the situation, and she had, the Executioner giving in to her demands immediately. Layloree had been right: she was a natural matriarch.

*But I do wish she had at least kept me apprised of whatever her idea is.* A dark chuckle frothed in my throat. *Maybe I am lending her more of my characteristics.*

When we got to the small passageway between the castle and the barracks, I set him down. Grey light filtered across the sky, dawn approaching already. "Where are the worst injuries? What hurts?"

"Everything." Shoulders's chest heaved. "Go back, get her out of there. Leave me here, I can take care of myself."

I leant against the back wall of the barracks to prop myself up, taking a deep steadying breath. "No you can't, and she will be fine."

"How do you know that?" He grabbed my collar, enraged brown eyes an inch from mine. "Get her out of there or I will tear this place apart."

I twisted his wrist, wrenching him off me. "How fruitful was that the first time you tried it?"

He glared but desisted.

I peered out. A pair of Regulars in green walked stiffly to the gates, ready to open them for the day. We just had to wait and hope no one came out from the barracks this early.

Pulling my jacket around his shoulders, I tried to tug it into place without touching his horrific burns, red blisters popping up across his ribs and sides. It wouldn't close, too stretched across the shoulders. "You really do have wider shoulders than me," I mourned.

"You idiot," he grated between his teeth. "Always joking around. You have left Evyn in a cell with a torturer!"

I patted his hand. "In case no one has told you yet, joking is how I deal with serious situations. I'll have you know I haven't left her in a cell with a torturer, I've left her with Aubin. Both of them. You would be forgiven for being distracted in the moment, but she asked me to trust her *three times*. I try not to make my soul companion repeat herself, no matter what my Skienien hindbrain is screaming."

He leant against the wall, trembling. "You are trusting those Aubins? One wants to forget her and one wants to know what she knows!"

"I'm actually trusting you and the Assassin. I once asked if there was a version of Aubin that fails her. You said there wasn't."

His eyes bulged. "None we had seen yet! Yet!"

I cut my hand through the air to warn him to keep his voice low. We had to hurry once those gates were open and get out before the corps came out for morning training. I did not want to attract attention to our position while there were potentially people waking up just on the other side of the wall to the barracks.

Hearing nothing, I whispered, "Something else you keep saying is that as soon as the Lonely Man meets Evyn, he changes. The Executioner is still the Lonely Man in this timeline no matter what he does or how old he is, correct? In this time, in this future, he never did – until now." My chest warmed. "That's what Evyn figured out. She had to get him to meet an Evyn, any Evyn, and she happened to be right there."

Shoulders gaped at me.

I turned away. Was he right? No, I had to trust Evyn, she had been sure she was on to something. I surveyed the gates, still closed, and returned to stand next to him. "How is Evie? What happened?"

"I... She..." His face creased in the shadows.

My heart twisted with grief. "Is she alive?"

"Yes, I'm fairly sure." His voice was full of pain. "This is what it feels like when the bond is cut, a lash that whips back at you like a rope under tension suddenly snapped. I've felt it before and mistaken it for something worse. It hurts. It hurts and I want her back." Tears coursed down his rough cheeks.

"It's alright." I patted his shoulder carefully, mindful that he had just been suspended and then sustained burns. "I swear, I will get her back. And would I lie to me?"

Shoulders shook his head, but whether in agreement or disbelief, I could not tell.

From our hiding place, I watched the Regulars shove the gates open before they went out. If they had taken up positions just outside, we would have to defeat them to get past them, but there was a chance they were out on patrol in the city.

I hunkered down to heave him up. "Come on, we need to leave, and you're going to have to hold yourself together until we get to the Assassin. Do you need something to bite down on?"

"No, I can deal with pain." He held himself upright next to me, digging deep from his reserves of strength.

He hobbled after me as we traced the journey that Evyn, Aubin and I had made a few turns of the glass earlier in reverse. The barracks stirred as we gained the gates; we had to leave quickly.

I looked through. The Regulars were indeed both posted to guard the gates, but they were investigating my pack, sifting through the lodestones with their heads close. Grabbing Shoulders's arm, I dragged him through the gates and around, past where my father's plaque should have been mounted on the wall to the scant cover of the other side of the gallows. I tugged him onward even though his face twisted in agony, until we were further down the street and out of the Regulars' interest.

"Slow down now, we've made it far enough." I pulled to the side.

He clenched his teeth together, pressing his palms into his eyes. "Now what?" His voice cracked, but he was still upright at least, refusing to fall or bend.

"We need to get to the Academy. I'll send the Assassin a message to meet us." Grabbing hold of the lodestone, I slipped into the blank space of connection.

*"You've got him then. Well done."* The Assassin sounded impressed.

*"He's in a bad state. Where can we meet you?"*

*"Get him down to the Academy via the main stairs, I'll meet you on the way."* He broke off the connection before I could inform him to expect just two Thorrns.

Taking his forearm, I led him back onto the street, focusing on the way to the Academy and mindful of the city waking up around us. I sang low under my breath; hopefully people would think we were drunk and not investigate Shoulders's stumbling steps any further.

The stairway down seemed infinite. He took each riser one at a time and I insisted on using each of the rest areas.

"Just keep going," he said, gasping at the pain. "I will handle it."

"No, we're staying together." A rapid rap of steps up put me on guard.

The Assassin rounded the corner. "At last. What happened?" He went to Shoulders's side, grabbing his arm to sling it over his own shoulders.

I stopped his wrist. "Don't, he's got burns." I opened the side of the jacket I had lent Shoulders briefly to show the Assassin.

The Assassin sucked air between his teeth at the red stripes. "Not much further," he said to Shoulders. "Come on, you can do this. What do you need?"

"Evie." He tottered, foot dangerously close to the edge of the stairs.

The Assassin's grip on his forearm never wavered. "You'll have to settle for cold lyneal tea. Choke it down at the next rest area." He turned his irate glare at me. "Where are the rest of you?"

"I left them with you."

"Me? You mean you left your Evyn and Aubin with the Evil Aubin?" The Assassin's mouth dropped open.

"I left the Spirit Shaper with the Lonely Man. Or Men, in this case." I raised a hand to forestall his protests. "It is at her insistence, she knows what she's doing, but believe me when I say I won't get any sleep for the foreseeable."

Muttering, the Assassin walked alongside Shoulders as he stubbornly limped to the next rest area. The Assassin pulled out a vial, a waft of what Evyn called peppermint when he unstoppered it. "Here. Drink this."

"We aren't safe yet." Tipping his head back against the wall, Shoulders swallowed hard, pulse pounding in his throat.

"You'll move faster if you can mask the pain with this. Drink it," the Assassin ordered, thrusting the vial at him. "Drink it voluntarily or I get the swordsman to hold you down and I'll force feed it to you."

I cracked my knuckles. "Better do as he says."

Outnumbered, Shoulders snatched the vial and downed it in one.

While we waited for it to take effect, the Assassin inspected the damage on him, lips thin. He tutted. "Sometimes I think I'm the only thing holding you together."

"Sometimes you are," Shoulders murmured.

I pressed my palms together between my knees. The Assassin never complained about how much he took care of, simply taking charge around Shoulders. Aubin had done that straight away when he grabbed me to scale the Tower and then fell through with us onto Earth. Had giving him a position, a rank and a place actually made him feel that he had to behave differently?

Skienien women had all treated me a certain way: a useful tool at worst and someone to care for at best, but all of them assumed they would take charge over my wellbeing. It removed my choice entirely when someone assumed I had no say in the matter.

I leant back against the cold bench, letting that thought simmer. This rest area was stone like all the others, benches cut around the periphery. "What did you learn here?" I asked the Assassin in a low voice. We were alone, but sound could echo through the stairs if we were not careful.

"The MasterMage is a shared position here, something that has never happened in any alternative history we've ever seen." Checking Shoulders's pulse and scowling as if the man's lifebeat had personally insulted him, the Assassin said, "It's MasterMages Waker and Liara."

That sent a barb straight into my stomach. "Liara is here?"

"A different one. She has red curls shot through with grey, laughter lines on her face."

"Laughter, eh?" Probably from all the hellish ways she and Waker were toying with everyone's lives. "I'll put a stop to that."

The Assassin ministered to Shoulders, distracted as he murmured, "What do you want to do?"

My blood surged, demanding blood in return. Knuckles creaking from how tight I held myself, I tried to relax, pulling calm down. "Different alt histories, different people. Unless we see otherwise, we have to assume they made different life choices. Ruining someone's life when they haven't done anything to deserve it makes you the villain."

The Assassin's face shifted slightly. Reading my Aubin helped me to decipher this one, but only marginally. Pain? Hesitation?

"I feel better," Shoulders slurred.

The odd expression quickly dropped from the Assassin's face and he rolled up his sleeves. "At last. Let's get you downstairs."

We limped into the Academy and to the room the Assassin had rented. Clean enough, it only had one bed, but what I said to the Assassin rang true: I would not be able to sleep tonight for worrying about Evyn.

What was she doing at this moment? This far away from her, her emotions were muted. Our bond was still new and only receptive at short distances. At least I would feel her pain if she were hurt, but by then it could be too late.

I tried closing my eyes, listening somewhere deep down inside for an echo of her. A frisson blossomed in my solar plexus, a small but powerful feeling. Was she feeling love?

I raised my arms up in a guard as someone walked into my reach.

"Peace, swordsman." The Assassin held up a blanket. "You fell asleep."

"I wasn't. I was trying to sense Evyn." I rubbed my sternum. "She's feeling love, I think."

One side of his mouth tipped up. "Love, eh." He sank down on the edge of the bed that Shoulders occupied, lying asleep on his back, chest and ribs bandaged. Perhaps I *had* napped briefly to miss that.

The Assassin's murmur was low in the basic but comfortable room. "Are you hungry? I've got cold meat and some bread."

I wasn't hungry, but I should eat to fuel what could be a long and fraught night, if I needed to rescue Evyn. "I'll take some. My thanks."

"Don't mention it." He moved soundlessly to the single table, cutting a generous portion and handing it to me.

I ate, watching him lining up his tinctures and potions along the table edge, shaking one or holding another up to the light of the glowstone, staring into their contents as though they held answers. I had met three Aubins now, each of them intense in their own way.

The Executioner had been possessed of a supreme confidence, and the Assassin's was not much further behind. My Aubin burnt with a similar flame to the Assassin's, though.

I put my plate to one side. "Assassin?"

"Yes?" He shook one of the vials, upending a cloud of flotsam inside.

"Would you ever want to leave Evie and Shoulders?"

He put his vial down with a clink, giving the question serious attention. "Not unless I thought I was a direct danger to them, no. I am given to understand there have been a few incidences of mind meddling, enchantment and spiritsight possessions amongst you precipitated by magic. That might explain why your Aubin is more sensitive to being close to you. He has actively, though accidentally, hurt you against his better intentions more than once."

"Would you not understand and forgive yourself, though? In his place?"

He turned his face away. "Perhaps. This is harder for me to understand because we are different people. I've accepted that my life is in service to Tuniel and now to Evie, to put what I feel at a very blunt level. In some ways, this Aubin is wanting a bit of independence from that. He is trying to see what he can be on his own, without you."

"He can be anything he wants with us," I said stubbornly, but the thought took hold. What could he do with a clean mental slate? No torture, no near-death experiences, no having to make and live with hard choices. What could he make of himself then? "He's capable. He could be anything, and I would support him to be anything."

"Would you?" The Assassin's voice was soft. "Or do you want him by your side, doing what you want him to do?"

The meal I had just choked down soured inside me. I put my head in my hands, unable to face him as I voiced my aspirations. "I want him to accept that he loves Evyn. I want him to live with us. I want us to train and work together every day. I love being with him, I love being around him, I love being belittled by him, I love it when he takes the wind out of my sails and when he makes Evyn smile. I want him to love being with us. I know he enjoys it." I looked up. "Or at least, he did."

"He's moving on," the Assassin said quietly.

That hurt, a pain that tightened my chest. "For the right reasons?"

"His reasons are the right reasons. I'm sorry, but if he asks to be let go, you have to let him go." With a brief smile, he went back to his bottles, leaving me to turn that over in my mind.

✳ ✳ ✳

I DID NOT SLEEP, instead sitting beside Shoulders. Thoughts of Evyn and Aubin chased around my head. As the Academy stirred for the morning, I pulled on a hood and went out to see what could be seen. I pounded up the stairs to the city, trying to feel if the bond got stronger with every step I took.

Entering the castle grounds, I engaged in some serious loitering. Morning training was progressing, so I walked toward the gardens, pretending that I had every right to be here. Checking left and right, I saw no gardeners and bent down as if I was one, tugging at some sad looking plant that no doubt Aubin would tell me was some rare specimen.

Footsteps grated along the gravel, along with a familiar voice that tugged at my heart. I glanced up. Walking along the pathways were Evyn and the Executioner. He had his hands behind his back and a frown on his face. Evyn pushed her hair behind an ear, her wild, wide gestures familiar to me; she was explaining something.

A touch lightly brushed my shoulder, although no one stood nearby. She paused but didn't turn toward me; she had just Found me and realised I was close.

I dug my hands into the soil, keeping my face turned to the ground and my breathing steady even as battle readiness flooded my limbs. They would pass me on their current path, and if the Executioner was anything as attentive to details as my Aubin, he would recognise me in a heartbeat.

Evyn pointed at something over the other side of the rambling gardens and ran toward it. The Executioner turned in place, feet grinding over the gravel, then ambled over to her.

A headscarfed form stood up as Evyn barrelled toward him. He had been hidden behind some gnarled tree, and I recognised Aubin's stance and bearing.

*Evyn has somehow convinced the Executioner to let them all go out for a morning walk.* Pride expanded my chest; she was in command of the situation and needed no assistance from me.

I stood and walked away quickly, unable to resist a final glance back as I reached the gates.

Evyn waved toward a patch of some tangled plant and Aubin waded in, tugging off a tall stem. He passed it to her and she turned it over in her hands, showing it to the Executioner. The two men stood well out of each other's ranges but always kept their bodies angled toward her, rather as the Assassin had.

In my chest I felt that tremulous bubble, soaring as Evyn passed the plant back to Aubin and their hands touched. Whatever had happened had changed a great deal for Evyn.

Exiting, I walked quickly down the boulevard, pulling over to a side street and laying a hand on my lodestone. *"They are getting on,"* I reported to the Assassin.

*"They're what?"* he asked.

*"Having walks in the gardens. Evyn's in full flow chattering away. They are getting on."* Great satisfaction in Evyn's ploy coming off saturated my thoughts. *"The Executioner is still the Lonely Man and, although he might not realise it, he's about to change. And I mean, he has to be a really Lonely Man. Everyone he works with is dead by the end of the day."*

*"Thorrn,"* the Assassin groaned. *"The jokes when you are on the edge of your reserves are truly terrible."*

I grinned. He didn't sound exasperated, more contented, soothed by my update. *"Anything from Shoulders?"* I asked.

The Assassin's thoughts turned grey. *"Nothing of use. He's miserable, as you would expect."*

*"Tell him that Evyn is fine. I'll be back later, I want to keep nearby to note how often the guard is changed."*

*"I can do that, and you're exhausted. Come, you know she's hale and well, and you'll be useless to her if she needs you later and you are fast asleep."*

Seeing Evyn had settled my nerves and tiredness did tug at me. The last sleep I had entertained had been back on my world and in another country. *"Very well."*

We passed each other on the stairs, just exchanging a swift nod with one another. I nearly fell into the bed next to Shoulders, passing out quickly and dreamlessly.

We both awoke when the Assassin returned. "All well?" I barked, sitting bolt upright, my father's sword half-drawn.

"Yes, calm down." He pulled his headscarf off his sweaty face, grabbing his waterskin with a scowl. He took a deep gulp, holding up a hand to delay our questions.

My stomach churned. "Well?"

He drew a hand across his mouth with a satisfied sigh, eyes bright on mine. "I saw Evyn and the Executioner out walking. This time she waited until the Executioner looked away and dropped a ball of paper on the floor. When they went back toward the castle I ran in and picked it up." He fanned it out to read aloud.

Both Shoulders and I listened, hands curling around the bed frame, as the Assassin read, "'Working on him and getting somewhere. Evie is alive and well, I can hear her occasionally telling someone to do one even from the top of the Tower. Telling him the truth helps because he knows what that looks and sounds like and he respects it. He's not quite in Torgund's pocket but is wary of him. Give it another night. Love you all.'" With a smug smile, he held the note up in the air between us.

Taking it, I cradled the sheet to my chest, careful not to crush it. "She is amazing."

"Yes." Shoulders smiled, the first since he had been sundered from Evie. *At last.*

Pouring a measure of water into a basin, the Assassin dashed and scoured the sweat from his face. "We'll take the night in shifts, swordsman. I'll go back now and wake you with the lodestone when the red moon sets."

"What about me?" Shoulders asked from his prone position, his voice a low rumble. "I can help."

The Assassin dabbed his face dry, considering. "You can go out with the swordsman if you want. We haven't met the other Thorrn or Evyn, so you can walk about with minimal subterfuge for now." He gave the black headscarf a dark look, holding it at arm's length. "I don't know how your Aubin put up with this."

My shoulders tightened. I shrugged to loosen them. *How* had *he put up with it?* "He had to bear it. Hiding himself was the only way. Besides, he lives the ruse with Tuniel every day, how is this any different?" My voice did not ring with conviction, even to myself.

The Assassin wound the headscarf in place slowly. "Yes," he said, voice muffled. "But everyone needs somewhere to be their true selves." He left without a backward glance, his words trickling through me like a new tenet, the edge of something I needed to grasp to understand Aubin.

"I'm trying to think through something aloud, Shoulders. I'm wondering if my Aubin has ever shown me his true self." I leant back. "Has the Assassin?"

Shoulders winced as he lowered himself back on the bed. "What do you mean? He's just... like this."

"Always calm and capable? That's not true, meeting that boy in Skien unsettled him for some reason."

"Well, what about your Aubin?"

I eased down, careful not to jostle him. "Trying to be the all-encompassing Ranger hero had clearly not been his true self, nor something he felt he could live up to. The apothecary was not enough, not everything he could be."

The edge of something stuck out at me, like a headscarf flapping in the wind. What was underneath? If I could grab and tug it out into the light, what would I find?

What could I already see without unmasking him, forcing him to show me? "It's the broken and bent man, still fighting to get to the truth through Waker's lies. It's the vindictive man, losing something precious and inflicting revenge on the perpetrator who would escape justice, despite knowing he would hang for it. It's the murderer, holding on with unrelenting force until I gave out underneath him, trusting that the spirit would be forced out of me."

No, that was not all. He was also the man who took himself away when he believed he was the one hurting us, and who had to do something when he saw people in trouble. "His true self is like anyone's, patched and brittle, made up of the experiences of the past and hopes for the future," I said aloud.

I frowned out the window. Of course it was dark outside, being in the Academy. *Hope. What does he have to hope for?* What pathway had his choices set him on? He saw failure after failure with each of his decisions, whereas I saw how he overcame the impossible challenges he had faced.

"He thought he failed Evyn when he believed Waker over her; I saw how he battled Waker even beyond her demise. He believed he failed Evyn when he stabbed Gavain; I saw how that changed him, how he carries that burden even now. The final failure has been too much for him. Instead of keeping me hale and well against all the odds, he nearly killed me by his own hand."

Shoulders gave a snort. He was asleep.

I sighed. "Good talk." I leant my head back for a moment, slipping into rest.

It seemed like only a turn of the glass when the Assassin shook me awake. "Disaster. Wake up, both of you," he snapped. "Torgund must have seen Evyn parading around the gardens. He's got her."

"My Evyn?" I asked stupidly, half asleep.

"Yes. Now he has the matching set," the Assassin spat.

I strapped my father's sword to my hip. "Our best chance is for you to scale the outside wall, Assassin, while Shoulders and I attack the inside. Hopefully the sentinels will be too busy with us to spot you and rain hot oil on you."

"That's suicide for you two," the Assassin said flatly, grabbing handfuls of vials and shoving them into his jerkin, hands shaking.

"Yes, but it is the only thing we can do at this point." I smiled sadly at Shoulders. "Want to see how far we get?"

He trembled but nodded firmly.

The Assassin thrust more daggers into holsters across his chest. "That's not the only thing. First we can try to get your Aubin out of the cells. He was thrown in there, I heard him yelling that Evyn had been taken."

Assaulting the cells was a much easier undertaking. "Good idea, and he can give us the latest intelligence, but I can't ping. Can you?"

The Assassin winced. "I make bad portals."

"I can't even do that," Shoulders said.

"Then it's the old-fashioned way. Prepare some of those special knives for application of somnus root into the bloodstream. We are attacking the cells now."

We stole up to the castle in the dark avoiding the patrol circuits and scaled the castle wall, one after the other. Shoulders needed help getting over the parapet, but then we were able to crouch and run in between the crenelations. Only the red moon was up and that was setting fast, the darkness working in our favour.

My heart rocked my chest as the Assassin picked the same lock Aubin had, darting in once the door was opened. I led the way through the darkened atrium and we attacked the gaoler all together; he was asleep before he could let out a shout.

I walked lightly up the cells, looking through the grilles to locate my Aubin. The cells were all empty and dark, apart from one with light ahead.

I peered into that cautiously, narrowing my eyes so as not to lose my night vision. I blinked hard, dazzled by what I saw. "Uh."

"Yes?" the Assassin whispered.

I cleared my throat and rapped my knuckles on the door.

"What the hell—" the Assassin hissed as I swung the door open.

# CHAPTER 28

Inside, the room was dominated by a fearsome rack lying horizontal with open manacles at either end. A teapot steamed on the surface and pulled up to the side were three chairs, occupied by Evyn, Evie and the Executioner.

"Evie." Shoulders gasped.

Evie stood and raced into his arms. She looked well cared for, clean and whole, and tears sprung to my eyes as the lines on Shoulders's face finally lifted.

"Evyn!" I smiled.

My Evyn gave me a wink and a thumbs up, leaning back in her chair with a hint of smugness in her face. *Well-deserved smugness.* She had somehow gotten the Executioner to bring Evie down from the Last Tower as well as convinced him not to hurt them. I beamed back at her.

The Executioner said, "I've heard much about you. And you." He appraised the Assassin, a searching up and down that made me imagine he was sizing him for a coffin. "Remarkable."

The Assassin closed his mouth. "What's going on here?"

The Executioner curled his finger around a teacup handle.

"What's going on is an interrogation, of course. The lady over there refuses to bond with the king. This one here has information that would be of value to him. As Chief Executioner my job is very simple: to secure these outcomes for my liege." He took a sip, placing the cup back in the centre of the saucer with a click.

I flinched, hand on the hilt of my sword.

He stood up slowly. "They were very staunch in opposing me and I had to use all my very best techniques. I left them in their cell to think about what torments awaited them in the morning, and, lo and behold, they have been rescued."

I slid to stand in front of him.

Frowning at me, he motioned me out of the way, and walked to the door. "I'll have to lock you in and replace the key, but I trust you can…?"

"Yes, Mr Tabreksson. I've got it all under control," Evyn said.

"Well then. Go well." He glared at all of us from the door, but his gaze softened when he looked at Evyn.

"Go well, Aubin," Evyn murmured, a triumphant smile on her face.

My heart hammered in my chest. "One moment. Where's our Aubin?"

The Executioner turned his head to look at me. A chill raced across my skin at his attention, and he smirked as if he knew exactly what he had done to me. "He's *hanging around.*"

My stomach clenched. *No.*

Evyn touched my arm, her touch sending a reassuring wave of love to assuage my fear. "He's joking, Thorrn. He's actually pretty funny, in a dark humour kind of way."

The Executioner's lips twitched, but the man looked as though he would rather crack someone's rib another way than by making them laugh.

She turned her face up to me, a soothing calm layering over me. "He's in the cells further along, unharmed."

"Do you want to retrieve him from me?" the Executioner intoned.

I gripped my father's sword. "Yes, of course."

"Then come along. I can lock you in with him just as easily I suppose."

I gave Evyn a quick squeeze and then marched out alongside him, keeping alert for his every move.

He stepped to one side to let me out and shut the cell door. It made barely a noise in the echoing corridor. He clapped his hands and the glowstones fired to a brighter hue, lifting the shadows around us.

Pulling out a single key on a string, he locked the door and tested the handle to make sure. "I always have to check," he murmured.

I stood ramrod straight, readiness to fight crawling across my limbs.

He beckoned me to walk next to him.

"Uh. Well," I said.

He chuckled. "Mm. Indeed." Walking alongside me, his steps were heavier and the gait more measured, but he was the right height for my Aubin. "Look after that soul companion of yours."

"Of course, sir, always." I gathered my courage. "What happened?"

He tilted his head. "A few conversations where she listened. Usually I am the one encouraging people to talk; I've never felt the need to unburden myself before, but having her hear me was... quite something." His face cracked, cheeks pushing up into a smile.

My heart relaxed an inch. "She... she has that effect on people. A kind of magic."

"It's no magic, boy. That is empathy. Come, he's in here."

The Executioner opened another cell door. Chained in the corner of the room was my Aubin, slumped on the floor in despair. His sleeves were ripped and his wrists torn and bloody where he had heaved against the manacles. His head wavered on his neck as he looked up at us.

The Executioner tutted at his counterpart. "I told you to stay put and stay quiet," he admonished my Aubin.

I frowned. "Give me the keys for these."

The Executioner reached into the inside pockets of his jerkin and passed me a small key. "Here you are."

I approached Aubin slowly in case he was disorientated. "Aubin, it's me, the Thorrn from your timeline. Are you hale and well?"

"Where's Evyn, is she alright?" he croaked, voice hoarse.

I smiled at him asking about her first. "She's actually a bloody genius, I'll tell you all about it. Let me see the manacles so we can get you out of here." I took care turning the band so it wouldn't drag on his raw skin.

His arms trembled trying to keep them raised, face fixed on the Executioner, breathing hard. I went to my knees to let his arms rest on me while I searched for the lock on his restraints. Once I found it I pulled the chains off slowly, mindful of the tears in his skin. My stomach lurched at the blood, but I shoved the nausea aside to help Aubin.

Once I released him and pushed the chains off, I lifted him up under his armpits to get him to his feet. "Feeling sick? Dizzy?"

"I'm fine, Thorrn." He swayed.

I clamped my hands on his shoulders and steadied him, looking into each of his eyes to make sure he could focus on me.

He blinked at me and then looked over my shoulder at the Executioner.

The Executioner had watched us in silence, face set. "I'm going to lock you in here now. I expect Evyn has already escaped. Oops."

"Won't Torgund be angry with you?" I asked.

He cocked his head. "Me? I left the jail cell occupants inside with doors locked, as per procedure."

I didn't know yet why he was helping us, but I was ecstatic he was. "My deepest and truest thanks, sir."

He looked out of the cell window at the dark sky hanging over the city. "I suspect you do everything wholeheartedly, boy. Oh, don't be surprised, I am very good at reading people. Deepest and truest love, deepest and truest friendship."

He fixed his counterpart with his light amber eyes. "I could have wished for such friends. Perhaps I should say, I would kill for them?"

We stared at him.

A smile flickered on his face, and he sighed. "No one has ever laughed at my jokes."

My heartrate accelerated. "I will gladly laugh at every single one but just not right now because I think I might pass out."

"Go well," he said as he left.

"Go well, Aubin," I replied.

The key snicked in the lock, leaving us in relative silence. I couldn't hear anything outside, not yet, only Aubin's shaky staccato breathing beside me.

He took a single shuffling step toward the door before his knees buckled.

"Whoa!" I grabbed fistfuls of his shirt, heaving him upright. He was heavier than I expected. "Aubin, hold fast there—"

"We have to get to her!" He pulled forward, rocking my stance. "I'll ping us out."

"Aubin! We don't have anywhere to go, Evyn has it all under control. She's hale and well, I swear to you."

He fought for a heartbeat more, out of habit, perhaps. Looking into my face, searching for the truth and seeing it, he sagged against me. "What is going on?" he asked, voice small.

"The Lonely Man met the Spirit Shaper, evidently." I replied. *As before, apparently, and over and over again if Shoulders is right.*

We would be better off sitting before he fell. I sank onto my knees, holding on as he did the same. He did not seem about to collapse in on himself, staring off to one side of my ear.

I uncurled my fingers from his – my, really – stained shirt. "Aubin, would you answer a question before Evyn and Evie come to ping us out?"

His gaze sharpened, snapping to mine. "Evie as well? You managed to rescue her?"

I ventured a smile. "Evyn did, yes." My clever soul companion, a natural at wrangling Aubins.

Now if some of that could come across to me, we might get somewhere.

He lifted a hand to his temple, exposing his raw wrists at the cuffs, and a bitter taste filled my mouth. He was struggling, and all I could think to do was badger him.

"Do you need help?" I took his hand. It was colder than usual, limp in mine. "What can I do?"

"I'm fine, Thorrn." He tugged free and pressed the heels of his hands to his eyes, his shoulders rounded. "What do you want to know? I did not get much intel from him, he knows the forms of interrogation and largely refused to speak to me."

I shuffled forward, knees grinding on the cold stone, careful not to knock against him, and kept my voice quiet and low to match his. "Not about the Executioner or this world. I was hoping you would tell me what made you want to rescue our Evyn from our tower."

His quick shallow breaths slowed as he scrubbed his face with a savage intensity, swirling over day-old stubble with a dry rasp. Most people were smaller than me, but he seemed smaller still.

My throat tightened, dry as the dust between the stones of the dungeon floor. I pulled out my water skin, holding it out to him. "Here. Nevermind." He was not in any state to answer such a question, just barely released from the terror of being locked away and fighting chains inside a cell.

The quiet spread out around and through me, my nerves unwinding slowly as Aubin drank. The promised heat of a confrontation hadn't happened, Evyn was unhurt and triumphant, and her smug success sent ripples of victory through me.

Aubin did not look victorious; his hands shook squeezing the waterskin. Pain had a way of grinding the edge from me and turning me inward; he wasn't immune to that either. Compared to the Executioner, he looked so much younger, especially sat across from me lost and broken. The lines on his face had made him seem so much more responsible, more learned and vastly more experienced, but in reality he was only a handful of turns older than me.

His whisper shattered the stillness.

"The day I met her, I was locked in despair and I hadn't even realised it. The work was the same as it had always been, but it grew harder every day. I know it is an undeniable truth that people get sick, bodies fade or grow tumours or have an inherent weakness never exposed before, when suddenly they need my help and I can do nothing for them except ease the pain. I know this happens to the young, the old and everyone in between.

"But it is one thing to know it and another to see it. I have helped babies into this world and had to watch them leave it, powerless to do anything else. I've ministered to children who have no hope of ever running or playing ever again. I have treated ancient repulsive lords who despite their habits are healthy as score-year-olds, and score-year-olds who suffer and die within a mooncycle. Genuinely good people live and die, and genuinely bad people live and die. There was and is and will never be any justice to disease and the whims of the body." His tones were quiet, soft and sad. "Swordsmen think the world is simple: a swing of their sword at just the right time and evil dies, good is saved. It is not like that in the world. Justice and fairness do not help, not in any way that matters."

I let that settle and sink in with me. Upholding justice and the spirit behind the king's laws formed a huge part of my core. What if it were as random as he described? It would be like living under Torgund constantly, something I would break under.

"That sounds awful," I said.

He shuddered. "Thank you."

"How did you endure it?"

"Looking back, I don't know. It must have crept up on me. I fell into apothecary when the Rushia woman took me under her wing, and Layloree's teachings were always about how exposing yourself to harsh reality makes you stronger. But after some measure of gaining strength, it chipped away at me. Not always, some cases slid off me at the end of the day, but enough left their mark that I was riddled with cracks, and I did not even realise it until I met her."

He tugged at his ruined shirtsleeves, wincing at his wrists. "Will you help me with this? I want to make a makeshift bandage."

"Of course." I opened my Ranger jacket. Pulling a knife from my belt, I tore into the bottom of my own shirt, cleaner than his.

Aubin watched, disgust on his face. "That's two of your shirts ruined now."

"The proper phrase is 'my thanks'." I passed him the fabric.

"My thanks." He wrapped it around his wrists with care. "I was passing the library when she came out, breathless with excitement. I saw earlier that you had been set to guard her so she was some person of importance and, while the castle was safe enough, I decided that her wandering around with no protection was unwise.

"I went up to introduce myself and we spoke. She asked what I did and I told her I was the King's Apothecarist, and then I found my mouth running on. I told her what I just told you, and she said... she said it must be a burden, to see injustice like that and be unable to do anything of substance to help. She listened, Thorrn. She didn't try to tell me what a good job I did for those who remained, or how some patients were saved by what I did. She listened to me complain how short I felt I came up to compared to what I *knew* needed to be done."

He bowed his head, hiding his reddening face. "No one had ever listened before. Prior to that I felt like I didn't have any option, that I just had to find a way to endure it, but hearing her say out loud what my heart had been crying out, I... I realised I did have choices." He looked up at me, eyes pale and shining with unshed tears. "Just one conversation and I determined to sell my shop and roll up my contract with the king. Isn't that ridiculous? A lifetime's career that I built solidly and steadily, and I decided to drop it all."

I touched his shoulder. "No, not ridiculous."

He straightened his collar, staring up at me, searching each of my eyes in turn. I squeezed his shoulder and he smiled, a taut and fragile thing.

Aubin went on. "Then Torgund took over, and I could see rafts of injustice heading down the canal for everyone, buoyed up on the shoulders of a misguided unit obeying mindlessly. It started immediately with your father, and who knows where it would have ended. Perhaps something similar to what we have here.

"When Torgund ordered Evyn's imprisonment, with guards to hold her up in the Tower and no hope of seeing the sunlight ever again, and myself to keep her drugged... I saw an injustice I could fight. I wasn't powerless. I could and would get her out of that tower, with a little help from a swordsman. And I would do it, whatever it took." He held my gaze.

I let that sink into me. We shared that fundamental truth, and it had rung through us both like the call to alarm bell.

He ran a shaking hand through his hair. "You know how it goes from there. You didn't trust my motives, which I could understand given I started our alliance with a lie. I didn't think you would believe the King's Apothecarist wanted to fight injustice." He waited for an answer.

I considered it. "The me back then would not have, you're right. I believed your reason entirely, and it fitted with what I thought I knew of you. I'm sorry I thought that of you."

He shrugged. "It's not your fault, it's how I acted around everyone. Shallow motives to make myself uninteresting, until I drowned in the persona I wore everyday." He turned over his torn cuffs, rolling them up his forearms. "My weakness was exploited. Waker could tear out my secret longings more effectively than any torturer would have been able to, and made me live the life I didn't even know I wanted. When I thought it had been snatched away, I did everything I could to get it back, thinking I had someone to save." He pressed the heel of his hands to his eyes.

I took his shoulders. It must have been so hard to endure his dreams being torn from him and used against him, contentment as a weapon instead of a comfort.

He fell into himself, chest caving. "I tried to heal alone but I couldn't. Your lashing served to bring me back to you both, and... I hated that it took that much to force me to face you again. I rebuilt the courage to try again, tried approaching Evyn, only to find I had lost her to a prince. He snapped her up, as he should have. Of course he would have." He laughed mirthlessly. "When I thought it couldn't get worse, she nearly died, and we nearly lost her entirely." He took a deep breath, which only shuddered out of him. "I can't keep losing her. I can't take it."

The old me would have told him to try, to press, to take hold and never let go, because that was how one protected what they loved. Evyn's experience and feelings had changed mine; no matter how hard one held on, life could be snatched away at any point. It wasn't anyone's fault or something I could fight, nothing we could prevent. It just *was*.

Pushing Evyn away meant he retained control at least. He was making a choice and choosing to lose her, rather than expose himself to the threat of loving and being destroyed when it all went wrong.

I patted his shoulder. "I know. I'm sorry." I meant it the way Evyn used it; *I'm sorry you are having this experience.* A phrase implying guilt, that a balance needed redressing, but also a simple empathic statement. *I am hurting because you are hurting. I wish you didn't have to go through this.*

He screwed the neck of the waterskin in his fist. "Being a Ranger is just another persona I pulled on, hiding underneath that head-scarf, but I struggled with what I wanted to do, who I wanted to be. My actions speak clearly: I can murder, and I can do so without hesitation. I can't defeat death but I can administer it as the cure, and it comes all too easily. I took a small measure of comfort in the fact that when I hurt you before, it was because of some enchantment, first Waker and then Liara. But in Rush, that was all me. I made a choice, I adhered to it and I saw it through."

Old arguments surfaced: *You saved my life.* He knew that, he could see it plain. That wasn't what he needed from me. "I'm sorry," I murmured. "I'm sorry you had to do that."

He pulled back out of my reach, voice hoarse as he demanded, "Why aren't you afraid of me? Why aren't you terrified of what I'm capable of?"

I smiled at him, heartened beyond words. "Because you're having a very human reaction to what you've done. You face it head on, giving yourself no respite or quarter, because you give no one second chances, least of all yourself.

"We're all capable of making mistakes, and we're all lost sometimes. You're human, Aubin. That's why I'm not afraid of you."

This time he didn't back away when I approached, and I put my arms around him.

He wrapped his around my torso slowly. "You've been unusually quiet," he said lightly.

"I'm learning to listen. I'm going to be the best you've ever seen."

He snorted with laughter. "Of course you are." He pulled back, rolling his eyes as he wiped them, and took a deep steadying breath. "Where are Evyn and Evie, and I suppose those others of us?"

"They're just in the other cell, they should be here by now."

He frowned. "I wonder if they are giving us time to talk—"

Evyn opened a portal through the door, tumbling in. "Yeah, I was. Hi Aubin." She waved shyly from the side, then gasped when she saw his injuries. "What happened?"

He stood up straighter, rubbing his wrists ruefully. "I tried to get free, I thought you might be in danger."

"I did say it would be alright." She scowled at the bandages, but kept her distance.

"The damage is superficial, Evyn." He pulled his shirt sleeves down.

"You sound like Thorrn." Evyn shot me a small smile, then met Aubin's eyes again. "How are you?"

"Much better. You were right, I did need to talk to him."

"What's this?" I asked.

Evyn smiled at me. "We did talk, a little, and I told him that you would listen. We all just need to talk to each other."

I raised my eyebrow at her.

She had the grace to flush. "I know that's what you kept waiting for, Thorrn. Thanks for your patience and all that."

*Patience.* That rang inside me, and Evyn's eyes widened at the same time.

"The Patient Slave," Aubin murmured.

I nodded to Evyn. "Spirit Shaper. You've fashioned us both, I think. For the better, in case that isn't obvious," I added. "And the Lonely Man, who doesn't need to be so lonely."

"Mm," he grunted. "What about Tuniel?"

"The Cold Mage?" The Assassin strode in over Evyn's open portal. "You shouldn't leave these lying around, Evyn, they let all sorts of riffraff in."

"What does the Cold Mage do?" Evyn asked him.

"That would be cheating." Evie followed after her husband, hand-in-hand with Shoulders, red-eyed as if he hadn't stopped crying since we reunited them. "Thanks for rescuing me, Evyn."

A beat of pride from her flared in my chest. She beamed. "You're welcome. Anytime."

The Assassin folded his arms as he addressed his wife. "Evie, this Aubin here has a request, if you please. He agreed to help me in return for a do-over. He wants to never meet Evyn and Thorrn, and—"

"Stop." Aubin squared his shoulders against the alts. Only this close could I see him trembling, a mixture of exhaustion and fear. "Don't you dare take them away from me."

The Assassin held up his hands. "Whoa, it was your idea! You want something else now, fire away." He cocked his head. "Be aware, though. One little tweak can change a great deal. It's your choice."

Aubin patted his side as if expecting to find his Battlemistress blades, coming up empty. He glanced up at his holsters, hanging on a hook on the wall.

I reached them down for him.

"My thanks." He hitched them tight around his hips. "What do you want?" he asked Evyn quietly, focusing on his belt and not looking her in the eye.

"Aubin," Evyn admonished softly. "We're here, aren't we? This is the timeline we want, the one with you in it."

"Yes. You here... and happy," I said. "I'm sorry you carry hard choices. If I could carry them for you I would, and I will, in future. You don't have to do the hard things alone."

"I'll help too," Evyn said. "You deserve to be happy, Aubin. You really do."

He stared at her, then at me, the pain slipping away from his eyes. He let out in a shuddering breath. "I'm sorry I ever went along with this. I don't want to change a thing, I would do it all again and more."

Warmth filled me up from the bottom of my lungs to the top of my head, pricking at my eyes. What was also pleasing was the tickle in my solar plexus; it pulsed with a strong, firm energy all of its own.

Aubin looked up at me, a soft smile as if he saw the shift of our feelings on my face, and down at Evyn, pink trickling up his neck to his ears.

A harrumph startled me. "Well, this is all very nice, but I for one have had enough of this world," the Assassin said, holding onto Evie's hand. "Take me home, my love."

Evie smiled up at him. "First, let's drop these intrepid explorers off. Skien, wasn't it?"

The Assassin shuddered. "Yes, Skien. It's just as bad as our Skien, I'll tell you everything."

"You'd better. Right you are, hang on to your hats." She opened a bad portal, the darkness seeming to crawl and reach into the world we stood on. "Oh! Do you three know how to behave in one of these?"

"Don't turn around, don't talk," I supplied.

"Don't talk?" She frowned at the Assassin. "That's a bit mean."

"They were bickering, I'd had more than a gutsful of it. It bought me five heartbeats of peace at least." Here with his wife, the Assassin faced the portal with more aplomb than he had the previous one, but he still kept a hand firmly wrapped around his blades.

I took Evyn's hand. She seemed to shiver with bliss, a shared golden glow lighting us up from inside and flowing up and down the bond, wrapping around Aubin as if it were its own thing, welcoming him back.

That light dimmed as we walked into the portal, the darkness enveloping us and dragging along my skin. Ahead of us was absolute nothingness except for the close heat that felt almost smothering with its intensity, until Evie closed her portal behind us. As soon as it slid shut with a snap, a room appeared.

It was a wide space with a long sofa and a short coffee table, littered with the square boxes emblazoned with images of pizza. My stomach growled; now that the peril was behind us, it was reminding me that it had been neglected.

The boy from before stood in front of a wide screen. Bigger than Evyn's moving picture box and much smaller than the cinema, it had a series of green and red lines intersecting horizontally. Four thicker green lines were imposed on top, all converging to one point on my right-hand side. Some writing flickered near the top, but I could not make it out.

"What does it say?" I whispered to Evyn.

She frowned. "King's Swordsman timeline alpha," she whispered back, and she and Aubin exchanged a tense look.

My hand tightened around hers. Was this something to do with us?

"Oh, hi," the boy said, turning away from the screen. "Welcome back and all that."

"Yes, hello." Evie smiled fondly at the boy. "I just need to take these alternative versions back to where we took them from, so I'll need a bit of help."

"Sure thing." The boy tossed his head at the screen, making his hair flop. "So, did you like the future you wanted? Ready to choose it?" he asked Aubin.

Aubin kept tight hold of his blades. "No, that's not what I want at all. I've changed my mind."

"Of course! You're the Lonely Man, you get to change it whenever-." The boy hooked his thumbs into his jeans, relaxed.

Aubin stared up at the screen above us, gaze scouring for answers in the bright lines. "What happened to the Evyn and Thorrn in that timeline we just left?"

"Oh, they died." The boy waved at the screen. The lines shifted, two thick green lines pulsing and then turning red two thirds of the way across the screen. The other two green lines continued and reached the end of the screen as before.

Evyn tugged my hand. When I leant down, she whispered, "Now it says, 'King's Swordsman timeline zeta.'"

The boy carried on speaking. "In this timeline, you won't be Gough's apothecarist at all, someone else is. During the Special Forces initiation test, the swordsman fails." His gaze flicked to me. "Sorry, man." He sucked in air between his teeth. "Then the King's Apothecarist, who isn't as observant, treats her minor bruising with bruswurt." He looked away from Evyn.

Grief swelled inside me, pulling like a bad portal, claustrophobic and clenching around my heart.

"Oh." Evyn's shoulders dropped.

"They died?" Aubin rocked back, hand on his blades.

I resisted the similar urge to touch my father's sword, as it would bring no comfort. We were useless, for there was nothing we could do, no action we could take, nothing to run to and no one to fight, because it had happened a score of turns ago, and Evyn and I were a long-lost tale cut short on that world.

The boy pointed at the two remaining glowing green lines. "Yeah, and so did the King's Apothecarist after Torgund looked for someone to blame. A version of you steps into the vacancy and... Well, the rest is history. Or future, if you want to get technical."

"The Executioner." Aubin tipped back a pace, hand to his mouth. "That's who I become. I'm some kind of evil monster." Pale horror drained his face of emotion, but now I knew his closed features hid his fear.

Evyn reached out to him. "Aubin, he wasn't evil, he just did what he was told. He pushed the little voice of misgivings aside and the responsibility for the decision up the chain. You, however, you found your voice. You can make a difference through your choices, and not just to change the past. You can shape your future too."

He settled at her words, and I felt something shift within me, grounding on her strong foundation.

A clap from the Assassin startled us all. "Great! Now that's settled, how about we do a bit of finessing, hmm?"

Aubin glared at him over his shoulder. "What do you mean?"

What was this? "I thought we settled all that." I tried to keep the panic out of my voice.

The Assassin flung his arms wide, encompassing this strange nowhere place. "You can have a nice tidy up. Any lingering regrets? You know all those things said in haste? Well, you can fix that, here and now. Limited time offer, as it were."

Aubin went very still. "Can I not smother Thorrn? I can't... stop thinking about it."

Compassion shone from Evyn's face, eyes watering. "Oh, Aubin."

My limbs flooded with a strange tingle, a sharp excitement that left me breathless. He wouldn't have left then!

"Hm. Hard," the boy said. Four lines appeared on the screen. They intersected, and where they touched, the points were green. The boy shifted some lines around but touch points went and stayed red every time, and after them two of the lines glowed red and flat. "No. Not unless he dies for good, and then she dies shortly after that."

The screen flickered red all over. A large message stamped itself in big angry letters across the screen, appearing and disappearing multiple times.

The boy flushed. "Aw, damn it."

"Turn that off," the Assassin said mildly.

Evyn reached blindly for me. I took her hand, her grip painful, and Aubin slid to stand in front of us.

Meanwhile, the alts on the other side looked faintly embarrassed. The boy waved at the screen, and it went dark and flat.

*What had that message said?*

Aubin nodded slowly, hand on his blade. "Then I'll keep that choice and I'll carry it. Not exactly gladly, but I feel better knowing there really wasn't another way to save his life."

The boy tutted. "Yeah, I mean, it was only last week you asked to make it—"

Evie slapped the boy's arm lightly with the back of her fingers.

"Ow. Sorry, yes, fine."

We stared at him.

"Moving on," Evie said firmly.

"Any other changes? Or is this optimised for good and all now?" the boy asked, this time with a surlier air and rubbing where she had tapped him.

"No, I think that's it," Evyn said brightly, keeping my fingers in a vice grip. "We'll just be going now, thank you." She turned to the boy. "And thank you."

"Yeah, well, ironing out these things is what I—"

Evie raised her hand again.

"Time to go, I think," Evyn said brightly. "Can we go home, please?"

"Yes. Onwards!" The boy turned in a complete circle and slouched away, Evie following, and we trailed after them.

"What did the screen say?" I asked them, trying to keep my voice to a murmur.

Aubin kept his face neutral. "I didn't quite understand it. Target scenario at risk, chosen course does not fulfil parameters. Evyn, do you have any ideas?"

She nodded, face pale. "It's computery, but I think it means that the choice you were thinking about wasn't going to meet their objectives."

"Their… plan?" My stomach sank. "You think they really do have some kind of plan?"

"Yes, I do, it was on the wall, Thorrn."

Aubin levelled a searching stare at Evie ahead of us, but she did not turn around.

"Here you go." The boy flourished, and a portal popped into existence ahead of us. We spilled out into Desoree's bar, next to the private room we had left. It was quiet, which meant it had to be closed: no Skienien bar was ever quiet when it was open. *Perhaps this is the early turns of the glass in the morning.*

I sighed in the fresh cold air. "I never thought I'd be grateful for the Skienien climate. I am never going time travelling again."

"It was interesting for sure. I can see why you do it," Evyn murmured to her counterpart.

Evie smiled sadly. "Yes. It's hard sometimes, though. I think we all try to do what we think is best, even if that's hard too."

I saluted. "Go well, Lady Evie."

"Bye swordsman, Evyn, Aubin." She lifted a hand in farewell as the boy sealed the portal, her sorrowful eyes the last thing I saw of that dark world before it vanished like a soap bubble.

"Bath, methinks," Evyn sighed. "And then a big dinner."

"Yes please." I grinned at her. "I wonder if Desoree would put on another platter of meat. I could use a good fight too, I was all wound up with nothing to battle in the end."

Evyn shuddered but turned thoughtful. "Maybe the meat we left is still warm."

What a thought. "I wouldn't want to eat it. Even though I knew it wouldn't be days old, the idea is still abhorrent." I waved her to the private room we had been afforded, but at the threshold we paused to look back over our shoulders at Aubin standing alone at the empty table, staring after us. "What are you looking at?" I challenged him. "Be off!"

"I…" His face paled.

"Who are you, anyway?"

Eyes bulging, he gasped. "It's me, it's Aubin, Aubin Tabreksson."

"Who?" Evyn cocked her head.

I squeezed her hand.

Aubin took a step back. "No. Oh no, something went wrong, no! Please, you have to remember me!"

I shook my head, smiling. "Sorry. Couldn't resist. Are you coming or not?"

He shot me a murderous glare. "Asshole. Am I... am I welcome?"

Evyn beckoned to him. "Of course you can come with us."

"Everyone is allowed a wobble, Aubin." I clapped him on the shoulder as he joined us.

He jolted, swearing under his breath, but his back relaxed under my hand. I gave him one final squeeze before steering him in with us.

There was no meat on the table, to my distress. "We'll find something else. Let's regroup with Layloree." I pulled out the lodestone that hers shared kinship with. I passed it to Aubin. "Here, she would relish hearing from you."

One side of his lips tipped up as he took it, eyes unfocusing. Quickly he was back with us, face hardened. "We have returned in the middle of a crisis. We've been gone for three days, not three turns of the glass as promised." He looked like he wanted to hurl the lodestone at the wall.

"What's happening? What about Layloree and Carreelee, and the refugees?"

He put his hands on the table, head lowered. "The Hudau has found the temporary refuge Desoree and I set up. Layloree is with them, but they are holed up in the warehouse with no way out. Their leader Brudamere is threatening to burn them all unless they give him the Oberrotian helper."

# CHAPTER 29



"Well, that isn't happening." Evyn grabbed his elbow with both hands, as though he would be plucked away any heartbeat. Or, more likely, that he would attempt to sneak off when our backs were turned.

Aubin touched her hand, hesitant and bereft. "Evyn, it's one life for many."

My heart lurched in my chest.

"No." She wrenched him around to face her. "You have to stop taking things on alone. You have a fully-trained swordsman who just said he had energy to burn, a fast pinger – that's me, by the way – a beast-shaper mage, Layloree – who is a force unto herself – and a whole gaggle of magic users with varying abilities. Those refugees aren't helpless, you know."

*Yes*. Evyn was right. What could I do with such capabilities?

Aubin smiled briefly. "If they turn their magic against the people of Skien, the Hudau would be proven right."

Evyn scowled, "Sure, yes, if they turned it against the people of Skien, but we are talking about a loud and violent minority. Everyone we met on our way in was uncomfortable that this was going on in their country but didn't know how to address it. I'm sure they would all cheer if those anti-magical bullies got what was coming to them."

I wrapped my hand around my father's sword. "If they want you, they can have you," I mused.

"Excuse me?" Evyn frowned, likely feeling the edges of my excitement. Curiosity mingled with uncertainty within her.

"I have an idea."

✤ ✤ ✤

WE CROUCHED ON A SIDE STREET, taking in the clear view of the front of a warehouse, our breaths mere puffs in front of us. Aubin set one hand on the stone wall next to him and explained, "Desoree started buying wool up by the barrel to store as a cover. It's bulky and needs a great deal of storage, but it's also warm for the people inside."

"Clever." Evyn hovered just behind me, hand on my back so I knew where she was.

"But flammable," I pointed out grimly.

In front of the warehouse were two scores of men, five holding torches that burnt with a snapping ferocity.

"Is Layloree ready?" Aubin whispered.

"Yes. Are you?"

He looked tired already, held together with force of will. His shoulders squared and he tucked the gauze on his damaged wrists underneath my Ranger jacket. "One moment." Standing, he paced a step over the icy ground and faced Evyn.

Her lips trembled, looking up into his face. "Be careful."

"I'll come back," he said. "Look after him, Evyn. He needs it."

"I know. I'll rein him in." Evyn wiped her face, stepping back from him. I steadied her steps on the icy floor, our pain as sharp as the surrounding cold. She took a deep affirming breath. "Now let's get those people out."

Aubin backed away, giving me a curt jerk of his head. He was ready as he could be for something as perilous as this.

I drew my father's sword. "Let's get started." I sent Layloree the signal, a quick flash of *"Go"* in the lodestone.

A cry went up from the crowd at the warehouse. "There he is!" We huddled to see.

Leaping over the eaves and slants of the roof above was a shad-owed shape. Much bigger than real life, Carreelee had had to store her mass somehow, but her features were Aubin's, perfected by Layloree's guidance.

She came racing over the tops, leaping from building to building with a loping grace, rolling when she landed. Aubin grumbled, "I can't do that."

"You'll go down in legend as doing that. Let's go." I hurried them to the edge of the side street as the men gave chase, pounding down the icy cobbles. Good, only half a score remained at the warehouse.

Aubin climbed, ready to join Carreelee and lead the mob around, misdirecting them with different targets. Whenever Carreelee tired, Aubin would take up the mob's attention, and vice versa. We needed the men to move north, to give as much space to the rescue effort as possible.

I stalked down the street, Evyn right behind me. We moved in synchrony, our bond stronger than ever and heightened by immi-nent danger. Worry for Aubin merged into a certainty that he would be fine, we were supporting him and he had accepted help at last.

"He's over there!" the mob screamed behind us.

Someone shouted, "How did he get over there?"

"He's magic, you idiot!"

*No, just and only human.* Evyn and I resonated with the satisfying fact.

We gained the warehouse with my sword aloft. "Men, I'm going to need you to clear away from the area," I said in Skienien in my best parade voice.

The men left to guard the warehouse had ice in their beards, that was how long they had been holding this stakeout. Runny eyes met mine in a series of icy glares.

I set my stance in a guard. "Go home. You don't want any part of this."

An older man with shaggy red hair stepped forward as the spokesman. Perhaps this was their leader, Brudamere. "Who the hell are you? Another meddler. What are you, Daronian?"

My height and colouring were Daronian, so it was a good guess. "Would you be Brudamere?"

"The same." His eyes narrowing, he thrust a finger at the warehouse. "Are you on their side?"

"Yes," I said firmly.

Brudamere spat to one side. It wouldn't surprise me if it froze instantly in this climate. "It's a travesty. No human should wield the power or the strength of the gods. Mages, mancers, dhampir, they are all doomed to fail and destroy others as they destroy themselves. Humans are weak, they crumble and fall, they use their skills for their own evil ends, and they twist the truth to make themselves the victim." His smirk turned knowing. "You know this."

*What a limited view of human nature.* "It's not up for debate. These people need help."

"What about all the people who are being destroyed by magic? As they struggle to control their powers, countless lives are lost!"

"I'll help them too. I'll help anyone who needs it." I looked around at the rest of the men. They shuffled their feet, not meeting my challenge. It was Aubin they wanted, a foreigner they could blame. They didn't want to hurt their own people, not really.

Brudamere snorted, then looked at Evyn behind me. "Is that little matriarch putting you up to this? You can be free of her, free to live a full life as a man on your own terms. You're strong, you can certainly live without her, without anyone."

"No thanks. I need my friends." I raised my sword. "Move away from the doors or I'll make you."

"Well." Brudamere reached out, and another man passed him a long-handled axe. "I was looking forward to a fight."

I grinned. "Me too."

Launching forward, I raised my sword to catch the handle as he swung his axe. He shifted backwards, and the head of the axe clanged against my father's sword, scraping down one edge and sending sparks shooting out. I blinked, dazed. A whoosh in the air rang like a warning. I jumped back as he swiped the axe to one side, but now he had to turn it. Darting forward, I swiped at his arm, cutting a slice into his fur, my sword grating against his armour underneath. *Damn and blast.*

Brudamere brought the axe back in another deadly arc, and I had to drop and roll away, jumping to my feet and bringing my sword up into a guard. He grasped the axe head high on the handle, ready for closer combat, and lunged forward. I made that costly for him, stabbing and reaching for his face; he twisted, hauling back and panting as he circled me.

I had seen enough; when he reached forward, his armour plates would bunch and move, exposing flesh under the joints. The next time he lunged, I would disable him.

Brudamere's eyes slid toward Evyn.

*He's spotted my weakness at the same time.* "Don't you dare," I growled. "Focus on me."

Brudamere swung his axe up and shouted to his followers, "Grab the matriarch!"

Evyn backed up a step, then another. "Are you sure?" she asked in Oberrotian. "You're not going to like this."

"Let them get a bit closer." I grunted, side-stepping Brudamere's downward swing and reaching in. This time I scored a hit at his shoulder.

He howled, staggering back.

I glanced at Evyn to find three men within two arms' length of her. My heart shrieked.

Evyn opened a small portal in front of her shins and a spray of seawater arced out, slamming against the men's legs and blasting them off their feet. She closed the portal with a snap. "That's got to be cold."

"She's a mage!" Brudamere shouted. "Kill her!" He swung his axe at my face in a killing arc, cold air slicing across my nose, followed by a splash of salty spray.

Brudamere stood in front of me, mouth wide and arm raised. His hand was missing, and the man let out a choking cry.

I stumbled to the side. He had swung into a dark tear in the air in front of me, the rain of another world pattering onto the head of his axe.

"Magic!" Brudamere stumbled back a step. This saved his hand, for the portal snapped shut, shearing his axe at the midpoint. He swore, staring at the stub of wood.

"Stop!" a woman's voice rang out.

Loping down the street were Battlemistresses in green and their men in grey, the equivalent of the Skienien army, the personal guard of the Chief of all Chiefs. At their head was Desoree.

Brudamere spluttered. "The army of the people on the side of magic users? This is a travesty!"

Desoree scowled. "The only travesty is how long it took me to convince Grendamere that the people of Skien means *all* the people of Skien." She glared at me. "Where have you been, Oberrotian?"

I kept my father's sword in hand, backing up to stand next to Evyn. "We were waylaid. My apologies."

She rolled her eyes. "What are you doing over here, then? Your army is on the east side."

"My army?"

She grunted, turning to Evyn. "This is why I don't ask men questions and expect sensible answers," she told her in Oberrotian. "Get over to the east side, Special Forces is over there providing us with assistance to secure the town."

"Alright." Evyn beckoned me. "Come on, looks like the Battlemistresses have it all in hand here."

I hugged her. "Well done on your new ranged ability!" I whispered to her. "Now we—" The lodestone on Amare flared hot. I flinched away from it but of course was unable to escape it, but it stopped building heat before it got unbearable. "That was Tuniel. She must be here!"

"Answer it then." Evyn linked hands with me.

I thrust one hand under my furs to put my hand on the lodestone. Immediately the grey stone streets fell away into blank white. *"Tuniel?"*

*"Thorrn, get to Aubin, quickly! He's hurt."*

No! *"Has he fallen?"* A fall from that height could be fatal.

*"He hasn't fallen but he's in the streets, here."* A map flashed into my mind, the streets of Keltskarr laid out in black lines. Aubin was two streets over. *"I am making my way there but you're closer."*

*"We'll save him."* I broke off the connection. "Evyn, we have to run. Aubin is in trouble."

*"Don't dawdle, go!"*

I grabbed her hand and took off in a sprint, dragging her along behind me, heedless of the frozen road.

Evyn gasped, stumbling. "Leave me, you'll get there faster!"

"I'm not leaving you alone in an engagement to take the town." I shortened my stride and Evyn ran as hard as she could. The two streets passed in a blur, my heart hammering in my chest. We had to reach him, we had to get there before the mob found him.

We turned the corner to find a score of men between us and Aubin. He was in a dead end, panting and blowing, Battlemistress blades raised and shaking in front of his face.

Directly in front of him stood a tall blond man in Special Forces red, and my heart stuttered. Gavain's face was hidden from me; he faced Aubin, back to the men of the mob, as if he were one of them.

He turned to face the mob, raising his sword. "Get back. Special Forces is here at the insistence of the Chief of all Chiefs, Grendamere the Great." Gavain couldn't speak much Skienien; this was a rote phrase Barlay must have given all of them.

He locked gazes with me and his blue eyes widened. He looked hale, red-faced still, but that could just be the cold wind and the exertion of fighting.

"You are surrounded!" he shouted to the men in between us.

"Sort of," I amended, keeping a firm stance as the mob turned around.

They glanced at one another, grimacing and looking away from each other's faces.

"Disperse now. Battlemistresses are securing the area," I announced.

Evyn put her hand on my elbow, and the mob looked at her. She cleared her throat. "Go home," she said in Oberrotian.

I repeated it in Skienien for them.

The men scowled and grumbled, but they shuffled away, heads down and turned away from us so we couldn't identify them, not the behaviour of people proud of their actions in the name of their cause.

When they were gone I let my stance shift toward a ready pose, keeping my weight balanced. "Well met, Gavain."

"Well met." His face fixed into a stony glare. He turned in place to face Aubin.

Aubin held his blades raised even though his arms shook. He had shifted all his weight onto one leg; the other must have sustained an injury.

He and Gavain locked eyes.

I pushed forward. "I can explain."

"What's to explain?" Gavain's lips barely moved. "This is clearly one of those alternative versions, here from another version of reality."

I looked between them. Aubin's teeth chattered from shock and pain, while Gavain loomed over him, still and stoic. Had he seen the truth?

"There you are!" Tuniel swept into the side street, bundled up in thick furs. "Swordsman, your heart seems to be coping admirably."

"Yes, MasterMage." Gavain saluted her, two taps of his fist against his chest.

"You do look a great deal improved." I reached my hand out to pat him on the shoulder.

He brushed my hand away. "You look hale and well. Do you need assistance?"

"No, Gav. We're fine." He was keeping it strictly to business. I could too. I turned my attention to Aubin. "What happened?"

He lowered his arms, still watching Gavain closely. "We got down off the roofs because that was going to kill us, but Carreelee got too tired and couldn't shape change anymore. I ran them down here but they cornered me, started beating me up." He touched the side of his head, looking at his bloody fingertips with a wince.

Evyn ran to him. He dropped his blades to clatter on the stones and swept her up, wrapping her in his arms and pressing her close. He closed his eyes briefly, pressing his cheek to her head. "We have to find Carreelee, I don't know where she is."

"Here." The squat mage waddled up behind us. "I wasn't expecting to have to use so much energy tonight. I need more stamina."

"You need training," I agreed.

She peered up at me, then at Tuniel.

Tuniel took a step closer to me, laying her hand on my arm as a clear claim. I leant into her touch. She met my eyes, happiness shining out of them. "Ranger, Special Forces is nearby. Perhaps we should regroup with them?"

"Yes. Good plan." Warmth flooded me, surrounded by my allies. "What does it mean that Special Forces came all the way here, to the interior of Skien?"

Gavain answered, from his post at the alley entrance. "Gough talked the Chief of all Chiefs around. There's going to be more of a concerted effort to help Skieniens accept the magic users among them."

I grinned. "That's wonderful news."

He did not look turn to face me. "I need to return to the contingent," he said stiffly.

"Of course. And... we'll talk," I promised him.

He grunted again. Was this some change of personality because of his heart, or the shock of seeing Aubin again?

Regardless, I would have to sort through it later. I paced up to Aubin. "Where are you injured?"

"Right leg, twisted my ankle. A few blows to the face." His lip was swelling. "This is what I get when I help people."

"And they will thank you for helping them." I ducked lower to pull his arm over my shoulder. "You get that too."

"Yes." He leant on me, fully and finally. He was heavier than he looked. "My thanks," he said.

The genuine sentiment made me chuckle. "Of course," Evyn and I said together.

Evyn's small steps acted as our metronome. The others pulled ahead, Gavain walking with Tuniel and Carreelee and keeping guard, and we had to follow a few paces behind.

Evyn smiled up at us. "Hopefully it's over for now, and I like Gavain's idea of pretending you're an alt. You can be Aubin again, if you wanted."

"Hm." The side of his lips went down. "I can reinvent myself. A new personality. It's easily explained away by being an alt."

"Or you can be you," I said.

"Whatever that is." He leant away from me to try putting weight on his hurt leg, hissing with pain, but his lips tipped up. "I could... try it out," he said quietly, as if testing the notion with us.

"Whatever you need," I said, and Evyn nodded enthusiastically.

She tugged at her plait. "We'll need to talk at some point about the others. Evie and the Assassin and Shoulders, and what they are doing."

Aubin's grip tightened around my shoulders. "It's suspicious in the extreme that they are keeping such a close watch on our timeline."

"Why?" I asked. "They might just want us and all their sideways versions to be happy, you know."

Aubin frowned at me. "A version of you and Evyn died, and they didn't try to prevent that. They even took us there, and it served as an abject lesson in what happens if we're separated or apart from one another."

"Whoa now, Evie happened to be captured there."

"What was she doing there? Did she find Liara, or not? We never asked."

I looked up and down the still streets. Over to one side the Battlemistresses were bringing order, dispersing the mob loudly. Tuniel and the others had walked to the other side, and waited for us at the end of the street. I helped Aubin hop along, careful of ice. "We still need to find Liara, and we will need the alts to do so. I think Liara is looking for Waker."

Aubin grunted. "Then let's hope she doesn't find her." His jaw ticked.

Evyn frowned. "Hang on. Something is nagging at me from where we've just come from..." She raised her eyebrows at Aubin, pointing accusingly. "Ah! Right! Yes! So, you did triage or whatever when Gerlay brought me to you. Did you have to do a diagnosis kiss?"

Aubin's lips twisted. "Well, yes."

"Ah! You did? Oh no!" She grinned, putting her hands over her red cheeks. "Nightmare."

"It's just a way to sample what you had ingested. You weren't in a state to tell me, and you didn't know in any case," he muttered.

Her cheeks flushed red. "I got a kiss and I wasn't even awake for it!"

"It wasn't a kiss in any real sense," he protested, loud enough to ring from the tall buildings around us.

"But he is a good kisser, Evyn," I said.

She put a hand to her chest, looking between us both with a big smile. "Do I finally get the Skien story?"

I rubbed the back of my neck, face heating. "We need more alcohol for this, but... Well. In Skien, men with a matriarch are considered to be somewhat kept in line. Men without a matriarch are considered potentially dangerous, like those rogues. A pair of men can travel together because they'll be the third segment of society... the Fikus."

Aubin looked up at the sky, fat flakes of white starting to spiral down. "And sometimes we had to prove we were, indeed, Fikus. And not rogue men prowling around."

"So we had to hold hands..." I swallowed hard.

"That soul jewel glowing on your shoulder..."

I winced. "And occasionally..."

He glanced at me. "If someone really wanted proof..."

I grimaced back. "We would have to..."

"I get it, I get it," Evyn said, chortling. "Oh man."

I shook my head, grateful for once that my face was burning, in this cold at least. "So that's why what goes on in Skien stays in Skien," I explained. "The whole world knows this."

She patted her flaming cheeks. "I'm just jealous of all the kisses."

I nearly said, *I'm sure he'll make it up to you.* Certainly things had changed between them, a willingness to try again in Evyn's every move and feeling.

Aubin had a half smile on his face, which broadened when he met my eyes, and he positively glowed looking at Evyn. For once he wore his heart openly, his feelings shining on his face, and he looked happy and grateful.

"Let's go home," he said.

# EPILOGUE: EVIE

As Davin closed the portal behind them, I nearly sagged. "Don't show them the actual projections!"

"I had to adjust things on the fly, it couldn't be a static model." Davin looked embarrassed at least. "Sorry."

"Well, that was fun," Aubin said, shaking out his hands. "Quite the close one."

Thorrn caught me up in his arms. "Are you alright? What happened? How did you end up there?"

I nodded to Davin, who pulled out the tracker. "Well? Are we on course?" I asked him.

"Yep. Looks good." He passed the device to me, but whatever he saw behind the visualisation was something only he could understand. I could just about make out small flickering shapes; the small potentials of futures yet to be. Compared with the more solid colours of the past, all done and set, the future was blurry, constantly shifting. More than a massive headache, it was a massive, massive problem.

Thorrn held me at arm's length, frowning. "Evie? What..." His eyes widened. "Did you do that deliberately? Did you go to that other world and get captured on purpose?" He whirled around to Aubin. "And you were in on it!"

"Yep." Aubin flicked his fingers wide. "Surprise!"

Thorrn gaped. When he turned back to me, his incredulous face wounded me, a jab across the bond that pierced my heart. "You lied to me. I thought you were in danger. I... I nearly died."

My hands trembled. I stilled them.

My husband snorted. "I can rewrite history so you didn't. Who's to say I haven't already?"

As Thorrn's anger rose up against him, I quietly thanked Aubin at the same time as I wished that he wouldn't step in. He was doing this to draw Thorrn's ire away from me.

*But I deserve it.*

"I'm sorry," I said, knowing the apology didn't even scratch the surface. "It was the only way. We needed them back together."

Shaking his head, Thorrn turned away. He couldn't leave, he couldn't make portals no matter how many times I showed him, but Davin wouldn't let him get lost in his realm.

"It really was the only thing we could do," I told his back.

Aubin slid next to me and squeezed my hand. "It's alright," he said in a low voice. "I know we agreed, but I also know it's not fair on him."

I turned into his chest, and he put his arms around me.

It hurt to lie to my soul companion, but I would spare him this. I would not involve Aubin and Tuniel either if I could, but I needed their help. Thorrn would probably understand, and might even back us, but there was a chance that big heart of his would rebel against the need. He had spent most of his life as a slave; he had no desire to inflict that on anyone, let alone a version of himself.

And, if that wasn't enough, he was a very poor liar. I was too, but I had something else I could do: I could care, and then I could do what was necessary despite that. Something Aubin understood, and it seemed that the swordsman's Aubin did too.

My nose stung, the precursor to tears. Aubin's eyes widened slightly, and I swallowed hard, forcing my throat not to wobble.

I had to lie to Thorrn, and by me, I meant Aubin. I couldn't directly lie to Thorrn and expect him not to notice my red face and sudden stutter; Aubin could tell him the moons were now all a funky pink and Thorrn would be convinced enough to go outside to check.

Aubin's gaze was steady, warm and full of resolve. His hands cupped mine. My fingers trembled; together, we stilled them.

After all, it was up to us, in the end, to make sure a future happened at all.

# THANK YOU SO MUCH

Thank you so much for reading. I hope you loved it as much as I loved writing it! I hope you'll come along for the next instalment of Thorrn and Evyn's adventures.

If you enjoyed this book, will you please review it? It really helps independent authors like me, and I do truly want to hear what you think. It only takes a few minutes, and it means so much to me. Thank you!

What's next for Thorrn and Evyn? Stay in touch with me and be the first to know when Book 5 is released. Join my newsletter and get my free gift to you, a novella called *Dough Boy*. Learn how Gavain and Thorrn's friendship started!

*The baker's boy gets by as best as he can, but when he defeats a rogue mage, he realises he might have a promising career as a swordsman for the king. But can he convince his father - and himself - of that?*

Gavain Gomoresson spends his days helping his father and dreaming of being something more. When a boy from Special Forces arrives to investigate the potential hiding place of a rogue mage, Gavain surprises himself - and his father.

Eager to try out to join the regular army, Gavain joins for Intake Sennight and meets with resistance; not only from the other recruits, but within himself and his father. Can he decide what his heart wants, and seize it?

Grab your exclusive copy on my mailing list – you won't find *Dough Boy* anywhere else.

Go to: https://www.beckyjamesauthor.co.uk/subscribe

# ACKNOWLEDGMENTS

A massive thank you to my wonderful beta readers, Angharad and Kristen Braddock. Without you, Thorrn and Evyn wouldn't be in reader's lives right now. I'm so glad you wandered into my timeline!

# ABOUT THE AUTHOR

Becky James is the author of The King's Swordsman series and coauthor of the Dark Tides series. Based in the UK, she has a deep love of the British countryside, canals, and all things fantasy; she devours anything that has magic, swords, good friends and good times. She is a massive extrovert, but nearly all her friends are introverts, so she knows how not to energy vampire them. She will still talk your ear off though.

Her series can be found wherever books are sold, and she is often floating around on Facebook and Instagram.

https://www.beckyjamesauthor.co.uk/

INTERVIEW WITH BECKY

HI BECKY! TELL US A BIT ABOUT YOURSELF.

I'm from Wales originally, then I moved to Scotland, now I'm trying out living in England. (I'll do Ireland one day to complete the set). I speak conversational Welsh, French and Japanese and eager to learn more languages. I am a massive extrovert, but nearly all my friends are introverts, so I know how not to energy vampire them. I will still talk your ear off though.

WHEN DID YOU KNOW YOU LOVED FANTASY?

I got into fantasy young, and I'm all for stories that use the settings / events to explore human nature and character-driven storylines. My first "grown up" fantasy writer was Eddings, and I love that balance of humour and heart.

Tell us a bit about your series.

I write upper young adult or what's called new adult sword and sorcery mashed with contemporary fantasy, about a cocky swordsman and his exasperated friends, and a fantasy romance series. I like noblebright, with worldbuilding threaded throughout the plot, and anything unexpected. I love it when a story comes full circle and closes off nicely, ready for the next. My stories are heavily UK influenced, from the mythology and folklore to the settings (semi-rural British countryside and our canals feature a lot. Slightly obsessed with canals). I'll feature the dreaming spires of Oxford next to steel-crash impacted Sheffield, and there needs to be more about the laylines influencing Milton Keynes and the real story behind the Magic Roundabout in Swindon.

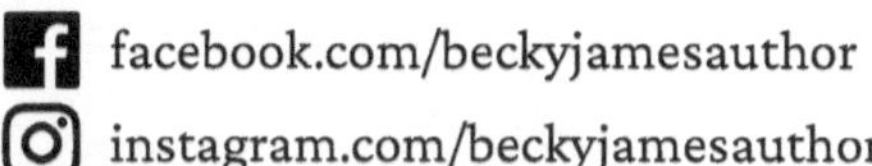

facebook.com/beckyjamesauthor

instagram.com/beckyjamesauthor

# ALSO BY BECKY JAMES

## OTHER SERIES

Perhaps you'd like to try a fae-filled fantasy romance? Step right this way!

*A Dram of Freshwater* is the prequel novella to *The Dark Tides* series.

THE WORLD IS ENDING. RORY CAN'T WAIT.

Stealing souls from under the noses of the guardians of the underworld is hard work, but for immortal Cat Sidhe Rory, it's all he has ever known. Hiding behind humour, he masks the dark waters closing overhead, but the longer he puts a smile on his face, the more real the threat becomes.

THE WORLD IS BEGINNING. DARLA CAN'T WAIT.

Darla is an explorer, endlessly fascinated by the land above. As a selkie, she remains trapped under the waves except for once every seven years. But, as luck would have it, now is her time to escape the waves. Desperate to sate her hunger for adventure, she finds her way to the surface, ready to experience all of the wonders of existence, including love, for the very first time.

But the fae world is ending. What will they risk to save it... and each other?

Grab your copy on my mailing list now!

https://www.beckyjamesauthor.co.uk/realmofdarkness

THEN, DIVE IN TO THE DARK TIDES...

### *A king with a broken crown.*

*Shay rules from the murky corners of the Topaz Court, a realm not many willingly travel to. It promises only one thing —Death. Duty eats away at the dark king, and as he escorts departed souls to the Otherworld, something—or someone— threatens to taint his kingdom and destroy the magic that sustains it.*

### *A selkie searching for answers.*

*Seven years ago, Neri's sister disappeared on dry land over the sands. Neri has prepared every day since to follow after her and find what delays her sister's return to the waves.*

*Death hounds after the selkie. Shay shouldn't stand in its way; to upset the balance is to risk everything. Not even when her spirit stirs something inside him, something he thought long lost...*

*As the threat to magic grows, the selkie might be the key. Together, Shay and Neri traverse the realms to save their homes, their families, and perhaps even themselves. Will they succeed, even under the shadow of death?*

✾ ✾ ✾

Book 1 will be published in Realm of Darkness! To preorder now, go here:

https://books2read.com/realmofdarknessset/

*WHEN DARKNESS FALLS, BEWARE OF THE CREATURES THAT COME OUT TO PLAY...*

*Fall under their spell over and over again in this ultimate paranormal and fantasy romance boxset! Over 40 full-length novels with heart-melting heroes and devastating anti-heroes, full of romance, magic, mystery, and adventure can be yours for an insanely low price.*

*Ready to be swept away? Your book boyfriends are waiting... Enemies-to-lovers, alphas, fae, werewolves, dragons, shapeshifters, vampires, gods, angels, demons, and more: with novels ranging from sweet to spicy, there's a flavor to sate your every craving.*

*You won't find these exclusive novels anywhere else, so don't miss your chance. Over ten thousand pages by New York Times, USA Today, and International bestselling authors and at less than three cents per book, this collection is a steal, but only for a limited time. Grab it today before it's gone forever...*

9 781916 877481